THE BALLAD OF BILLY LEE

The Story of George Washington's Favorite Slave

A Novel

BY LEN LAMENSORF

DERIVED FROM THE PLAY

The Ballad of Billy Lee

Introduction By Joseph J. Ellis

Note From Ron Chernow

SeaScape Press™ 5717 Tanner Ridge Ave.
Westlake Village, CA 91362
Phone: 818-707-3080
Website: www.lenlamensdorf.com

SeaScape Press™ os a trademark owned by Leonard Lamensdorf
First Printing 2012
Second Printing 2020

10987654321

Printed in the United States of America

Publisher's Cataloging-in-Publication

Lamensdorf, Leonard
The Ballad of Billy Lee: an historical novel / by Len Lamensdorf
Includes bibliographical references.
LC Classificaton: PS3562 A4635 B35 2020
ISBN: 9798648069909
Ebook ISBN: 9780-852381-6-2

Washington, George, 1732-1799
Relations with Slaves-Fiction
Slavery-United States-History
18th Century-Fiction

THE BALLAD OF BILLY LEE

Billy Lee, an African-American slave, was at George Washington's side for over thirty years. Though never a relationship between equals, it was an intimate and enduring connection. A superb horseman, bold soldier and a literate aide, Billy Lee stood next to Washington when he crossed the Delaware, galloped at Washington's side in battle-a slave armed with a pistol, carbine and spyglass-served with him in Valley Forge and through the difficult years to the final victory at Yorktown. He was responsible for Washington's public and private papers at conventions and congresses, but Billy was a slave, always hoping to be freed, and his slavery cost him the love of his life. Yet his loyalty to Washington was unwavering. This unique and remarkable "buddy" story delves into the quest for freedom, from the tyranny of England to the chains of slavery.

This novel is an enhancement and adaptation of Len Lamensdorf's play The Ballad of Billy Lee.

Joseph J. Ellis, Pulitzer Prize and National Book Award winning historian, called the stage play of The Ballad of Billy Lee "one of the most poignant untold stories in American history."

After viewing the stage version of The Ballad of Billy Lee, Pulitzer Prize winning author Ron Chernow wrote to Len Lamensdorf: "You have done a beautiful job of coaxing [Billy Lee] out into the sunlight and giving him the attention that he most assuredly deserves. My sincere congratulations. . . I share your strongly held view that it would be wonderful if more Americans were acquainted with the remarkable Billy Lee."

Also by Len Lamensdorf

Novels:

Kanes World

In the Blood

The Will to Conquer

Trilogy:

The Crouching Dragon

> *The Raging Dragon*

> *The Flying Dragon*

Gino, the Countess & Chagall

The Murdered Messiah

The Mexican Gardener

Plays:

The Ballad of Billy Lee

The Guest House

The Survival Game

Film:

Cornbread, Earl & Me

> Executive Producer & Screenwriter

> Nominated for 5 Image Awards

> A new version of this film will be released soon

CRITICAL PRAISE FOR LEN LAMENSDORF, whose novels have won Gold and Silver Benjamin Franklin Awards, three" Ippys," (the Independent Publisher's Award), and the *Fore Word Magazines* Book-of-the-Year Award.

The Ballad of Billy Lee: "I always imagined [Billy] much as you presented him: garrulous and funny, warm and achingly human, as well as very perceptive about the momentous events he observed from Washington's side. I especially liked the way that you concentrated on his craving for freedom ... "

– Pulitzer Prize winning author Ron Chernow.

"*The Ballad of Billy Lee,_* should be regarded as a historical dramatization in which Billy Lee's voice and words, though impeccably rooted in the historical evidence that has survived, represent Lamensdorf's imaginative recreation of a man otherwise lost to us forever."

– Pulitzer-Prize and National Book Award author Joseph J. Ellis.

"Move over, J.K. Rowling… *The Raging Dragon* is a heart stopping, history-packed jaunt through Paris at the turn of the 1960s. From old airplanes to far older castles, from the famed Sorbonne to the eerie catacombs, readers will devour this tale to the exciting end."

– *Gayle Lynds, New York Times best-selling author of Mesmerized, The Coil, and The Last Spymaster.*

Gino, the Countess & Chagall. "… [is] a rollicking travelogue and art history saga ... voluptuous, lusty, lighthearted."

– *Publishers Weekly.*

Gino, the Countess & Chagall. "Lamensdorf presents a glowing tribute to the world of art through the life of a talented and charming painter who personifies a zest for life."

– *Publishers Weekly.*

The Crouching Dragon. "… an unusual, intriguing adventure tale, with a touch of fantasy gaming… Suspense-laden."

To Erica, my oft amusing muse

Matthew, Cole, Lauren, Derek and Kirsten
Always cherish your freedom

TABLE OF CONTENTS

INTRODUCTION

The following introduction was written by best-selling author, Professor Joseph J. Ellis, Pulitzer Prize and National Book Award winning historian in connection with author Len Lamensdorf's play The Ballad of Billy Lee, first staged in Santa Barbara, California,. on December 10, 2006, starring Henry Brown. This Novel is an enhancement and adaptation of the play, the two intertwined like the strands of DNA, or perhaps more aptly, like the lives of George Washington and Billy Lee.

Welcome. You are about to see one of the most poignant untold stories in American history. Suppose I said that an African-American slave, by the name of Billy Lee, was George Washington's most constant and intimate companion during that last quarter of the eighteenth century.

On a day-by-day basis, Billy Lee laid out Washington's clothes, combed his hair, saddled his horse, and accompanied him wherever he went. He was the only rider who could keep up with Washington during fox hunts at Mount Vernon. He was at his side when Washington assumed command of what became the Continental army outside of Boston in 1775. He was alongside him during the humiliating defeat at Long Island, in the boat with him crossing the Delaware on Christmas Day of 1776, with him to accept the British surrender at Yorktown. He waited in the background as Washington chaired the Constitutional Convention, and he accompanied him on the triumphant trip to his inauguration as president in 1789, though had to drop out because of bad knees before reaching New York.

It does not end there. Billy Lee sat beside Washington during his retirement years on the piazza at Mount Vernon overlooking the Potomac, when tourists and guests would flock around, and Washington would often refer questions about specific battles in the war to Billy's memory. When Washington died in 1799, Billy Lee was the only slave that Washington freed outright in his will - his other slaves would only be freed upon Martha's death - and Billy Lee chose to stay on at Mount Vernon as a free man until his own death in 1828, receiving visitors and recalling the stories of his life with "the General."

Washington was notoriously adverse to intimacy, and up until now his wife Martha, and his close friend and quasi-son, Lafayette, were regarded as the only intimates permitted to occupy the space around Washington that was off-limits to everybody else. Now a third person, an African-American slave no less, must be added to the list.

The evidence of Billy Lee's role as Washington's man-servant has always been "out there," though scattered in little tid-bits, like a Trumbull painting or several nineteenth-century prints with Billy Lee in the background, or the casual mention of his presence beside Washington by visitors to Mount Vernon, or the recorded conversations with Billy Lee by journalists and early historians after Washington's death, preserved in dated memoirs and early histories.

But until Len Lamensdorf gathered together these scattered pieces of evidence, then put his own imagination to work in recovering the story they tell, it was impossible to appreciate that there was a story at all. Recovering it, to be sure, requires dramatic license, since the documentary record is too small and spare to permit straightforward scholarly treatment. The following film, then, The Ballad of Billy Lee. should be regarded as a historical dramatization in which Billy Lee's voice and words, though impeccably rooted in the historical evidence that has survived, represent Lamensdorf's imaginative recreation of a man otherwise lost to us forever.

There are several reasons why we should rejoice at Billy Lee's recovery. First and foremost, his own life is an extraordinary story of a witness to the most dramatic and consequential events in American history, from the roller coaster ride during the War for Independence, to the Constitutional Convention, to the establishment of the United States as a viable nation-state. These are not small matters. Like Washington himself, Billy Lee was present at the creation.

Moreover, once you come to understand the intimate, long term relationship between Washington and Billy Lee, you begin to recognize why Washington's views on race were different from most of the other prominent Virginia planters, most especially Jefferson. For Washington never subscribed to the dominant opinion that African-Americans were biologically inferior to whites, so that any plan for gradual emancipation must include XIV Introduction a provision for the removal of all ex-slaves to Africa or some location in the Caribbean.

Washington believed that African-American slaves were not the product of inferior genes, but rather the product of oppressive conditions as slaves. He was able to see them as fully-endowed human beings, burdened by their status as slaves just as he himself would have been if raised under the same conditions. There was a law in Virginia, for example, requiring that all freed slaves be removed from the state within one year of their emancipation. Washington simply defied the law, presumed that all the slaves be freed in his will would be allowed to remain on the premises at Mount Vernon, and no one ever had the audacity to defy his presumption.

Why Washington was immune to the prevalent racism of his time has always remained a mystery, though truth be told, no serious scholars have given the question the attention it deserves. Once you know Billy Lee's story, however, at least part of the answer becomes clear. Washington spent the bulk of his adult life in the presence of a wholly dedicated, highly intelligent, thoroughly competent AfricanAmerican slave who, on a day-by-day basis, demonstrated the inherent fallacy of racial stereotyping. Human intimacies triumphed ideological prejudices.

This is one of my many conclusions as an American historian after seeing The Ballad of Billy Lee. You are likely to have conclusions of your own, about both Billy Lee and George Washington. But I do think that it is fair to say that, after viewing this film [the play on DVD], your understanding of the troubled, traumatic, and tumultuous history of our racial origins as a people and a nation will never be the same.

Joseph Ellis
Springfield, MA
2010

PROLOGUE

To: Editor, The National Intelligencer

From: Marcus Ames, Reporter

Date: July 4, 1825

The interviews lasted many hours across several days. He was not what I expected. An elderly, but still muscular mulatto man with two bad knees, hobbling about from chair to chair in his white-washed cottage at Mount Vernon, talking non-stop about his days with the General, as he called him.

I took extensive notes, and a much longer story will follow, but for now you need to know that this Billy Lee claims intimate knowledge of General Washington over a thirty-year span. It's all oral testimony, few documents to back it up, but his command of detail is extremely impressive.

Little things, like what Washington talked about in the boat crossing the Delaware, what he had for breakfast most mornings, how he liked his hair tied, his favorite horses, favorite dogs, favorite cuss words.

Big things too, like his reasons for insisting that Martha bum all their correspondence, what he thought of Hamilton, Adams, Franklin, and Jefferson. (Wait 'till you hear his thoughts on Jefferson.) How he managed the excruciating pain he suffered from his terrible teeth virtually his whole life. And - you won't believe this - how beautiful women threw themselves at him throughout his life. How Washington dealt with them-sometimes with Billy's help.

I realize this report arrives far too late to make the Annual Independence special issue and a bit early for the Jubilee issue in 1826. But it does seem to me that we're onto something bigger here. If he's telling the truth, this Billy Lee is God's witness. This strikes me as a big story. I presume your permission to pursue it.

Know that Mount Vernon has the look and feel of a rotting ruin. The mansion is going to seed, the slave population has been depleted by sales of whole families to plantations further south, all of which

Billy says the General would consider a betrayal. He's been at Mount Vernon for a long time, but claims all his friends are either dead or gone. He is, I would guess, about seventy-five, and obviously headed for the hereafter, where he says he will ride again with the General. My intention is to get his story before he goes.

For our illustrator, if you decide to go all the way with this, Billy Lee is a light-skinned negro just short of six feet, with deep creases in his face that all flow upward, like a permanent smile. He conveys the impression of someone present at the creation. I do believe he is the genuine article.

CHAPTER 1

The Squire and the Slave

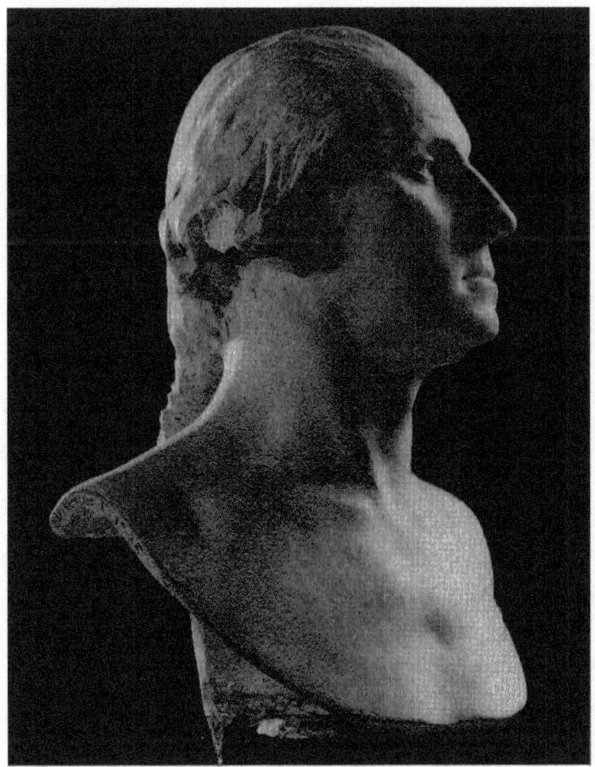

Figure 1 George Washington bust by Jean-Antoine Houdon.

The first time I seen the General was at a foxhunt I was surprised how big he was. I was pretty tall mesself but he was inches taller than me, big head, big butt, big, strong hands. I was smilin'to mesself when he swung aboard his horse—I was feelin ' sorry for the horse. Then we started ridin. 'He fooled me again. Whether he rode at a canter or a gallop, he rode like he was glued to the saddle. Did't bounce at all,

*din't stand in his stirrup, jes glided easy like. Damn, I thought, I got to
show him what I can do.*

It was the Fall of 1768. Red, yellow and brown autumn leaves
were swirling and spinning in the air and the cerulean blue Virginia
sky was clear and bright, when a young mulatto man, Billy Lee, galloped his well-lathered sorrel up to George Washington. Although
Washington didn't stand in his stirrups while riding, he was standing
in them now, surveying the terrain while a pack of seven specially
bred foxhounds bayed away, frantically searching to recover the scent
of a very fast and very frightened red fox.

"Where are the other riders? Washington asked, "and who the
hell are you?"

"Somewhere back over that hill, General. They cain't keep up
with you, so I come mesself. My given name is William Lee, but folks
call me Billy."

Billy was again struck by the size of the man and the chiseled
shape of his huge head with its profusion of reddish-brown hair, pulled
back and tied. His eyes were deep-set—a grayish blue, and at first
look rather chilling. He was the biggest and most impressive white
man Billy had ever seen. And when he stood in the stirrups, his head
silhouetted against the brilliant sky, Billy thought if you powdered his
hair white this man looked like the picture of God in Mama's bible.

Washington was also the best-dressed fox-hunter that Billy had
ever seen. Billy's master, John Lee, usually dressed in every-day
clothes when on the hunt, but Washington wore a vivid scarlet coat
with brass buttons, black breeches and stockings and a fine pair of
long, polished leather boots. He wasn't wearing his black hunting cap,
which hung instead on his saddle. The other hunters were a motley
crew, wearing all manner and color of clothing, but they wore their
black caps held by a cord below their chins. Billy wore an ordinary
brown shirt, breeches and shoes, but he also wore a little red cap on his
head—designating him as the huntsman.

As Washington eased himself back into the saddle, the hounds
flushed the fox out of a thicket and resumed the chase. Billy bolted
after them, leaving Washington to utter some inaudible profanity as
this presumptuous black boy surged ahead, soared over a high white
wooden fence and through apparently impenetrable brush and trees,

then landed gracefully and galloped after the hounds. Washington caught up with Billy at the foxhole, where the hounds were digging away in a frenzy of sweat and saliva.

Washington, visibly impressed, had to catch his breath as he spoke, "Where did you learn to ride like that?"

"Colonel Lee taught me the simple stuff. After that I got bettuh and fastuh on my own. I guess it jes comes natural to me, General."

"Don't call me 'General,'" Washington said with some impatience. "My rank in the militia was Colonel."

Billy just smiled back, unfazed. "Well," he said, you jes look like a General to me, sir." Billy thought that, no matter what Washington said, he liked being called "General."

By then the other riders had at last caught up, and the leader, Colonel John Lee, a stout, rosy-faced and cheerful man, released a lean, fierce-looking English terrier he was carrying across the horn of his saddle to dig out the poor, trapped fox.

"I see, Colonel Washington, that you've met my boy, Billy," Lee announced in a triumphant tone, "I do believe he can give you a run for your money on horseback."

"He already has, Colonel Lee," Washington acknowledged, "quite a run indeed. Do you mean to tell me this young man is a slave? He doesn't carry himself like a slave."

Billy shifted in the saddle, then blew a loud note on the small brass hunting horn he carried around his neck, declaring the demise of the poor fox.

"I know what you mean," Colonel Lee retorted. "Not only that, he can also read and write. Billy copies all my correspondence for the Burgesses."

Washington looked at Billy skeptically. The other hunters—slave owners all—evidently didn't like the idea of literate slaves, and they looked askance at John Lee.

Lee, oblivious of his neighbors, warmed to the subject. "Billy is quite a talker, too. Probably because he has spent so much time inside our home. His mother is our cook, and Billy always helps her out. When he was seven or eight years old, I asked him if he wanted to grow up to be a cook like his mother. No, he said, he wanted to be a master like me, because the food's better and you get to tell people what to do." Lee laughed out loud, and Washington smiled. He was not particularly interested in the youthful history of a slave, even a clever one—who seemed not to know his place.

Billy didn't believe this discussion was doing him any good. He sensed that Washington regarded him as a questionable curiosity, so he busied himself polishing his horn and smiled away.

What was going on in Washington's mind was not clear until later. He was not the kind of man to speak his mind when it was only half made-up. Indeed, he was not the kind of man to speak his mind at all unless absolutely necessary, regarding casual conversation as an unnatural and unnecessary act.

Washington cantered over to Colonel Lee in nonchalant fashion, and the two men exchanged words. Billy had a hunch the General was offering to buy him. He didn't know whether he liked the idea or not. In fact, he had lived his whole life on the John Lee plantation, and although he was aware of his status as a slave, he was comfortable where he was. Billy and the other slaves sometimes talked about freedom, but it was an idea that, until now, had never held any reality for him, personally. The possibility of being sold had never seriously occurred to him before, and he realized that there was no way to know how this monument of a man would turn out as a master. Billy briefly lost his almost perpetual smile; it didn't please him that a couple of white men might be casually talking about buying and selling him. His life might be about to change radically—without any decision from him. When Lee shook his head and Washington shrugged, Billy didn't know whether to feel relieved or disappointed.

But soon afterward, Colonel Lee died suddenly. The slaves on his plantation were badly frightened. Their expectations ran all the way from being sold to the West Indies—a real hellhole for slaves— to being set free. Billy's Mama was a short, squat, dark-skinned woman, with surprisingly broad shoulders and large hands, yet her touch with food was light and inventive. Mrs. Lee was very proud of her cuisine and had no intention of setting any of her slaves free— least of all, Billy's Mama. Mama hadn't any thought of freedom. She was worried about the struggle of having to live and work on her own in the white world. But Billy's ideas had changed dramatically after the encounter with Washington had taught him how vulnerable he was. Now, the very idea of freedom excited him.

Washington went to see the widow Lee to offer his condolences, and to learn if he could buy Billy. Mrs. Lee brought Washington to her kitchen where Billy and his brother Frank—a somewhat younger, darker-skinned lad—were standing together, looking scared. Mama was working, but wearing a sullen expression, giving sharp looks around from time to time.

Washington offered a price for Billy that he knew was low. The widow, disappointed shook her head, and suggested a higher price. They dickered for a while and finally agreed on a price. It was excruciating for Billy to stand there and learn how much money these white people thought he was worth.

Suddenly, Washington turned to Billy and asked him if he wanted to be purchased and brought to Mount Vernon.

Billy thought it was nice to be asked, but what he said was, "I don' wanna be separated from Mama an' my brothuh."

Washington was not deterred. "Mrs. Lee," he said, "I'd be happy to buy Billy's mother and brother, too, if you'll quote me a fair price."

Billy smiled, but the widow said, "I'm not selling the mother." Billy's smile evaporated.

"Then perhaps I shouldn't buy Billy," Washington said.

Feeling helpless, Billy's attention skittered between Washington and the widow.

Mrs. Lee said, "That's up to you, Colonel Washington, but I'm going to sell Billy to someone, one way or another."

That immediately clarified what had become a confused negotiation. Billy and Washington glanced at each other and both knew instinctively that this deal was going to happen. Frank vaguely understood, too, and he leaned against Billy, who put an arm around him.

"I'll buy Billy's brother to keep him company," Washington said.

The widow agreed, and the haggling on a final price went quickly. Washington and the widow scribbled a note confirming the sale. Billy and Frank picked up their clothes, while the widow embraced their Mama, both women quietly shedding tears. Washington stood silently as the boys hugged Mama. The widow, accepting the currency from Washington, was unable to say anything more. Mama forced a smile and murmured to her sons, "Do what Colonel Washington tells you," in a shaky voice. "Yes, Mama," Billy said, hugging his mother for the last time. Frank just nodded, unable to speak. Washington walked on ahead, apparently oblivious to the emotion of the moment, looking for all the world like a man who had made a good bargain for a pair of fine horses.

Billy didn't look back; he didn't want to start crying again.

CHAPTER 2

Price and Place

Figure 2 Idyllic image of Mount Vernon with Washington speaking to an overseer.

The General bought me in 17 an' 68 for sixty-one pounds an 'fifteen shillings. Truthfully, I din't really know then if I come cheap or 'spensive, but I liked to think I musta been worth more. I'd already learned that bargainin ' wi ' the General was like bonin ' a catfish. Aftuh a piece you jes wanna get it done. So he got it done. I said my goodbyes to Mama—knowin 'in my heart I'd never see her agin—an' moved all my belongin s, which wasn't much, up to Mount Vernon. Been here evuh since.

Inevuh did find out what the extrafifteen shillings was for—maybe for my good, strong teeth. The General had nothin' but trouble wi' his own teeth, tormented him all his life. You kin be sure he ʸspected mine an 'Frank's the day he bought us.

The Mount Vernon estate turned out to be much larger than Billy expected. Colonel Lee's plantation was several hundred acres, but he never owned more than a couple dozen slaves. The five farms that made up Mount Vernon totaled thousands of acres, and the Washingtons owned more than a hundred and fifty slaves. Some lived on one of the four outlying farms, but almost half of them worked at or around the Mount Vernon mansion and lived in a large two-story, white-framed building called the Family House. The first floor contained a big dining room and kitchen. The floor was earth, pounded hard and flat. Most of the slaves lived on the second floor, where there were some partitions for families, but most of the young unmarried slaves lived in large, open rooms, almost like barracks— one for the women and one for the men.

Sometimes, at Washington's request, Billy stayed in a cramped room up under the eaves in the Mansion, but most of the time he lived in the Family House in a small cubicle of his own, an arrangement that offended some of the other slaves. They couldn't see why an eighteen-year-old newcomer should have better, more private, living quarters than slaves who had lived at Mount Vernon for many years. At the Lee place, Billy had known everybody and everybody had known him. At Mount Vernon there were far too many people, spread over large distances, for Billy to know them all, and apparently, most of them were not at all interested in knowing him. His open ways and easy smile had carried him a long way at the Lee plantation. At Mount Vernon, there was little response to his early, friendly overtures; for the most part he was simply ignored. Of course, there were young black ladies who might have been interested if they weren't afraid that other young black men wouldn't like their attention to the new boy.

Even without being told, Billy understood right away that there was an unspoken hierarchy among the slaves. Those who worked in the Mansion were considered superior to those who worked in the fields. And lighter-skinned slaves, such as Billy, were ranked higher than the darker-skinned slaves. The darker skinned slaves deeply resented this differentiation, and this made for some built-in conflicts within the slave quarters.

From the beginning, it was evident to everyone that Billy was in his own unique category. He didn't work in the house or in the fields. His sole assignment was to act as Washington's huntsman when he went on a fox hunt, which happened as often as three times a week. Washington provided him with his own uniform to wear to the hunt, a plainer, less expensive version of what he himself wore. Billy liked the fresh, new clothing, but that was a further source of irritation to the other slaves, who made fun of his fancy coat and breeches. The little black cap made them laugh. Billy joined in the laughter—it seemed to be the wisest thing to do. But no matter how shrewdly—and good-naturedly—Billy reacted to the jokes, he continued to receive a certain amount of derision. Caesar, a gigantic dark-skinned man, became his chief tormentor, often asking, "Are you really a slave, Mr. Lee?"

"You kiddin' me, Caesar? A' course I'm a slave."

Caesar shook his head. "Cain't hardly believe it. Look at you. All you evuh do is dress up in fancy clothes an' ride horses now an' agin. Don' seem like slave work to me."

Caesar liked to loom over Billy when he spoke, a big black shadow that threatened to swallow him up. The last thing Billy wanted to do was fight with Caesar, who outweighed him by at least fifty pounds and was known for raising roof-rafters single-handed.

Billy knew he needed to justify his soft job as best he could. "It does seem very easy, Caesar," he said, "but it's harder than you think. I spend five hours wi' my ass on that hard saddle ev'ry time the General orders me to ride the farms wi' him, an' more hours when we go fox-hunting. Did you ever ride a horse?"

"A plough horse," Caesar said disdainfully.

"A horse is a horse, Caesar. Just imagine havin' a saddle on that plough horse, your ass bouncin' up an' down for hours, and you holdin' onto the reins so long you think your ass is gonna bleed an' your arms fall off. Sometimes I cain't sit down for the rest of the day."

The other slaves were laughing at Billy's way with words, and Caesar didn't quite know what to do. He finally said, "Jes 'membuh what I tole you."

"Yessir, Caesar, "Billy said, "an' thanks for settin' me straight." As Billy turned away he rolled his eyes in mock relief, and a few of the slaves had to suppress their laughter in order to avoid setting off

Caesar. But not all of them laughed; some, at least privately agreed with Caesar that Billy's duties were pretty easy for a strapping, muscular young man, compared to the long hours and excruciatingly harsh work often imposed on field hands. Even some of the house-hold slaves had more extensive duties and often put in far longer hours than Billy.

In fact, Billy truly enjoyed hunting. Washington provided him with fast and powerful horses from a stable full of excellent animals and personally rotated among three of them so his mount was always fresh. Billy was directed to do the same. Billy's favorite was a horse called Chinkling, named for his breed, a fast and powerful animal who seemed to hate being headed, and responded enthusiastically to Billy's constant urging for more speed. Billy rode stretched low over Chinkling's back, his head alongside the horse's neck, in contrast to Washington, who always rode severely erect. Billy never used a whip. For Chinkling, Billy's knees were just as powerful a stimulant as any whip.

There were often guests at Mount Vernon, and apparently many of the men were chosen for their skill and enthusiasm for fox-hunting. Between the hunting and the management of his far-flung properties, it seemed that Washington was always on horseback. In the beginning, Billy's duties were limited to the fox-hunt, which left him with a lot of free time—the free time that inspired the contempt— or was it jealousy—of Caesar and others. In response, he began to spend his spare time at the stables helping the stable-master feed and groom the horses. If the opportunity arose, Billy would saddle Washington's mount of the day. However, Washington seemed to prefer doing it himself, which Billy found strange. Billy watched in awe as Washington lifted his saddle with one hand and slung it on the horse's back. Billy tried to emulate this feat of strength, but he couldn't.

Washington soon noticed Billy's additional effort in the stables, which told him he hadn't been keeping this strong, young man busy enough. He promptly informed Billy that assisting the stable-master would now be part of his regular duties. Billy ruefully realized that he had outwitted himself. Washington was as clever as he was physically imposing.

When he first began riding with Washington, Billy rarely spoke, watching and listening as he tried to figure the man out. Billy quickly learned that Washington hated idle talk even more than Billy loved to chatter, and since Washington was the master and Billy the slave, silence tended to trump conversation in their many rides together. During the chase in a fox hunt, of course, talking was not possible—except for essential information exchanged or orders given. Both men were fully engaged, virtually always out-riding the other riders, occasionally making eye contact with knowing looks affirming their superior speed and agility. Billy liked to believe he was earning Washington's confidence even though the man never uttered a word of encouragement.

In fact, Billy was right—up to a point. Washington was convinced that he had made a shrewd decision in buying Billy for his huntsman. He was a superb young horseman, inspired at seeking out and finding excellent terrain for the hunt. Billy's conduct with Washington's guests was always correct, accommodating, without any attempt to become familiar. He never presumed on his close physical contact with Washington to be the chatterbox Colonel Lee had warned about.

At that time Washington's body-servant was a white man named Tom Bishop, an indentured man. He assisted Washington at and around the mansion, but he seldom accompanied Washington when he rode to inspect his farms and would have been worthless at a fox-hunt. Tom seemed to Billy to be a cheerless sort, but since Washington preferred silence, perhaps that was satisfactory to Washington. Billy couldn't help thinking it might not be particularly pleasant to have a surly, apparently unhappy man help you dress and tend to your personal needs. He also learned that Tom's term was running out, and the word around Mount Vernon—from Tom's black slave girlfriend—was that when his indentured time was over, Tom intended to leave Mount Vernon. Billy wondered whether being Washington's body-servant would be a good job.

Washington was thinking along the same lines. He wanted an efficient servant, not a companion, but Tom's value was limited. He could read and write fairly well, but his horsemanship was such that Washington had given up bringing him along on inspections. Washington recalled that Colonel Lee had touted Billy's skills at reading and writing, and he already knew that the young man rode very skillfully. One day, when the fox-hunt was over, Washington told

Billy to follow him to the Mansion as soon as he had stabled his horse. Billy couldn't think of any recent transgression of his, so he didn't believe he was about to be punished. Still, you never knew around these white folks.

As soon as he had cleaned himself up, Billy presented himself at the Mansion. Washington led him to the room outside his bed-chamber, where Tom was folding and hanging some of Washington's clothes.

"Tom," Washington said, "this is William Lee—Billy. He is going to be your assistant. I want you to train him to help you with your duties. Billy, you'll take your orders from Tom. Tomorrow, when I ride my farms, I want you to ride with me."

This all came as a surprise to Billy—and to Tom as well. Not that Tom particularly cared; his time would be up in a couple of months, and he was planning to leave anyway. He didn't know much about Billy, but he was young and Tom would give him the hardest and heaviest work.

That is how Billy became Washington's body-servant in addition to his regular fox-hunting duties. At first he was only an assistant, but Billy's natural energy and enthusiasm outshone Tom's laconic service, and when Tom's term expired, Billy became Washington's only body-servant. The other slaves quickly became aware of Billy's new status, which didn't change their attitudes towards him. In fact, some thought he had somehow charmed his way into a much more difficult job than he had had before, and they laughed about it.

In addition to becoming familiar with the General's preferences in food, clothing and other personal matters, Billy learned to speak two languages. The first was his natural way of talking—the way he spoke to most folks, especially his own people. The other was what he thought of privately as the "White Man's Tongue," the more formal manner in which he spoke to the General's friends, such as the governor, and other important white people

As Washington's body-servant, Billy laid out his clothes and helped him dress, brushed his thick reddish-brown hair, of which he realized Washington was very vain, and tied a queue in it. Billy didn't prepare Washington's meals, but he served them to him, especially breakfast, often some kind of fish, and almost always hoecakes— pancakes made with corn, melted butter and honey—accompanied by three cups of tea. Then, routinely, regardless of the weather or the season, they would ride to one or more of Washington's five farms to inspect and manage them.

When Washington viewed his properties, he kept records, gave orders to the overseers of each farm and sometimes to individual workers. Billy became a kind of secretary. Washington gave him a notebook and a pencil—a thin stick of graphite gripped in wood or wrapped in string—and told Billy what to write. Sometimes the notes were very specific: "1 keg of #6 nails for Samuel," the black overseer of River Farm, and sometimes they were very broad and general: "Wheat not growing properly, may need to rotate crops."

In addition to the slaves he owned, Washington also bought indentured servants and artisans, usually for their special skills. He was continually expanding and improving his property—during peace and war—and some type of construction was always underway. The work required skilled carpenters, joiners, masons, brick-makers and painters. Washington sometimes went to the harbor at Alexandria to meet a boatload of artisans, and often purchased the craftsmen he needed, just as if they were slaves. Also, like slaves, sometimes the indentured men ran away. Washington responded exactly the same way he did for runaway slaves . He posted and advertised the name and description of the men, and offered a reward for capturing and returning them. For example, two white carpenters named Spears and Winters ran away and tried to escape downriver. They were apprehended almost immediately and returned to Mount Vernon. Billy concluded there wasn't much difference between white and black people at Mount Vernon—Washington owned almost all of them.

Washington often surprised Billy by jumping off his horse to actually assist in the work. He might pick up a shovel and dig, or help move a heavy rock, or assist a carpenter lining up his work. One time he joined several men who were trying to raise a wooden partition that had been nailed together on the ground. His strength made the difference. Of course, when Washington pitched in, Billy had to do the same. It wouldn't look right for Washington to be digging a ditch while Billy sat on his horse, idly watching.

One afternoon, Billy was taking notes beside an irrigation ditch. "Three shovels of dirt per minute for Caesar," Washington dictated, "four for Pompey, and none at all for Samson, who claims he's too sick to work and is just sitting there on the ground like a lump." Billy wrote the numbers and the names in his notebook as Washington paced back and forth beside the ditch, periodically cursing beneath his breath, while the white overseer, Valentine Johnson, kept wrap-ping and unwrapping his whip around his wrist. "Worthless ass-holes.... pieces of pure shit....y ou, too, Johnson, just watching this goddamn fiasco." Johnson did not seem particularly disturbed at the tirade. He had heard it before. His head was down, eyes looking at the ground, hand wrapping that whip.

Billy also said nothing. He had learned from experience that there was no talking to Washington when he was in mid-eruption, for then he entered a zone where his furies detonated a long string of interior explosions that simply had to run their course.

"I got the numbers, General," Billy semi-whispered as Washington continued pacing. "Nothin' more to do here. Maybe we should head on back." Washington silently nodded, then mounted up, and Billy let him ride ahead for several minutes, allowing some space for the after-shocks.

What you folh don' unnerstan "bout the General, 'cause it don' fit wi what it says in the booh, is that he was what I call a full man. Brimmin' ovuh, he was. Some men, famous men too, they have an easy time bein 'what we want 'em to be, 'cause they got no fires. But the General had some big fires burnin' inside him. It took a heap a tryin 'for him to stop from burnin' up. The books wanna make him inta a statue, an 'I reckon they's a reason for that, but I kin tell you, he was a full-up man, alius threatenin' to ooze out ovuh the top. I don' think you'd wanna work for him.

Billy realized—as perhaps Washington did not—that as soon as they were out of sight Johnson was going to whip the shit out of those slaves. He couldn't help feeling sorry for them even though the whippings might cause a problem for him, personally. It was well known that Caesar was Billy's implacable enemy, and he had been present when Washington castigated the men, and precipitated their whipping. Not that Billy had any real sympathy for Caesar, but he certainly didn't want to be at odds with this monster.

Washington kept talking as they rode along. "The problem isn't really Johnson," said Washington, exhaling deeply. "The problem is my workers just won't work. They're eating me out of house and home, costing me more than they earn."

Billy let this thought settle. Johnson was probably unfurling his whip now, and Caesar was being forced to take off his shirt. That's the way it worked. Johnson was a little man, a little white man, but he had the big whip.

Billy would have liked to tell Washington that the problem was that Washington didn't have workers, he had slaves. There was no reason for them to work their butts off. Washington wasn't going to pay them a big bonus for working hard. It wasn't that they were lazy; it was that they were slaves.

Although Washington had been opening up to him a bit more these days, Billy was certainly not going to tell him how to run his plantation. In all likelihood, in some locked-off compartment of his brain, Washington also realized that the problem was that the men were slaves. But he was not prepared to consciously consider that problem, which well might overturn his whole world. He kept riding, looking straight ahead. He had obviously recovered his composure and with it his preternatural calm, which some observers likened to a Roman stoic, others to an Indian chief. This was his other, more familiar, zone. No one could tell what he was thinking, much less feeling, at such moments, and Billy knew well enough to let such silences alone.

The truth was, Washington had never given slavery much thought at all. Like most Virginia planters he had been born into it. He had inherited his first slaves from his father's estate when he was eleven years old. He referred to his slaves the same way he talked about his livestock, and felt no compunction about shipping trouble-makers off to the death camps that were the sugar cane fields in the West Indies. That wasn't just an idle threat. Some years earlier, Washington had sold Tom, an incorrigible slave who had run away and been caught several times, to Barbados, locked in chains, knowing he would be dead from overwork in a few years. The story was well-known to the slaves at Mount Vernon and retold as a cautionary tale for years thereafter.

Washington had no wish to consider the problem—if it were a problem—at this time. And since indecision was the cardinal vice in his mental universe, he decided to decisively ignore the matter and change the subject.

"By the way, Mrs. Washington is going to need you to serve at the Belvoir dance tonight," he said to Billy, who just nodded. They rode the rest of the way in silence.

CHAPTER 3

Neighbors

Billy was standing with his arms folded, his back against the wall, decked out in his best butler livery. He and others from Mount Vernon had been recruited to assist at a Farewell Ball being held at Belvoir, the magnificent estate of the Fairfax family several miles upriver, where the Washingtons and Fairfaxes were co-hosts. Car-tons and boxes were piled here and there, the remaining furniture was draped, and the estate, despite its grandeur, had an already abandoned look.

Washington clearly had Belvoir in mind when he remodeled Mount Vernon, but he could not afford the expensive stone, let alone the scale of Belvoir, so he used wood, painted and stippled to give the appearance of stone. On the other hand, Mount Vernon's setting above the Potomac was the equal of any estate in the Tidewater.

Washington had moved from his mother's home to Mount Vernon soon after his half-brother Lawrence had married Ann Fairfax. Her family, led by the eccentric patriarch, Lord Thomas Fairfax, was probably the largest landowner in Virginia, a living vestige of an almost feudal aristocracy. Colonel William Fairfax, the patriarch's cousin had taken over the day to day responsibilities for operating the North American properties. George Washington, age sixteen, had gotten his first job, joining his best friend, William's son, George William Fairfax, in surveying the family's vast holdings in the Shenandoah. He remained there for several years, developing his fascination for western lands and acquiring his first individual holdings. When Lawrence died, George applied for his former office in the Virginia Militia, and thus began his second career. His subsequent role in the French and Indian wars would always be a matter of controversy, but in the Tidewater he was a hero.

Figure 3 Young George Washington as surveyor.

Those days were long past as Billy observed the dancers at Belvoir. It had long been rumored that Washington was enamored of Sally Fairfax, his best friend's wife. That hardly mattered now, as the couple were moving to England, and George Washington and Sally would never see each other again. There would be correspondence, and towards the end of their lives, almost confessional letters, but the realities of their relationship would never be fiilly known.

The ballroom at Belvoir was big enough to accommodate fifty couples, but almost twice that number crowded the space that evening, and the flaring gowns of the ladies kept brushing against Billy as they danced past his station. He didn't mind at all.

Part of his mind was still back there at that irrigation ditch, where Washington had temporarily lost control. And yet here was the General on the dance floor, the model of composure, bowing with dramatic flair as each Virginia damsel approached him with her dance card, indicating that she was next in line to place her left hand on the muscular arm of the most impressive physical specimen in the room— Virginia's greatest military hero in the French and Indian War, and the best male dancer to boot.

"The general had a real big ass, an' thick legs. So if you was to describe him by his parts, he might sound downright clumsy. But the truth was that on the dance floor, as on horseback, he was a glidin' man, whose body had that built-in music. The ladies could trust that his han' at they waist would guide them gracefully to the next step. I really do think he was a bettuh dancer than a rider, though I's prob 'ly prejudiced–is that how you say it?–'cause I could always out-ride him, but he could out-dance me any time."

Billy watched Martha watching all this, a petite but handsome and well-coiffed lady, adept at carrying on a meaningless conversation about the weather or the surging price of negroes at Richmond, all the while keeping an eye on her husband, and on the tightening grip of those Virginian beauties swirling away in plain sight. Billy wondered what the beauties were saying, if anything. And what Martha was thinking, if thinking was the right word.

The last dance of the evening required the hosts and hostesses to take the lead. As Sally danced with George William, Martha danced with Washington and whispered "At last" in a tone that Washington found difficult to decipher. George William and Sally drifted off the floor, and the guests formed a circle around the Washingtons as he showed off his most sweeping style. Martha touched his powerful right arm, tossed her head backward, hair almost trailing to the floor, then let out a loud and blissful "Yes!" The guests broke out into spontaneous applause. Several of the most coquettish ladies, who concealed their jealousy behind forced smiles and barely touched their satin gloves together in a mockery of clapping, whispered how inappropriate they considered the intimate style of the Washingtons.

Figure 4 Martha Custis.

***

As soon as they returned to Mount Vernon, Martha took Washington by the hand and led him up the stairs to their bedroom, humming the last tune of the dance as she skipped up the stairs.

Billy retired to the alcove he was assigned to when directed to stay overnight at the mansion, a small cubicle immediately adjacent to the Washingtons' suite.

After the Washingtons were in their bedroom, Martha let down her hair, then turned her back to Washington. "Dear, unbutton me, if you would."

"Did you enjoy yourself tonight, my dear?" he asked as Martha let her gown fall to her feet.

"Well, there are at least three women who were hoping that you would be unbuttoning their gowns at this very moment," she whispered with a smile. "Watching them simmer was interesting."

"I'm only interested in whether you're simmering right now," Washington whispered.

Martha turned, placed her arms as far around her husband's waist as they would go and put her forehead onto his chest. "Are proper ladies allowed to simmer, dear?" she asked teasingly and then began to raise up his shirt. "Tonight I think I would rather melt than simmer," she said seductively.

Washington took Martha's face into his hands as he took off his shirt and tossed it aside. "Dear, about those flirtatious women tonight," he stammered, "is there something I can do....? Something I shouldn't do....?"

"It's not what you do, my dear," Martha observed, 'it's who you are. And, God knows I'd be the last person to want that changed." She reached down and began to unbuckle his belt. "The last person." As she led him to bed, Martha whispered into his ear: "Just remember, you married the wealthiest widow in Virginia."

"Was that the reason I married you?" Washington asked as he lay down beside Martha.

"You tell me," Martha teased. "I always thought you were on the rebound from the *lovely* Sally Fairfax.

"God, I was so young then," he sighed as he stroked Martha's hair.

Martha turned on her side to face Washington, took his face in her hands, then murmured, "So show me tonight that you're not yet an old man."

"My simmering.... melting.... wealthy... wife," Washington chuckled.

"Stop talking," she declared as she pressed against him.

CHAPTER 4

Family and Friends

It was true that Mount Vernon was much larger and more elegant than the Lee plantation and better organized, but at the same time life there lacked many of the intimate personal qualities that Billy was fond of. His relationship with the Lees had been relaxed and he had enjoyed a good deal of personal freedom. Mrs. Lee had taught him to read and write, and Colonel Lee had begun his training as a horseman. He had few specified duties, and because the Lee place was so much smaller he hadn't had to deal with large numbers of other slaves, all engaged in various farming and construction enterprises.

Billy had believed that having his brother Frank with him at Mount Vernon would help him avoid feeling lonely, but Frank was years younger and almost lost without his Mama. Billy found him one day, huddled in a corner of the Family House, weeping.

"What's wrong, Frankie?" Billy asked.

"I wanna go home."

Billy wondered why he had thought a twelve-year old boy would be good company—brother or not. Billy sighed. "This is your home now."

"I miss Mama."

"Me, too. But we ain't gonna see her agin, no more."

This brought a new freshet of tears. Billy moved protectively, so that no one else would see his brother crying. People who showed weakness—especially slaves—suffered for it.

"Wanna go ridin' horseback with me?" Billy asked.

This interrupted the flow.

"Don' know how to ride, Billy."

"Come on, I'll teach you."

"What if I fall off?"

"You'll get back on again."

Billy asked the General for permission to use one of the older, softer-riding horses to teach his brother to ride. Washington had no objection.

At the last minute, Frank tried to back out, but Billy wouldn't let him. There was some cringing, some shaking, a little whimpering, but in a few sessions, Frank gained confidence and was able to canter around the curving driveway with reasonable confidence.

"When do I get my own horse?" Frank asked.

Billy barely resisted the urge to knock him silly. Stiffening his resolve, he decided to continue training Frank. Perhaps one day he would be a huntsman, too, although he didn't believe Frank showed any real zest for horsemanship, just a mild interest in having fun.

Billy decided he would also teach Frank to read and write. Mrs. Lee had started Billy reading books around the age of five. For some reason she hadn't done so with Frank. Maybe the Lees had decided having one literate slave was enough for the whole plantation. Still, he was thankful he had been that slave.

At first, Frank balked at learning to read. "What good will it do me?"

"You kin read a bible jes like Mama's."

"I know all them stories already."

Billy laughed. "You can learn all kines a' good things iffen you can read."

"Like what?"

"Like how to do more than break your back diggin' ditches. They's lots a' jobs 'round the plantation you kin do if you kin read and write."

Frank was suspicious. "Cicero is a good carpenter—kin he read?"

"You bet he kin. You see them rolls a' papuh he uses when he's barn-buildin'? Them are plans, an' they tell him how to put up the walls an' raise the roof." He felt silly having to explain this to his own brother, but Frank wasn't dumb, he was just ignorant—an ignorant slave. Billy didn't even tell him how reading and writing would help him get and stay free. Frank's eyes were barely open to the realities of his world.

When Billy showed his brother how to perform some of his duties as a butler, Frank perked up a bit. He liked the livery Billy wore—the handsome, well-cut clothing appealed to him. Washington noticed Billy training his brother and thought he would look well at formal functions. He offered to dress Frank accordingly, and on occasion the boy proudly carried a tray or poured wine from a pitcher. Many of the other slaves didn't like Frank's new clothing and his job—the same ones who thought Billy was guilty of putting on airs. Billy learned, ruefully, that instead of having a companion, he now had another person to defend. He could only hope that some day in some way, his investment of time, energy and affection for Frank would pay off.

***

When Billy came to live at Mount Vernon in 1768 at age eighteen, there were two other youngsters living there: Martha Washington's children from her late first husband, Jackie, her son, age fourteen, and her daughter, Patsy, twelve—the same age as Billy's brother, Frank. Patsy was a delightful child, open, friendly and good-natured, a favorite of virtually everyone, black and white. She was slight, graceful, with a tumble of brown hair and large, oval eyes. But she suffered from sudden, seizures—the "falling-down" disease—sometimes called "epilepsy," which did not have any generally recognized successful treatment. Everyone at Mount Vernon was alerted to her problems, but what to do about them was another matter. Many slaves were frightened by her attacks, and even some supposedly sophisticated whites thought anyone having these attacks was somehow possessed.

One day, Martha entered a first floor parlor and was astonished to see Billy sprawled on the floor, his body arched over Patsy's twisting body, her hair flailing, her skirts askew, muted screams coming from her throat. Martha also screamed, thoroughly mistaking the situation, and then instantly realizing she had misunderstood, she covered her error with a cry of, "Oh, Patsy!" and dropped to the floor beside them.

Billy, unfazed, never looked up. "She was bitin' her tongue, Ma'am, and I eased it outta her mouth."

He was holding Patsy firmly, but gently and her spasms were gradually subsiding. Billy had understood the source of Martha's first response, and although deeply hurt, he knew enough about white folks not to let it plunge him into bitterness.

"Thank you, Billy," Martha said, composing herself as well as she could.

"May I carry Miss Patsy to her room?" Billy asked.

Martha's hesitation was very brief. "Of course, Billy."

***

That evening, Martha told George about the episode.

"I wish we had an answer to her problem," George said, "but none of our doctors seems to be very helpful."

Martha continued to stare at him, and Washington knew there was another unresolved issue. "What is troubling you, my dear?"

She hesitated, reluctant to express her concerns. "Billy was very helpful, today."

George, accustomed to her style, immediately realized that Billy— somehow—was the problem. He could also wind his way around a subject if necessary. "Please tell me about the entire episode, again."

She told him.

"Finding this young, black man, crouching over your daughter, frightened you."

"Yes."

"Do you think there is any danger there?"

She did not respond.

Washington realized she was being foolish, but he did not want to say so. He also understood that her feelings arose, not from a particular fear of Billy, but from deeply ingrained attitudes toward black men, especially slaves. It was as much a part of his culture as hers, but she had been sheltered from reality by two husbands and their families. And her bigotry ran far deeper than his.

Washington said, "We must be careful not to lose the good will of those who serve us, but at the same time, we must pay attention to everything that happens at Mount Vernon."

It was a weak speech, but it satisfied Martha.

***

Jackie Custis was a different story. Martha's son, her eldest child and her favorite, had been indulged since birth. At age fourteen, Jackie was of average size and build, neither handsome nor homely, neither bright nor stupid. He was, at best, indifferent to his studies, and in a contest, it would probably have turned out that Billy could read and write far better than he did. But Jackie was crafty, and knew how to wheedle whatever he wanted—special clothing, a new saddle for his horse—from his mother and stepfather. George would have exerted more discipline, but he did not believe it was his place to do so.

In the early days, Jackie had tried to take over Billy, in effect to make him his personal servant, but Washington had immediately been aware of this, and sternly advised Jackie that Billy was his—Washington's—body-servant, not Jackie's. This did not please Jackie, but there was no appeal. Billy was clever enough to try to mollify Jackie from time to time with little services and favors, but Jackie was largely oblivious to the good deeds of others.

It was common knowledge that the Washingtons had their disagreements about Jackie, who stayed pretty wild until, a few years later, he met a pretty young lady from a very fine family, Miss Eleanor Calvert. Then, all of a sudden, Jackie became very polite, smiled a lot, stopped ordering folks around. He surprised everybody at Mount Vernon—maybe everybody in the state of Virginia. When Jackie and "Nelly" married, Martha and George—and Patsy—were thrilled. Patsy was very happy to have a new "sister."

But the same year Jackie got married, Patsy had her worst attack of epilepsy. In the past, notwithstanding the severity of these attacks, somehow Patsy had survived, but this time, despite all the efforts of family and doctors, she died in agony. Martha was deeply despondent. Even George, who had never gotten down on his knees to pray, did so for Patsy, but to no avail.

It was a strange time. Pasty dies an' later Jackie marries. Washington's best fren', George William an' his wife Sally 'migrates to England. For the nex' several years, Jackie an' Nelly was very happy. He was a terr 'ble farmer, but a fertile fathuh. Nelly has seven chillun, only four a'whom survives. One a' 'em they names for the General— George Washington Parke Custis, but again, tragedy almos' buries the good news. The year this son—called "Wash"—was born, Jackie dies. But thass 'nothuh story.

***

And then there was "Preacher," a man around forty years of age in 1768, whom Billy had carefully chosen to befriend when he arrived at Mount Vernon. He was tall and angular, with sharply chiseled features and a shaved head. His eyes were kind and his smile serene. He often carried a small, well-thumbed, leather-bound book, which the others thought was a bible. It was, in fact, a book of prayers, and it was the source of his sobriquet. Preacher could actually read the prayers, but no one seemed to know where and how he had learned to read. Other slaves often asked him for a blessing, which he was happy to give. On occasion, the General allowed him to perform a pseudo-marriage ceremony for slave couples. It pleased the slaves and helped to preserve tranquility at Mount Vernon. Preacher did not pretend to be authorized by the Anglican church or any other organized religion.

His given name was Vitruvius, but it was not an easy name and very few could pronounce it properly. Billy had seen the name etched into wood at Preacher's bedside. He had copied it down and later asked the General about it. The General was startled, but then smiled. He gave Billy the correct pronunciation and told him the name was that of a great Roman architect. He said when Vitruvius was born, Washington's father, Augustine, had thought the baby's face resembled a face on a Roman coin he had once seen—somewhere.

"I've known Vitruvius—Preacher—since childhood," the General said. "When my father died—I was eleven years old—he left me ten slaves, including Vitruvius, whom I called "Vitty," who was at or near my age. Vitty and I had played together when we were younger. He had always been a slave, but somehow it was different now that I personally owned him. I was a child, myself, but I owned him."

Suddenly, the General seemed embarrassed by these personal comments. "You'll find him a very good man," he said. "He's a good carpenter and a loyal, trustworthy, man. He knows most everything about Mount Vernon and its history." The General turned abruptly away; the reminiscences were over.

Billy cultivated Preacher very slowly. He knew he would need a counterweight to Big Caesar, but he couldn't be too obvious, or folks wouldn't believe that Preacher was independent—everyone would believe that Preacher was merely Billy's "man."

It was obvious that Preacher was well-respected and that many, young and old, sought out his advice. Preacher's wife, Lily, was a cook in the Main House and their daughter, Phyllis, was a seamstress. They were, for Mount Vernon, a professional family, well-liked, well-respected.

Billy's first approach came when he found Preacher sitting alone reading his prayer book in a corner of the Family House dining room.

"Vitruvius," Billy said, enunciating clearly.

Preacher looked up sharply, then smiled. "Ain't heard my full name in so long, I almos' din't recognize it. How come you know that?"

"The General tole me."

"Ah. My former playmate."

Preacher then told Billy what he already knew, and more

"He's a fine lookin' man, today," Preacher said. "Tall, strong, nice head a' hair, big nose an' chin. You'd a seen him at ten or eleven, you wouldna thought so. Very tall for his age, so thin he looked like a coat rack—all angles an' awkward. Strong already, but clumsy. Thought he might fall down any time. Ass looked too big for his body, nose too big for his face. But he was stubborn, tried hard at everything. Couldn' please his Mama, much. She jes thought he was a big ugly kid. Nevuh showed no love for him. I felt sorry—I was a slave and my Mama was kinduh to me.

"George learned to read and write—got help from Lawrence, his half-brother, fourteen years olduh. George worshiped Lawrence. Good, kind man. Sickly, but good an' kind."

Billy didn't learn these things in one sitting. His talks with Preacher stretched across days, weeks, months. In time, he felt he knew a great deal about the General, and all of it would help him as he made his way through life at Mt. Vernon.

Preacher said he never did understand the relationship between George and his mother, Mary Ball Washington. George resembled her very strongly, which wasn't flattering because she was not a pretty woman. But the same, strong features looked fine for a man. Still, Preacher knew that George felt she had stood in his way, more than once. Lawrence had wanted George to enlist in the British navy. Mary had flatly refused. "They'll chew him up and spit him out," she said.

"They'll use him, abuse him, and in the end he'll have nothing—not even be able to buy a cheap commission."

Fact is, she was probably right, but George lost his one chance to visit England, and he long regretted it. The only time George ever left the country was to visit Barbados with Lawrence, who was hoping the hot climate would help cure his consumption. It didn't work, but George had a wonderful time living a full, social life away from the lowering eye of his mother. Unfortunately, he became infected with smallpox. He recovered, but for the rest of his life his face was marred with tiny scars.

"Took him a long time to accept all that scarrin,' Preacher recalled, "small as it was. Early on, he was always searchin' his face in a mirror, hopin' the marks was gonna disappear. 'Course they din't but he was free of the pox forevuh."

Preacher hesitated. There was more to the story. "Me an' an olduh slave, Leander, accompanied George to Barbados as his servants, and Lawrence brought a couple a' his slaves.

"It was George's first—and only—time away from home, an' he went a little wild, goin' to parties every night, dancin' till dawn." Preacher took a deep breath before continuing. "George got involved wi' a pretty young Creole girl—they say that's where he got the pox. Fact is, after we got back to Mount Vernon, we heard she died a the pox. Some folks said she was pregnant an' her baby died, too."

Preacher paused again.

"Come on," Billy said. "Don' leave me hangin.'"

Preacher sighed. "It's jes a rumor, but we heard the baby was George's. Don' know 'bout that, but I do know he was mighty sad when he come home. Maybe 'cause he d been so sick. Maybe 'cause Lawrence don' get better. But maybe...." His voice drifted off.

"When did the General and Miz Washington get married?" Billy asked.

"In '59," Preacher said.

"Pretty long time, but they ain't had no chillun," Billy said.

"Thass true."

"Miz Washington has two chillun," Billy said, slowly leading up to his real question for Preacher. "The General looks very fit an' strong, but do you think maybe the smallpox keeps him from havin' chillun?"

"We all been wonderin' 'bout that for a long time," Preacher responded. "Mr. Washington not only got smallpox in Barbados, he also got malaria an' the consumption. Some folks believe all that sickness make him unable to have chillun. Don' know iffen that's true, jes like we don' truly know if he got that Creole lady in Barbados pregnant."

Billy didn't question him further, but he tucked those stories away in his memory. He might have use for them some time down the line.

CHAPTER 5

Philomena

Soon aftuh I get to Mount Vernon, I meet this young an'pretty slave, name a' Philomena. She's a couple years younguh than me—mebbe sixteen—but b 'lieve me she's a full developed lady. When I was at Colonel Lee's, slaves was kep'apart unless the owners wants 'em togethuh, so I ain't spent much time wi 'young women. At Mount Vernon, Phil an 'me get real close real fas 'an 'soon she tells me she's gonna have a baby—my baby. Shocks me, but seems they's oney one thing to do—I gotta marry this gal. She says gettin 'married's fine wi' her, so I ast the General if it's all right wi'him. He ain't too happy, but he agrees. We has Preacher do the honors, an 'jes like that, we's married.

So one mornin, 'I wake up wi' 'nothuh person in my bed—my very own wife. Not even sure what that means, but it's a done deal. Some parts of it is fun—you kin easy guess what that is—but then they's the responsibility, an' the fact a' gettin' along with 'nothuh person. We's both young, an' not much experience at any a' this, but we struggle along.

Then, jes as fast, Phil's burstin' wi' that baby, gettin' sick mos' ev 'ry mornin,' an' not able to work in the fields at all. They's ladies there who acts as midwives, an' I ast what to do. They tell me ain't much I kin do, but they keep Phil calm an' quiet—much as they's able. I try to show I care, but don' really know how to act. I'm sure sorry Phil's got so much pain. I'd seen ladies pregnan' afore, but nevuh with these kinds a 'problems.

About six months along, Phil wakes up in the night, screamin.' I ain't sleepin' in the same bed no more, but I'm oney a few feet away. I run for the midwives, an' they come lickety split. Got me some boilin' water, listenin' to that poor lady's screams behine me. 'Most evabody in the Fam 'ly House is awake—cain 't sleep wi' all that noise.

I'm pacin 'up an' back. Midwives is workin' hard—whatevuh they's doin—I leans in, but they shove me away. "Get mo' water," they say. I kin barely catch a look at Phil's face, an 'she loo fa scairt to death. She's screamin'—cain't believe her voice holds up.

But soon, she sounds a bit hoarse, an' then some weakuh. An' fin'ly don 'hear her at all. Silence is very loud—even louduh as minutes go by. Kin oney hear the rustlin' a' midwives skirts. Then, they ain't no sound at all. One a'the midwives comes to me, an 'takes my hand. She got tears in her eyes.

"She's gone, " she whispuhs.

I cain't unnerstan' what she means. "What you sayin'?" I ast.

She puts an arm 'round my shoulders, an' says, "Philomena is gone to heaven."

I throws her arm off an' hurry to Phil's bedside. Kneel down, touch her face. "Phil," I whispuh, "please talk to me."

No answer. I whisper agin, "Honey, I'm here. Please tell me you's here."

Midwife comes up to me, kneels 'aside me, "Billy, I'm sorry, she cain't hear you." Pauses. "She's daid."

Word cuts to my heart. I throw my arms 'round Phil, huggin' her, kissin' her, pleadin' wi 'her to be alive. But it ain't so. I fin'ly has to give up. I kisses Phil's mouth, an' then they close her eyes an 'pull a sheet ovuh her head.

That's when I sees the little thing wrapped in a blanket, lyin' on a chair. I knows what it is—it's the baby. I go ovuh. I kin see it ain't breathin '—so small, so small. Ain't never gonna breathe. It's a tiny boy. My son. I start sobbin.'

Lordy Lordy, I cain't believe it. But it's true. Midwife takes little critter away, an' I don'stop her. I'm helpless—helpless. Young, an' dumb, an' helpless. They try to lead me away, but I ain't goin.' I'm stayin' wi' my Philomena. Day goes inta night, night inta day. I hardly move at all.

Next day, we bury Phil an' the tiny baby. Lots a weepin' 'round Mount Vernon—some of it mine. Nevuh lost nobody before—not to

*death. Strange kinda feelin. 'So final, an 'nowhere to go. General an'
Mrs. Washington is kine to me, don' expect too much from me. But
I tell the General, work is good for me. I wanna keep workin'—do
evathin 'I kin to put this sadness behine me. It's many weeks afore I
feel like a human bein 'again. Cain't help thinkin 'some times' bout
the General an' that girl in Barbados. Mebbe we got more in common
than we know.*

CHAPTER 6

Two Saturday Nights

The General taught me a lotta fine words an' the idear s that went wi' 'em. One a' my favorites was "hierarchy," which means who's on top, who's on the bottom, an' who's in-between. Thasspretty clear in the army where evabody's got a rank, an' you kin draw youself a chart an 'fill in names by ev'ry rank.

Same thing was mos'ly true at Mount Vernon, where the General was on top, Miz Washington's a tad lower an' us slaves is at the bottom. Below the Washingtons was Mr. Lund Washington, the General 's cousin, who was the manager a 'Mount Vernon for many years.

Then comes the overseers, who's in charge a' runnin' the individual farms. Some was white an' some was black. Unduh them was the artisans, people wi' special skills, like joiners, masons, weavers. They was mos'ly white an' free or Ventured servants.

Finally, at the bottom, come me an' my people, the black slaves.

Billy tried to be very careful how he spoke to other slaves, but if he forgot himself and spoke the "White man's tongue" to ordinary folks at Mount Vernon—say the field slaves—they thought he was looking down on them.

What made it worse was that slaves who worked in the Mansion House thought they were better than the ones who worked in the fields, and the field slaves resented the "airs" of the Mansion slaves. Billy tried to stay friends with everybody, but it wasn't easy, especially because he was so close to the head man—the General. That made him the number one slave—if there was such a position.

But the lines weren't really sharp and clear. After the Revolution Hercules, a slave, was Martha Washington's favorite cook. There wasn't any worker—slave or free, manager or overseer—who stood higher with her than Hercules. He got whatever he wanted, including elegant clothing, even fancier than any the General ever wore, even a velvet waistcoat and a gold-headed cane. If he wanted a young woman to spend the night in his quarters, no one would complain.

Billy could read and write and was the best horseman and fox-hunter anybody had ever seen, but he didn't have any construction skills such as a mason or carpenter. Theoretically he would have ranked higher than a field hand, but lower than a manager or overseer. That wasn't the whole picture. He was with the General almost every day. Besides Mrs. Washington and Lund Washington, anybody at Mount Vernon who wanted to get the General's attention, had to go through him.

But even that wasn't the whole story. As long as he was with the General, and in his good graces, Billy was a powerful figure. No overseer was likely to interfere with him. But when he was alone, especially in the Family House, he was just another slave and vulnerable to the jealousies all around him.

One Saturday evening, while the slaves were dancing in the Family Room, Big Herman, the hulking, heavy-set white overseer at Dogue River Farm, stumbled in. He was very drunk, and when he first came in he was staggering around, swinging his arms to the music. It was easy to see his eyes weren't in focus.

Several dozen slaves were dancing a Virginia Reel—doing a pretty good job of it—and they tried to ignore Big Herman. He soon wandered close to the dancers and bumped into a young lady, but she regained her step and kept dancing. Jason on the flute looked over to Billy, who, because of his connection to Washington, was considered to be in the know when it came to dealing with white folks. Jason's eyes were asking the question, "Should we quit?" Billy shook his head and strummed strongly on his banjo, a skill Junius had taught him..

Herman didn't notice anything. He bumped into another dancer, this time a strapping young buck, and that young man didn't give ground. Herman bounced off like he had hit a brick wall, lost his footing, and fell back. His face was turning purple. Herman stiffened up and, walking like he was on a tightrope, stepped back in the line and started dancing again. He was clumsy as an ox, and he messed up the line. Folks began dropping out, one by one and two by two.

Herman found himself turning and turning in the middle of the floor, all alone, while the music was still playing.

Herman staggered to a halt, spun around, blinked his eyes and yelled loudly, "Stop that fiddlin,' nigguhs!"

The others looked again to Billy. He gave Herman a big smile, still strumming away."You's a fine dancer, Mr. Herman," he said. Some of the slaves started to giggle–very low, but Herman heard them.

He took two steps toward Billy–wobbly steps–then said, "Stop that music, nigguh!"

Billy signaled to the other musicians and they all stopped playing. Herman didn't know what to do. He was standing in the middle of several dozen black slaves, looking foolish. And he sensed it.

Herman started laughing—not really laughing—but forcing it out. Loud, coarse, as if he were throwing up more than laughing. His eyes weren't laughing, but he was slapping his hands and pretending to laugh. Then he stopped suddenly and screamed, "You dumb nigguhs, you think you kin dress up like white folks, play white people's music an' dance like white folks–but you cain't. You jes a bunch a' animals pretendin' to be people! Pigs an' cows dancin' the reel!"

Herman was laughing again, and the younger men were moving toward him—very slowly, but their eyes were dark, hard and fixed. Billy realized that somebody was about to be beaten up real bad, maybe get killed, and it was probably going to be that stupid oaf, Big Herman. Which wouldn't be good for anybody. Billy stepped forward and slammed a chord on his 5-stringer.

"Le's dance evabody–take your partners an' dance!" He nodded to the other players and they started sawing away on the fiddle, tooting on the horn and blowing on the flute. Some young ladies, smarter than their men, began to pull them onto the floor.

Herman staggered backwards out of the Family Room. He was moving pretty fast for a big man, trying to pretend he was full of dignity and leaving because he wanted to. But he wasn't fooling anybody— not even himself. Then he was gone, and everybody was dancing.

But it ain 't like before. When you's a slave, the massuhs kin always stop you in your trach–jes like that. Turn you from a man to a dog. An' I hates it! But what kin I do? Tell the General that Herman, the big nasty overseer, said some mean things to me an'my feelin's was hurt? The General wasn't right there, so I went back to being a common slave—way down at the bottom of the hierarchy. An' the rest of the slaves could see that there wasn't a damn thing I could do about it.

***

Then there was another Saturday night that started with innocent dancing. As usual, a couple of men had fiddles, another a flute, and Junius, a house slave, had a banjo. Soon after he arrived at Mount Vernon, Billy had talked Junius into teaching him to play it."It was a simple darn thing," Billy exclaimed, "but it made good noise."

The slaves came in from the outbuildings around the Mansion and from the farms farther out and mixed with the Mansion slaves, most of whom lived at the Family House. The General didn't mind the slaves getting together, as long as there was no loud ruckus and they didn't get too drunk to work on Monday morning.

Usually, the gatherings were cheerful, but sometimes there would be friction. Caesar, a mean-tempered man, was probably the strongest slave at Mount Vernon; he had helped build a barn by lifting heavy beams into place single-handedly. He lived at Muddy Hole Farm, several miles from the mansion, and he was married to Jezebel, a very pretty and flirtatious woman, who lived in the Family House because she worked as a maid in the Mansion. Jezebel and Caesar only got to see each other on Saturdays and Sundays, and Caesar wanted to do more with Jez than twinkle her toes.

Caesar regarded Billy as a slimy toady who sucked up to the masters. Caesar also feared that Billy was canoodling with Jezebel. It was true that she flirted with Billy during the week when Caesar was away, but she flirted with a lot of men. Billy tried to stay away from her. He thought he could take care of himself in a fight, but Caesar was just too big and strong.

One Saturday night, Jezebel sashayed up to Billy and dragged him onto the dance floor, saying, "Caesar's real sick and ain't gonna be coming tonight."

"That so," Billy said.

"I been waitin' to dance wi' you for a long time, Billy. A long, long time." She was sliding up and down against him, and Billy was getting pretty worked up, but he knew that Jezebel was nothing but trouble, and as soon as there was a break in the music, he headed into the kitchen adjoining the dining room, hoping to escape. But Jezebel was only a few steps behind him.

"Where you runnin' to, Billy boy?" she asked in a sultry voice.

Billy didn't want anything to do with Jezebel, but he wasn't going to run away from a woman, either. As he turned to face her, Jezebel was on him, but instead of a kiss, she suddenly screamed.

Surprised, Billy stepped back, and took a blow to the head that sent him reeling into Jezebel, who screamed again, but managed to shove Billy aside, which was a good thing because it saved him from suffering another blow with the flat side of a metal meat cleaver brandished by Caesar.

Although he was groggy, Billy moved quickly to put the big wooden serving table between him and Caesar. Even in the faint light of a pair of oil lamps, Billy could see that Caesar was glaring at him with undisguised hatred.

"Hold on, big man," Billy said."You got no call to be mad at me."

"You been aftuh my woman an' I's sick of it."

He began circling the table while Billy retreated, searching for a weapon. He had a pocket knife, but that was no match for the cleaver.

"I ain't never laid a han' on Jezebel," Billy said, "cept maybe to dance wi' her right out in public where evabody could see."

"I seen her grab your balls," Caesar snarled.

Scared as he was, Billy couldn't help laughing."You're crazy, Caesar. Jez never grabbed my balls, an' b'lieve me, if she did, I'd have known it. Tell him, Jez, it wasn' me."

"You's dreamin,' Caesar," she said."Never touch no man like that 'ceptin you." She pressed against the door, hoping to escape, all the time thinking *these two niggers can cut off each other's balls for all I care.*

Caesar hadn't taken his eyes off Billy."Think you kin fool me, Billy?—you wi'your fancy ways an' fancy words. Thinkin' I'm so dumb you kin lie to me an' get away wi' it. Thinkin' you's better'n me.

"Ain't nobody better'n you," Billy said."Evabody knows—you's the strongest man at Mount Vernon."

Billy spied a big black iron cooking ladle, hanging on the wall. It didn't have a sharp edge, but it had a long handle and a heavy spoon. He pulled it off the wall.

Caesar laughed harshly."Gonna cook you some soup, Billy? I'll chop you in little chunks an' put you in it." He lunged across the table and tried to hit Billy with the business end of the cleaver, but he came up short and one corner of the blade dug into the wooden surface—so hard that it stuck there. While Caesar tried to yank it free, Billy hit Caesar's extended arm with the cup of the ladle. There were two sharp noises, the sound of the cup breaking off the ladle, and the sound of Caesar's forearm cracking—which resonated like the report of a rifle, echoing off the kitchen walls, and intercepting Caesar's follow-up scream of pain. He let go of the cleaver, grabbed his broken forearm with his other hand and hopped around the room, forgetting all about Billy Lee.

Jezebel was about to run out of the kitchen, which Billy would have liked to do, too, but he yelled, "Don' go, Jezebel, we gotta help Caesar!"

Caesar was still hopping around, moaning loudly, the jagged ends of the broken bone sticking through the skin, bleeding profusely.

"Git a fork from the drawer!" Billy shouted to Jezebel, "an' some a' the dish rags from the shelves. We's gonna splint the big man's arm!"

Caesar sagged to the floor, holding his arm and moaning, bathed in his own blood. Jezebel nervously handed Billy a fork and some rags.

"Don' fight me, big man," Billy pleaded, "I'm gonna fix your arm."

Caesar's eyes were glazed, and he didn't have the strength to resist. Billy used the fork and some rags to tie a tourniquet on Caesar's arm, cutting off the blood. Then, with Caesar screaming again, Billy pulled from both directions on his forearm, forcing the bones back under the skin and, using the ladle handle as a splint, tied it tight against his forearm with the rags.

"Bring me that bottle a' whiskey from the top shelf," Billy yelled to Jezebel.

He pulled out the cork with his teeth, told Caesar to hold his head up and back, and poured whiskey slowly down his throat. The big man choked and shuddered, but didn't try to pull away.

"Feel better in a little while, Caesar. But now we got to git you to bed."

Caesar looked at Billy with a mixture of fear and gratitude, as Billy, with Jezebel's help, lifted him from the floor and half-carried, half-dragged him from the kitchen into a pantry next to the kitchen, where they piled some sacks and made a makeshift bed for him.

"You see, big man, your wife's crazy 'bout you—she'd do anything to help you. She don' give a damn for little, ole Billy Lee. Right, Jezebel?"

"Right," she whispered, but unbeknownst to Caesar, she fondled Billy's balls on the way to the pantry.

CHAPTER 7

Race and Racing

Ev'ry spring an' fall, I an' the General drove down to meet wi[9] the other folks in Williamsburg. Partly, he went 'cause he 'd become a membuh a' the House a' Burgesses, but that din 't keep him from havin' a good time. He had a fancy coach, come all the way from London, painted green an' polished to a shine it was, wi' the General 's mark—his coat of arms—on the side. Took six horses to pull it, plus our ridin' horses, trailin' aftuh. Trouble was, the wheels kep[9] fallin' off, so the trip was always trouble, an' the General stomped an' cuss 'd so loud as to make the leaves fall off en the trees. But once we got to Mrs. Campbell's, right there on the Duke a' Gloucestor Street, he stopped cussin' an' started drinkin.' We alius had a good time in that ole capital place.

Washington was holding a glass of Madeira in one hand, his cards in the other. Edmund Pendleton, a prominent member of the Burgesses, known affectionately as the Silver Fox of Virginia politics, sat across the table, smoking a cigar and smiling at his cards. Billy stood against the wall between the two players, intently watching the game.

"Come, come, Colonel, they can't be that bad," said Pendleton, as Washington squinted hard at his cards.

"Well, you're going to have to pay to find out, Mr. Speaker," Washington replied, tossing a pound note into the pot while taking a sip of his wine and gesturing for Billy to fill his glass.

Pendleton made a face of mock surprise, puffed on his cigar, then looked at Billy."Would you fill me up too, Billy, before your master empties my pockets?" Billy leaned over Pendleton to pour the wine, and Pendleton pulled his cards tight against his chest."Don't you peek now, Billy boy," Pendleton joked, "your master doesn't need any help."

Billy smiled back at Pendleton."I 'spect not, sir. He don' usually bet 'less he's got him a good hand."

"Ah, exclaimed Pendleton, "you have just given me a highly useful piece of information, Billy. But can I trust you to tell me the truth? Colonel, you tell me. Can Billy be trusted?"

"Well, Mr. Speaker," replied Washington, enjoying the repartee, "I would say you could trust Billy when it came to horses, but not when it came to women. About cards, I couldn't say."

"That really doesn't help me much, does it, Colonel?" Pendleton observed, puffing away, looking intently at his cards."Now the real question, Colonel darling, is, can *you* be trusted? And I have over the years adopted a simple rule of thumb that never fails to provide the answer."

"And what pray tell, is that?" asked Washington.

"No planter in Virginia who refuses to smoke cigars can be trusted. It is, I can assure you, an infallible rule, sir, and this is a test you do not pass," Pendleton declared triumphantly.

Billy watched Washington shift in his chair, then raise his glass towards Pendleton."I give you a toast, sir, to tobacco. It is a noxious weed that has destroyed the economy of Virginia, fills the air with poison, and attacks the constitutions of our best men, among whom I would count you, sir. This test of yours, I most happily, and even honorably, prefer to fail."

"Well done, well done! Pendleton shouted, rising to touch glasses with Washington."An act of defiance to my, and Virginia's, fondest illusions that leaves me totally confounded. So I must decide with my infallible principle exposed at last. This throws me onto my last line of defiance, which is, when in doubt, always call. Best go down on the offensive." Pendleton tossed his pound note into the pot, then revealed his hand: two pair, aces and jacks, and puffed away.

Washington remained expressionless, then slowly laid down three kings.

"I done tole you, sir," said Billy, grinning sheepishly.

"Yes you did, Billy," Pendleton exclaimed with great energy, patting Billy on the backside.

"I feel somewhat embarrassed to beat you with kings, sir." Washington observed as Billy filled his glass again."Especially at a moment when even one king seems one too many for my taste."

Pendleton squinted at Washington querulously, presented his glass for Billy to fill, then said, "We seem to be moving from poker to politics—a dangerous trend."

Pendleton proceeded to explain that, while there was a clear consensus in the Burgesses that British taxation was unacceptable, the delegates were divided between those wishing to issue a plea to Parliament and the king for a policy change and those preferring economic pressure in the form of agreements to boycott British goods.

"Count me squarely in the latter camp," Washington responded without pause, "and I intend to offer a proposal to that effect in the Burgesses. Mere supplications only reinforce the presumed superiority of our Lordly Masters in Great Britain. We are their equals, not their subjects. Equals have no need to plead."

Washington did not mention that the proposal he planned to offer had been drafted by George Mason, Washington's good friend, who was not a member of the Burgesses, and that the proposal also called for an end to the slave trade. Billy, who had seen the proposal, wondered what, if anything, that meant for him.

"You know then, Colonel Washington, that we are going down a road that just might end in an open break with—how did you call them?—our Lordly Masters in Great Britain," Pendleton said."That would mean war, and I know of no man among the Burgesses who is currently prepared to contemplate that."

"I contemplate it, sir," Washington responded."I do not wish it, but I also do not see how we can defend our rights and honor without being prepared to threaten the resort to arms in response to these abuses, and mean what we say."

Pendleton, now deadly serious, looked Washington in the eye, for several seconds."Do we have the cards, sir?" he asked.

"What do you mean?" said Washington, waiting for Pendleton to clarify his question.

"Could we actually win a war?" Pendleton exclaimed, "or would we be bluffing?"

"I cannot say for sure that we would win," Washington responded."But I can say that if we are not willing to fight for our liberties we can never retain them."

Pendleton raised his eyebrows, then offered his glass to Billy for a final drink."Billy, you have a very brave master, perhaps foolishly so, but no man in the House that I know sees the course so clearly, and no man in America that I know is equivalently prepared to face the consequences."

"Like I tole you, sir," said Billy matter-of-factly, "he aint a Muffin' man, in cards or nothin' else."

"I can see that quite clearly," Pendleton concluded as he rose from his chair."Let's just hope that the British *are* bluffing. God help us if they're not."

"With all due respect, Edmund," Washington observed with conspicuous resolve, "God will have nothing to do with it."

Pendleton smiled and raised his hand to touch the shoulder of the much taller Washington, "You're absolutely right, George. Absolutely right. But in the absence of God, you're the next best thing."

***

Washington and Billy were standing outside Christiana Campbell's inn, the morning after Washington had laid down his three kings to the chagrin of Edmund Pendleton. Their destination was the race track at Williamsburg, where Washington had a horse scheduled to run in the third race. The Duke of Gloucester Street, where they stood, had the look of a miniature Parisian boulevard—Virginia version—with neatly manicured lawns and trim red brick buildings on both sides. It was twenty-feet wide and one mile long, now full of walkers and riders, stretching from the College of William and Mary at one end to the Governor's Palace at the other. The race track was just beyond the palace.

Let's walk to the track," said Washington."We can take our horses with us in case we change our minds and decide to ride."

Small talk was not one of Washington's strengths, so as they ambled down the Duke of Gloucester Street, the onus fell upon Billy to break the silence.

"Do you think Mr. Pendleton was upset at losin' last night," he asked.

"Mr. Pendleton is a Virginia gentlemen," Washington replied, "a special breed that knows how to lose with style. Besides, he used the loss to extract from me a political commitment more valuable than the money in the pot. The Silver Fox was the real winner last night."

Billy nodded, and waved to the blacksmith, an elderly ex-slave who had shoed the big white stallion that Washington was racing that day, when a shout came from behind.

"Colonel, Colonel Washington!" It was George Mason, whose plantation at Gunston Hall was only a few miles south of Mount Vernon. Mason was so devoted to his impressive estate that he had chosen not to run for election to the House of Burgesses, but he, like Washington—perhaps even more so—was an ardent supporter of non-importation as the preferred response to British taxation, and he was in town to assure that the Burgesses enjoyed the benefit of his practical wisdom. He had already provided Washington with a draft of his proposal.

"Headed to the track?" he asked. Washington nodded and Billy tipped his hat."Good seein' you here, Mr. Mason," he said with a smile.

"Are you going to ride today, Billy? If so, I know how to bet," Mason observed.

"No sir," Billy replied."General says they won't let slaves ride down here when people's bettin'."

"Huh?" Mason exclaimed as they walked."Colonel, may I suggest you consider freeing Billy for the day in the interest of my wager," Mason joked. Washington gave Mason his best squinty stare, a mixture of ice and incredulity, then shifted the topic."Bet on the horse, sir, not the rider." Mason started humming to assist the mood shift.

Off to the left a crowd of about thirty, mostly men, gathered in front of Raleigh Tavern, Williamsburg's chief watering hole. Some kind of auction was going on, and as they drew nearer a large sign announced the kind of auction it was:

Thirty Choice Virginia Born
SLAVES
consisting mostly of boys and girls,
from 13 or 14 down to the
ages of 2 or 3 years

Two of the toddlers were crying, one teen-age girl was trying to comfort her younger brother. Billy thought the way prospective buyers handled the young girls exceeded the requirements of commerce. The older boys were standing rigidly as prospective buyers poked and prodded them and inspected their teeth. Their eyes showed a combination of fear and barely repressed anger.

"Oh, God," Mason moaned."They're all children."

Washington immediately understood what Mason meant. Several owners had obviously decided to cut their costs by selling slaves too young to do heavy work in the fields. This meant breaking up families, which was considered taboo within some but not all of the upper reaches of the planter class of Virginia, which was where both Mason and Washington located themselves.

"I can't look at this," Mason exclaimed."Let's move on." It was obvious that he was one of those would not split up families. Washington had not yet declared himself. He stared silently at the scene, and Billy stared at him.

As they walked away, Billy decided to break the silence: "Ever see anythin' like that afore, General?"

Washington nodded and said he had bought and sold many slaves, to be sure, but something about this auction had touched him as nothing had before.

Perhaps it was the children who were being sold without their parents. But he chose not to answer Billy's question, although his body language betrayed his revulsion as he quickened the pace to put space between himself and the horrid scene. The sobbing of the small children followed them down the street, only gradually merging into the sounds of the crowd. No one spoke until they reached the race track.

"Your bay's lookin' good, General," Billy observed as they entered the oval track, a belt of plowed dirt half-a-mile long. The horses were lining up at the far end and the bay was suddenly acting up.

"Don' pull on the bit," Billy yelled to the rider, a local white jockey."Jes ease up on him, an' he'll calm down."

Mason left them to place his bet.

"Ain't you gonna go bet, General?" Billy asked."I'll save our spots here."

Washington did not answer. The gun sounded and the horses bolted from the starting line, the riders rating them to conserve energy for six laps around the track.

"C'mon," Billy cheered as they rounded the first turn.

But Washington turned his back refusing to watch.

"He's lookin' good, General," Billy shouted, not yet noticing that Washington's attention was elsewhere. As the horses galloped past on the second lap, Billy realized that Washington had moved off several paces and was staring into the distance.

"What's the matter, sir? Somethin' wrong? Somethin' I done?" Billy asked.

Washington did not turn around., but he spoke forcefully."It will never happen at Mount Vernon. As long as I live, it will never happen at Mount Vernon. You have my word on it, Billy," and then he abruptly walked away.

It took a minute for Billy to understand what Washington was talking about, distracted as he was by the cheering crowd and the now-sweating horses galloping past again. Then it hit him, and he started running to catch up with his fast striding master.

"General, I hear ya," Billy sputtered."Kin I tell your promise to the othuh folks back home?"

"Tell every slave at Mount Vernon, Billy. Every one of them."

They took a side street back to Campbell's in order to avoid the auction.

CHAPTER 8

Gathering Clouds

Figure 5 Boston Tea Party.

I was thinkin' my life was goin' good, learnin' how to keep the General happy, makin' friends among the black folks, avoidin' Big Caesar an'his kine. But things was changin.' The Burgesses passed their non-import act, an'the Governor sent 'empackin. 'Me an'the General went to the Virginia convention where they made him commander a' the militia, an'Patrick Henry says, "Give me liberty or give me death!" Sounds like he means it A 'course I'd a liked my liberty, too, but I wasn' thinkin' a' dyin' to get there.

Somehow, I din't figure how serious these people really was. When I heard 'bout the "Boston Tea Party," me an' the othuh slaves at Mount Vernon thought it was funny. Gang a 'white folks strippin' off

*they clothes, paintin' they selves like injuns an' dumpin' crates a'tea
in the bay. But the colonials ain't laughin, 'the General ain't laughin.
Brits sure ain't laughin.'*

Martha was deeply concerned as soon as she saw the grave
expression on her husband's face."What has happened, dear?"

He shook his head."There's been a military engagement at
Lexington and Concord, two towns near Boston."

Martha sighed audibly as Washington continued."British troops
marched out of Boston in broad daylight, planning to lock up guns and
powder the local militia had stored. The Brits had no idea there might
be any opposition until they came upon hundreds of men— most of
them farmers—lined up in a park. They wore no uniforms, but they
were carrying muskets. British, of course, were dressed in their fine
red uniforms, wearing those tall hats that are designed to make them
look like giants."

Billy couldn't help noticing that Washington seemed to enjoy
telling the story. His brow was furrowed, but his voice was firm and
strong.

"The British troops laughed, and their officer told the farmers to
get out of the way. They didn't move. He told them again, but they still
didn't move.

Somebody fired a shot—nobody knows whether it was the British
or the Colonials—and there was an exchange of gunfire."

"Oh, my," Martha said.

"There were dead and wounded on both sides. Bodies lying on
this green parkland. The British were surprised by the opposition,
but they resumed marching. The colonials—they called themselves
"minutemen"—followed right after them. The shooting continued—
the colonials taking advantage of the terrain, firing from behind trees
and bushes, the soldiers in their neat ranks, firing when ordered to.

"The British took so many casualties their officers finally ordered
them to turn back without collecting the guns or the powder. The
Brits weren't exactly running, but they were retreating as fast as
they could." Washington paused for a moment."The world's greatest
soldiers, stopped by a bunch of farmers. I never had much respect for
those Massachusets people, but after this..."

"I hate to say it, General," Billy said, "but this don' sound like no
argument 'tween old friends, this sounds like a war."

Figure 6 Battle of Concord and Lexington.

Washington nodded. "I'm afraid you're right."

It didn't seem to Billy that Washington was afraid, at all.

"They're calling a second Continental Congress in Philadelphia," Washington told Martha, "and I'm a delegate."

"Of course," Martha said."And I know you'll stand up for our freedom."

Billy was surprised. Some wives would have urged caution, but it appeared that Martha was fully committed to her husband's cause.

"I'm hoping for peace," Washington said, "but it will be very difficult to achieve with the King as stubborn as he is, and Lord North vilifying the colonials almost every day."

In fact, Washington had almost certainly already made up his mind before he left for the convention. He had written to his old friend, George William Fairfax, that while he was unhappy, "that a Brother's sword has been sheathed in a Brother's breast...the peaceful plains of America are either to be drenched in blood, or inhabited by Slaves...." And he wasn't referring to Billy and his black brethren.

When Billy was preparing to help Washington dress the next morning, the General told him to lay out his best blue and buff uniform from his militia days. Billy was thinking about asking, why, if Washington was hoping for peace, was he dressing in a military uniform? But he was wise enough not to give voice to that question.

Billy brushed the General's hair until it was almost falling out, and tied a blue silk ribbon in it. Billy also wore his best clothes, including a jacket and breeches that looked like a uniform. The General gave Billy a fine three-cornered hat. It was too big, so Mrs. Washington showed Billy how to put a cotton kerchief inside to make it fit.

Billy noticed that Washington was having unusual difficulty with his dentures, and he was concerned that if the General had to speak at the convention—which was virtually a certainty—that it would be especially difficult for him.

"I got an idear for you, General—could help soothe your gums."

Washington responded with a forced smile, clearly indicating that Billy was right about his pain."What are you suggesting, Billy?"

"Slaves—when they got pain—mix up some laudanum, using the poppies you grows here at Mount Vernon."

Washington frowned."I don't believe in using such medication, Billy. I've never approved of it."

"General, the mos' 'importan' thing is for you to do a good job at this here Congress. Anythin' that Stan's in the way ain't good for nobody."

For a moment, Washington was silent. The pain in his mouth had reached almost unbearable levels in recent months, and he had to admit that Billy was right about the importance of the coming meeting.

"Have some made up for me, Billy."

'Yes sir!"

They rode away from Mount Vernon, Washington in his chariot, Billy and other servants and retainers on horseback, trailing behind, while Martha, Jackie and Nelly waved goodbye.

As they neared Philadelphia, they were met by a throng of nearly five hundred riders, cheering Washington, who gravely acknowledged their accolades. Billy was relieved when they finally reached their lodgings—for once the coach had not broken down.

***

At the meeting, Billy sat next to the General, handing him papers as requested, There were many speeches—Samuel Adams, John Adams, Jefferson, Franklin and several others. They spoke passionately, claiming they wanted peace, but conditions had to change— the colonials were the equals of Englishmen in England, not their inferiors. Washington listened politely, but said very little. Whenever anyone else spoke, they looked over at Washington to gauge his reaction. Sometimes he gave a little nod, but nothing specific enough that anyone could determine precisely where he stood. He was the only one in uniform, and was chosen to chair no less than four military committees. At one point, when it looked like the delegates might be about to select a commander for their troops, Washington abruptly left the room, leaving Billy sitting alone and wondering what was happening.

Later, when Washington returned, Billy noticed that he was hurriedly writing on his pad. Of course, the General was always writing something. When he rode his property he routinely made notes, or had Billy make notes, of what needed to be done. He wrote letters to his friends—to governors, military officers, and other important people. He wrote so many letters that some people wondered how he had time for anything else. When his papers were accumulated and catalogued years later, it was estimated that he had written more than ten thousand letters in his lifetime—and that did not include military orders and other writings. Most of the letters were in his own writing. Others he dictated to a secretary, word for word. Sometimes, with Joseph Reed, Tobias Lear and Alexander Hamilton, men who understood his thinking, Washington would tell them what he wanted and they would write the letter or order. He would read their work, perhaps cross out a word or write between the lines, then sign it.

Washington kept copies of everything he wrote—everything he received. Usually, he entrusted these materials to Billy, who, during wartime, kept them safe at headquarters, occasionally in his saddle-bags, and sometimes sent them by courier to Mount Vernon.

Once in a rare while, Washington would tell Billy to write something simple—say, a note to Lund Washington instructing him plant the walnut trees as soon as the frost broke. He allowed Billy to word these letters himself, and Billy was proud to do it. Billy tried to copy the General's handwriting, and he became pretty good at it. Washington would give a quick look to Billy's work, then sign it.

But that was much later, after Billy had spent years by his side in wartime, and he had learned precisely how far he could trust him. In 1775, at the second Congress, Billy noted that Washington was writing something which didn't quite look like the usual notes. Washington looked up, as if he were following the debate on the floor. The delegates were once again discussing who should lead the army. Hancock was looking smug; after the events in Massachusetts, where the fighting had begun, he apparently believed he was the obvious choice for commander.

Washington pushed the paper he had been writing on in front of Billy, who read it quickly. He couldn't quite catch the drift. The General had written something about not being qualified to head the army, but if chosen he would serve without pay. Billy was bewildered; no one had offered the position to Washington, although rumors were rampant that the delegates thought the leader should come from Virginia, the richest and most powerful state, and that Washington was the logical choice.

John Adams was on his feet, bellowing in his strong, but raspy voice, "Mr. George Washington is the best man—the only man— suited to head the colonial army."

There was a gasp from Hancock, but almost everyone else was on their feet, yelling "Hear! Hear!"

Washington finally stood up, acknowledged their cheers, accepted the commission and said he would serve without pay, which led to another round of cheers.

Then Washington said, "Lest some unlucky event should happen unfavorable to my reputation, I beg it be remembered by every Gentleman in the room, that I declare with utmost sincerity, I do not think myself equal to the Commission I am honored with."

His words were drowned out with more cheers. Billy applauded, too, smiling because he was proud to be Washington's man, and also because those were the very words that Washington had scribbled on the note he had showed Billy—before he was named Commander-in-Chief.

CHAPTER 9

The Battle of Boston

Figure 8 Washington takes command.

We was oney in Philadelphia for three weeks. I must say, I never saw so many good-loofan' black women in one place, lots of 'em free, too, mos ly 'cause a' them Quaker folks. But the big thing that happened was that they made the general a General. I alius tole him he was one, but the Congress made it official—even though they din't yet have an army. He worried a heap about it, says he 'd rathuh sneak off west a 'the mountains an' live in a wigwam. I tole him I wasn't goin' out there to get kilt by Injuns. He just swatted his big ol 'thigh an'says I ought not to worry, 'cause we was goin 'to Boston to get kilt by redcoats.

"I know you been appointed head of the army, General, but this don't look to me like much of an army." Billy made this observation as he and Washington rode among the American troops bivouacked outside Boston. The soldiers wore a strange collection of odd and unmatched clothing, lived in a bewildering variety of shelters made of boards, sailcloth, turf, bark and bracken, with a few real tents mixed in. Horses and other animals wandered about, eating garbage and defecating where they chose.

As Billy and Washington approached a small bridge, three Virginia militiamen, soon joined by several of their compatriots, lined up to urinate off the bridge, cheering and jeering at two proper Bostonian ladies walking by.

"Virginia is here to link up with you Yankees," one soldier shouted at the ladies, "and we're ready for y'all to link up with us any time."

As the women walked quickly on, Washington and Billy rode onto the bridge and the Virginians, all farm boys and self-described sharpshooters, kept shouting invitations for the women to join them in a sectional union.

"That's quite enough," intoned Washington in his most authoritative style.

"Who the hell are you?" yelled the apparent leader of this pack."And what's that nigger doing here? We don't want no niggers fighting with us."

Washington dismounted, intending to deliver a lecture about discipline, assuming that they knew he was their Commander-in-Chief. Billy remained on his horse, hand on his carbine, more aware than his master that they were dealing with some free-spirited rednecks who recognized no authority outside of their own rollicking souls.

The first mistake one soldier made was to bump Washington, done casually, but not quite inadvertently. This invasion of the sacred space prompted an instinctive swing of Washington's elbow into the soldier's face, breaking his nose and producing a sudden flow of blood. As another soldier approached— it was unclear whether he intended to assist his friend or accost Washington—he was immediately leveled by Washington's fist, a blow that broke his jaw.

This both surprised and provoked the other Virginians, but Billy spurred his horse into the group, knocking several of them to the ground. When another soldier came at Billy, who was dismounting, he butted him in the chin with his carbine and he rolled unconscious into the others; one last soldier attempted to confront Washington, but he was dispatched with a blow to the back of the neck that flattened him.

Figure 9 Washington physically ends riot (Billy on horseback in background).

The remaining Virginians just stood there—or crouched on the ground—somewhat dazzled, mostly stupefied, because they had no idea who had just humiliated them. Billy sensed this immediately."They don' know who you be, General."

Washington, who had re-mounted, found this difficult to digest. What kind of idiot could not read his rank from his uniform? And he was not exactly ordinary in his appearance, not the kind of mountain you could mistake for a molehill.

"These boys don' unnerstan,' General," Billy explained as he also re-mounted."They know heaps 'bout fightin,' not much at all 'bout soljerin'. Nothin' at all 'bout rank. They don' hardly figure that you's a General, head a' the army."

The Virginian whose nose had just been broken confirmed Billy's conclusion. He cupped his nose with one hand and made a sloppy salute with the other."We was jes fimnin' here, sir. Din't really mean to—"

"—Your intentions are not relevant, mister," Washington interrupted."Gather your men and report back to your unit. Since you appear to have a great urge to relieve yourselves in public, you are hereby ordered to dig latrines for your regiment until this engagement ends."

Despite his bloody, broken nose, the man had to struggle to keep from laughing out loud."We ain't exactly got a regiment, sir," he replied."What we got is a bunch of good ole boys who can pick off a British officer at two hundert yards, straight through the gizzard. That's what we do, sir. We don' dig latrines. Make us do that and most of us will jes up and leave."

Washington looked down at this soldier for several seconds."Any man who tries to leave will be regarded as a deserter, mister, and will be shot down like a dog. Do we understand one another?"

The soldier did not respond, just stood sheepishly beneath Washington's ferocious gaze."Do we understand one another?" Washington repeated.

"Yes, sir," the soldier shouted, coming to attention, an obviously unaccustomed posture. He had little respect for this officer's rank, but plenty of respect for his physical prowess.

As Billy and Washington rode off, Washington started to ponder out loud."We may need these men today," he observed, "but to win this war we need a disciplined core of regulars who are prepared to go the distance."

Billy chuckled."Them boys ain't goin' no distance, General. When this bus'ness in Boston is finished, they's goin' home."

Washington just stared ahead, saying nothing as they rode past an older soldier, squatting to take a crap on the side of the road. Washington shook his head in disgust. Billy laughed out loud."Ya got to 'membuh, General, them Yankee farmers, they think the whole world is they personal latrine."

This drew a thin smile from Washington, who gestured for a turn toward his headquarters, which were set in a magnificent, two-story white-columned and lemon-colored brick Georgian mansion, standing among other opulent homes on what was known colloquially as Tory Row. The contrast between Washington's lodgings and those of his soldiers was both ironic and startling.

There, to his great pleasure, standing with her arms on her hips at the picket fence, was Martha, accompanied by her son, Jackie, and his wife, Nelly."We heard you were desperate for recruits, General Washington," she joked, "so we decided to volunteer for duty."

Washington leaped off his horse. Martha slipped into his arms as Washington, almost giddy with delight, tumbled over backwards when her body hit his. Nelly and Jackie smiled indulgently and slipped away to the mansion.

"I wrote you that I was very close," Martha said as he cradled her face in his hands, "but we made such good time on the ferry from Annapolis that we seem to have beaten the mail."

Washington lifted her off the ground in a bear hug as Martha giggled."Do you like my little surprise, George? Or should I say General Washington?" Martha semi-whispered in a mischievous tone, thrilled that she had contrived to arrive sooner than expected.

She started to assure her husband that all was well at Mount Vernon, when she noticed blood on his right elbow."What's this, dear? Are you hurt? Let me tend to it," she said worriedly as she tried to take off his coat.

Washington laughed, grabbing Martha in a gentle head-lock. "It's not my blood, dear. Belongs to a lad now sporting a broken nose," he explained. "Billy and I had a bit of a scuffle with some unruly troops."

"Yes, Ma'am," Billy volunteered, "some Virginny boys was pissin' offen a bridge—"

Washington cut him off."No need to go into the sordid details. Suffice to say that Billy showed that he knows how to use the butt of that carbine."

"They got my blood up a bit," Billy replied, "mos'ly 'cause they was goin' aftuh you, partly 'cause they calls me a nigguh. Don' like it when white folks call me that."

An awkward silence ensued. Martha finally broke it. Looking at Washington as she tried to read his eyes, she said, "We don't want that word used in our presence, right, George?" Washington nodded, saw that Martha was expecting more of an answer, then in a low voice, muttered "No, we don't. Now, let's go inside and get you unpacked."

Somewhat bewildered by this conversation, Billy prudently ducked his head and led the horses off. Two sentries saluted as Martha and George entered the beautifully appointed Cambridge house and then Martha whispered into Washington's ear."Did I say the right thing, George?"

Washington nodded, put his finger to his lips to signal the subject was too sensitive to address in public, then assumed command of the scene by saying, "My oh my," in mock disbelief at the size of Martha's baggage train.

Martha did a twirl, hands on hips, and mocked his mocking tone. "It's all essential, George, for Nelly and me. You never did understand what a woman needs to wear, especially a woman whose husband is Commander-in-Chief of the Colonial Army."

"It's the Continental Army, dear. We're no longer colonies."

Martha shot back, "You get my point. And I intend to stay for the duration of this campaign, however long it lasts."

Shaking his head and putting up his hands in surrender mode, Washington had the last word."I am certain that, when news of your arrival reaches General Howe in Boston, he will immediately recognize that his situation is hopeless, sue for peace, and the war will be over."

When the baggage had been deposited and the soldiers saluted themselves out the door, Martha leaned against the closed door of the bedroom and let out an exasperated sigh! "I said the wrong thing to Billy, didn't I?" she exclaimed."I could tell by your look that you disapproved."

"No, dear, you misconstrued my wince. We've all heard that word used a thousand times, but it was still wrong for Billy to use it as he did."

"You mean in the presence of a white woman?" Martha asked rhetorically.

"Yes," said Washington throwing his coat on the bed."Since we left Mount Vernon almost six months ago, Billy has been at my side constantly. And today, as I explained, he was magnificent."

"So what's your point?"

"My point is that Billy has presumed—and I'm guilty for letting this happen—certain familiarities. It was probably inevitable. Unlike Mount Vernon, Billy is now with me twenty-four hours a day, seven days a week. Certain lines have been crossed that would never have even been approached back in Virginia. Out here, it's not obvious that Billy is a slave, and he doesn't feel obliged to act like one. Billy forgets his place. So your rebuke today served to remind him, and me as well."

***

We stayed up there 'round Boston through the winter. First time I felt real cold. The General kep' tryin' to find a way to get at them redcoats in the city. One time he thought we might sneak our boys 'cross the river on ice skates, but nobody else thought that was a good idear. Then General Knox, who was the fattest man I evuh seen, come up w' a bettuh idear. Drags fifty-eight big ol' cannon down from Fort Ticonderoga ovuh icy roads, 'cross frozen rivuhs, through snow an' sleet all the way to the 'merican camp. On Washington's orduhs, they's planted them cannon on Dorchester Hill overlookin' Boston town an'the harbor. Brits cain't figure out how we got all them cannon up there an' behine barricades, star in' down they throats. General Howe figures there wasn 'no sense in jes sittin' there an' gettin 'blowed'ta bits, so one day in March the Brits jes sail away. I recall thinkin' them masts loofa like a forest movin' 'cross the water. Evabody was congratulatin' the General. That college there in Cambridge even says he was one a 'theirs now. He din't pay it much mind. Said the big battle was gonna happen down in New York. So that's where we heads in April a' '76.

CHAPTER 10

The Declaration

I 'membuh that day so clear—the day that fancy lookin 'paper come down from Congress. Lord knows I wasn 'spectin 'nothin 'like that, an' at first I didn't know what to make a' it. But it change my life forevuh.

"We got a packet here, General. Come from that Hancock man down in Congress wi' all kines a' fancy seals an' stamps markin' it as somethin' special."

Washington looked up from his desk, which was overflowing with dispatches and intelligence reports on the enormous British fleet arriving off the coast of Staten Island with the largest expeditionary force ever to cross the Atlantic, estimated at thirty-three thousand troops.

It was July 7, 1776. Martha was planning to go back to Mount Vernon, stopping in Philadelphia to undergo inoculation against smallpox at Washington's insistence, while Washington remained at Manhattan, engaged in some combination of planning, wondering and worrying how to deploy his army—about half the strength of the burgeoning British force—to repel the imminent invasion.

He had a keen sense that this was an overcrowded moment. Pieces of paper were building up on his desk faster than they could be read. Aides were shuffling about like frightened birds before a hurricane. There needed to be a calm epicenter in this storm, and he was by disposition and rank the designated source of serenity, the center that must always hold.

"Open it up, Billy. I've been hoping to hear that Congress has scared up some more troops for us. Otherwise, it may come down to you and me against thirty-three thousand British and Hessian regulars."

Billy barely smiled."There's a covuh lettuh here from Mr. Hancock, sir."

"Please read it," Washington sighed."Probably another plea to defend New York at all costs."

"It's got a whole lot of titles for you, General, His Excellency an' such an' such," Billy said as his eyes scanned the parchment.

"Skip all that," Washington impatiently requested, gesturing to move on with his hands.

Billy started reading:

"It gives me pleasure to inform you that on July 2nd last the full Congress approved a resolution that these thirteen former colonies are now independent states and no longer members of the British Empire.

"A formal document declaring our independence and the principles on which it is based was approved and sent to the printer on July 4. A copy of that document is enclosed, and you are hereby requested to have it posted outside your headquarters and read aloud to all the officers and men under your command."

Figure 10 Young Thomas Jefferson.

"Don' know who wrote this, General," Billy concluded, "but Mr. Hancock signs it in his own han'. Does this mean what I think it means?"

"Yes," Washington blurted as he rose from his chair, smiling broadly."It means we have crossed the Rubicon and there's no turning back. It means we are no longer living a lie, Billy."

"Well, we been fightin' for more'n a year, so I guess it's good to know we been doin' the right thing," Billy said with a faint edge of sarcasm as he handed the packet to Washington.

"Billy, I want you to post this on the officers' bulletin board right away." Washington then summoned an aide, instructing him to make copies for dispersal to all the regiments after the reading at headquarters.

Billy tore down the orders-for-the day to make room for the three printed sheets, then nailed them neatly, side by side. As the officers and men of headquarters gathered for the reading, Billy began to read the front sheet silently to himself, barely moving his lips as his eyes grew wider with each word. Then his eyes came to words that stunned him: "We hold these truths to be self-evident, that all men are created equal, that they are endowed by their creator with certain unalienable rights, that among these rights are life, liberty, and the pursuit of happiness."

He backed away from the billboard, visibly shaken. But he recovered his composure sufficiently to take his accustomed place behind Washington as the Declaration of Independence was read aloud. It took eight minutes to reach the last line: "we pledge our lives, our Fortunes, and our Sacred Honor."

"The oney words I'm hear in ' is words I's repeatin' in my head: 'All men are created equal, that they are endowed by their creator'—I figure that's God—'with certain unalienable rights'—don' know what 'unalienable' means—but I sure unnerstan' the rest, 'that among these rights are life, liberty and the pursuit of happiness.' Life... liberty... liberty!"

There was an awkward silence as the troops, who were at attention, waited to be dismissed before reacting. Washington broke the silence."We are now a free and independent nation!"

This let loose a volley of huzzas and hoorays and hats tossed in the air. The officers just smiled at this momentary breach of discipline, waved "dismissed" to nobody in particular, then joined the celebration.

As the men milled around, slapping each other on their backs and retrieving their hats, Billy leaned forward and whispered into Washington's ear as he shook hands with his aides."S'cuse me, sir, but kin we have a word?"

Washington nodded, finished his handshakes and gestured Billy back into his office.

"This is a big day, General—yep, a really big day," Billy began.

"Indeed, it is," Washington replied, tossing his own hat into the air in imitation of the troops, but catching it like the Commander-in-Chief."Today we know, officially and beyond any doubt, what we are fighting for. From now on, nothing less than American independence will do."

Billy took off his own hat and looked like a man at church about to recite a prayer."Yessir, sure enough. But the words I read—we all heard 'em—say somethin' more. Say all men is equal. Says a man's rights is his own. Cain't be taken away. Ain't that right? Ain't that what it says?"

Washington began to catch the drift of Billy's questions, and as it settled in, his head rose up, his chin extended, his facial expression froze, and his posture stiffened like a statue, poised to deflect what he knew was coming.

Billy rushed on."Don' them words from the Congress mean I'm a free man, General? "

"No they don't, Billy."

"It says all men are created equal. I'm a man, ain't I?"

"Yes you are, William Lee, and a fine man at that."

"But I ain't free."

"No."

"Will I be free?"

"Some day you will be. Just not now."

"Then that Declaration is jes words. Says all men is free, but don' mean it."

"Billy, that's not what it says," Washington attempted to explain.

"Pardon, sir, but that's *zackly* what it says," Billy came back.

"Well, that's not what it means," Washington replied huffily."Be serious, Billy. This is about American independence, no more and no less."

Washington was bone certain that he was right about his reading of the Declaration. Like many others, even firebrands like Tom Paine, his eyes passed over the opening section of the document as a mere rhetorical overture to the main music of American independence.

But Billy's eyes had a different focus: he read the opening section as a profound and powerful, indeed lyrical, declaration of human equality and freedom. This was the music he heard more clearly than Washington because, as a slave, it spoke directly to him. History would eventually show that Billy was right, but in the crucible of that crowded moment on the verge of an enormous British invasion, it struck Washington as both bizarre and irrelevant.

Billy had a mind to reiterate his reading of the words, but it was clear from the General's stare that this was an argument he was not going to win.

"Jes one more question, General. If we win this war an' hold on to 'merican independence, will I be free?"

Washington looked at Billy in a way he had never done before, seeing a side of him he had never known, or perhaps had never allowed himself to know. He did not stammer, quite the opposite. He knew he needed to be crystal clear precisely because his thoughts were confused.

"I can make no promises, Billy. None. But I will take your request under advisement. I surely owe you that."

I din't argue no more wi' the General—no point to that. I went back to my room, feelin' upset an' b 'lievin' them white folh had fooled me with they fancy words. But then I started to think—right then an' for the first time—that this war we was fightin' was now 'bout me. Mebbe this ain't the way to say it, but I begun to feel I had a dog in this here fight.

CHAPTER 11

A Different Declaration

In November a' '75, LordDunmore, the Royal Governor a' Virginia issues a proclamation, offerin 'freedom to slaves what runs away from they ownuhs an' joins the British. In fact, some slaves run away from Mount Vernon. I think they's crazy trustin' them crafty Brits. But then the 'mericans says the Declaration of Independence wi' all its talk 'bout liberty, don' include us slaves. Confuses me plenny. Whose side should I be on?

There was no slavery in Great Britain. A black slave named James Somerset had escaped from his master in 1772, and when his master sued to retrieve him, a British judge held that slavery was against the law of the land, and they set Somerset free. Slaveowners in America were deeply concerned by this decision, fearing their "property"— their slaves—would be taken from them. But then the government in London ruled that what happened with Somerset didn't apply in the colonies.

That relieved the minds of the slaveowners, temporarily, but after Dunmore's proclamation, white plantation owners became concerned again—afraid their slaves might rise up and kill them all. They needn't have worried—the British didn't really want too many black soldiers, themselves. They didn't trust them much more than the slaveowners and used most of them for construction work and very few as soldiers. They wouldn't allow the blacks to bivouac with white regulars, and as a result virtually all of the slaves who signed up died on ships—just like so many of their ancestors had when they came over from Africa.

Meanwhile, Washington had a major problem with recruiting a sufficient number of soldiers. The militias served their brief terms and went home, and even after the Congress gave Washington authority to enlist a regular army, it was difficult to persuade young men to join up at the pathetic pay they were offered. Billy was secretly amused. He understood that early on the Americans seemed to have believed they would have all the soldiers they wanted, as if recruits would be falling out of trees, lining up, pleading to be sent out to shoot people who looked exactly like them—people they had previously thought of as their "brothers." Billy realized that, as usual, when a war starts, most people don't think that they're the ones who are going to be killed.

Billy believed the solution could be enlisting black soldiers. But then the Americans held a Council of War, and they voted unanimously "to reject all slaves," and then to reject all negroes in the army, free or slave. Billy thought that was crazy, especially after black freedmen had fought so well at Lexington and Concord and Bunker Hill.

Billy decided to speak to the General."Now that you's in charge a' the army, mebbe we kin get some black folks fightin' for you."

Washington frowned, but Billy said, "Start wi' some freedmen, an' if that works, mebbe some slaves."

"I trust you, Billy," the General said."You'll always be at my side."

"Thankee," Billy responded, "but I ain't talkin' 'bout me. Down at Mount Vernon, we got a freedman, Junius, workin' as a carpentuh. He's a big , strong feller, kin handle a musket good, an' tole me he'd like to fight for the rebels. I think he'd make a mighty fine soljer."

"I need Junius at Mount Vernon, I can't enlist him."

"Maybe some othuh folks. They's plenty a' black men in Alexandria an' Williamsburg who'd want to be in *your* army. Billy said it with a strong *your,* knowing that almost everybody had heard of George Washington and knew what a fine man he was.

Washington shook his head."I don't think the other planters are ready for that."

Billy shut up, feeling deeply disappointed. He felt even worse when Washington wrote up an order saying, "Neither Negroes, Boys unable to carry arms, nor Old Men, are to be enlisted."

The General handed the order to Billy to carry to the other officers and to be sent to every unit in the army.

Billy couldn't help saying to Washington, "Is this 'cause a' what I said?"

"No," Washington responded, "that's what Mr. Hancock, President of the Congress tells me he wants. I believe the army should be controlled by civilians—the people in Congress—so I'm doing what he asked."

Billy was thinking that he was "people," too, but he knew there was no use saying it.

But that wasn't the end of it. The militia units continued to dis-solve after a few months and recruitment never met the army's needs. Billy was gratified to read the letter that Washington soon felt compelled to send to Hancock: "I've been told that free Negroes who've served this Army are very unhappy at being turned away. They may seek to enter the British army. So I'm going to have to depart from what I wrote you before and let them be enlisted. If I'm doing wrong, tell me, and I'll put a stop to it."

Of course Hancock never told Washington to "put a stop to it." From that time on, there were thousands of Negroes fighting in the rebel army-often side by side with white soldiers. Some of those men compiled outstanding records. For example, Lafayette employed a black freedman named James Armistead as his principal aide. Armistead was one of the most successful spies for the Americans during the war. Acting as a double agent, he learned that Cornwallis had moved his forces onto the Yorktown peninsula, information that proved to be a turning point in the war.

Meanwhile, Billy restrained himself from telling the General that he had been right about the need for black soldiers. And he did not bring up again his continued confusion about the Americans' Declaration of Independence and the British threat to free runaway slaves.

CHAPTER 12

These are the Times

Figure 11 Washington in thick of battle of New York.

We din't do no winnin 'at New York We was first class whipped on Long Island, then agin at Kip 's Bay, where the General darn near got hisself kilt tryin' to rally the troops. Fact is, me an' John Reed gotta grab his horse's bridle an' drag him away from the front. I got mesself 'tween the General an' the Brits. They was shootin'point blank but never hit either one a'us.

We left three thousan' boys behine at Fort Washington, an' then we had to watch from 'cross the river when the Hessians massacres 'em aftuh they surrenduhs. I give the General my spyglass an' he watches 'em nail our boys to trees wi'bayonets. Says he nevuh forgot that. I heard him tell folks aftuh the war that we should nevuh have tried to defend New York. But I kin tell you for a fact that, at the time, he took it personal an' he took it bad. Tole me straightaway that he mighta jes lost us the war right then.

Washington, with Billy beside him, watched as the last remnant of the Continental Army made it across the Hudson River into New Jersey. A young aide-de-camp, Alexander Hamilton, rode up and declared, "That's the last of them, General. I estimate that slightly more than three thousand made it across."

"How many did we start with, Hamilton?" Washington asked with conspicuous impatience.

"You mean at the start of the battle, sir?" Hamilton asked.

"Yes, at the start of the wretched battle, Colonel Hamilton, if you please." Washington was obviously in a sour mood, and poor Hamilton was the closest available target for his frustration.

"About fifteen thousand, sir, but that includes militia and some of them ran away, so they should not be counted as casualties."

Hamilton's horse reared and Billy reached across to grab the bridle."Just stay put wi' me for awhile," Billy quietly advised Hamilton.

Washington rode forward alongside the column of bedraggled and obviously beaten troops. An elderly black soldier gave him a tired salute as he rode past. A thoroughly frazzled woman, either a soldier's wife or a camp follower, looked up through her matted hair and made an obscene gesture while mumbling something about bullshit officers. Washington just rode on in stony silence.

"Best let him go on up ahead for a while," Billy told Hamilton. Hamilton nodded. He was a rather short young man who appeared taller because of his erect military posture. Washington, who had an uncanny eye for talent, had plucked him from the ranks as one of his aides after the debacle at Kip's Bay.

"You is now a membuh a' the General's family, Colonel, sir," Billy remarked as they rode forward through the stumbling residue of an army, about thirty yards behind Washington.

"Any pointers on how to get along with my new 'father,' Mr. Lee.?"

"Jes call me Billy, if you would," Billy responded."He's been my mastuh goin' on nine years I do believe. He 'spects a lot a' any man he takes on. But he also 'spects a lot a' himself, which is why you don' wanna go ridin' up there right now. He knows he just got his butt whipped by General Howe, an' he takes it all mighty personal."

Hamilton took all this in, especially Billy's use of the word "master," which surprised him because he had assumed that Billy, like all the other black soldiers in the army, was a free black, probably once a slave, but no longer. This struck Hamilton as strange, given the cause for which they were supposedly fighting, and the fact that Billy was evidently extremely close to Washington and deeply trusted by him. But it was also the kind of sensitive matter that a newly-arrived aide should not explore.

At this point Washington turned in the saddle and gestured for Billy and Hamilton to come forward and join him.

Washington was all business as they came alongside."Colonel Hamilton, take a detachment of fifty able-bodied men, no wounded or sick soldiers, and establish a defensive position on this side of the river. If and when Howe's advance units reach the river, put up a show of force to discourage their crossing and send a courier to apprise me of their arrival. God knows how close Howe's army is, but if it were me, I'd be right on my tail."

Hamilton's first reaction—his unspoken thought—was that fifty able-bodied men would be hard to find in this column of sick, wounded, and wasted men. Also, that fifty men, no matter how able-bodied, had zero chance of holding off Howe's advance guard if Howe was in hot pursuit. But Hamilton, braced by Billy's advice, swallowed his doubts and questions."Yes, sir," he almost shouted as he saluted and then galloped off.

"Billy, I want you to ride ahead," Washington ordered, "and find us a place to rest for the night. High ground, if possible, where we can put up a respectable fight if Howe comes on."

"Will do, General," Billy responded."But if Howe does come on, we got nothin' respectable on our side to do any fightin.' Jes look at these boys, General, they is—"

"—I know the condition of my troops. Just find us the best location for the night, Billy. If Howe comes across the river in force, we're all going down. Find us a place where we can all go down with honor."

Billy wheeled his horse, but said nothing. He realized there was little chance they would find sleep and less that they would some-how manage to go down with honor.

***

"General Washington, I want to thank you for granting me this interview, most especially given our....uh...challenging situation."

Washington was seated in his tent at his portable desk, reading after-action reports by candlelight as Billy brushed his hair. The interviewer was a short, rumpled young man, early thirties, with a slight cockney accent, who had embedded himself with the Continental Army during its desperate march through New Jersey in order to write an account of the ordeal for two Philadelphia newspapers. His name was Tom Paine, and it had only recently been revealed that he was the anonymous author, almost a year earlier, of *Common Sense,* a pamphlet that had energized and inspired the people.

"The honor is mine, Mr. Paine," said Washington as he rose to shake Paine's hand.

Billy said, "Mine, too. The General tole me to read your words when we was starin' down the redcoats outside Boston las' year. You was the first man to speak out in a way that ordinary folks kin unnerstan'."

Paine shuffled his feet."Well, Mr. Lee, you are precisely the kind of reader I was aiming at. A hard-working American who values his freedom and is willing to fight for it rather than succumb to slavery at the hands of our British betters."

Billy gave the General a quick look. Paine, like Hamilton, obviously presumed that although Billy was Washington's servant, he was not his slave, a misconception that was becoming increasingly frequent as the army moved through northern states where there were more free blacks than slaves. Billy wondered when Washington would finally get the message.

"What can I do for you, Mr. Paine?" Washington asked, eager to change the subject and unwilling to correct Paine's misconception. He shot a look at Billy, which Billy read as an order to remain silent. Billy needed no such order. This had happened many times before.

"Well, General," Paine explained, "I'm writing a story on the current crisis. In fact that's what I'm calling the piece, *The Crisis*. I want Americans to know how profoundly endangered our cause truly is, but I don't want to provide the British with information that might embolden their effort. Am I correct, sir, in thinking that we are quite vulnerable?"

"You are correct," Washington spoke the words with full gravitas."And I appreciate your sensitivity on this matter. We are down to about three thousand troops, less than half of them ready to fight. For the life of me, I don't understand Howe's caution. If it were me, I would be coming on full bore."

"Thank God they have Howe and we have Washington," Paine declared as if from a pulpit, although he was, if anything, an outspoken enemy of organized religion."There are some reports, unverified, that Howe is settling in for the winter at New York—some rumors that he has taken up with a Tory woman, a Mrs. Loring, quite a fetching lady I'm told."

"Let's not give General Howe any reason to leave his love den," Washington said."When you write your story, Mr. Paine, I ask that you provide no information on the depleted size of our army, or its currently crippled condition. Put an emphasis on—"

Paine interrupted, not wishing to be told what to write."—I know what to say, General, and I believe I know how to say it. Listen to this;" he referred to some notes he pulled from his knapsack: 'These are the times that try men's souls. The summer soldier and the sunshine patriot will, in this crisis, shrink from the service of their country—'"

Washington interrupted Paine."—My God, man, we know how bad the situation is. We need your gift for crafting inspiring words."

"And you will have them, sir. I go on to say, 'but he that stands by it now, deserves the love and thanks of man and woman!' By God, General, the man who stands by his country now will be a hero forever more!"

"Splendid!" Washington said."Get your essay finished and rush it to the printers in Philly as soon as possible. That's an order, Mr. Paine."

Paine saluted, and the three men chuckled companionably for a few seconds. Washington looked down at his papers to signal that the interview was over, but as Paine half-bowed and headed out of the tent, Washington suddenly rose and said, "Mr. Paine—for your ears only. Howe may have gone into winter quarters and our tattered fellows may require time to heal, but I folly intend to strike a powerful blow before this army beds down for the winter. You may not reveal this, but I trust this knowledge will move you to write an even more uplifting story. You provide the inspiration, Mr. Paine, and I'll furnish the troops!"

Paine's eyes widened."What a story! I can hardly wait for you to give me permission to write it. We desperately need good news."

Figure 13 Thomas Paine.

As soon as Paine had moved out of earshot, Billy said, "I know you wrote to your fren, Governuh Trumbull, 'bout how a 'lively blow' would raise the spirits a' the people, an' Joe Reed sent you a note 'bout attackin' Trenton, but I din't know you's made up your mind."

Washington smiled."Tom Paine did it for me—said just the right words. Times that try man's souls are times for soulful men to act."

Billy resumed brushing Washington's hair."Yessir," Billy said, "that Mr. Paine got a fine way wi' words, but I think he'd be surprised to learn I'm your slave. Colonel Hamilton, Mr. Paine—all these fellers thinks I'm a free man. They figure if I ever was a slave, you must a' freed me, 'specially aftuh the Congress come out with that Declaration a' Independence."

Washington did not immediately respond, and for a moment, Billy felt a pang of uncertainty. He wondered if he had gone too far. What he yearned for was freedom, not embarrassing the General. But the General gave no hint of any internal debate, no flash of his eyes in anger. His expression never changed.

After a lengthy pause, Washington uttered two familiar words."Under advisement."

Washington pretended to read the scattered papers on his desk. He had long ago perfected the art of silence, the postured inscrutability that came across to most witnesses as omniscience, even when Washington himself was experiencing deep doubts about the matter at hand. Billy had learned the gift of silence from his master, and he continued brushing the General's hair without a word while his pulse was beating faster than it did on a fox hunt. In Billy's case the source of the suppressed excitement was singular. He knew that he had stepped over a line to make the case for his freedom, using Paine's misunderstanding as a weapon in a way that violated the Virginia code between master and slave. But it was that very code that Billy had hoped the Declaration of Independence had made obsolete. He would persevere until Washington's understanding matched his own. It might take as long or longer than this revolutionary war, but his stake in it was even greater than that of men already free.

In Washington's case the tension was double-barreled. He had just made an impulsive statement to a prominent journalist about some bold stroke. His trademark was an almost preternatural control, and he had just violated it. Moreover, the combination of Paine's misguided assumption and Billy's edgy violations had opened up a crack in his mind that he did not like to acknowledge, but knew to be there. Namely, it was beginning to be more and more difficult to maintain that Billy didn't deserve to be free; that most of the arguments buttressing slavery were slowly but relentlessly falling away. If the Americans were not, indeed, fighting for individual freedom, what were they fighting for?

At this stage, however, it was just a crack in a still-frozen facade. He could seal it with silence, which is what he was doing, but the crack was now present. In fact, now even the silence seemed to have a crack in it. Best to move away from it before the crack widened in his mind.

"Time for bed, Billy. Wake me at dawn tomorrow."

CHAPTER 13

Trenton

I'm real surprised when the General tells Tom Paine he's gonna put on a big attack afore the end a' the year. General alius plays his cards close to his vest an' here he goes, practically promisin' victory. That tells me he 's more 'n jes upset 'bout bein 'kicked outta New York—feels he's gotta do somethin 'to keep the army togethuh. Paine an' Hamilton give me an openin' to push him 'bout settin' me free, but I know his thoughts is elsewhere, an 'I pull back pretty quick.

There was very little time left in which to mount a major offensive. Although Congress had recently voted Washington almost dictatorial powers, the fact remained that the enlistments of thousands of Continentals would expire on New Year's Day, 1777. Washington had two weeks to avoid a looming disaster. The situation was even worse, psychologically, than it was materially. Fear and depression stalked the land. That was why Washington had virtually implored Tom Paine to write an inspirational essay.

Billy had never seen the General with such a solemn mien. He was noted for his stoicism, but now his mood verged on despondency. Billy thought it would have been a good time for Martha to be with the General, but circumstances made that impossible. Not-withstanding his mood, Washington worked methodically, combining status reports of his own troops with information compiled by his network of spies about the British, and especially the Hessians. He consulted his own engineers and reviewed maps of the areas in question.

Then he convened his general staff and informed them that he was considering an attack on Trenton for Christmas day. The officers, confused by swirling rumors, were surprised and pleased to learn Washington's intentions. He asked for their opinions of his plan, but he did not permit the usual meandering discussion. Greene promptly said he was strongly in favor. Knox said, "Getting my cannon over the river will be the biggest challenge, but I guarantee I'll do it!" The others quickly agreed and after brief consultation, Washington told them of the three-pronged attack he planned and sent them off to prepare.

Afterwards, Billy said, "That was one of my favorite staff meetin's, General. No wishy-washy, shilly-shallying, up an' down an' sideways an' back, mebbe so an' mebbe not. You got 'em straight down to work. Ev'ryone a' 'em knows zackly what he's sposed to do."

"Yes," Washington said."Now we'll see if they do it."

Washington was writing on small pieces of paper. One fluttered to the floor and Billy picked it up.

"That's the secret password for the sentinels, Billy," Washington said, 'Victory or Death.'"

A chill went through Billy. He had never heard Washington say anything quite so ominous.

***

Chris'mas night. Wors' weather I evuh seen. General's got his heart set on attackin 'this dingy little town called Trenton. Soljers mannin 'the town is all Hessians—Germans paid by the Brits to kick the crap out a'us. We knows what they's like. So we's by the Delaware River. It'sfreezin' cold, the river's risin'an'the wind's blowin' hard 'nough to knock you down—carryin' snow, sometimes sleet right in our faces. Rivuh's filled wi' chunks a' ice, current's fiowin' fast. We's jammed inta flat-bottom boats wi'tall sides, evabody standin 'cause they's no place to sit. I'm standin 'next to the General. He mumbles, "The only good thing is that the Hessians will think only a lunatic would attack in this weather." I jes nods.

Boat's slippin' an' slidin,' bouncin' offen hunks a' ice, boys throwin' up an'pis sin' down they legs. They was all shiverin', din't have coats, some don'have shoes. Boat crews was usin'poles an'oars to git us 'cross. Takes near twenny minutes. When we finally bumps the shore, I jump offfast as I kin an'run to git our horses.

Figure 14 Iconic painting of Washington crossing the Delaware (Although not shown, Billy was standing next to him).

Washington had split the army into three parts, fifteen hundred with Cadwalder and Reed, seven hundred under Ewing. Twenty-four hundred, led by the General himself plus Greene and Sullivan, were crossing the Delaware in the big, flat-bottomed boats. And then there was Knox, 6'3" and 320 pounds, getting his eighteen cannon across the river, as much by will power as strength.

The attack was running late; it would be daylight before they reached Trenton and the possibility of a surprise had dwindled accordingly.

Billy told Washington that his horse, Blueskin, was calm and steady. Didn't know how he'd be in battle, but he sure looked good.

"How about you, Billy?" Washington asked.

"Strong an' ready, General," Billy replied firmly, but then he always said that, even when he was quaking in his boots.

Washington mounted Blueskin and Billy mounted his regular horse, Chinkling, leading a replacement bay, just in case. As they rode past the trudging soldiers, some men were mumbling the standard profanities and soldierly complaints: "How come only officers get to ride?" "You sure can pick 'em, General—one fine night for a fight!" There were others who grumbled, "'Bout time we gave them lobsterbacks some a' their own shit," "Hey Billy, tell the General I need to get home for spring planting."

But most of the soldiers said nothing, proud that their general was sharing their misery in this obscene weather. They leaned into the freezing rain, stomping and stumbling in the red-stained snow where the bleeding feet of the men ahead had carved a trail. A few flickering lanterns threw this tableau into odd and fantastic shapes, as the whistling wind made strange music with the contrapuntal beat of crunching snow, rattling canteens, cartouche boxes, and jiggling bayonet belts.

As they neared Trenton, the last stretch was sharply uphill over rocky, icy ground. Blueskin was moving slowly, but steadily, when his hind legs skidded out from under him, threatening to throw Washington and crash onto him as he fell. Billy saw it coming, a split second too late to help. Washington instantly and instinctively countered the shift in balance, grabbed Blueskin flowing mane and forced the horse's head up with Herculean strength. Blueskin scrambled his hind legs until they found purchase, and under Washington's calm, almost incredibly powerful control, righted himself and continued the ascent. Washington leaned low and spoke to his horse."Good fellow," he said."Saved both of us from execution."

The soldiers who had watched this astonishing event gaped in amazement at their commander's physical strength and preternatural calm—reassured once more that they were following a real leader.

Billy's response was subdued."Fine move, there, General. You's the oney man—'cept mebbe me—who could a' done it."

Washington shook his head."Would have been a hell of way to end my military career."

"I always said you was strong as a horse. Aftuh this I'd have to say, maybe you was even stronguh."

The troops had split up, General Sullivan's troops going down another road, and soon a courier came back from Sullivan with a note saying their guns were too wet to fire. Washington frowned and told the messenger, "Tell the General to go to the bayonet."

Moments later, Greene rode up. He spoke almost in a whisper: "I've heard from Cadwalder and Ewing. They haven't been able to cross the river yet, and they won't be able to join up with us in time for our attack." Greene waited, unsure what reply he wanted to hear.

Washington knew better than to hesitate. "Go forward, sir. The assault goes on."

Greene showed a tight grin as he saluted, and cantered away.

Everybody was late, and when they finally reached their positions, it was almost daylight. Amazingly, they had all reached the points assigned for the start of the attack at virtually the same moment. Greene's men had come upon some pickets and exchanged fire, but the sentries, not understanding this was part of a major attack, had merely slipped away instead of hurrying into camp to warn their leader, Colonel Rail, and the rest of the Hessians.

Knox, who always managed somehow to get his cannon where they were needed, had brought all eighteen of them to a knoll overlooking the town, the exact location that Washington had selected for the placement of the artillery.

Greene's men came out of the woods running. The Hessians, now alerted, came stumbling into the streets. But the wind had turned, and snow and sleet were driving into their faces, and they remained confused about the nature and numbers of their attackers, Greene's men opened fire, but the Hessians didn't panic. They formed lines, waited a moment, fired, and then pulled back in an orderly fashion.

Greene's and Sullivan's troops came together. Washington and Billy cantered to higher ground where they could see the entire field of battle. Billy had the spyglass Washington had given him, but they were so close there was no need for it.

The Americans kept charging ahead, while the Hessians continued piling out of houses and barracks, drums beating, officers yelling in German, guns firing. Greene, knowing where Knox and his cannon were located, swerved his men to avoid the lanes of artillery fire, and Knox's cannon opened up.

Figure 15 General Hnery Knox.

At Washington's orders, the cannons had been loaded with projectiles filled with bullet-sized pieces of iron, fifty to a round, designed to take out six to eight infantrymen in an open field. But the Hessians, by mistakenly concentrating their forces, presented a dense target that a single canister could penetrate three or four rows deep.

It took less than two seconds for the canister rounds to hit the Hessians. Heads and arms went flying backwards, bones mixing with iron to fill the air with shrapnel that leveled the row behind. Men whose legs had been blown off, tumbled face down to the ground, screaming as their intestines flowed out. They tried to prop their remaining torsos on their elbows before they died.

The Hessian soldiers in the rear, following the rules of their training, rushed to fill the gaps and met the same fate, slipping on bloody body tissue and intestines as they staggered forward, before being disemboweled and decapitated.

Greene and Sullivan resumed their advance on the Hessian flank.

Billy understood that Washington was champing at the bit."You stay here, General, the boys is doin' jes fine." He held out his spyglass, hoping to distract him.

Washington reined Blueskin around and the horse reared as Washington intended."Neither of us can stand being here, useless, while our boys are being killed." He kneed Blueskin and the big stallion broke into a powerful gallop as Washington raised his sword. Billy had anticipated the move and, however reluctantly, he surged Chinkling until he was beside the General. The Americans, seeing their commander join them in battle, cheered and redoubled their attack. Blueskin shuddered at the gunfire, but continued running.

The Hessians, surprised by the ferocity of the assault, continued to fall back, but seeing the American commander standing tall in the stirrups of his great stallion, with a shimmering blue-grey coat that looked almost white, several fired at him. Billy was almost tempted to ride behind the General, since bullets and grapeshot never seemed to find him, but he remained stalwart, riding stirrup to stirrup with Washington as he shouted encouragement to his men.

The bullets whizzed by, but none of them hit either Washington or Billy, and Billy wondered if the aura surrounding the general was somewhat more expansive than he had thought. Then a Hessian, trapped apart from the main body of his fellows, ran towards Washington, his bayonet fixed. Billy had not unlimbered his carbine, but he whacked the Hessian on his head with his spyglass. The Hessian fell like a stone.

With the streets of Trenton filled with American soldiers, Knox ceased firing his cannon. The Hessians began a full-scale, but disciplined retreat towards an apple orchard, planning to make a last stand out of range of Knox's guns.

As Greene's men closed in, the surviving remnant of the Hessians formed a double line and fired a final volley, wounding some of the Americans. The Hessians then threw down their muskets and surrendered.

Greene yelled, "Cease fire!" but several of his soldiers, their blood up and angered by the final Hessian volley, fired into the Hessian front, killing or wounding most of the front row after they had surrendered. Then two American soldiers hurried up and bayoneted the wounded Hessians, shouting "Remember Fort Washington!" Greene winced and looked away.

Meanwhile, Washington had ridden through the slaughterhouse on King Street, the main street of Trenton, Billy close behind. Prescott had to be spurred over the dead bodies and pieces of dead bodies on the ground. A wounded Hessian officer, barely able to walk, grabbed Washington's foot at the stirrup. He did not speak English, but silently guided Washington and Billy to his fallen commanding officer, Colonel Johann Rail, lying near death on the porch of a house on King Street. Washington and Billy dismounted and approached the stricken Hessian.

"To whom do I have the honor?" Rail managed to utter in heavily accented English, despite his pain.

Billy responded, "This is His Excellency, General George Washington, at your service, sir." Washington was taken by Billy's deco-rum. He was behaving as a fully trained aide.

"Ah," said Rail, his voice breaking as he spoke, "you are just as tall as they said, General Washington. Congratulations, sir, on your tactical brilliance today. Textbook use of canister against infantry."

"Thank you, Colonel." Is there anything we can do for you?"

"I fear the wound is mortal, sir, but you could grant a dying man his last request."

Washington nodded."It would be an honor, sir."

"It is about honor. Would you allow the regiment to retain its colors? We have never lost them in our two hundred years of existence. The survivors could eventually bring them back to Prussia after the war."

"Consider it done, sir." Washington saluted Rail, who made a gallant attempt to return the salute.

Washington and Billy then remounted and headed over to Greene's troops, who were rounding up the Hessian survivors in the apple orchard. Once again, their horses had to navigate the bodies of dead and wounded Hessians littering the ground, as three overwhelmed medics began to identify the likely survivors and mark the foreheads of the others with an X.

"You know, it's odd," Washington observed to Billy as they rode."We've rarely had to witness the mangled horror of the battlefield after the battle, because we were usually retreating."

"I guess thass true, General," Billy replied."But do recall what we saw them Hessians do to our wounded boys at Fort Washington aftuh they surrenders. The Hessians is mighty lucky to be fightin' agin you."

Greene saluted as Washington and Billy rode up."Splendid job, Brother Nat. Splendid. Casualties?"

"I understand their commander is dying. If he does, they will have lost twenty-two dead and eighty-four wounded. We've captured nearly nine hundred of them. Another six or seven hundred have escaped across the river. Shall we track them down?"

"I think not. We have other goals to follow up on. What are our casualties?"

"In battle, two killed, although we hear two sentries froze to death during the night. We've also had four slightly wounded, including your cousin, Captain William Washington."

Generals Knox and Sullivan appeared, Knox's horse sagging beneath his enormous weight, but his broad face wreathed in a beatific smile.

"A splendid result, gentlemen," Washington exclaimed."All our officers and men are to be commended. When we return to camp there will be extra rations of rum for every soldier."

Even as the men were cheering and waving their hats (those who had them), two Continentals began pushing an apparently stubborn Hessian soldier with their muskets, and when he resisted their efforts, one of the Continentals knocked him to the ground with the butt of his musket, cursing him as he went down, and the other American, also cursing, bayoneted the Hessian through the throat.

"General Greene," Washington shouted, "arrest those men immediately!"

"Yes, sir."

"They are to be disciplined, General," Washington said angrily, "and they're fortunate that I'm not in a mood to have them executed. We are neither British nor Hessian. We do not abuse, let alone murder our captured enemies."

"Yes, sir, but I know these men to be good soldiers. And they lost some of their closest friends at Fort Washington. Don't you think—"

"—It's not what I think or what you think, General. It's what discipline and human decency demand. I'll rely on you to devise a suitable punishment."

"Yes, sir."

Billy noticed that, in these circumstances, Washington had ceased calling Greene, "Brother Nat," his favorite nickname for his favorite general.

Billy and Washington then rode back up the hill where Knox had returned to begin hitching up his cannon."Henry, you earned your pay today," Washington yelled as they came up."The Hessian commander, Colonel Rail, complimented us on our use of artillery."

"I told you we'd have them out-gunned, but even I didn't think they'd have only one four-pounder. And we took that out in the first volley. Turkey shoot after that, General. Doesn't it feel good to be on the giving rather than the receiving end for once?"

Washington nodded and Billy smiled and said."I do believe the Bible says somewhere that it's a heap bettuh to give than to receive. So what we done today is the Lord's work, an' what them poor Hessian boys felt was the wrath a' God."

"Billy's making you into an instrument of God, Henry," Washington joked."How do you feel about that?"

"I take my orders from you, General," Knox joked back."But I always presumed that you took yours from the Almighty himself."

Billy smiled to himself, recalling that when he first met the General, he had thought that he resembled the picture of God in his mother's bible.

CHAPTER 14

Valley Forge 1 Conditions

Figure 16 Misery at Valley Forge.

Ya don' need to know 'bout all the fightin' an' sufferin' we done ovuh the next year. It's all in the books. Princeton. Brandywine. Germantown. We done good at Princeton, but aftuh that mos'a the time our boys fought hard, but got licked. The General thought hard about keepin 'Howe out a 'Philly but nothin 'worked. What you need to know is that men kept goin' into an' outta the army. The General called it a turnstile. But they was a group, some black boys in it, too, who signed up for the duration. They was like the current in our rivuh, the raisins in our dough. The way I think 'bout it, we had the General, who wasn 'goin 'nowhere else, and then the for-the-duration boys, who had nowhere else to go. We all got frozen togethuh at Valley Forge.*

"General, I tole you I would stick with you to the end. Pardon me for sayin' it straight out, but I do think we's pretty close." Billy's comment had no discernible impact on Washington's erect posture and steely gaze as he rode through the Valley Forge encampment much in the manner of a Roman proconsul savoring a recent triumph.

"Keep it down, Billy," Washington whispered."The men might hear you."

"I don' think I'd be tellin' em anythin' they don' know, General. A man don' need to be told he's starvin.' All he gotta do is lissen to his stomach growlin.'"

Washington knew that Billy was right. They were riding, as they did almost every day, over blood-stained snow, past the frozen corpses of dead horses and groups of shivering soldiers, some of them cutting up canvas tents to make shoes. Half the men were classified as too sick for duty. Most of the men, sick or not, huddled in the one thousand log huts the General had ordered built, like hiber-nating bears who might not make it through the winter. The huts had fireplaces and chimneys, but the only wood they had was soaked through and sent out more smoke than heat. The windows were made of sheets of paper dipped in fat—they let in a little light. The doorways were covered with rags and torn sheets.

Someone had brought in the smallpox, and it began to spread. Washington tried to have all the men inoculated with pus dug out of the sores of the sick ones, but the doctors didn't get them all. Billy had been inoculated by Colonel Lee, long before he was sold to the General, and starting in '77, Washington had sent orders home to Mount Vernon to have everybody inoculated, slave and free.

Washington had gotten smallpox, himself, years earlier, when he went to Barbados with his brother Lawrence. He recovered, and although his face did not have the deep pits of many who survived smallpox, he had many tiny marks—shallow scratches—but he was free of the pox forever.

Billy had been thinking about that since Preacher had told him the story about Washington's trip to Barbados. He had wanted to ask the General about it for some time, but didn't have the nerve.

When Washington ordered the vaccinations at Mount Vernon, Billy thought he had found a way—an indirect way—to ask the question. At least he thought it was indirect.

"General," Billy said, "evabody at Mt. Vernon knows pretty well you figure you got more slaves than you need, but they keep havin' babies and they's more mouths to feed."

Washington looked steadily at Billy, who now didn't know whether to go forward or not, but he swallowed hard and plunged ahead."I think they's crazy, but some a' them slaves been whisperin' that you wants to have 'em vaccinated 'cause that'll keep 'em from havin' babies."

He forced a laugh to show how ridiculous he thought that was, but the General exploded—so quickly and fiercely that Billy had no hope of heading him off.

"That's a lie," Washington yelled and added half a dozen other expletives."The vaccine won't make anybody sterile—it'll save their lives. Who is telling this terrible story?—I'll whip his butt till he bleeds out of every hole in his body!"

"It's jes word a' mouth, General. Crazy talk, but I'll tell the folks it ain't true whenever I gits back there."

A suspicion began to form in the General's mind. As soon as the fog of anger dissipated, his intellect could operate clearly again."This is about Barbados, isn't it? Barbados and me. Somebody thinks the smallpox I got there made me sterile—and then they concocted this crazy story about me crippling the lives of my own people."

Washington leaned very close to Billy, staring into his eyes."I wasn't sterile when I went down there, and I'm not sterile now. Do you understand me, William Lee?"

"I do sir, I surely do. Yessir, never been nothin' you said that was clearer to me. 'Course it ain't really any a' my business, General."

Washington did not look away for a very long time. Billy blinked once or twice, but he didn't back away. He respected the General, but no longer feared him as much as he had when he first went to Mount Vernon.

Besides, the General hadn't answered his real question: why hadn't the General and Martha had children? He was no closer to solving that mystery. What about Martha? Could she still have children? Did she want any? Billy's mind was too active, too curious, to simply abandon this mystery.

In the meantime he was witness to what seemed a happy marriage. The General and Mrs. Washington got along fine when they were together, and wrote to each other regularly when they were separated. Each time Billy brought him the mail, the General always asked if there was something from Mount Vernon. He opened the letters from Martha before anything else—even letters from Congress. Every once in a while there would be a separate envelope enclosed with Martha's regular letter, marked "private" and carefully sealed. The General would respond with a separate sealed note, and Billy seldom saw what he had written, and then, only inadvertently. Billy recalled that Martha had a private desk in her sewing room at Mount Vernon with separate drawers under lock and key. Once, Billy had walked into the room while Martha was sitting at the desk with one of the drawers open, and he had seen it contained papers folded like letters. Martha had quickly closed the drawer and Billy pretended he hadn't seen anything.

***

There were other troubles at Valley Forge besides smallpox. Some soldiers caught pneumonia and died. They succumbed quickly because they were weakened by the terrible conditions and the lack of decent food. Washington had gone into Valley Forge with twelve thousand men, and would come out with three thousand less. Women were dying, too. There were many women following the army, even some children. Some of the women were wives of officers and even ordinary soldiers—or just girlfriends. Some were whores. Washington detested that, but it wasn't easy to get rid of them. Not only people were dying, but horses and dogs as well. The smell from dead animals, foul latrines and unwashed men filled the air.

Perhaps saddest of all for Washington was the quality of his troops. Most of the skilled farmers and mechanics had gone home. Most of the men who were left were indentured servants, former slaves, young men who had just arrived from England and Ireland, none of them more than twenty-five years old, some as young as fifteen.

Washington told Billy, "You can't expect men like these to be fighting for some big idea like 'freedom'" And yet, some of them were fighting for just that, and that core gave Washington heart.

Nevertheless, in his official correspondence with the Continental Congress Washington himself described the condition of the army as deplorable, warning that when the spring came there might not be any army at all.

But as he and Billy rode past the clutches of men huddled around small campfires, Washington was determined to project the serene self-confidence of a natural aristocrat trotting to his appointment with destiny. And he expected Billy to do nothing that contradicted his self-conscious embodiment of what the troops and officers referred to, quite simply, as "The Cause."

"Whatevuh you want, General," Billy sighed."But seems to me we's just pretendin,' puttin on a show, bein' like actors."

Washington smiled."Precisely. And that's just what we should be doing, and what the men expect us to do. So lift up your head, William Lee, square your shoulders, put on that good old boy face for me."

"We all be foolin' each othuh, an' knowin' it all the while. But I'll play along iffen you want." Then he sat taller in the saddle, grabbed Washington's elbow, and whispered into his ear."Slaves is real good at foolin,' you know, 'cause that's how we get by." Washington just shook his head with a look of mock exasperation as they approached another huddle of troops around a campfire.

One young soldier limped over, patted Blueskin's flank, then grabbed Washington's left ankle above the stirrup—a move oddly reminiscent of the officer who had led them to the dying Hessian Colonel Rail. Billy wasn't sure about the soldier's intentions and he reached for his carbine, but Washington gestured for him to put it away.

"What can I do for you, soldier?"

"Sir, Private Dawson. We're all from Dan'l Morgan's outfit, and we've got a man who claims to know you. We're pretty sure he's just tellin tall tales—"

"—Let me meet him," Washington interrupted as he dismounted, Billy close behind. Five soldiers straightened up as Washington approached, a young lieutenant ordered, "Attention!"

Washington smiled in recognition and said, "Lieutenant John Marshall, it is a pleasure to see you here."

"The privilege is all mine," Marshall responded.

They shook hands,and Washington gestured to the soldiers to be at ease. Marshall was almost as tall as Washington, with a mop of black-as-night hair, a pistol and tomahawk in his belt, and a bandage around his right hand.

"How'd you get that injury, Lieutenant?" Washington asked.

"Piece of shrapnel at Brandywine, sir. It'll be perfectly fine by the time we leave this God forsaken place in the spring."

Washington nodded his approval, then said, "I understand one of your men claims to be an acquaintance of mine."

A soldier stepped forward, saluting nervously, the man behind him giggling at his imminent exposure as a fraud."Private Phillips, General. Remember me from Cambridge when you put me straight on that bridge?"

"Ah, yes, Phillips, good to see you again," suddenly recognizing the man whose nose he had broken two years before."I can see your nose has healed." Washington looked over at the other soldiers."I recall that we had a spirited conversation that day about the importance of latrines."

"Yes, sir," Phillips answered with obvious relief, "I've taken your words to heart ever since. Also got me five more redcoat officers since then, just like I promised."

Playing along with the charade, Billy extended his hand."Good to see you agin, Mr. Phillips."

Then, silence. Phillips was grinning, Washington was re-creating the distance he customarily kept with enlisted men, Billy was back at his usual place a half-step behind Washington, Marshall was looking at his Commander-in-Chief with barely concealed veneration. Silences never seemed to bother Washington, but after four or five awkward seconds, Phillips broke the spell.

"Lieutenant Marshall here is the most decorated officer in Colonel Morgan's unit. We're all sharp-shooters, sir, but Lieutenant Marshall is the sharpest of us all. Also the fastest runner. We men call him Silverheels. He's also—"

"—That's quite enough," Marshall interrupted, looking up at the sky."His Excellency is not interested in such trivia. He has more important matters to occupy his mind."

"Quite the contrary," Washington retorted."I always want to know about officers who have earned the respect of their men. This war has become a kind of testing ground for talent, Marshall. And you are apparently one of its looming discoveries. I'd be interested in your assessment of our current situation."

"To be truthful, sir, pretty miserable. My men are down to half-rations, about a third are sick or recovering from wounds, not ready to fight. We've lost three men and half our horses to exposure. But what you said about a testing ground seems right to me. If we can survive this winter and come out the other side in the spring, I don't think there's any way the British can beat us. These men, like me, are signed up for the duration. We all expect to win. Just get us through this," Marshall spread his arms as if to envelop the whole panorama of suffering, "and we will."

"Very impressive, Marshall," Washington said in his most measured mode, "especially since it lines up almost perfectly with my own thoughts on the matter."

"Yes, sir."

"Now, I must get back to headquarters," Washington declared as he remounted."And you, Phillips, good to see you again. Take care of that lieutenant of yours. We're going to need men like him after we win this thing." Lieutenant—my regards to your family.

Washington was shaking his head and smiling broadly, uncharacteristically cheerful on the ride back.

"What's got you so bouncy, General?

"These are some of the men we once feared would go home after the next battle, and now they say they've signed up for the duration. I was thinking that we don't deserve men like that. And if we do find a way to win this war, men like that will be the reason."

"Let me tell you, General, they's thinkin' that *you's* the reason. And, no offense, sir, but I'm thinkin' that evabody's foolin' evabody else."

***

They was one bright spot for me at Valley Forge: Margaret. I thought then, an' I still b 'lieve now that she's the fines' lookin' woman I ever seen. Margaret Thomas ain 't very tall, but she's round in the right places, an' she's got a walk that'd set your blood boilin.' I jes loved to watch her walk–comin' at me an' goin' away. She don' throw it around like some ladies–she knows how to move it jes right. Her

*skin's real smooth an'even, like coffee wi'a little milk in it. Thass how
I like my coffee."*

Billy had previously seen Margaret in Cambridge and New York,
but although he had realized she was a particularly attractive woman,
and that she was working at headquarters, everything had moved too
fast at Cambridge. New York had been disastrous for the army, and he
had no time for personal thoughts.

The first time Billy paid Margaret any serious attention was when
she walked into Washington's headquarters in Valley Forge, which
occupied a fine fieldstone-faced house that had been rented from the
Potts family. It was a very cold day, but she was only wearing a light
green dress with a deep front, nipped at the waist, with a flowing, tan-
colored wool shawl draped over her head and shoulders. She marched
in, swept the shawl off with a graceful swing and gave Billy a dazzling
smile. She had fine teeth, pretty lips and green eyes that flashed right
through him. He couldn't help noticing how nicely she filled out that
green dress.

Then Caty Greene, the wife of Washington's favorite general,
Nathanael Greene, spoke to Margaret. Caty was visiting the Potts
house, ostensibly to settle some housekeeping matter; Billy believed
she was really interested in speaking to Washington. Greene's quarters
were in another farmhouse, some distance from the Potts House, but
somehow, Caty often found reasons to be at Washington's headquarters.

Margaret made some notes on papers she was carrying. It was
obvious that she could read and write, which always impressed Billy,
no matter whether the person was white or black, but especially if they
were black. Caty noticed Billy staring at Margaret, smiled and brought
her to meet him.

"Margaret Thomas, this is William Lee, known to one and all as
Billy. He's General Washington's valet, but also his trusted aide."

Billy immediately realized that Margaret didn't look nor act like
a slave. He already thought she was special because she was literate—pretty and smart—and she moved like a lady. When he looked
into her eyes, none of that seemed to matter.

Margaret put out her hand and said, "It's a pleasure to meet you."

Billy was surprised. In those days women, especially black
women, didn't offer their hands for you to shake, even if you were

black, too. Billy took her hand (which felt quite smooth—no hint of field work—or laundry washing, either) and nodded, not quite sure what to say. Margaret had to take her hand back, and Billy missed it the instant it was gone.

Billy managed to croak out, "Nice to meet you."

Both ladies smiled, and then they turned back to whatever they were working on. Billy pretended to be studying some field orders. When he looked up, Margaret was gone, but Caty Greene was still hovering about, gazing towards the steps to Washington's room.

Billy approached her and said, "I seen Miz Thomas afore, but I don' recall what her service is?"

Caty responded, "I thought you'd find her attractive. Margaret works for Mrs. Thompson, who is in charge of housekeeping here at headquarters. Mrs. Thompson is a very good worker but her eyesight is failing and Margaret helps keep Mrs. Thompson's records."

"Yes, Ma'am."

Billy had another question, but was afraid to ask. Caty understood."Miss Thomas is a single woman, a free woman, and she works for our army as a paid employee. We're very lucky to have her."

"Thankee, Miz Greene," Billy said. He wasn't certain whether the news was good or not. A free woman. Impressive, but would she have any interest in a black slave—even a valet to the head of the Continental Army? The idea struck him more forcibly than ever before that his status as a slave might be an enormous impediment to the realization of his hopes and dreams.

But at that particular moment, Caty spoke, interrupting Billy's chain of thought.

"Mr. Washington seems rather thin to me, Billy. Are you sure you're feeding him well enough?"

Billy laughed."The General sure ain't gonna feast when his men is starvin,' Miz Greene. He eats a fair amount, but he's a very big man."

Caty smiled."He certainly is. And very good looking, too."

"Nevuh noticed," Billy said, "but I guess some folks would think that."

Caty continued, "You work closely with Mr. Washington. You must be aware that the General and I have the same color hair and eyes?"

"That right?" Billy said."I'll pay more 'tention."

Billy knew that Washington liked Nathanael Greene—whom he often fondly called "Brother Nat"— more than almost any other general with the possible exception of Knox. Greene was not an impressive physical specimen—he suffered from asthma attacks and walked with a slight limp from a childhood accident—but Washington had found his judgment to be excellent. Billy also knew that women found Washington attractive, and always tried to dance with him whenever there was a party. At Valley Forge, there hadn't been any parties—not like the ones at Mount Vernon in peacetime, or even in New York, before the disastrous campaign there.

Figure 17 Gen. Nathanael Greene.

Caty, with her cascades of reddish-brown hair and luminous blue-gray eyes (she was right, her hair and eyes were similar in color to the General's), was easily the prettiest woman in the camp. A vivacious woman in her early twenties, she wore deeply scooped gowns that clung to her body, and her movements were alluring— not extravagant, but not quite innocent. A few of the wives were less than charmed, even though Caty was always smiling and pleasant to everyone. But it was obvious that the officers delighted in Caty's company, smiling, laughing, often trying to divert her with little jokes and compliments.

The remarkable thing about Caty was that she was pregnant when she came to camp; she gave birth to a son in early February, a son she named George Washington Greene. Not even pregnancy had seemed to interfere with her flirtatious nature or the attraction she held for men.

While Caty spread her attentions around, Billy was well aware that she focused much of her charm on Washington. She sometimes touched his hand or laid her fingers on the arm of his uniform, and she was able to coax the occasional smile from him, not an easy task because of his ill-fitting teeth.

As the months in Valley Forge continued, with slender rations, widespread illness, painful and ugly deaths, Caty spent even more time at Washington's headquarters. She told Billy she thought the General was sorely in need of diversion, and she was happy to provide it. Billy was surprised that she spoke so frankly to him—a black slave—but he felt certain she wanted him to repeat this message to Washington. Instead, Billy spoke to Amos, one of the black valets at Greene's headquarters. The valets, black and white, slave and free, formed a kind of intelligence service, sharing information about their masters, trying to anticipate problems, and also just plain enjoying the gossip. Billy did more listening than talking, but now and then he would share some meaningless story about Washington.

Amos told Billy that General Greene and his wife argued quite a bit. He was aware of her flirtatious nature and concerned that she might embarrass him in some way, even get involved with another man. One of Caty's female servants told Amos that Caty had found a letter from General Gates' wife to Nat Greene, and Caty was certain he had been having an affair with her. Greene denied it—said the connection was all in Gates' wife's imagination.

Billy was not insensitive to female charm himself, and he knew that there were numerous infidelities among ordinary soldiers as well as officers, but he believed that a liaison between Washington and the wife of one of his generals would have disastrous consequences. Surely, Washington was aware of the danger, but he was a man, a strong and virile man, and he had been away from home for a considerable length of time. Billy wondered if Caty were trying to seduce the General to get even with her husband.

Caty had become even more attentive to Washington of late. Billy was with him almost everywhere he went at Valley Forge, but one day, she somehow managed to slip past him at the Potts House, and when Billy went upstairs, he was astonished to find her in the General's bedroom. The door was open and both of them were dressed, although Washington had his jacket off and his hair was loose—not tied in the usual queue. The General had kept his small, personal desk between him and Caty, but they both were surprised when Billy walked in.

Billy said, "'Scuse me, General, some dispatches has come in from Philly, an' I thought you'd like to know. They's in your office downstairs."

"Of course," Washington said, pulling on his waistcoat with Billy's help.

Caty curtsied quickly and hurried away. Billy followed the General downstairs. When the General reached his office, he looked about with a puzzled expression on his face."Where are the dispatches, Billy?"

"Sorry, General, I jes realized you seen 'em yesterday." Washington looked at him sharply."I see," he said, and Billy believed he did.

***

It was late February, close to the General's birthday on the 22nd. I had a hunch that Miz Washington would join the General in camp, jes like she did at Cambridge an' Morristown. She couldn 'get there too soon if we was goin' to avoid problems wi' Caty Greene. I was doin' my best to help the General avoid any—uh—temptation, but it would be a lot easier when Miz Washington was in camp.

Sure enough, to Billy's relief, Martha arrived at Valley Forge a few days before the General's birthday, bringing wagonloads of provisions and her own cheerful, little self. The General was thrilled to see her, but she was astonished to see how pale and thin he looked. Pale and thin, but safe and secure. Billy always thought it was very kind of Mrs. Washington to share winters in camp. That was true, but it was also probably true that she was smart enough to protect her investment in George Washington.

As Washington and Billy rode up to army headquarters at the Potts house after one of their daily tours of the camp, Martha came out and leaned against the white picket fence, followed by Caty Greene.

"George, I don't know why you feel the need to go out in weather like this," Martha declared, and she rushed forward to close Washington's coat collar around his neck.

"The men need to see me, dear," he responded, giving her a quick hug.

While Martha grabbed Washington by one arm, Caty stepped forward to grab the other and usher him into the farmhouse."The women need to see you, too, General," Caty gushed, "and we have arranged a dance tonight for the general officers and their wives. I fully expect one dance, with Mrs. Washington's permission, of course."

Washington and Billy exchanged perplexed looks.

"Caty," said Martha, "my one concern is that my husband will be trampled by the stampede of officers rushing for your hand."

The idea of scheduling a dance amidst this frozen version of hell struck Washington (not to mention Billy) as bizarre, like ordering tea in the middle of a battle, or dismounting to admire the sunset during a fox hunt. But, then, wasn't that Caty's whole point, to provide a little feast as a way of mocking the prevailing famine? It was a perfect Caty kind of idea, simultaneously outrageous and then, once it settled in your mind, the kind of bold statement of defiance that you wish you had thought of yourself.

True enough, some of the men freezing out there in their huts, once they heard the music wafting through the frigid night air, would invent new profanities to defame the presumed privileges of the officer class. But Washington knew enough history to realize that enlisted men had been doing that since the Peloponnesian Wars.

And the fine farmhouse where George and Martha were staying had already become the butt of jokes about the Big Hut where His Excellency lived like a King.

Washington hoped that out there—among the men who counted most, men like Lieutenant John Marshall—the sound of music in the air would bring a smile, as a statement that their cause and its indomitable leader, were not freezing to death in this wintry mix of suffering and sleet. Indeed, let the musicians play louder, so the sound could carry all the way to Howe's headquarters in Philadelphia, where it would be heard as an ominous signal that the Continental Army was still alive and well, and would be coming to get them as soon as the snow melted in the spring.

"It's clear I have no say in this matter," Washington mumbled as he handed his coat to Billy and headed for the fireplace, Caty clinging to his arm.

"No, you don't. Martha and I have decided—" Caty proclaimed.

"—Actually, it was very much Caty's idea, dear," Martha said while brushing the snow off Washington's collar.

"You will have a grand time, General," Caty said while doing a twirl in front of him."And I will assume the responsibility for protecting you from all those wives who claim you are the next dance on their cards."

"Now, *that* will be a sight worth seeing," Martha observed with an arch tone and a shake of the head.

"Billy, I believe I'll need you tonight to protect me from these women."

"Yes, sir. I'll show up. But you's on your own wi' the women," Billy replied while going out the door."Hessians I can handle. Horses, too. But women......," and he waved himself away.

***

Billy looked over the punch bowl as the four musicians took a break—two violinists, a bass player and someone who played an instrument he had never seen, a sort of horizontal harp. He would have been thrilled to join the group with his banjo, but the truth was, he did not read music, and the classical pieces they played were not part of his repertoire. Still, the room where the dance was being held was so crowded the musicians were forced to play in an adjoining room. If he had been posted in that room, Billy would not have been able to keep an eye on the General.

In fact, the main room in the Potts house was far too small for a dance. But while there were more than a dozen generals in camp, only a few of them had their wives with them, and most of the others were not anxious to parade their girlfriends before the Washingtons. Despite the invitation from the wife of the Commander-in-Chief, some of the remaining wives had begged off for a variety excuses, legitimate and otherwise. Even so, the cramped space could barely contain the crowd of couples, including the Washingtons.

Washington and Greene were huddled in deep deliberation. Greene, the more animated, had ridden the northern loop through the encampment that day, Washington the southern loop. They were comparing notes on the morale of the troops. Washington was telling Greene about his earlier meeting with Lieutenant Marshall. Because Greene had recently been appointed Quartermaster General—a position he had not sought and had only accepted because of Washington's urgent request—Greene was offering his analysis of the supply problem that, unless solved, put the very survival of the Continental Army at risk.

Off to one side stood Mrs. Washington, wearing one of her most elegant Mount Vernon gowns, gesturing gracefully as she made conversation with three officers' wives, a task for which she had no peer, at least so Billy thought. He had often watched her perform this diplomatic chore, somehow making it seem like a delightful game rather than a boring duty. He noticed that she periodically stole glances at her husband, trying in vain to make eye contact. She was also stealing glimpses at her co-hostess for the evening, the flirtatious Caty Greene.

Caty preferred talking to men rather than women, or rather they preferred talking to her. In any room of handsome women, Mrs. Washington could usually hold her own. But with Caty in the room, a new and almost impossible level of other-worldly glamour entered the equation. Without make-up, she was a stunning work of nature. With it, she was preposterously gorgeous. Yes, Billy thought to himself, Caty Greene was the most beautiful white woman he had ever seen.

And it was clear from the way she carried herself that Caty knew it. No one without personal knowledge would ever have guessed that she had given birth to a child only a few weeks earlier.

When the musicians began to play again and the dancers returned to the floor, Billy watched Caty glide behind the General, tap him on the shoulder, throw open her arms, and say something Billy could not hear. The General excused himself with General Greene, bowed to Caty, and they proceeded to dance. All eyes in the room were on them, but they were both used to such attention, and both had mastered the art of not noticing. The crowded space meant that they had to dance very closely together—which Caty had craftily anticipated when she arranged the dance. They appeared to be making pleasant conversation throughout the dance.

"Well, my dearest Caty, it would appear that your party is a complete triumph."

"Hmm, I like that 'dearest' very much. Would you really like me to be your dearest?"

"Well, of course, you already are."

"That's not quite what I mean, George. Know that I can be very discreet."

"Every eye in the room is on us now. You must know that, too."

"I do. But my eyes are only on one man, and I very much want to have him."

"You already do. Brother Nat is a very lucky man."

"You could be lucky, too, if you would just let yourself go."

"That is not what I do, Caty. You know that."

"Well, you need to do it. *And you* know that."

"The music is about to end."

"To be continued."

Billy watched as Washington kissed Caty's hand, delivered her to General Greene, then made his way over to Mrs. Washington and her small coterie of officers' wives. The General and his wife were an exceedingly well-matched couple, Billy thought, as he noticed how they read each other's body language. In one sense, it was easy, of course, because everyone deferred to them—Billy thought of the house slaves at Mount Vernon smiling away—but they also had an emotional bond, an honest affinity, that was rock-ribbed. They could play roles together because, when they were alone, they did not need to play roles at all.

Billy felt a pang of longing. He, too, would like to have a mate who was well-matched to him—a source of love and understanding. He had had plenty of women in his time, but he really yearned for one special woman who would share his life and his dreams. He had lost Philomena, but now his thoughts flashed to Margaret Thomas. Was it possible that this lovely creature could be his?

Billy smiled as the General and his missus led off the last dance of the evening. For a full minute they were alone on the floor, swirling gracefully as they chatted as only a couple comfortable with their prominence could do."Ah, the General loves his lady," Billy said to himself.

"She propositioned you, didn't she?" Martha asked George."Well, urn, yes, she did."

"Bitch. No wonder they call her the Cleopatra of the camp."

"Calm down, dear. I parried her thrusts."

"George, this is probably the most gorgeous woman in America, and she wants to thrust with you. What am I to think? And do?"

"Do you honestly think that I can be tempted?"

"Yes, who wouldn't?"

"Do you think I will act on that temptation?"

"No. I know you better than she does."

"Yes, you do."

"So what do I do?"

"Nothing different. Kill her with kindness. Embrace her requests. Make her feel guilty."

"Guilt is not an emotion that Caty recognizes. Rumor has it that she is sleeping with half of your senior staff."

"Martha, I cannot ask Brother Nat to send her home without starting a scandal. I need you to handle this. Can you do it?"

"One question—do I have your unconditional love?"

"Yes."

"That's all I need to know."

CHAPTER 15

Valley Forge 2 Relations

I was seein' Margaret at headquarters 'most ev'ry day, an' I'm thinkin' on her more an' more. Ain't thought this much 'bout one particular woman evuh before, not even, Lord forgive me, Philomena. Margaret's very polite to me. Sometimes, she'll be passin' by an' give me a very nice smile an' a nod. Othuh times she don' even seem to notice me. A lot a men taifa to her, not all a' 'em black, but she never says more 'n a few words to any a' 'em—far as I knew. Still, I'm worryin 'that one day she 'Il meet a man she likes an' that'll be it for me.

Billy finally figured out where Margaret lived. He never actually followed her—didn't want to be caught at that—but one day when he was out riding with the General, Billy saw her go into one of the hundreds of ramshackle log huts that dotted the landscape all over Valley Forge.

The General noticed Billy staring after her."Isn't that the young lady who's on Mrs. Thompson's staff?" he asked.

"Yes sir, I believe it is."

Washington smiled. "Is she one of your many lady friends?"

"No, General. I hardly knows her any bettuh than you do."

Washington shrugged in disbelief, and they cantered away. But seeing Margaret going into that hut troubled Billy because he thought that she might be living with some man—some soldier. Billy almost gave up right then, but he felt so drawn to Margaret that he couldn't help watching for her and talking to people about her. He just couldn't get up the nerve to speak to her when she came into headquarters, which she did quite regularly. He might smile a bit, but he didn't say anything. He was surprised that he felt so tongue-tied; he was usually able to talk to anyone and everyone—male or female, black or white.

One dreary afternoon when he was carrying papers to be delivered to General Greene, Billy decided to walk instead of ride, and he just happened to be dressed in one of his best uniforms. The route he took through the muck and mud and filthy snow and ice, just happened to pass by the hut that he had seen Margaret entering. As he approached, walking very slowly, a pair of ladies came out of the cabin. One of them saw Billy, and they both turned quickly and went back inside. He heard voices and laughter—women's voices, women's laughter— and when he was right in front of the oil-cloth draped doorway, out stepped Margaret.

She was fixing her hair and straightening her skirt. She looked at Billy as if she were surprised to see him and said, "Well, hello, Mr. Lee."

"Hello," he answered—not much of a reply, but he didn't know what else to say.

She was smiling very warmly, and Billy could hear giggles from inside the cabin. Margaret looked around as if she were annoyed at the sounds.

"Don't mind these ladies, Mr. Lee. It's been a long winter and they're a little funny in the head."

That got a big laugh from inside and a smile from Billy. "I know how that is, Miz Thomas. I gits the same way sometimes when it's really cold."

"I hope you don't giggle," she said.

"No, Ma'am," he said, "but I sure don' mine the sound a' ladies laughin'—that's music to my ears." That earned Billy a cheer from inside and a very, warm smile from Margaret.

"Where are you going on this cold day?" she asked.

"It's a military secret," he said, holding a finger to his lips.

"I should have known," Margaret said. "It's clear that you're a very important person on General Washington's staff."

Billy laughed. "I do my best."

"Folks say your best is pretty good."

That raised another laugh inside, a different kind of laugh. Margaret was looking at Billy rather frankly—up and down, head to foot and in-between. Billy was thinking he would have blushed—if he knew how—but then there was silence, and he still didn't know what to say next.

"I guess I'll be on my way, Miz Thomas," Billy said.

"Margaret," she said.

"Pardon."

"Call me Margaret."

"A pleasure," Billy said, really smiling, "and I'll be pleased if you call me Billy or Will, as you prefer."

She smiled. "I like Billy," she said .

He tipped his head and said, "I sure like Margaret."

And then Billy was on his way. He knew she would be watching him, and he began to feel like he was walking on the edge of a cliff, being careful to put one foot in front of the other, hoping he wouldn't stumble and make a fool of himself. Afterwards he laughed about it— but he was damn glad he didn't trip or fall down.

***

I'm sure Margaret don 'mind the fact I dress nice an' work for the Commander-in-Chief On the othuh hand, she's free an' I'm a slave. No matter how tall I am an' how erect I start, 'how fine a horse I ride, an' what clothes I 'm wearin ', I still ain't free—so I cain't never stand as tall as Margaret, not unless I become free. I ain't been thinkin' 'bout that for a while, but aftuh meetin' Margaret, it begin to seem real importan.'

Even though Martha Washington was going to stay in camp until the spring campaign began, Caty Greene kept hanging around headquarters. Billy didn't see how Caty could corner the General alone when both he and Martha were in the way. Billy didn't make his opposition too obvious—he didn't want Caty Greene as an enemy. Trying to assess Caty's intentions, Billy spoke to Amos, one of General Greene's valets, who told him that when Caty was "interested" in some man she would often spend time with the man's wife or girl-friend. Caty was almost always the prettiest girl in the room, and she wanted her 'target" to see how she compared with his lady. That made sense to Billy; Caty *was* younger and prettier than Martha Washington. Of course, Martha wasn't too bad looking herself, and she had one big advantage: She was in bed with the General every night.

One day, Martha was preparing to have the first of a series of teas at headquarters for some of the officers—not generals, but lieu-tenants and captains. Billy was there, Margaret, too, and Caty just happened to be there—as usual. She said she'd like to be a guest at Martha's tea. It was true that Caty's husband was a general, and she hadn't intended to invite any generals or their wives, but Martha recalled that George had asked her to accommodate Caty, and she reluctantly agreed. Caty then said, "I think it would be nice if you also invited Margaret and William to tea this afternoon."

Martha was plainly stunned. She'd never invited any of the valets or the staff—black or white—to tea before, and she considered the idea outrageous,

Caty smiled and said, "All the officers know Billy and they probably know Margaret as well. But if you believe—"

Billy could see a huge funnel cloud forming—one that could blow him and Margaret into oblivion. Whatever Caty Greene was aiming for, it wasn't going to be good for Billy, and it had the potential to destroy his relationship with the General. Martha's expression was beginning to knot into a disbelieving frown, but she hadn't yet formed her response into words—and it would soon be too late.

Billy spoke quickly. "It'll be a privilege for Margaret an' me to serve tea to the officers—a great privilege, an' we thank you for the offer. If it's agreeable to Miz Washington, we'll leave immediately to dress propuhly an' return promptly. Do we have your permission, Miz Washington?"

Caty looked frustrated, Margaret disappointed, but Martha wore a beatific, even triumphant, smile. "Of course, Billy, Margaret." She turned to Caty, and bestowed on her an even brighter smile. "Shall we go up to my quarters, my dear?"

Billy hustled Margaret out of the room, and they both hurried to get dressed appropriately. When Margaret returned to headquarters, she was wearing a nice, trim-looking blue dress and neat shoes—not washerwoman clothes at all. Billy had put on his newest uniform jacket and buffed up his shoes.

Just as Billy was going into the parlor, Washington called him into his office. He was surprised to see Billy wearing his best jacket, but he thought that anything that helped anyone's morale at Valley Forge was a good thing.

"Billy, I have some papers I want you to distribute promptly to all of the generals.

"Uh..." Billy swallowed hard. "Kin I put that off for an hour or so, General?"

Washington frowned. Billy did not usually respond to an order this way.

"And what, may I ask, is the reason for this delay?"

Billy thought he might choke, getting the words out. "Sorry, Sir, but I been invited to tea."

Washington could not have been more astonished if Billy had told him he was going to the moon. In fact, he couldn't believe he had heard Billy correctly. "You're going to tea?"

"Yes sir."

"Where, pray tell, is this hallowed event taking place—an event that takes priority over my orders."

"Right here, General. I mean in the parlor. Miz Washington an' Miz Greene is givin' a tea an' they invited me—an' Margaret Thomas."

The concept of two black people, one of them a slave, invited to a formal tea at his headquarters, was an idea that Washington could not readily assimilate.

"Wait here," he said and stood up

"—A' course we declined Miz Greene's offiih," Billy added. "Wasn' right at all. I said Margaret an' me would help serve the tea—cain't no way be guests." He hadn't wanted to tell the whole story, but he thought this was a time for candor.

The General stomped out of the office.

Billy knew where he was going and more or less what was going to happen. While he and the General had spent a great deal of time together in the nine years since he had moved to Mount Vernon, and especially during the war years, there were lines too fixed to cross, even if he were being pushed across that line by some damn general's good-looking wife.

Washington accosted Martha: "What were you thinking when you invited Billy to tea with the officers and their wives?"

"It wasn't my idea—it was Caty Greene's. She invited herself and the two negroes."

"I should have known."

"You told me to kill her with kindness—embrace her requests."

"Good Lord," Washington said, "my very words. I didn't mean that kind of ridiculous request."

Martha nodded. "We might have been compromised, but Billy stepped in, saying just the right thing—offering to serve tea to the officers and ladies. You're right about him—he's got very good judgment, for a slave."

Figure 18 Young Martha at Mount Vernon.

Washington returned to his office, made no comment about the tea party, but handed the papers to Billy, and said, "Make certain these papers are distributed by the end of the day."

Billy couldn't get out of there quickly enough, but even without Washington's comments, he knew he had escaped a dangerous, even potentially devastating trap.

It ain't like I nevuh been to a formal tea afore. The Washingtons offen served tea at Mount Vernon, an' usually I was there, playin' butler an' caringfor the General an' Miz Washington an' they guests. Naturally, I ain't part a 'the ceremony -1 mean they din't serve tea to me, but I watched it many times. Like a lot a' things in the General's life, I tries to commit to memory everythin 'I see, so I don' make no mistakes.

Billy was still wondering why Caty Greene wanted both Margaret and him to be invited. Then he remembered what Amos said about Caty arranging things so she'd be compared favorably with some other woman if she was interested in that lady's husband or boyfriend. Maybe what Caty wanted was for Margaret to see Billy—a slave— dealing with white people in a social situation. Maybe she figured that Margaret was not only free, she was smooth enough to handle herself properly in any company. What about Billy? He realized then that he was being tested, and got just a wee bit nervous.

When the officers and their ladies saw Billy and Margaret at the tea, they were more than a little surprised, but soon relaxed when they realized they were only present to serve.

Caty attempted to include Billy and Margaret in the conversation, but Billy just smiled and skillfully avoided any but minimal responses and Margaret followed his lead. Caty managed to elicit from Margaret that she had family in Philadelphia, but nothing more. Billy believed nobody would ask him such questions. They wouldn't be comfortable inquiring how and when he was born, and how and when he became a slave—and how he liked it. He almost smiled at the thought of answering such questions.

But then Caty Greene asked, "How long have you been with the Washingtons, Billy?"

All the others froze, but Billy immediately realized he would have to avoid being humiliated by telling details about his sale by

Colonel Lee's widow and purchase by Washington—maybe including the price paid for him. "I been wi' the Washingtons for almos' nine years now," Billy said. "I first met the General when I was fox-hunting wi' Colonel John Lee from Westmoreland County. Mr. Washington was a colonel then—in the Virginia militia—but it was clear he would be a general some day—some day soon. ""

Billy thought he had dodged the question pretty well, and he doubted Caty would press on with her questioning, but even as she opened her mouth to say—God knows what—Martha jumped in, saying, "George says that Billy is as fine a horseman as he's ever seen."

"Thankee, Ma'am," Billy said, nodding modestly. And then Martha said something about the medical needs of the soldiers at Valley Forge, and the conversation veered off in another direction. When Billy gave Caty a quick look, he saw her appraising him with a faint smile—a smile he interpreted as acknowledging the skillfulness of his evasion, although she was so crafty he couldn't be certain.

After an hour or so, Martha stood up, signaling to everyone that it was time to leave. Billy was pleased when some of the ladies nodded to Margaret and even smiled at him (they didn't curtsy, of course). The men knew Billy and a couple of them shook hands with him. He'd remember who did and who didn't.

Billy was happy to escape from the tea without suffering any major damage, and he thought he now had a perfect opportunity to walk Margaret home.

"May I accompany you to your lodgings," he said, trying to behave like a gentleman without sounding silly.

Margaret said, "I was hoping for a horseback ride."

"You wait right here," Billy said, and he hurried off to saddle his horse.

When I gits back to Margaret on my horse, Chinkling, I starts to dismount. She waves me off an' says "Give me a hand up," which I do, an' in a moment she's sittin' behine me. Margaret 's holdin' tight even though I'm walkin' Chinkling as slow as possible. I kin feel her body heat right through my jacket—I ain 't wearin' my greatcoat— an' some of the nicest parts a' her body is pressin' agin me. I's gittin' pretty hot myself. An' when my horse skids a step on the ice an' her hands slip lowuhI'sfeelin' even hottuh.

When they reached Margaret's cabin, Billy slipped from the saddle, reached up and pulled Margaret into his arms. He thought this might be the best chance he was ever going to have, so he kissed her—thoroughly. She was mumbling something but at first he wasn't listening. Then he finally understood.

Margaret was saying, "We should go inside."

Billy didn't feel much like meeting the ladies who lived with Margaret, and he held back, but she pulled him right past the oilcloth covering the door and into her cabin. There wasn't anyone else there. He didn't know how that had happened, but he wasn't thinking about anything but loving up Margaret. With remarkable speed she spread Billy's jacket and her shawl on some straw, undressed (while Billy did the same), and pulled him down with her for some of the most enthusiastic lovemaking he had ever enjoyed.

Billy, something of a connoisseur in these matters, thought it was even better the next time. Then Margaret pushed him away and got into her clothes—almost as fast as she got out of them. Billy was ready for some more loving, but Margaret wasn't having any, helping Billy get into his clothes as fast as he had shed them, while doing the same for herself.

She lighted a candle, and she looked beautiful—as if she'd been fussing with herself for an hour instead of just a minute. Billy was looking more lopsided in his clothes than she was, and she laughed— that rippling laugh he had heard before. He quickly straightened himself up. She gave him a quick kiss and began moving him out the doorway.

"Margaret," Billy said, but she was already pulling that oilcloth shut.

"Goodnight," she whispered.

It was too late for Billy to say something romantic. He pulled his hat on, and stumbled around until he found his horse near a campfire. The soldiers sitting there were smiling at him, one saying, "You've got a fine ride there, Billy," but he pretended he didn't hear. He climbed on his saddle and rode back to the General's house.

Billy suddenly remembered the papers he was supposed to distribute. He tethered Chinkling and hurried into Washington's office. The General was sitting at his desk, stony-faced.

"I know it's pretty late," Billy said, "but I kin still pass out those orders real fast."

"Mrs. Washington's tea ended hours ago," Washington said, his face set, his expression grim.

Billy thought maybe a humble tone would help. "Been a strange day, General. I kind a' lost track a' time. I sure do 'pologize."

Washington correctly suspected that Billy had gone off with that pretty black woman from housekeeping, but he thought it would be unwise to bring that up just now. For the first time, Washington was fully aware that he had no constructive means with which to punish Billy for his transgressions. Billy was a slave, but there was no overseer around to whip him—not that Washington would ever have considered such treatment. On the other hand, it did not seem appropriate for him to pass out the kind of punishment that one gave to an errant soldier—twenty-four hours of sentry duty, or some such.

For years now—all of the time Billy had been at Mount Vernon and at his side during the war—Billy's conduct had almost always been exemplary. There had never been a serious reason for him to consider any significant punishment. It seemed to Washington that the only course available to him was a reprimand, not necessarily delivered at this exact moment.

Equally important, Washington would have to pay close attention to Billy's relationship with this black woman, particularly if that relationship were going to lead Billy to be lax in his duties, diverting him, even partially, from his responsibilities to Washington, himself. Earlier, he had told Martha that he was not concerned about that woman, but now he realized he had been mistaken. She was a threat of as yet unknown dimensions.

As so often in perplexing circumstances, Washington followed the route that had always been eminently successful for him: Silence.

Without a word, he stood up and left the room.

Billy did indeed feel fully chastised, even fearful. He had never had a confrontation like this with Washington before. He did not want the situation to be repeated. Billy went out to stable Chinkling and then went in to bed. He rose before dawn to distribute the orders to the generals.

***

That same morning Margaret walked into headquarters and acted like every other day—nothing special, polite, but she didn't even offer Billy a warm look. He was relieved because he din't want to have any further problems with the General.

A few days later, a keen look from Margaret told Billy it was all right again. In the evening, he slipped away from headquarters and went to her cabin. Sure enough, she was alone. They enjoyed an hour of very intense love-making, and then Margaret escorted Billy out of the cabin—not too early, not too late, but always with Billy wanting more. They got together regularly after that, but Billy was increasingly concerned that the General would find out and be very angry.

In fact, Washington was already convinced that Billy was deeply involved with Margaret Thomas. He observed Billy's conduct carefully, and thus far, at least—with the exception of the overnight delay in delivery of general orders—he had not found that Billy's service to him was deteriorating. Washington had always been aware of Billy's interest in and attraction for the ladies. This was normal for a virile young man, and Washington was not foolish enough to interfere, at least not at this point.

A few weeks went by, and various signs told Washington the relationship was ongoing. He decided to let Billy know that he was aware of Billy's current "infatuation" and give him an opportunity to reassure his master. "You're looking very happy these days, Billy. Got good news from somewhere?"

Billy shook his head and said, "Maybe 'cause it's gettin' a little warmuh 'round here."

Washington gave Billy a sharp look and said, "I see." Then he walked—almost stalked—away.

Billy concluded that the General had figured it all out, and he told Margaret the next time they were together.

"That's all right," she said.

"It is?"

"Sure." She paused a second, while Billy waited for her to tell him why it was all right.

"Because we're getting married." She smiled—her biggest, prettiest smile.

No one had ever surprised William Lee more than Margaret did when she said that. He just looked at her—his eyes wide open. Neither one of them said anything for a long time. Then Margaret's eyes got very narrow. Billy could sense her whole body tightening up, even though he wasn't anywhere near enough to touch her.

Her eyes got even narrower. Her shoulders rose up—slowly.

"You think I'm not good enough for you 'cause I'm a washer-woman?" she said, her voice pitched a little higher than usual and sounding tight and strained.

Billy knew he had to say something.

"You's a fine woman, Margaret Thomas," he said.

Her eyes were still narrow. "That don't mean nothin,'" she said. Her voice didn't have its usual elegant edge. This woman was getting angry—slowly, but no question about it.

"You think you can climb in bed with me any time you please, and that's all?"

"I never said that."

"You never said nothin,'" she says. "You just used me."

Billy was shocked and very worried. The word that Margaret had spoken wasn't "used." It was a very crude word, a word that Billy didn't even want to think of, and that Margaret had never said to him before.

He steeled himself and said, "You're a fine woman—"

"—You said that!"

"Lemme finish! You's the best person I ever met an' I never had more respect for any woman than I got for you."

She sighed—she sighed so deeply that it seemed to Billy she was blowing the air right out of the room. And then she started to follow that sigh, walking straight out of the cabin.

"Wait a minute," Billy said.

She didn't wait; she kept on moving. Billy grabbed her arm and she tried to pull away, but Billy was very strong. A lot of ideas were racing through his head.

"I really care for you," he said—speaking very strongly. "I truly do."

Her head was still turned away, and she was still trying to pull out of his grip.

"Dammit!" Billy said. "You gotta let me think!"

She still wasn't looking at him. "You mean you never even thought about marrying me?"

"No! I mean, Yes! I did."

She was easing up a little bit.

"Margaret, I figure you're too good for *me*. You's free an' I'm jes a slave. I cain't do a thing I wanna do,'thout the *massuh* givin' me permission."

She wasn't pulling so hard against his hand. "You're hurting me," she said.

Billy didn't know whether she meant his hand or his words. He released her arm. She was still standing there, but she wasn't turned away as much. She was almost looking at him. Almost.

"You're smart, Will. You can read and write and do both of them very well. You can add and subtract and keep a column of figures in your head. You're tall and strong and you ride a horse as well as the General."

Billy was thinking how much he cared for this woman. He thought she was very fine in bed, but it was more than that. The words came out, even before he thought about them—words he had never said to any other woman.

"I love you, Margaret Thomas."

She turned all the way and almost smiled. Almost.

Billy took the deepest breath he had ever taken, and said, "I'd like it fine if you'd marry me."

There was one long minute. Then he turned her and kissed her hard and she kissed him back just as hard. She pulled away and smiled and said, "Let's go tell Miz Washington and the General. They can get a minister to marry us."

Billy temporized. The realities of what he had just agreed to struck him forcibly. What would happen if he told the General he wanted to get married? Would the General consider that to be a stabilizing factor for a lusty young man? Or would he consider it to be a threat to the quality of Billy's service to him? Washington had steadily refused to free Billy, and it might be clear that his marriage—to a free woman— would inevitably bring up the issue of Billy's freedom sooner or later. Would marrying Margaret help or hurt his prospects for freedom? He was afraid to find out, just yet.

"I don' know if I wanna bother the Washingtons 'bout my personal life," he said.

"You think they won't give you permission to marry because you're a slave?"

Billy thought there was no point in being evasive on this particular topic. He said, "Plenny a' slaves gits married at Mount Vernon, an' the Washingtons tries to keep 'em togethuh. The General hardly ever sells any slaves an' one a' the reasons, he says, is he don' like to break up families. In fact, he jes don' do it."

"Good," Margaret said. "Then he sure won't stop you and me—me being free."

Billy was thinking hard and thinking fast. "The General prob'ly gonna tell us to wait 'til the war's over. He'll likely say this ain't the right time."

"White soldiers are getting married almost every day. Why can't we?"

Billy was thinking harder and faster. He truly loved this woman and wanted to marry her, but he didn't want to take a chance on somebody saying "No," because that might end everything. There might be no way back from "No."

"Let's not take no chances," Billy said. "We kin have a minister wedding aftuh the war. Now, we'll Jump the Broom."

"Jump the Broom?"

"It's a custom black folks brought ovuh from Africa. You take a broom an' sweep up, cleanin' away the ole stuff in your life. Then your friends hold it an' you hold hands an'jump over it—an'jes like that you's married."

"I know all about that Jump the Broom stuff. We ain't in Africa now. We're in America. I want a real wedding."

"We'll have it for sure, honey. But first we's gonna jump the broom. That way we'll already be married an' ain't nothin' nobody can do 'bout it."

She was standing there thinking. Billy didn't want her to think too much so he grabbed her and kissed her, and pretty soon they were enjoying some serious love-making. When they were done and Margaret was stretching luxuriantly, Billy said, "Far as I'm concerned, we's married already."

Wrong thing to say. Margaret sat right up—fast. "Come on," she said, "we're gonna get Amos and Mavis and Antoine and Rebecca—all our friends—and have them witness us Jumping the Broom."

"All right," Billy said. He wasn't fully happy, but he certainly wasn't feeling sad.

They dressed quickly and went off to talk to their friends, quietly, not making a big thing of it. Billy spoke to three of the black men who were on the staffs of Generals Greene, Sullivan and Knox. He made it clear that they were not to share this information with their officers. They readily agreed—having a secret wouldn't be easy in an army camp, but they would certainly try. They all liked Margaret and they were happy for Billy. Margaret also confided in some of her friends, who agreed wholeheartedly.

They planned to meet that evening at the big barn two hundred yards from Washington's house. Mainly black people worked there, and they were confident they could persuade them to stay quiet.

At the same time, Billy felt troubled. This was the first time he had withheld any significant information from the General. What and when would be the reckoning? But then he was swept up in the excitement of the moment.

Jeremy took some brandy from Knox's storeroom and Mavis brought beer from Sullivan. They all had their regular allotment of rum; everybody received rum, soldiers less than officers and blacks less than whites. Then Margaret and Billy set off for the barn. But a few yards from the barn, they saw a lady standing in front of them. It was pretty dark, but Billy was sure it was Caty Greene. "Oh, oh", he was thinking, but he hoped he could bluff it through.

"Evening, Miz Greene," he said. "You's pretty far from your quarters on a mean, bittuh night like this."

"So are you, Margaret,"—she wasn't talking to Billy. "What brings you here?"

Margaret didn't get flustered. She said, "Some of us black folks are having a little party. I hope you won't report us—just an innocent little gathering for some hard-working people."

The barn door was open a crack and a little light was spilling on the snow and bouncing up so they could see Caty Greene's face fairly clearly.

"You're dressed every nicely, Margaret, for just a little party." Billy was about to say something, when Caty cut in. "You, too, Billy. That must be your best uniform, right?"

"Yes, Ma'am."

"What are you celebrating? Please tell me—I love a party."

Billy decided there was no use lying. Caty Greene could make things very unpleasant for a slave who lied to her.

"Fact is, Miz Caty, Margaret an' me's gettin' married tonight."

"Oh," she said. "I didn't know General Washington had granted you your freedom, Billy."

That set both Margaret and Billy back a bit.

"Not yet, Miz Greene, but I have no doubt it will be pretty soon."

There was an uncomfortable silence, then Caty spoke to Margaret. "Are you sure this is what you want, Margaret?"

Billy couldn't help holding his breath.

"Yes, Ma'am," Margaret said. "This is exactly what I want."

"I see. Do you have a minister?"

"No," Billy said. "We'll have a minister wedding latuh. Tonight we's going to Jump the Broom. Do you know 'bout that, Miz Greene."

"Yes, General Greene's valet told me all about it."

Right then Billy knew that Amos was the one who had told Caty, and maybe General Greene, about their plans. Had she come to stop the ceremony? Billy felt his hopes and dreams might be slipping away. In a flash he could be banished to Mount Vernon and reduced to a menial house or field slave.

"Billy and I have the highest regard for you Ma'am," Margaret said. "We'd appreciate it if you didn't share this information with anybody else?"

Billy admired the way Margaret had spoken. Smooth, he thought, very smooth.

Caty said, "I'll keep your secret on one condition—"

She paused and this time both Margaret and Billy held their breath.

"—that you invite me to the wedding," Caty said, and it was all Billy could do to keep from hugging her. In fact, Caty did hug Margaret. Billy thought he'd have to file that away in his memory. Margaret and Caty were much closer than he had ever imagined; maybe even closer than he and the General were.

The three of them walked into the barn, and the presence of Caty Greene stopped everybody dead—as if they were in a tableau.

Caty waved a hand and said, "I'm here for the dancing."

Her words unfroze the tableau, and everybody went back to what they had been doing.. Margaret's friends had brought candles, and they had set them in makeshift sconces all around the room. The flickering candles cast a warm glow—but not enough light to reveal it was really a shoddy, ramshackle barn. Nor was the candlelight sufficient to warm up the barn, but when all the folks were moving around, the conditions became more tolerable. Jeremy had swept the floor clean except for a little pile that was reserved for Margaret and Billy.

When Caty Green removed her coat, she revealed a lovely, deep-cut floral-patterned gown, proof enough that Caty hadn't merely stumbled onto the celebration, but had dressed carefully in anticipation of it. The slaves tried to avoid staring at her, but she was a dazzling sight.

Billy had dressed in his finest livery uniform, and Margaret wore a splendid white satin dress with décolletage that matched Caty's. Missy had "borrowed" the dress from an officer's wife and she had also wound some bright flowers in Margaret's hair. Billy wondered where they had come from in the dead of winter. They didn't last long, but even so, they were a pretty carmine color that set off Margaret's green eyes.

Billy had brought his banjo and started playing with the others. The wind was howling outside so they could play as loud as they wanted. Jeremy had a little flute and Felix a snare drum, and they did their best to play together. The rum was getting to them so their playing was a bit out of tune, but nobody cared. Jeremy grabbed Billy's banjo and Margaret grabbed Billy's hand. Everybody began singing a song called, "Jump the Broom."

Jeremy and Mavis spoke the opening words:

All hold hands
And say a prayer,
Before we dance
We'll clear the air.

Then everybody sang the chorus:
Jump the Broom,
Jump the Broom,
Everybody step back
(Beat) Make Room.
Bride's a 'comin'
So's the Groom
Everybody step back
(Beat) Make Room.

Jeremy and Mavis then spoke the following:
Sweep your life,
Sweep it clean,
Do it right,
No in-between.

Then everybody chimed in with the "Jump the Broom" chorus. Jeremy and Mavis then spoke the following:
Pick your partner,
Choose her well,
Treat her fine
Or live in Hell.

Then everybody ended with the "Jump the Broom" chorus.

Margaret and Billy both took hold of the broom and finished sweeping the room. Everybody cheered. Two men held the broom level to the floor, up about a foot. Billy took Margaret's hand and she held her skirt up with the other.

"I'm marryin' you right now!" Billy said.

"And I'm marryin' you back!" she answered.

While everybody was laughing, they jumped the broom. Then they kissed—so long and strong that folks yelled for them to get it done with. Jeremy started out on the banjo and the other musicians played along. Margaret began swaying and then dancing, and soon, nearly everybody was on the floor, dancing. The black guests performed some of the same dances as white people, swinging in big circles, bowing and curtsying. Caty slipped into the line and joined in. None of the blacks had ever seen a white lady dancing with a black man, but they just kept dancing, and after a while, Caty dropped out, still smiling and clapping as if she had done this every day of her life.

Then, when the guests started dancing two by two, Caty came over and took Billy's hand, which Margaret gracefully gave up. Billy held Caty so far from him that she started laughing, and Billy relaxed a bit. The others pretended to ignore them.

Caty said, "You're a very lucky man, Mr. Lee."

"Yes, ma'am, I sure agree wi' you."

"Margaret's not going to be satisfied for long with being married to a slave."

That was a thought Billy had shoved to the back of his mind.

"I 'spect the General to set me free any day, now."

"The fact that you're married to a free woman ought to help."

That was the very fact that Billy had been worrying about, but he said, "I believe you're right."

A little later, Caty slipped away, giving Margaret a big hug and smiling her way out of the barn. No one was sorry to see her go. Once she was gone folks began getting noisier and noisier and drunker and drunker, and some couples were disappearing in the hay.

After a bit, Margaret and Billy snuck away. Everybody else was too drunk or too busy to notice. When they were alone, Billy told Margaret, "This is the finest, happiest night of my life.

CHAPTER 16

Forging an Army

If Caty Greene believed she could devote herself to seducing George Washington, Martha had other ideas. Soon after the tea party that Caty, Billy and Margaret had attended, Martha organized a sewing circle, and she drafted all of the officers' wives to work with her—especially Caty. Instead of flouncing around in low cut dresses, Martha had Caty and the others patching and sewing, not just for officers, but for ordinary soldiers. They made socks, shirts and blankets and patched everything they could. At first, Caty was a little withdrawn (perhaps sullen), and kept a sharp eye out for the General. Her interest in sewing was minimal, but Martha kept the ladies in their places, working for hours on end. Gradually, Caty loosened up and got into the spirit of their endeavors. She wasn't really an evil person, just remarkably self-centered.

Martha dragged Caty along on her regular tours of the encampment, going from hut to hut in the dead of winter, bringing items the women had sewn and patched. Billy sometimes accompanied the ladies, acting primarily as a packhorse.

The boys felt pretty good about having officers' wives, including the Commander-in-Chief's wife, visiting them and bringing along whatever they had worked on. Sometimes, just looking at the soldiers was painful. Almost all of them were thin, many were sick, some were dying. An unfortunate number had an arm or a leg amputated. When a limb became infected, there was no other choice. Some of these men still wanted to be soldiers, and Billy had seen men with only one arm he thought were braver than some with two. The General tried to send home all the badly wounded men he could.

Even in these circumstances, Caty could be flirtatious, and the men loved it. She was earning her title as "The Cleopatra of the American Revolution."

One day Billy was with Martha and Caty when they entered a hut where sick soldiers were lying on crude benches, tattered rags and even directly on the dirt floor. Martha was bundled up in a heavy coat and a scarf that encircled her neck, but Caty's coat was slanted to reveal her cleavage. Even in this freezing weather she generated her own heat. One of the prostrate soldiers was buck naked. The ladies didn't even blink. They just smiled and handed out blankets, pants and whatever else they had.

Martha was also carrying paper and writing materials. She asked, "Does anyone here want to write a letter to his mother, or wife, or girlfriend?"

A man with no pants and one arm said, "I'd sure like to write to Mama, Miz Washington, but my writin' arm is gone. Can you help me?"

"Of course, Martha said, "You can start right now. First tell me your mother's name and address." She was poised to write with a thin stick of graphite wrapped in string.

The soldier smiled and gave her the information, then said, "How do you start a letter?"

Martha smiled. "Let's begin with "Dear Mama.""

"That's good," the soldier with one arm said. "Dear Mama, I want you to know that I am just fine and expect to be home soon."

As he rambled on, another soldier—the naked one—asked Caty, "Would you please write a letter to my mom?"

Caty cheerfully agreed, and America's Cleopatra sat on a log next to the naked soldier and wrote a letter for him.

***

They was othuh folks that helped the General through that fearsome winter. The Frenchman, the Marquis de Lafayette shows up. Rich as he is, he don'bring much. Most importan', he brung hisself. He's a skinny little guy wi 'a big nose, an 'I don' think he was twenny years old, but he was full a'energy an' smiles.

Figure 19 Marquis de LaFayette.

Benjamin Franklin had recommended Lafayette to the Congress, and they made him a Major General. Washington said they had given him this elevated commission because they hoped he would help get the French into the war on the American side. He came from a famous military family, but he didn't have much military experience himself, so Washington was very leery of him at first. Fortunately,

Lafayette proved to be good-natured and humble, and he said, right away, in rather stumbling English, "I don' expect a command, *Msieu le General*—I'm happy to be your aide and do whatever you want me to."

It was immediately evident that he meant it, and he was as good as his word. After a while, Billy believed that Washington thought of the Marquis as a son. He never had blood children of his own, only stepchildren from Martha. It also seemed apparent that Lafayette, whose own father had died young, thought of the General as a father. Billy wasn't entirely pleased by this relationship. He had believed that he was the young man closest to Washington.

And then there was von Steuben.

By March of 1778 the snows had mostly melted at Valley Forge, new recruits were arriving each day to fill the spaces left by troops whose one-year enlistment had ended and about three thousand other unfortunate souls who had not made it through the winter. A wide meadow had been transformed into a make-shift parade ground, where a full brigade of five hundred troops was moving back and forth, performing left, right, and oblique turns with impressive precision, while local visitors, some who had traveled from Philadelphia to watch the show, periodically broke into applause.

In the center of the field the drill-master stood atop a wooden box, formerly a container for artillery rounds, barking out commands in a thick German accent, studded with profanities that moved rather incomprehensibly from German and French to fractured English then back again. Gesturing flamboyantly as the troops moved to and fro, he looked for all the world like a slightly crazed symphony conductor in an ecstatic trance.

"Nah! Das ist shit on a spit."

"Nein! Nein! My lovely bastards."

"Ya! Asses in, shoulders back, peckers up."

The drill-master was a stout, full-throated Prussian officer with a large, florid face, a prominent and long nose and receding gray hair. He had recently arrived from Prussia, and he faced the troops wearing a resplendent parade uniform, complete with rows of shiny medals. He styled himself Friedrich Wilhelm August Heinrick Ferdinand, Baron von Steuben, and claimed to be a close confidant of Frederick the

Great as well as a general in the Prussian army. Both of these claims, it turned out, were fabrications, the kind of inflated credentials that Washington had come to expect from European expatriates, most of them former French officers, who arrived in camp as self-appointed saviors of the languishing American cause.

Figure 20 Gen. Von Steuben.

What made von Steuben different, apart from his flair for multilingual profanity, was his apparent gift for drilling troops. Washington spoke hardly any French and no German, but Captain Benjamin Walker, a William and Mary graduate who spoke fluent French, had volunteered to assist Steuben by translating the baron's commands for the soldiers.

At first, the men hated the whole process—this bombastic foreigner yelling at them in strange languages. He swore like crazy in bastard English, German and French. The men just stared. Finally, he turned to Captain Walker and said to him in French, "These men don't understand me when I swear at them in German or French. Will you please swear at them in English?"

Walker did what Steuben had asked, and the men began to laugh. That made Steuben even angrier and he swore at them even more. But little by little—while they were laughing—the men learned how to march and maneuver.

"This man is making these Continentals into a real army," Washington whispered to Billy. "I didn't think it could be done."

Watching the final results of this transformation from the sidelines was a small crowd of dignitaries, including, on horseback, Generals Washington and Greene, Billy, and the Marquis de Lafayette.

"The baron is obviously a fraud," Greene observed with a smile, "but a lovable fraud."

"Indeed, that he is, Brother Nat," Washington replied, "but he just might be the kind of indispensable fraud we desperately need."

Lafayette nodded, although the truth was that his English was still a work in progress, so it wasn't entirely clear to him just what Greene and Washington were talking about.

Billy saw the scene from his own unique angle. "That man knows more cuss words than any slave at Mount Vernon. An' he does make those boys look pretty."

It was obvious that Billy was somewhat dubious about the exchange between Greene and Washington; for what their more experienced eyes were witnessing as they watched the orchestrated maneuvers of von Steuben's "lovely bastards" was a new level of discipline within the Continental Army that Washington hoped would make it capable of competing with British regulars on the battlefield.

Greene tried to explain this achievement to Billy. "It's not just about looking pretty, Billy. On the battlefield the British troops consistently out-maneuver us, allowing them to deliver maximum firepower at the point of attack, and to maintain discipline during a strategic retreat."

"Seems to me," Billy replied, "that our boys already know how to retreat real good."

"If we're going to win this war," Washington chimed in, "we need to make the British run away. And the baron is teaching the men to move in unison without thinking, just like the British and Hessian professionals."

"Without thinkin'?" Billy exclaimed. "I thought thinkin' was a good thing, General."

"It usually is, Billy," Washington responded with growing impatience. "But in the heat of battle unthinking obedience to an order often makes the difference between winning and losing. The baron is preparing us to win."

Billy just shook his head. He couldn't understand how these smart men could believe that thinking wasn't a good thing.

At that moment a loud round of applause rang across the drill field as von Steuben brought the troops to a final halt, shouted "Dismissed," and then proceeded to take several swooping bows to the crowd, much like an opera singer at the end of a bravura performance. He then began to walk jauntily across the field towards his Commander-in-Chief, accompanied by Captain Walker, who had generously agreed to remain as an interpreter until von Steuben's broken English moved past his limited vocabulary of colorful profanities.

"Impressive, Baron. Very impressive indeed," Washington declared as he and von Steuben exchanged salutes. "I would like your candid assessment of our rag-tag army."

"But be gentle, if you can," Greene said. "His Excellency and I have come to feel a special bond with these men, most especially the for-the-duration boys who made it through this horrid winter." Walker translated both generals' comments to von Steuben.

A conversation then ensued that Billy found difficult to follow, since von Steuben's remarks needed to be translated by Captain Walker. Washington noted, with some satisfaction, that this impromptu assemblage of the top leadership of the Continental Army revealed the extent to which the war had become an international effort.

Von Steuben explained—through Captain Walker—that he was struck by the difference between these men and Prussian soldiers, who accepted discipline instinctively and without question and then performed like machines in battle. He was impressed that the American troops demanded to know why certain maneuvers, like moving from column to line formations, were critical skills on the conventional battlefield. But once you explained it to them, they picked it up quite quickly. Billy understood that very well—thinking was good. He smiled to himself.

"Does it trouble you?" the General asked von Steuben," that the soldiers often speak to each other in the ranks, and seem to enjoy spitting every few paces?"

When Washington's words had been translated, Von Steuben laughed. "These actions show clearly," he said, "the camaraderie and deeply personal spirit among these men—something most Prussian, and for that matter, British or Hessian regulars, simple don't possess."

Billy's ears perked up as von Steuben explained, "My goal is to give American troops the basic military skills of professional European soldiers, while retaining the sense of initiative, the almost spiritual commitment to the Cause, that makes them special." He smiled broadly again. "That is why I call them 'lovely bastards.'"

Lafayette seemed most impressed, almost transported to some Gallic version of Nirvana by von Steuben's assessment. His reaction gushed out so furiously that Walker could barely keep up with his translation. But the gist of Lafayette's reaction appeared to be that he had crossed the Atlantic to campaign with troops who were fighting for a cause they believed in deeply, and that he shared just as deeply.

Billy said, quietly, "Like I thought, the baron an' the marquis wants our boys to keep on thinkin' when they fight."

"That's not quite what I heard, Billy," Washington said. "The baron seemed to be saying that our troops feel a personal commitment to our common cause and he wants to layer the discipline over the top of that feeling."

Billy shrugged. He thought that was pretty close to what he had been saying. Washington was a bit miffed by the smug expression on

Billy s face. He said stiffly, "A British regular will hold his position in line while the man next to him is being disemboweled by a cannon ball. That's not a natural act, Billy. Our boys need to be capable of the same kind of discipline. And that only comes with experience and training."

Billy pondered that for several seconds. "That may be so, General, but I'd like to add one thing."

Washington looked over to Billy and smiled. "And what might that be General Lee?"

"When our boy is gettin' blood and guts spread all over him, he's gonna know zactly why he's stayin' put."

Washington smiled more broadly while staring straight ahead. "Point taken, and well said. Just what the good baron was suggesting, and more succinctly put."

"Is 'succinctly' good, General?"

"Very."

Now Billy had the broadest smile as they trotted back to headquarters.

***

Billy's good humor would soon be tested. The General was drafting final orders for leaving Valley Forge, and Billy realized he could no longer postpone informing him of his new personal situation. This was not an interview he had been looking forward to. Washington was studying some dispatches, and Billy waited quietly until he had his attention.

When Washington looked up, Billy said, "There's somethin' real importan' I have to tell you, General."

Washington noticed that Billy seemed very jumpy and, unusual for him, his brow was furrowed. The General was immediately on alert, setting aside the papers on his desk and focusing directly on Billy. There were times when his firm expression and unblinking eyes so intimidated even strong men that they immediately changed their minds, withdrew their requests, lapsed into silence.

"What is it, Billy?"

Billy had decided that long explanations would not be helpful. He spoke directly: "Uh, a few weeks ago, Margaret Thomas an' me got married, an'—"

"—married?" Washington interrupted. What minister married you?"

"We din't have no minister, General, we did an ole African ritual an' pledged ourselves to each other."

"Then you're not really married."

"Oh, yessir, General. Lotta black folks gits married this way."

"Whatever this 'ritual' may be, I don't recall you asking for my permission to marry—or whatever you believe you have done."

"We knows how busy you is, General. We din't wanna bothuh you wi' our personal stuff."

"I do not remember any slaves at Mount Vernon marrying without the permission of Mrs. Washington or me."

"That's jes it, General. This ain't Mount Vernon. It's war an' some private things happens. You cain't always follow the usual rules."

"I'm extremely disappointed that you have undertaken this course of action without informing me. This is the first time you have ever done anything like this."

Washington was once again deeply concerned that his closeness to Billy during the war had undermined his authority and encouraged Billy to engage in improper and even dangerous conduct. He would have to be even more careful about keeping Billy in his place.

"We're leaving camp, Billy," Washington said in a stern voice. "We will set this matter aside and discuss such issues after the war."

"Uh, that won' work, General," Billy replied. "Margaret wants to travel wi' us aftuh we break camp, an' naturally, as her husband, I agree."

"Impossible," the General said. "I cannot approve of such a course of action."

"But, General, we's married, an' lots a' officers an' even plain soljers got they wives traveling wi' the army."

"You are neither a soldier nor an officer, Billy. The subject is closed. Dismissed." Washington directed his full attention to the papers on his desk.

Billy was stunned. It took a minute for him to realize he would have to walk away. He had feared that Washington would be displeased and unhappy, but it had not occurred to him that he would flatly refuse permission for Margaret to follow the army. He was plunged into despair—and he could not begin to think of a remedy. This was the lowest point in his life. It seemed to him like a funeral—a complete collapse of his hopes and dreams. Even worse, he would now have the painful and humiliating task of telling Margaret.

"That's an outrage!" Margaret virtually screamed. "I'm going to talk to that man, myself." She started to move past Billy, who quickly took her arm as firmly but gently as he could. He tried to embrace her, but she pulled away.

"That ain't gonna work, honey," Billy said. "I heard the man's words an' I seen the way he looked. It's no good talkin' to him right now. Maybe when we break camp, you kin go back to your family in Philly for a while. I know for sure I'll get the General to change his mind pretty soon an' I'll send for you." He din't really believe that, but he had to say it.

Margaret got even angrier than before, but her voice was cold—more distant than he had ever heard from her before. "That's what I get for marrying a slave."

Her words struck Billy even harder than when Washington had told him that the Declaration of Independence didn't apply to him—that he was still a slave. He steeled himself and said, "Margaret, I know we kin work this out real soon. I love you, baby, an' I plan to spend the rest a' my life wi' you."

"Beginning when, Mr. Lee?"

Billy was going to say, "Real soon, honey," but he would have had to speak to Margaret's back. She had turned abruptly and stomped away. Billy had to face the fact that he would be leaving Valley Forge without her. He tried to tell himself that this was just a temporary setback. But he didn't really convince himself. For a moment he thought desperately of running away. But, in the present circumstances, that might be considered desertion. A runaway slave who was a deserter. He could be shot or hanged. And why would Margaret join a desperate fugitive? That could make her a criminal, too.

Billy steeled himself. He would have to be very clever to deal with his new circumstances. His relationship with the General was now at risk, and he would have to rebuild trust in order to avoid an even worse disaster. He had been betrayed again, but he dared not show it. He would have to be a better "slave" than ever. The thought turned his stomach, but survival was the most important goal. Every slave knew that—even clever and love-struck ones like Billy Lee.

CHAPTER 17

Monmouth

The General gits all kines a' advice from his War Council 'bout where to head aftuh we break camp at Valley Forge. But truth is he ain't sure whether our boys is ready for a big fight, so we heads towards New York, jes bidin' our time, when we accident-like run smack inta the rear a' the redcoat army. It was at a place called Monmouth Court House on one a' the hottest summer days I kin evuh recall.

Washington was anxious to take advantage of this opportunity and deliver a punishing blow to Clinton and Cornwallis who were planning to move their troops to Sandy Hook to embark for New York.

The General met with his officers, Greene, Wayne, Stirling and Lee and gave them orders to find and attack the British. Lee dissented, arguing against any kind of major engagement. Washington overruled him, but nevertheless put him in charge of the operation.

Charles Lee was a tall, gangly, ugly-lookin 'feller, but he 's suppose to be one' a'the few trained officers in the Continental army. He sure was an odd duck—one time in Jersey in '76, while the General's waitin 'for him to bring up his troops, Lee's havin' his-self a fine time wi' some ladies—at a tavern. They's only a handful a' soljers protectin' him, an' the British surprise 'em, capture the sentries an' bust inta the tavern. They find Lee upstairs wearin' a dressin' robe—an' nothin' else. They capture him an' the seven or eight dogs he alius has wi' him. After a while, the General trades some British officers we captured for General Lee. I guess they threw in the dogs for free.

With the battle looming, The General told Billy to ride to the top of a nearby hill and report what he saw. Billy asked permission to bring some of the other officers' aides and servants along. Washington shrugged. Billy gathered his friends and they all rode to the top; Billy was on Chinkling and he was trailing the reins of Blueskin, one of the General's favorite horses. At the top of the hill, Billy whipped out his spyglass—showing off for the others—but all he could see was men running here and there in the smoke.

Next thing he knew, a British cannonball roared through a sycamore tree right over his head. Billy didn't know whether he should stay or go, but the others prudently scattered as fast as they could.

A single rider was galloping up the hill at breakneck speed, and Billy's first thought was that the rider should slow down before his horse collapsed in this heat. When the rider pulled up next to Billy, he was so out of breath that Billy had trouble understanding what he was saying.

"Lieutenant Brewster.....with an urgent message......from General Washington....for Billy.....Lee.....Do I have the honor..."

"Ain't no real honor, Lieutenant. But, yes, I's Billy Lee."

"General Washington requests...that you join him...in the field... as soon as possible, sir."

"Don' call me sir. I ain't no officer, Lieutenant. An' the General gave me orders to come up here. I also got his horse, Blueskin."

"Beggin' your pardon, uh, Mr. Lee. I don't know whether the General wants his horse or you. What he really said was to get your ass down there as fast as possible. His words, Mr. Lee, not mine."

Billy grabbed the reins of Blueskin and bolted past the still-recovering Lieutenant Brewster, down the hill. Within two minutes he was at Washington's side, pulling Blueskin to a sliding stop.

The first wave of retreating Continentals were sweeping past, and Washington was obviously in a foul mood. The General had believed he was going to celebrate a great victory that day, and he had come upon the army in a helter-skelter retreat.

"Total chaos here, Billy. That goddamn Charles Lee has apparently ordered a retreat just when we had the redcoats on the run. I need you to deliver orders to the other generals. Leave Blueskin here. Meanwhile I'm staying on the sorrel."

Billy immediately recognized that this was a critical moment, not the occasion for questions or explanations. God help Charles Lee when the General met him on the field. But the airbursts, the increasing sound of musket balls whistling past, told him that the advancing

British wave was coming on fast. The General, sitting astride his horse in the midst of the action, was surely at risk. But his blood was up, and no amount of pleading could persuade him to dismount or move to the rear, so Billy merely nodded.

Figure 21 General Washington rebukes Charles Lee at Battle if Monmouth

"Folks has ast me 'bout this partie 'lar moment time an' agin. Some stories already got into the history books 'bout it, but the stories don' come togethuh. Some things I can tell you on the Bible. The General sees Lee leadin' a retreat. Lee has his dogs wi' him, all seven or eight a' 'em. I kin say for a fact that General Washington relieved him of his command on the spot. But zactly what he said to Lee, well, I ain't gonna repeat it. I did hear the General—in full voice—use some words I nevuh heard him use before or since. Well, mebbe once later, 'bout Mr. Jefferson. But I jes don 'feel right sayin' any more 'n that. But let's make it plain—Charles Lee understood ev'ry word.

As General Lee, stunned and indignant, rode off in disgrace, Washington assumed command of the retreating American troops. He drew his sword and rode forward, yelling at the men to turn and fight. Billy rode beside him, his carbine in one hand, but mostly trying to keep his body and his horse between the British and the General. Bullets were whizzing past, shells were exploding, but even as men were dropping around him no bullets hit Washington—or Billy. Some of the men were falling down from heat exhaustion. The temperature was over 100 degrees, and most people were finding it difficult to breathe. Everybody was pouring sweat—even the General—and Billy had rarely seen him perspiring.

Figure 22 Washington rallying the troops.

Washington told Billy, "Ride to Lafayette and Wayne—tell them I want them to make a stand where they can delay the British advance and retreat as slowly as is prudent. Then come back."

Billy didn't feel good about leaving Washington, but he crouched low on Chinkling's back and rode him as fast as he dared toward the battlefield. He found both officers under heavy fire, doing just what the General wanted, slowly drawing back their troops, using the maneuvers that von Steuben had so recently taught them. Some of their men were collapsing, felled by the dense, heavy and humid heat. Wayne told Billy, "it's even worse for the Brits—their soldiers are dressed in thick woolens and they're carrying heavy field packs. We've passed many of them, dead or dying."

Billy galloped back to Washington and reported what he had seen and heard.

"Good," the General said, then sent Billy to Lafayette and Stirling with similar orders. They promptly swept to the left of the advancing British. Greene had already begun a sweeping motion to the right. Washington continued to ride up and down the lines, exhorting his men to stand and fight. All along the front, men cheered him and turned back to face the British.

As Billy hurried back from his courier duties, Washington suddenly disappeared from sight. Billy's heart constricted. He and everyone else feared Washington had been shot, and there was an audible intake of breath all across the battlefield, but while his dead horse lay motionless on the ground, the General leaped free, jumped to his feet and continued to rally his men. When everyone realized Washington had not been wounded, they cheered lustily.

Meanwhile, Billy raced back to where he had tethered Blueskin and brought the horse at a gallop to the General.

Washington yelled, "My poor horse dropped dead from the heat!" He swung aboard Blueskin and continued rallying his men. When they saw him mounted again, they cheered even louder than before and redoubled their efforts. The sound of musket-fire became a roar, the clouds of muzzle smoke intertwined with dense and humid air. Visibility was poor, but flashes from muskets and cannon ricocheted through the air like fire and lightning. Men were screaming, horses neighing, and bodies littered the field—alive, dead, nearly dead.

By this time the leading edge of the British assault force had crested a ridge about one hundred yards from the General. The British stopped to fire a volley, and about a third of the soldiers forming a line behind Washington went down. The British halted to fix their bayonets and prepare for a charge. But the Americans had retreated to defensible positions, while the British troops, still disciplined although exhausted, were exposed in open country.

"What do you want me to do now, General?" Billy asked with obvious urgency. "I don' think we kin stay here long."

Washington spoke firmly, but coolly. "Ride up and down the line, Billy. Tell the men to await my signal, then fire one volley. After firing, they are to move back one hundred yards, re-loading as they go, form on me again, then fire another volley at my command. If necessary, we will repeat this maneuver until we stop the British advance."

Billy understood that Washington was proposing a strategic retreat, the acid test of von Steuben's success in instilling discipline amidst the chaos of battle, because retreating soldiers were most disposed to run away as fast as they could. And they had, time and again, in the past. What would they do now?

Billy pounded his heels into the side of Chinkling, leaned over his neck to present a smaller target, then rode down the line at maximum speed, yelling all the way. "Fire on the General's command! Then move back slowly, re-load as you go!"

It worked. The first American volley caught the British fixing bay-onets and took out half of the first line. When the survivors marched forward—a highly disciplined and brave move on their part—they were cut to pieces by the second American volley. Out of the six hundred British soldiers who had started the attack, only three hundred fifty were left standing.

Washington ordered a third and final volley that reduced those numbers even further, then led a bayonet charge against the shriveled line of the survivors.

As the American troops charged forward, Washington took off his hat and waved it in the air. "It's a fine fox chase, my boys," he shouted, as they streamed past him, repeating a familiar line he had used at Princeton. Billy blew his horn in celebration.

"Looks like you an' me is back where we started, General."

Washington put his hand on Billy's shoulder. "Indeed, we are. And you were truly a sight to behold riding down that line."

"Do I hear you admittin' it, General, that I can out-ride you?"

Washington laughed. "Never said that. But you did look magnificent draped over Chinkling's neck. Next time we see the baron, remind me to tell him that his bastards were truly lovely today."

The fighting was over, and the British troops slipped away. Washington decided that his troops were too exhausted to follow, and he signaled the cessation of hostilities—to the relief of his own officers and men. It remained unbearably hot on the battlefield. Billy brought their horses to a shady spot where he could tether them, removed their saddles, then sloshed water over their backs and allowed them to sip some water—slowly. It would have been too dangerous to allow them to drink as much as they wanted. Billy was careful, too, wetting his lips and tongue, then spitting the water out. Neither he nor the horses would eat anything until long after darkness fell.

The General walked slowly back towards their original encampment. As he strolled, he came upon Lafayette, lying on a cape spread on the ground under a leafy oak, sound asleep. Washington nodded his head, slowly lay down on the cape next to Lafayette. In seconds, he was asleep, too.

The General alius thought a' Monmouth as a victory. It wasn' really. Though we kilt more a' them than they kilt a' us, Clinton's army 'scaped to Sandy Hook to sail away. But our boys had bravely held, an' turned a defeat inta at least a stalemate. General believed they had proved Americans could stand up to the Brits an' battle 'em stroke for stroke. General Lee ended up bein' court-martialed an' got run outta the army. I never felt a second a 'sympathy for him.

CHAPTER 18

Yorktown Ironies

It was kinda strange. Once our boys showed they could match the redcoats at Monmouth, you'd think the General would be lookin 'for a fight all the time. But he went jes the othuh way— avoidin' straight-up attacks. I knew the man well, so I understood it din't come natural to him. Down deep, he was alius hankerin 'for a big battle that'd end the war. I did hear him say once that winnin' battles was good, but winnin'the war was bettuh. I couldn 'for the life of me see how we was winnin'the war. Things went bad in the Carolinas, an' that traitor Benedict Arnold was making all kines a' trouble in Virginia.

But then Cornwallis does the General a big favor. He gets hisself stuck on a narrow spit a' land near a place called Yorktown. The French is in the war now on our side, an' the top French general, Rochambeau, brings thousans a' troops up to join Washington's army. Meantime, the French navy appears in Chesapeake Bay an' cuts Cornwallis off from gettin 'supplies or reinforcements.

***

As we head towards Yorktown, we's also gittin 'closer to Mount Ver-non. A note come from Mr. Lund that a British warship's anchored in the Potomac. Mr. Lundfears they'splannin 'to destroy Mount Vernon, but the British Captain comes ashore an' tells him he got no hostile intentions. Mr. Lund'so relieved he sends a boatload of provisions to the British ship in thanks. He also tries to get back some slaves that has run away an' gits taken up by the Brits, but the Captain refuse.

Washington was furious and he told Billy, "It would have been less painful to me if Lund refused and they burned down Mount Vernon."

Billy was surprised. "You really mean that, General?"

Washington's jaw stiffened. "It is humiliating for me to have my own people collaborate with the enemy—and I'm going to tell him so, myself. Bring me my horse, Billy, we're going to Mount Vernon!"

They rode at high speed for a long day, avoiding large towns and stopping only to briefly nap and rest their horses. Along the way, Washington told Billy, "Lund's note doesn't answer all questions. I must determine whether any other property of mine has been disturbed by the British."

"Don' sound like it, General."

They rode a little further, and then Washington said, "Under the piazza there's a storage area we excavated when we expanded the Mansion. It's hidden by brush on both sides, but it's there. Half-way in there's a big iron safe, which we bought from England years ago—before you came to Mount Vernon. Preacher—Vitruvius—and I and an ironmonger built the safe together. I believe Preacher and I are the only ones living—besides Martha—who know it's there."

Billy knew there had to be more to the story, and he waited patiently, as they cantered along the dusty highway.

"In the safe," Washington said, "are some of my most private and valuable papers, including the deeds to most of the land I own."

Billy was astonished by this revelation. Although he had never been in the storage space under the house, he knew it existed, but he knew nothing of the "safe."

"I have to verify that my papers are still there," Washington continued.

"What could happen to 'em?" Billy asked.

"The British were coming and going, slaves were running away. At one time, Lund himself went out to the British warship. Lund didn't say anything was disturbed, but he may not have known about the safe. It's too important. I have to be sure."

They reached Mount Vernon without incident, and had barely dismounted when Lund, Martha, Jackie and Eleanor and their four children appeared. Even before embracing his family, the General dressed down Lund Washington. "You disgraced me, sir, when you dealt so amiably with the enemy. I would rather you refused to comply with their orders, even if they had responded by destroying Mount Vernon."

Martha was shocked, but said nothing. Lund reddened, and mumbled his apologies in a stricken voice. "I am sorry, General. I thought I was doing the right thing. I assume you will wish to terminate my service here. I will vacate my lodgings immediately—"

Washington waved him off. "—That is not required, Lund. But be certain that such conduct is not repeated in the future."

Lund nodded several times and hurriedly withdrew. Only then did Washington embrace his family. It was the first time he had met the children.

Washington told Billy to get Preacher, and the three of them approached the piazza storage area. Billy and Preacher cut away the brush, and then the three men climbed down into the dank, dark, rat-ridden corridor. Preacher had brought candles and he lit one as soon as they entered. Bats flew at them and they waved their arms to drive them away.

Soon they reached an iron door, about four feet wide and four feet high, niched into an iron framework above a cement foundation.

Washington produced an iron key, plunged it into the slot and turned it. The key made a fierce grating sound, but the tumbrels didn't turn. Washington hesitated, then tried again with similar results.

"Excuse me, sir," Preacher said. "If you keep pushin' that hard, the key may break off. Try wigglin' it 'til it starts."

Washington nodded and did what Preacher had said, and in a minute the key began to turn, still screeching loudly, but slowly opening the lock. The hinges, however, were rusty, and it took the combined efforts of all three of them to swing the door open. Inside were several shelves with papers neatly stacked on them.

Washington hesitated for a moment, then said, "I trust you not to reveal what you have seen here." His look was the firm, almost fierce stare that had terrified many men, but both Preacher and Billy were familiar with it, and although they nodded strenuously, they were not frightened.

Washington quickly riffled through a pile of legal documents, which Billy assumed were deeds. Washington scanned them and then replaced them on the shelves. Next, he viewed the other papers in the safe, most of which seemed to be letters, although Billy could not tell who had written them or what the subject matter was. Again, Washington seemed satisfied with what he found.

"Nothing missing," he muttered under his breath, then gestured to Preacher and Billy to help him swing the heavy iron door shut. It squealed in protest, as did the key when Washington turned it. Less than fifteen minutes after they had entered the storage area they exited the sunken corridor, and Billy and Preacher replaced the brush, covering it.

Washington said not another word and strode off to enter the Mansion.

Billy was burning with curiosity to know what had been in the documents that the General valued so highly that he had been willing to leave the army to confirm their safety.

"Prob'ly never know what's in them papers," Billy whispered to Preacher.

Preacher smiled. "Not unless you got 'nothuh key," he said, and turned abruptly away.

***

Apart from the occasional illumination round coming from the British side, the night was pitch black. It had rained for two straight days, so the trenches were flooded and the sappers and miners were ankle deep in mud as they dug away, cursing the conditions. Private Joseph Plumb Martin, one of the for-the-duration New England lads who had signed up before he could shave was now a grizzled five-year veteran. He was in the middle of a curse when he crawled into the ankles of another man.

"What the fuck," Martin exclaimed. "Who are you? And what in God's name are you doing out here?"

"Soldier, I believe the proper question is, 'What is the password?' And the proper answer tonight is 'Virtue Triumphs.'"

It took Private Martin about two seconds to process the presence of a superior officer conducting a personal inspection of the trench lines surrounding Yorktown. And it took another few seconds to realize that the officer was none other than General George Washington, an improbable but quite palpable presence, standing erect in the trench, drenched by the rains and backed only by a black soldier or servant— it was hard to tell which.

"Beg your pardon," Martin somewhat haltingly explained, "but passwords don't mean dog shit out here, General, 'cause any talk is liable to draw fire from the British redoubt over there. I don' think it's a good idea for you and your man to be standing straight up like you are."

Washington started to respond, but before he could utter a word, Martin grabbed him by the coat and pulled him face-down into the mud. Billy was about to laugh at the scene, when two British sniper rounds whizzed past his left ear. He fell to his knees behind the prostrate Washington in the trench, then threw his body over him.

"What are you doing, Billy?" Washington asked in a muffled voice.

"I'm makin' sure you live long enough to free me, General," Billy responded.

"Please get off me, Billy. No British ball is going to get me. Never has and never will."

Billy thought—based on good experience—that was probably true, but the General had never said it in quite those words before, and he was troubled that he might be tempting fate.

Just then three members of Washington staff, led by Colonel Alexander Hamilton, came crawling forward in the trench, all apparently concerned that their commander had been wounded.

"Virtue Triumphs," Hamilton semi-shouted the password.

"Well," Washington responded, "sometimes it does, and sometimes it doesn't, Colonel Hamilton, but there's no need to share the password with the entire British army. According to Private, uh, uh—"

"—Private Martin, sir."

"Yes, according to Private Martin, silence is the best password out here tonight. How close would you estimate we are to the British redoubt, Martin?"

"About a hundred fifty yards, sir. Rough guess."

"Are you sure you're not hurt, General?" Hamilton intruded.

"Not a scratch, Colonel Hamilton. Perhaps a few bruises where Billy's damn elbow got my ribs."

"Sorry 'bout that," Billy observed. "Jes tryin' to do my job."

"You might have over-done it," Washington remarked as he started to stand up and another British illumination round lit up the landscape. "Meanwhile, about this British redoubt that Private Martin here -who obviously knows more than the rest of us put together—thinks it's about one hundred fifty yards from our position—"

"—Only a rough guess, General," Martin blurted out.

"Yes, that's my problem, Martin. I'm intending to order an attack on that redoubt tomorrow. And we need to know more about its location and disposition than a rough guess can provide."

"Uh, oh, I think I know what's comin' nex'," Billy whispered to Hamilton. Billy knew that muskets couldn't fire accurately at that range, but snipers with rifles could.

"Colonel Hamilton, I would like you to join me atop that little rise over there as we measure Private Martin's rough guess against what we see."

"Uh, General, I don't think you want to do that," Private Martin suggested. "The British have already got us spotted. They've got the range. You go up there, exposed like that, and they're going to—"

Washington cut him off. "—Thank you, Martin. Now, Hamilton, you've been pleading with me for a major combat assignment, and I'm leaning toward giving you command of the American force leading the assault tomorrow. So you need to do the reconnaissance with me now. Are you ready?"

Thrilled at receiving the news of his imminent combat command, Hamilton never wavered. "Yes sir, let's go."

While Billy watched more or less helplessly, the two men clambered up the rise, then stood up to survey the terrain with their telescopes. It took the British snipers about thirty seconds to identify them, so within a minute bullets were whizzing in the air and splattering the mud around them. Shortly thereafter, the illumination rounds became continuous, and cannon balls began landing to their front and rear as British artillerymen inside the Yorktown garrison began to bracket their position.

Down in the trench two of Washington's aides, Williams and Lassiter, pleaded with him to come down, then stopped abruptly as one of the cannon balls landed between them and skipped into Lassiter's ankle, nearly severing the poor man's foot.

"Ain't no use yellin' at him, boys," Billy calmly observed. "He does this kinda thing all the time."

Private Martin just shook his head and looked on with some mixture of awe and admiration as both Washington and Hamilton appeared oblivious to the streams of death flowing past them.

"I now see the best attack route into the redoubt, sir," Hamilton declared. "I think we can get down now."

"Stay with me for a little while longer if you would, Colonel Hamilton. It does the men good to see that their commanders are prepared to run the same risks we ask of them, don't you agree?"

Hamilton sensed, correctly, that he was being tested, and his response demonstrated that he was determined not to be found wanting. "However long you wish, General. I shall not budge until you do."

Washington looked approvingly at Hamilton as the bullets and cannon rounds continued to fill the air around them. "Just a little while longer and we will have made our point."

Down in the trench, Billy had begun to grow impatient with Washington's prolonged risk-taking. "Time to come down, General. Mrs. Washington would scold me if I din't tell you so."

Hamilton made a gallant gesture of deference as Washington began his way down the hill and back to the relative safety of the trench, where Billy greeted him with a smile of relief.

"Please drop the Mrs. Washington line, Billy," Washington complained. "It's getting stale."

"Point taken, General," Billy responded. "But I ask you one favor in return. Please don' scare the pants off me again. If you die, I lose my job."

CHAPTER 19

Surrender

Next day it was ovuh. Lotta cannon fire back an' forth, but Brits ain't gettin' outta the trap. They's a big assault, Hamilton leadin 'on one flank, wi 'the French poundin 'the othuh. Ain't long afore there's a commotion on the British side an' out come the white flags. The battle a' Yorktown is ovuh. Funny thing is, that's the first an' last time in the General's life anybody surrenders to him in battle. 'Bout time.

***

It was quite a scene. Washington was seated on Nelson, his favorite battle horse , while Billy was mounted on reliable (and still fast as a deer) Chinkling, just to his rear. Looking to his right Billy could see the officers and men of the Continental Army lined up in a row two ranks deep and half a mile long. The officers had on their best uniforms, but the bulk of the troops wore tattered smocks, weathered hunting jackets, and soiled headbands. Some were barefoot. Billy was better dressed than most of them.

On the other side of the narrow pathway the officers and troops of the French army were bedecked in their white uniforms, with brightly colored borders, plumed hats, glittering swords, officers decorated with silk sashes, sparkling badges and buckles. This was a professional European army decked out in its most splendid finery. And they were looking across at a motley collection of proud ruffians, mumbling profanities while spitting tobacco.

As Billy leaned forward to look all the way down the line, he whispered to Washington, "Them French boys sure looks fine, don' they General? Put our boys to shame."

Washington gestured Billy back to his position, then looked down the long pathway between the two armies. "Here come the proper objects of shame, Billy."

Marching out of Yorktown were six thousand British and Hessian troops, muskets shouldered, colors not flying but "cased" as Washington had insisted in the surrender agreement. Matters of military etiquette were not part of Billy's department, but he had stood behind Washington when he pounded his fist on the table and instructed all his aides that the British were not to be accorded the honor of flying their colors at the surrender ceremony. When the British had protested that this was an abject humiliation, he had only smiled.

Somehow, after nearly two weeks of intense and incessant bombardment—the French gunners were reputed to be the world's best—and after suffering nearly a thousand casualties, the British and Hessian troops had managed to preserve their full dress uniforms intact. And here they came, marching out in their resplendent red, every button polished, officers' swords drawn and gleaming in the early autumn sun, the music of fifes and drums mixing with the bagpipes of one Scottish regiment, all determined to be glorious in defeat. Billy thought it was disgusting that they should look so good.

Only as the British troops trudged closer could Billy make out what was causing a commotion within the American ranks. The British officers had ordered their men to do eyes-right, thereby looking only at the French troops as their conquerors, ignoring the Americans. This provoked a chorus of cussing from the American side, blended with raunchy threats of, "Let's roast the lobsterbacks alive," and "Tell 'em to insert their bayonets up their own assholes."

This in turn provoked the British soldiers to respond with their own colorful description of the Americans as "ruffians, a raggedy mix of hoodlums and barbarians."

Washington sat super-erect, pretending not to notice this ongoing exchange as the head of the British column drew near.

"I do believe them redcoats is sufferin' over this surrenduh, General," Billy observed.

Washington responded without turning his head. "They can't stand it and don't understand it, Billy. Losing to the likes of us is inconceivable to them."

In fact, some of the Brits were singing, under their breaths, a derogatory song:

If ponies rode men and grass ate cows,
And cats should be chased into holes by the mouse,
If summer were winter and the other way around,
Then all the world would be upside down.

"Cain't let them get away with that, General," Billy said.

Washington agreed. He called his soldiers to attention and had them raise their guns. Startled, The British turned to look at the Americans—suddenly fearful they might be about to shoot them down. That stopped the singing, and now the Americans were laughing—and spitting.

As the head of the British column came abreast of Washington it became clear for the first time that the British commander, Lord Cornwallis, was not leading his army, and had, in fact, delegated the surrender ceremony to a subordinate, a mere brigadier, General O'Hara, rather than face the disgrace himself.

The British officer turned his horse away from Washington and offered his sword to General Rochambeau, the French commander, who sternly declined it and pointed him towards Washington as the true Commander-in-Chief.

Billy could not see Washington's face, and he presumed incorrectly that the General was savoring this moment of triumph as the glorious climax of almost endless suffering and sacrifice. He was stunned when Washington refused the sword and gestured towards one of his subordinates, General Benjamin Lincoln, to receive the sword, instead. Washington would not accept surrender from an inferior officer.

After Lincoln ordered the British officer to have his men stack their arms in an adjoining field, Washington turned back towards Billy, who could now see his flushed face, set jaw, and cold-as-steel eyes.

"General, I kin see you is brimmin' right now," Billy whispered.

"I'm well under control," Washington answered. "But if that British lackey had smiled at me for three more seconds, I would have strangled him with my own bare hands and then trampled his body into the dust."

Figure 23 British surrender at Yotktown.

CHAPTER 20

Right of Return

Early that same evening Billy heard the sound of piercing screams and shrieks coming from the woods. His first thought was that a group of drunken Continentals had gotten hold of some Hessians and were beating or even executing them in a final act of retribution. But only a few paces outside his tent he was suddenly in the middle of over a hundred black men and women, many disfigured beyond description with smallpox markings. They were all former slaves from Tidewater plantations who had run off to the promised protection of the British army as it passed through. They had suffered through the bombardment at Yorktown and a virulent smallpox epidemic in the close quarters of the British garrison, and then been callously expelled from the encampment to find their own fates after the surrender ceremony. It was clear to Billy that many of them were headed for the hereafter, and all of them were desperately fleeing to nowhere in particular.

Then he heard a woman's voice shout his name. Before he could turn his head, he was almost knocked over by two black women, who frantically grabbed at his shirt while sobbing in uncontrollable heaves. They were, it turned out, two house slaves from Mount Vernon, Lucy and Esther, who had bolted a year earlier in response to false promises of freedom with the British army, and were now marooned, with nowhere to go.

Billy grabbed them both in gentle headlocks until the sobbing subsided, offering assurances that they were now safe. Lucy was the first one to regain her composure. "Billy, kin you take us to Mount Vernon? Please. We gonna be punished for runnin' away? We promise nevuh to run away agin."

Billy tried to grapple with the incongruity of the situation, but the emotional overload was too much. He had just witnessed the surrender of the British army and the culmination of a glorious American victory. But that victory now meant that Lucy and Esther, if they were lucky, would become slaves again. Did that mean that the cause was not so glorious? Or did it just mean that freedom under the auspices of the British army turned out to be more oppressive than slavery at Mount Vernon?

Such questions quickly evaporated under the more pressing and immediate problem of how to answer Lucy's desperate request. Two young black women were sobbing in his arms amidst a scene of utter chaos. Billy knew that he couldn't really speak for the General, but that in fact was precisely what the situation demanded.

"Ladies, let me ask you. Do either one a' you have any sign a' the pox? Any marks or agues?" It was dark and he was more or less futilely searching their faces and arms for evidence as he spoke.

"No, Billy," Esther blurted back. "Lotta folks come down wi' it all 'round us, but me an' Lucy sleeps outside when it starts. In the mornin' you kin 'spect us up an' down. We got no pox."

"Alright, you kin stay with me tonight," Billy replied, "an' I'll tell the General you was kidnapped by the Brits an' you 'scaped. I'm pretty sure he'll want you back."

Lucy and Esther wrapped themselves around him again, sobbing with joy this time.

Billy shuddered at the sights and sounds of slaves running about the woods like lost souls, screaming to the moon for someone to help them. God only knew what was going to happen to them.

"C'mon, ladies," he said, "let's get you outta here."

Next day, all day, Billy rehearsed the conversation he planned to have with Washington about Lucy and Esther. Should he reveal that he had all but promised their return to Mount Vernon without consequences? No, probably not. In fact that just might draw the wrath of God from the General, who was jealous of his own prerogatives. Should he bring them along for the interview, hoping that just the sight of their plight would do the deed? Hmm. A bit risky, since they might expose his premature promise.

By late afternoon he had still not worked out his approach when the General sent an aide, John Laurens, to fetch him for some undisclosed duty. Billy liked Laurens, a South Carolina boy whose father had served as president of the Continental Congress, and who was perhaps the only South Carolinian alive who openly advocated an end to slavery.

"The General says to come on now, Billy," Laurens urged, "says it's important."

Billy was ginning up his courage, but had still not got the words right when he entered Washington's tent.

"Ah, Billy, been looking for you all afternoon."

"Yes sir, well, I got a matter to raise wi' you, too, if I kin."

"As long as it's not going to keep you busy tonight, Billy."

"Beggin' your pardon, sir, but it ain't 'bout me. It's 'bout two house slaves from Mount Vernon who turns up here at Yorktown, an' I was jes wonderin'—"

"—Ah, you mean Sally and Esther."

Billy was suprised, but haltingly corrected Washington. "Uh, well, it's Lucy an' Esther, General."

"Yes, of course, Lucy. Well they were apparently carried away by a British patrol several months ago. God know how they survived their imprisonment with Cornwallis' army. Reports indicate that most of the captured slaves contracted smallpox. But I understand they're fine and eager to resume their duties at Mount Vernon."

Billy's mind was now racing. The General didn't acknowledge that Lucy and Esther had run away, for that realization might have required him to recognize that almost every slave at Mount Vernon wanted to be free. And that recognition would have required a drastic alteration of his self-image as the benevolent patriarch of Mount Vernon. Even this rock-ribbed realist had a blind spot when it came to his own slaves. But in the present context his illusion worked perfectly for Lucy and Esther. The last thing he needed to do now, Billy told himself, was to correct Washington's misconception.

"Thass right, General," Billy half-lied, "these women cain't wait to get back to Mount Vernon."

"Splendid," Washington declared. "Now, you need to know that I have decided to host a dinner tonight for all the British, French, and

American senior officers. I need you to deliver my invitations, brush my best uniform and polish my brass and boots, then come along to help out when the British squirm beneath our hospitality."

"Wouldn't miss them Brits squirmin' for all the wort' General," Billy observed. "But you got to make me one promise."

"And just what is that, Billy?"

"If Cornwallis don' squirm enough, you won' kill him on the spot."

Washington laughed out loud.

CHAPTER 21

Toast

Cornwallis, it turned out, claimed he was still indisposed, and could not attend the dinner; another pathetic attempt at a slap in the face for the American leader. His place was taken by General Charles O'Hara, the same non-descript and nonchalant Irish officer whom Washington had almost strangled for trying to surrender to the French commander the previous day.

Speaking to Nat Greene and Hamilton who sat beside him, Washington said, "Since the British have just lost the climactic battle in a war that will cost them their entire empire in North America, O'Hara's conspicuously affable and upbeat demeanor is surely a feeble façade."

"Perhaps," said Hamilton, "they are blissfully unaware of the scale of their disaster."

Washington nodded. "You may be right. This entire catastrophe seems inconceivable to them. Our ragtags have defeated the greatest army in the world."

"In that sense," Greene observed, "Cornwallis' absence is the most telling presence at the table.

The American officers laughed, which only briefly caught the attention of the British and French officers.

Billy was stationed directly behind Washington, wearing his best shirt and white gloves. His initial and most important duty was to fill the wine glasses of all twelve American officers in preparation for Washington's introductory toast. The etiquette of the occasion was edgy, since the American and French officers had just spent the last two weeks attempting to annihilate the troops under the command of the British officers, who had only the day before been forced to witness the ceremonial humiliation of their entire army. Washington's to ast, therefore, was a touchy affair. On the one hand, the very fact that he had convened this gathering suggested that he would set a gracious tone. On the other hand, as Billy alone knew, only yesterday he was on the verge of doing serious harm to General O'Hara, now smiling with apparent ease and preparing to raise his glass no matter what Washington said.

Washington rose to his full six-foot-three-inch height, a figure impossible to ignore.

"Gentlemen, join me in a toast," Washington intoned, "to honor the Master we all serve."

Billy did not permit himself a smile, but his first thought was that no one in the room understood as much about serving a master as he did. His second thought was that the General had carefully prepared this toast to sound a high-toned note that skirted the awkwardness of the occasion. When the General wanted to be diplomatic, no one could best him, because he had a flair for elevated talk that allowed him to levitate to a higher altitude where all constituencies could comfortably congregate. But Billy didn't believe either the British or the French gave a damn about such diplomatic niceties, or appre-ciated the grace and wisdom of his words.

Perhaps it was a function of the seating arrangements, which had the American delegation divided between the two ends of the table, and the French and British delegations facing other across the middle. But for the rest of the dinner there was a salvo of toasts between the British and French officers in which the bravery and honor of the other side was the common refrain. "The other side" did not seem to include the Americans.

All of the Americans were painfully aware that no one toasted Washington for hosting the dinner, or the Franco-American alliance, which had made possible this stupendous victory. Laurens and Knox, Stirling and Wayne at the far end of the table conversed with each other. Washington did the same at the head of the table with Hamilton and Greene. Between them the French and British appeared to commiserate and bond as European aristocrats who had more in common with each other than they did with the Americans.

Hamilton whispered to Greene, "If you didn't know that the French were America's indispensable allies, you could have thought they were allied with the British."

Washington heard this exchange. "We can't afford to offend the French at this point," he murmured. "But I'll feel far happier when all foreign troops have returned to Europe."

Hamilton and Greene agreed.

On the way back from the dinner, Billy asked Washington what this love-fest between the French and British meant. "Was strange to me, General. Seems like we was invisible at our own party."

"Nice way to put it, Billy. I should have anticipated it. I have fought against officers from both of those countries, and I have fought alongside them. But I keep forgetting." Washington began to chuckle.

"What you been forgettin,' General?" Billy asked, somewhat relieved that Washington, who normally could not tolerate the smallest slight, apparently had his emotions under control.

"Think of it this way, Billy. In England and Europe, all officers are aristocrats who share a common code as gentlemen. It's a club of sorts. And they don't think Americans can be members. That's why General O'Hara didn't want to surrender his sword to me. Beneath him, you see."

"Mighty arrogant if you ask me, General. 'Specially when you jes' kicked their ass to kingdom come."

"That actually made it worse for the British officers tonight, Billy. Their presumed posture towards us is condescension. It's very hard to condescend towards someone who has–how did you put it? -just kicked their ass."

"That explains the Brits," Billy replied. "But how come the French—who's our allies, right?—how come they seems to be sidin' wi' the enemy tonight? Still don't make no sense to me."

Washington paused for several seconds as they trotted on. "No, it really doesn't. But honor is a complicated thing. Perhaps they just felt sorry for their aristocratic brothers. Or perhaps they realized that our triumph means the beginning of the end for their aristocratic world."

"Don' know what that means, General."

"None of the American officers sitting at that table would be eligible for commissions in the British or French army. And none of us would make the guest list for a fancy party in London or Paris."

"Not even you, General?" Billy asked, somewhat bewildered.

Washington smiled. "Not even me, Billy. The British army rejected me long ago. Though I must say that, if I were to apply now, they might have second thoughts and make me a captain or major."

Billy couldn't help laughing. "General, folks who's that stupid deserves to lose wars."

"And that is precisely what they have done, Billy. Perhaps that's really why I invited them to dinner tonight. God's word, I didn't really understand my own motives until just now. I wanted to make my presumptive superiors feel their inferiority. O'Hara's rather strenuous pomposity makes me believe that I succeeded. Do you agree?"

"Outta my range, General. As I see it, don' make no difference what General 0"Hara thinks. They done lost an' we done won. And that's all they is it to it."

"You do have a way of bringing matters back to basics, Billy. And your instincts are impeccable." Washington couldn't understand why he had chosen to have this philosophical discussion with Billy, and he decided to return the conversation to practical matters. "By the way, bring those two house slaves to see me tomorrow morning, so we can get the basics straight with them before they return to Mount Vernon."

"Sir, I think in all honesty you need to know—"

"—That they really ran away, right?"

"How'd you know?"

"You just told me."

Billy fell silent.

"Tell them to keep on lying when they see me tomorrow. Martha will be overjoyed to get them back. Their lying will make it easier for everyone."

This was an uncharacteristic insight from the General, Billy thought. He could do curves as well as straight lines. Hadn't really seen that before. But he kept such thoughts to himself and simply said "Yessir."

CHAPTER 22

Speeches and Silences at Newburgh

Aftuh Yorktown, I thought the war was ovuh. But the General says it ain't over 'til a treaty's signed an' the British army sails home. As it turns out, that takes two more years. We spent that time in Newburgh, New York, waitin' an' continuin' to drill the troops. Later on the General tole me the army was best ready to fight when they was no more fightin' lef' to be done. Most a' the fightin' at Newburgh was among ourselves, 'bout what we was owed for our service in the war. I had some thoughts on that. The General had some thoughts a 'his own, which some say was the best he ever had. I dunno. I think he did right by the army, but he din't do right by me.

***

It was January of 1783 and a light snow was falling outside as Washington sat in front of a roaring fire, coat unbuttoned, boots off, feet propped up on a small stool while Billy brushed his hair. Alexander Hamilton had just arrived from a visit to Philadelphia and was reporting on the current debates within the Continental Congress about the disposition of the Continental Army.

Washington was making guttural sounds as he listened to Hamilton, who said, "The news isn't good. A proposal to provide all of the officers with a pension of half-pay for life, failed miserably. Then they tried a cheaper one: full pay for five years. But it's clear that's headed for the legislative graveyard, too."

Hamilton attempted to conclude his report on a light-hearted, if caustic, note. "It would seem to me, sir, that Congress has concluded that the army has managed to survive without pay, shirts, and shoes—

often without food—quite well for the past eight years and wishes to do nothing that might disturb that longstanding pattern."

Washington nodded. "Thank you for your succinct summary of our predicament, Colonel." He turned his head slightly towards Billy. "You've brushed away some of the gray hairs, Billy, but this news guarantees that I'll be growing many more to replace them. Now just tie it up, please." He then reached down into a bowl of nuts and began to munch away.

"Not good for your teeth, General," Billy observed while tightening the knot and smoothing out Washington's little ponytail. "How 'bout a glass of Madeira to go wi' it?"

"Wonderful idea, Billy. Can I persuade you to join me, Colonel Hamilton?"

"Absolutely," Hamilton replied, "but then I have to be on my way."

Billy poured two glasses, and as Hamilton rose to accept his glass, Washington also rose.

"Let me propose a toast to the officers of the Continental Army. Men of virtue, and virtue will be their only reward."

Hamilton sipped his wine and managed only a brave smile. "If we truly are men of virtue, as I believe we are, then knowing that should suffice. But I just don't understand—"

"—Don't try, Hamilton, it's just too painful," Washington interrupted. "The Congress wants us to dissolve and disappear as soon as the peace treaty is signed. Then they won't have to bother with questions of compensation. They want us to believe that glory is a dearer currency than money"

Hamilton shrugged while putting on his coat. "Perhaps our true compensation will come in the history books."

Washington mused, "Let's hope that posterity is kinder to us than our politicians." Hamilton saluted himself out the door.

"Miz Washington should be down for dinner soon," Billy observed, "but afore she comes I'd like to raise my ole question wi' you."

"Old question?" Washington asked.

"Yes sir. You an' Colonel Hamilton be wonderin' how the Congress will treat the army. I'm wonderin' how you'll treat me. I don' want no pension. But I do want my freedom. I think I deserve it jes like the army deserves its reward. We both stuck it out till we won the war. I do believe it's time for you to decide on this. I been mighty patient."

Washington had been expecting this, but hoping it would be indefinitely deferred. In fact, his thinking had expanded a great deal during the course of the war. He had almost imperceptibly moved from thinking as a dull-minded Tidewater slave owner to being the leader of a cause that he fully recognized was incompatible with slavery. He knew that Billy's question was wholly appropriate and unavoidable, but he had not yet acknowledged—even to himself— that his own response should be just as obvious as the principles for which he had fought over the past eight years.

Nor was that all. Billy had been there all the way. He had saved his life on more than one occasion. And in all the less dramatic, more mundane matters, Billy had never failed him. The war had proven to be a test of many things—the sheer stamina of the army, the shabby resolve of the Congress and that vast imponderable called the American people—but if it was also a test of Billy's loyalty, he had passed the test with flying colors. Even when Washington had refused his permission for Billy's "wife" to accompany the army, his loyalty had not faded.

But in other regions of his mind nothing approximating clarity was possible. The man whom he had become while commanding the army in the North was glaringly at odds with the man who had come of age in the slave-drenched South. If he spoke to an inveterate enemy of slavery like Lafayette or Laurens, he went one way. If he spoke to old cronies like Lund Washington, his manager at Mount Vernon, he went the other.

It was an awkward realization, but while others considered him the most decisive man of the era he had to admit to himself that he had as yet refused to follow indisputable logic and experience to their ultimate conclusion about this most sensitive and controversial subject.

Sincere, intelligent men, strong friends like Lafayette and Laurens, honorable men like Hamilton, even the inescapable and insufferable Quakers—who refused to fight for the nation, but fervently told him how he should live his life—told him what he ought to think, but never fully convinced him.

He was all too aware of all the dangers of granting Billy's request. Perhaps it was his unspoken fear that freeing Billy might well ignite a fiise that led inexorably to that huge barrel of explosive material that was slavery itself. He had justified his delays by repeatedly telling himself that he wouldn't answer Billy until he had worked out the solution to the larger problem. But in the meantime, he couldn't even be sure of what impact freeing Billy might have on the other slaves at Mount Vernon. What looked and felt utterly right now, north of slavery, might seem odd and troubling once he returned to Virginia.

And perhaps it was something more basic, though so elemental that it clogged up his thinking without really being a thought at all. Perhaps it was that freeing Billy or any slave for that matter represented a crack in the world into which he had been born and come of age, and he could not imagine living anywhere else.

These chaotic and tortured thoughts were streaking through Washington's mind at a high velocity, but still he had not spoken, delivering another one of those long silences for which he had long been famous.

Billy had patiently watched Washington's impassive face, once again impressed that strange and turbulent storms might thunder behind those unblinking eyes without betraying a single sign to the outside world. "General, would you like me to repeat my question?"

Washington shook his head, thereby prolonging the silence. At long last, he spoke. "I cannot give you an answer, Billy, before conferring with Mrs. Washington. But I will do that as soon as possible. And now" — the subject was about to shift, Billy thought —"it's time to dress for dinner."

Billy masked his disappointment. He had hoped for a prompt and positive response and now he would have to wait until....when?

***

If Washington needed an excuse to prolong his procrastination— and he clearly did—an excellent candidate arrived in early March of 1783. One of General Knox's valets told Billy there was a petition circulating among the officers. Gates, who had received all the credit for the victory at Saratoga when the actual fighting was led by Benedict Arnold, was trying to take over the army again. The officers were angry with Congress, and even good men like Knox were being tempted. The plan was to push the army to rebel, overthrow Congress, take over the government and install Washington as king—temporarily, perhaps, until Gates himself assumed power.

Billy didn't like to spread rumors, but he felt compelled to tell the General what he had learned. He brought him the anonymous letter Knox's valet had quietly given him, which requested that all the officers in the Continental Army meet at the New Building in Newburgh, a capacious structure originally designed to serve as a combination chapel and dance hall, there to denounce the Congress for failing to make good on their promise of pensions. If a permanent peace with Great Britain was signed, the army would march on Philadelphia and demand their just reward. If it was not, and the war continued, they would refuse to take the field until assurances of their pay and pensions were authorized.

"Thank you, Billy," Washington said, clapping him on the shoulder. "I can always rely on you." Billy bit his tongue keeping himself from repeating his request for freedom.

Washington immediately sent his own letter stating that no one other than the Commander-in-Chief—namely him—was empowered to call such a meeting. He ordered a meeting of the entire officer's corps, five hundred strong, to gather at the New Building on March 15. Then he sent all his aides and their respective staffs into high gear, preparing for his presentation to the officers of the Continental Army.

It almos' seems like we was gittin' ready to go inta battle. The General had lotta meetin's wi' his personal staff to help decide on what he should say where he should stand, what he should wear. Colonel Hamilton stayed up two nights writin' the speech, an' the next day the General crossed out some a' the words an' adds some a 'his own. My job was to get his dress uniform cleaned an' pressed, an' to polish up his boots an' brass. All the aides was assigned spots to sit in the audience when the General spoke so as to stop any shoutin' an' start some cheerin.' I tole 'him I'd be standin' behine him agin the wall, an' though I cain't bring my carbine 'cause weapons ain't allowed in the buildin 'I'd be ready if trouble happened.

Billy found the General sitting by his portable desk, writing something in big letters. "Why you doin' that, General?"

Washington laughed. "I can't read my speech unless I can see it."

"Why don' you wear them eyeglass things that Doctor Rittenhouse feller sent you from Philly?"

"That would make me look feeble," the General said.

Billy shook his head. "Ain't no way you kin ever look feeble, General—not unless you's gonna shrink 'bout a foot."

Washington grinned, but kept writing laboriously in large letters.

***

"Well, General, you look jes fine," said Billy as they prepared to leave headquarters on the big day. "You got your words ready?"

"I'm clear about what I want to say, Billy, but I don't know how they will react. I love these men, and I want them to know that, but if they even contemplate defying the Congress, they will stain the very cause we have fought so long and hard for."

"Yessir, seems right to me." Then Billy pulled the spectacles out of his vest pocket. "I brung these along jes in case. I know you don' like to have the men see you wearin' eyeglasses, but mebbe you ought to keep 'em ready."

Washington took the glasses, put them in his coat pocket and sighed. "A concession to age, though Franklin once tried to convince me that they were emblems of wisdom."

"Yessir, I do b'lieve Dr. Franklin was right."

When Washington entered the New Building five hundred angry officers were stirring in their seats. Billy whispered, "These fellers looks like they's ready to go to the bayonet." General Gates sat at the front in the seat reserved for the chairman of the meeting. This was richly ironic because Gates had been a behind-the-scenes instigator of the mutiny, the coup, or whatever one wished to call it. It was clear that many of the officers had not expected Washington to show up personally. Certainly Gates was stunned. Washington studiously ignored him, his aides fanned out into the audience, Billy took up his post to the rear, behind the podium. Washington strode briskly to the lectern; Gates slipped quietly away.

Billy knew that Washington was not a great orator, but over the next twelve minutes he delivered a speech that matched the drama of the moment. The oratorical crescendo came early :

"As I have never left your side one moment, but when called from you on public duty. As I have been the constant companion & witness of your Distresses, and not among the last to feel, & acknowledge your Merits. As I have ever considered my own Military reputation as inseparably connected with that of the Army. As my Heart has ever expanded with joy when I have heard its praises—and my indignation has risen, when the Mouth of detractions has opened against it, it can *scarcely be supposed,* at this late stage of the war, that I am indifferent to its interests."

But at the end, as the General looked up at the officers, there was no ringing round of applause. It was another one of those awkward moments of silence that Washington seemed to generate, though on this occasion he was the one to feel the pressure to move past it. Nothing less than the honor of the Continental Army, perhaps even the fate of the American Revolution, was at stake, and yet the cavernous room remained eerily quiet. Billy watched, motionless, as Washington's right leg briefly trembled behind the lectern.

Washington reached into his breast pocket and spread on the podium a letter from Joseph Jones, a delegate to the Continental Congress who empathized with the army's plight. Then he pulled from his coat pocket the Rittenhouse spectacles and put them on. As he adjusted them, he looked out at the audience "Gentlemen, you must pardon me," he said in a low tone, "for as I have grown gray in the service of my country, I now find myself growing blind."

This simple gesture was a perfectly aimed shot into the hearts of the assembled officer corps. First came a vast intake of breath, then a rippling of applause, then a standing ovation, then battle-hardened soldiers crying uncontrollably. The subsequent reading of the letter from Jones was merely epilogue. All prospects for mutiny by the Continental Army ended at that moment. Washington turned the meeting over to Gates, who realized that he had just been humiliated, and the officers subsequently voted unanimously to proclaim their confidence in the Continental Congress and in Washington as their designated liaison with the government.

Billy handed him his hat as they departed the New Building.

"One a' your fines' moments," Billy said softly.

"Couldn't have done it without those spectacles, Billy," Washington whispered back. "I had thought about using them at the start, but it worked better to save them for the end."

"My, oh my," exclaimed Billy as they exited the building, "we been together all this time and you still got surprises for me all stored up."

"Well, to be honest," Washington replied with a wink, "today I even surprised myself." And then his aides began gathering around him to offer their congratulations for a masterful performance. Billy never mentioned that he had seen Washington's leg tremble behind the podium.

****

A few days after the Newburgh speech a dispatch arrived from Congress, apprising the Commander-in-Chief that a preliminary agreement had been signed in Paris, suspending all hostilities in anticipation of a formal peace treaty. Even the ever cautious Washington, who had once declared that the Continental Army would not disband until every British soldier had vacated American soil, was now prepared to acknowledge that for all intents and purposes, the war was over.

Billy had the honor of hand-carrying copies of the General order to all the regiments, in which Washington (with a silent assist from Hamilton) announced that they had at last won the war. The last sentence suggested that celebrations could now begin: "An extra ration of liquor to be issued to every man tomorrow, to drink to Perpetual Peace, Independence & Happiness to the United States of America." Billy was beaming. He figured that he would use his ration to toast both American independence and his own.

To say that Washington's mind was moving in the other direction would not really be correct. It was having a difficult time moving at all. When he told Billy that he needed to confer with Martha about freeing him, he was just searching for a convenient and credible excuse to delay the decision. But having created the excuse, he felt obliged to honor it, thereby transforming it from a dodge to a crucial consideration. It helped that Martha was one of the few people who was allowed to inhabit that interior space where he could afford to expose his confusion. (Icons were not allowed confusion.) The fact that Billy, by virtue of his position, had also occupied that same space on multiple occasions then streaked through his mind and only upped the emotional ante of his decision.

***

It was Martha's last night in Newburgh. She had stayed another winter with her man, the war was at last won, and the roads back to Mount Vernon were becoming more negotiable, so she had announced her decision to go home and leave the culminating ceremonials of this post-war phase to her husband. They had already celebrated the peace treaty with a fine dinner and some French wine. Washington had some amorous thoughts about spending their last night together, but when he entered their bedroom, Martha was already in her nightgown, sitting up in bed reading *Tristram Shandyx* the current rage among the wives of the senior officers. This did not look encouraging to George.

"What are you reading, my dear?" Washington asked as he tossed his coat on the chair.

"The latest sensation from Mr. Sterne," she answered, closing the book. "It's all sentiment and innuendo. Much too indirect for your taste."

Washington arched his eyebrows in mock disbelief, but decided not to reply, lest he be drawn into a conversation about the virtues of a fictional world where hearts ruled heads—a world that, as Martha fully understood, he regarded as *terra incognito*. Besides, his own head was preoccupied with Billy's request and with anticipating Martha's reaction to it. He decided, reluctantly, he would have to discuss it with her that evening—it would be his last chance until he returned to Mount Vernon, whenever that would be.

"I've been brooding about something for several weeks, dear, and I would appreciate your opinion," Washington said as he searched for his nightshirt.

"Well, if it's about the fatal charms of the promiscuous Caty Greene, I don't want to hear any more. In fact—"

"—No, it's about Billy. Once again, he has asked me for his freedom. And I think he has a point. He has served me loyally and well. Now he wants his reward."

Martha carefully set aside her book. "Billy's a fine fellow, no doubt, but if you set him free you could start a revolution at Mount Vernon. There are many slaves who have served us well across the years, George. What about them?"

"Billy's in a special category He's fought beside me for many years—saved my life a couple of times."

"I see you've been thinking about this for a while."

"The war has changed a lot for me. Frankly, sooner or later we're going to have to free these people. It's not moral and it goes against the very cause we've been fighting for."

Martha's expression was frozen. "Are you saying we fought this terrible war not to free ourselves, but to free our slaves?" Her voice had risen as she spoke.

"The fact is, we can't support all the slaves we have, Martha. Half of them aren't doing a darn thing. We spend more on their food, clothing and upkeep than they earn for us."

"You never spoke this way before the war." Martha was temporizing, almost overwhelmed by what her husband was saying, and feeling tentacles of fear about her future.

Washington had not expected this response from Martha, and he began to feel defensive. "After watching thousands of black soldiers fighting bravely, some dying in battle, and living day and night with Billy, I freely admit that my ideas have changed."

Martha gathered herself before she spoke. "Some of the Mount Vernon slaves are yours alone, George, but even more are my dower slaves and their offspring. You can't set any of them free—they belonged to my late husband and now to his children or their descendants. There are bound to be bad feelings—even worse. If you're planning to set your own slaves free, I'm totally against it."

"Your slaves and mine have intermarried. I've sworn never to break up families."

Martha sighed. "You see, it won't work."

"I'm only talking about freeing one man—Billy." His voice had become almost plaintive.

Martha forced a smile. "Stop worrying about it. We'll figure it all out at the right time."

"That's what I keep telling Billy. I don't think that tune will play forever."

Martha blew out the candle, then turned on her side, her back to Washington. "The last time I looked," she murmured, "there were no free blacks at Mount Vernon. Remember how you told me, and I agreed, that it's different up here? Well, it's not different down there."

Washington lay on his back, looking up at the ceiling, saying nothing. Within a few minutes he could tell from Martha's breathing that she was asleep. Behind his stare several new thoughts were racing through his mind. In the real world interests trumped principles. What it came down to, then, was his interests versus Billy's. It was a close call because Billy had done everything right to earn his freedom. He had been blind not to expect Martha's opposition—but in a sense he welcomed it. She had made this impossible decision for him. He did not allow himself to think it was a cowardly excuse. His family came first; his wife came first.

It wasn't clear, but it was clear enough. As he turned on his side and closed his eyes, he had made a decision. He needed to find the right moment to apprise Billy. That would be difficult.

***

I b'lieve it was June a' 1783 when the General calls me in. He had jes written his circular letter to the gov 'nors a 'the states, an 'I helps make copies for him, the big point bein' that he was steppin' down as head man a 'the army. He seemed to me to be a mite nervous, not like him. I soon found out why. My freedom would have to wait, he said. It could come some day, but not now. Said he had talked it ovuh wi' Mrs. Washington, an' they both agreed. He seemed to be layin' it off on her. I din't say so at the time, but I din't b 'lieve him. Only time he ever lied to me. Damn near broke my heart. When Parson Weems writes that the General could not tell a lie, I reckon he din't know 'bout this time.

CHAPTER 23

Washington's Farewells

Figure 24 Washington's farewell at Fraunces Tavern.

In early November, 1783, Washington had met with the army—the ordinary soldiers—and told them the peace treaty had been signed in Paris and the war was finally over. They cheered when Washington very emotionally thanked them for their service and referred to them as one "patriotic band of brothers." He said he hoped the states would honor their promises to pay their pensions

"I ask you to return to your homes as citizens of the United States, not as Virginians or New Englanders."

Billy said his own goodbyes to the other valets of the general officers, and to his other friends as well. He was surprised at how difficult it was for him.

Later, at Fraunces Tavern in New York, Washington said his farewells to his officers—some of whom had served with him for seven years. If anything, those farewells were more emotional than the ones with the regular soldiers. Billy was especially moved when Washington embraced the officers one by one. Tears flowed freely; the marble man was drenched with them— his own and his officers. Some of the officers even embraced Billy, who gave way to emotion, himself, time after time. He was astonished at how close he felt to men like Knox and Greene.

The final farewell was a more formal affair at Annapolis, Maryland, where the Congress was sitting temporarily. On December 22, a ceremonial dinner was held in Washington's honor, one of the most elaborate events of the entire revolutionary era. The General stirred some of the attendees when he called for a strong central government—which always struck some people as code for a monarchy. After the dinner there was a dance, with ladies lining up to dance with Washington—just to "touch" him.

Caty Greene, dancing with Washington, said, "I've heard that King George said that if you don't make yourself king you're the greatest man in the world." Washington laughed, "At least I'm one of the tallest." Caty said, "No man I've ever known, and I've known more than my share, has ever given up the kind of power you possess."

Washington replied, "My dear Caty, you have never known me." As they finished dancing Washington kissed Caty on the cheek.

Figure 25 General Washington dancing with Caty Greene at officer's ball.

***

The next day the Continentals staged the official ceremony, led by Thomas Mifflin—who, with General Gates was among those who had been trying to force Washington's resignation. Now Washington was proving all his critics wrong, surrendering his authority voluntarily, stating, "I retire from the great theatre of Action.... I hereby offer my commission and take my leave of public life."

The man who had known how to stay the course, now showed that he knew how to leave it—perhaps one of the greatest acts of renunciation of power in all history.

Billy had brought horses to the door, and as soon as Washington finished speaking, he strode to the door, mounted his horse, and he and Billy cantered off as the crowd cheered.

Billy said, "And to think, you coulda' been king."

Washington didn't respond as they rode away.

Billy couldn't help wondering if the time was getting closer when he would be reunited with Margaret. Mrs. Thompson, who had retired in 1781, before she left had given him an address in Philadelphia that Margaret had given her. Billy had written to Mar-garet a few times, but had never had a response. Maybe his letters hadn't reached her—with the army on the move or holed up in some smaller community, such as Newburgh, who could be sure that the mail was being handled properly? Washington always seemed to get his mail, but maybe it was different for a general. Billy kept the freedom question out of his mail and, mostly, out of his thinking. It would all work out, somehow. He was sure of that. Meanwhile, he was missing Margaret more than ever, now that officers and men were being reunited with wives and girlfriends everywhere.

CHAPTER 24

Tripped

My life don'change much 'til April a' '85. I'm helpin'the General survey some property near Alexandria when I slip on muddy groun'an' pitch on my face. My face is fine, but my knee is broken. The General sends a horse an' cart to get me back to Mount Vernon. Doctors say they ain't nothin'they kin do. Thass pretty sad, but I'm still ridin 'wi'the General, though it hurts plenny.

The General enjoys bein 'home, but ain't no way the people gonna let him live his life out in quiet an' peace. Evabody's worryin about how the 'mericans gonna run they country. They has a Constitutional Convention in Philly in '87, an' guess who's named president a'the convention?

Billy told Washington his knee was feeling well enough that he could go with him. Washington agreed .

Going to Philly. Made Billy think of looking for Margaret, but there wasn't any time. He was at the General's side every day. At night he tried to sleep in his room, but the pain in his knee was fierce, and he took more than a nip of whiskey to help him through it, which meant that he had to cover his breath with sarsaparilla tea. The taste was bitter, but it hid the whiskey.

It's a long, hot summuh, an' they's a lotta arguin 'an 'deal-makin.' The General don' say much, but when he speaks, evabody drops whatevuh else they's doin. 'Lots a'negotiatin'done at night. The General speaks his mind in private like he nevuh does on the floor a' the Convention. He convinces lotta people they should favuh a strong central govament. Convention fin 'ly agrees on this constitution thing. They sends it out to all the states for 'em to say yes or no, an'evabody goes home.

179

Figure 26 Washington at the Constitutional Convention.

***

Once we's home an' figure we's gonna be here for a while, I gits back on the subject a 'Margaret. I gits a note from my fren Ennis in Philly says he's found Margaret livin'wi a free black fam 'ly Isaac an'Hannah Sills. I writes to her an'she's kinda coy but seems like she might be okay livin' wi' me again. Writes she ain't feelin' well, an' would be hard to travel jes yet. I goes to the General an' asts him to help me get back togethuh wi'her. He ain't happy at all, but I gits the clear feelin 'he's feelin 'jes a bit guilty for separatin 'me from her aftuh Valley Forge. General says he 'll write his fren Clement Piddle an' ask him to find Margaret an' send her, by boat or land, as necessary, to Mount Vernon.

The General wrote privately to Biddle, not showing his letter to Billy. Washington told Biddle, he had heard Margaret was unwell, but he (Washington) was willing to reunite them. "I had conceived that the connection between them had ceased, but I am mistaken...1 never wished to see her more, yet I cannot refuse his request...as he has lived with me so long and followed my fortunes through the war with such fidelity."

Weeks went by and nothing happened, except that Biddle eventually wrote that he couldn't help with the situation. He didn't say why, and neither did Washington.

"Whass the mattuh, General? What's goin' on? Billy asked.

"I'm sorry, Billy. I've done all I can."

Billy didn't think that was a satisfactory answer, but there didn't seem to be any way to do anything about it. Once more his hopes of being reunited with Margaret were dashed.

***

Except for being separated from Margaret, Billy wasn't sorry to be back at Mount Vernon, and he was hopeful that he was going to be all right—that his bad left knee would heal. But then, in the Spring of '88, when he was picking up mail from the post office in Alexandria, Billy fell again. This time he broke the other knee, the right one, and it was a severe break.

The doctors told Billy that his knees were not going to get better, and he realized that he couldn't ride regularly with the General any longer. That was a terrible blow for Billy, but he told the General that he believed his brother, Frank, could replace him. Frank was younger, but he was a tall, upright young man, and Billy had taught him to read and write quite well. He hadn't been in the war, and wasn't a crazy rider like Billy, but he could handle a horse. Billy had taught him that, too.

The General said plainly that no one man could truly replace Billy, but he made Frank the butler in the Big House, and picked another young man, Christopher Sheels, as his body-servant. Christopher was the nephew of Frank's wife, Lucy. Billy was proud the General had to split Billy's job in two, and he was glad the work stayed in his family.

But Billy couldn't stand just lying around. He thought about the time he had learned to fix some boots for the General, and he said to him, "You gotta bondsman bootmakuh name a' Jimmy Forrest. I'd like to train wi' him an' make mysel' useful."

Washington liked the idea. When Billy started, he could only make minor repairs, but after a while he became very skilled. He made some fine shoes for the General—even better ones for Lady Washington. When Jimmy's indenture time ran out, he left Mount

Vernon, and Billy was fully in charge. Billy thought it wasn't as good as riding to hounds, but it was better than doing nothing.

The General was writing letters to dozens of people to help get the states to agree on the new constitution, and even more people were writing to him, or coming to Mount Vernon to talk about it. Christopher brought newspapers from Alexandria, and they were full of articles about the constitution. Billy read some of the articles and he was astonished by them. Many were positive, but some were so mean-spirited that Billy wondered if their writers lived in the same country. Of course, not everyone had nice things to say about Washington, but he didn't complain and soon there were enough votes to get the new government underway. They voted in a new Congress and then they elected Washington the first president. It greatly pleased Billy that the General received one hundred percent of the electoral votes. Not that he was surprised—who else could they choose?

In Billy's opinion, there were many fine men at the convention. Billy liked Franklin because he always seemed to have a twinkle in his eyes and something clever to say. Franklin had inspired some rueful laughter among delegates to the convention when he said, about the new country, "We'll all hang together or we'll all hang separately." Billy noticed that the portly gentleman was kind to everyone, slave and free, but especially to the ladies. He certainly wasn't handsome, not tall and quite bald—he rarely wore a wig— but he was very charming and had many lady friends.

Billy thought that John Adams was pretty smart, but seemed to be in love with himself, his speech dotted with "I" and "me" and "myself." Still, Billy was not unhappy when Adams was named vice president instead of Jefferson. He didn't trust Jefferson, whom he thought of as a sneak who said one thing in public and did quite another behind people's backs.

***

While Mr. Washington 's president, that ol 'Jefferson tells lotta lies 'bout him—an 'pays for newspapers to say the mos 'terr 'ble things. 'Nothuh thing 'bout Jefferson. He could write some a' the fines' words you 'd evuh read—like his Declaration a 'Independence—but he was the wors 'public speakuh in the whole Congress. Kinda mumbles—

talks so soft you cain't even hear him. Cain't even make his own words soun 'good.

Hamilton an' Jefferson hates each othuh somethin 'fierce. The General makes Hamilton head a' the money departmen'—the Treasury, an' Jefferson is Secretary a' State. I think the General hopes that'll keep Jefferson out a'the country, but it don 'work out that way.

Figure 27 Alexander Hamiltom.

***

For Washington, the most difficult part of being president was that he had to live in New York. The General had bad memories of the battles he had lost there and the people -Tories they called them -who strongly favored the King of England.

Billy told the General he wanted to go to New York—especially to see him sworn into office. Both Mrs. Washington and the General said "No." They appreciated the fact that he wanted to serve, but they knew he couldn't walk much, and it was hell for him to ride a horse. The truth was, Billy didn't see how he could do much good in New York. Besides, he didn't think the Washingtons wanted to have many slaves in New York. There had been a major fight over slavery in the convention. Northerners said they wanted to end slavery altogether. Southerners said," Slaves are our property. Are you planning to pay us for them?"

The delegates finally, reluctantly, agreed they were going to stop buying African slaves in thirty years. Billy thought to himself—*As if thass gonna do me any good.*

The biggest fight was over voting. The Northerners didn't want to count slaves at all. The South wanted to count *all* their slaves. Not let them vote, just be counted. They finally split the difference. Three-fifths of the total number of slaves in every district would be counted.

Some folks say this is disgustin '—treatin' a black man like sixty percent of a white man. Mebbe so, but I think, Hell, at least they's countin 'some a'us- afore it was like we was invisible.

But I'm gettin' off en my track. The General sees how set I am on goin 'to New York.

"I understand, Billy," he says, "and I would like to have you there, but the trip is too difficult. You'd suffer a great deal of pain traveling to New York, even if you rode in a carriage."

"I don' need no carriage, General," I say. "I can make it on a horse. I'll take it slow, sir, jes so many miles a day, but I'll be there."

Washington looked at Billy for a minute, but didn't say a word. Later, Christopher told Billy the General had said that if he was really going to New York, he should leave early—give himself plenty of time.

Billy had told the General he could ride to New York on horse-back. The truth was, Billy wasn't really sure. He packed his things, slung his banjo on the saddle and put his roll on the back of Sarge—the horse with the softest ride. As he was about to leave, Tobias Lear, the General's secretary, rode up to him.

"Mr. Lear," Billy said, "how you be?"

"Mr. Washington wants us to ride together," Mr. Lear said, looking serious.

There was no way for Billy to say, "No."

Some a' my frens is wat chin' as me an' Mr. Lear rides away. We ain't doin' no trot, canter or gallop—jes a nice slow walk. I fix a smile on my face an' don' let go 'til I'm outta sight. Fact is, mos' ev'ry step that horse takes goes right up my body an' stabs my head. I try to ride on the grass 4ongside the road, but sometimes they's roch an' stones an' holes hidden in the grass, an' ev'ry bump jes jump right to my brain. I'm happy Mr. Lear don 'try ridin 'hard. That woulda drove my bones right through my knees.

Every time Billy and Lear reached a town—or even a farm—there were folks out on the road preparing to greet the General when he came by. They were playing music, singing songs, putting up colorful flags.

Lear said, "I recognize the farm we're coming to. We'll stop there for the night."

I don' think we's gone twenny miles—an 'I'm half dead. Farmer smiles when Lear tells him he's ridin' to New York for the General. Lear says, "Mr. Lee is one of the General's closest aides. I'm sure he 'Il be pleased to hear you've offered him your hospitality." Farmer nods real quick, an' shows me a nice little room near the kitchen.

I don 'sleep hardly at all. I lie there, movin 'my knee here an' agin, try in 'to find a good place. I put a bandanna 'tween my teeth, an' bite on it 'steada 'screamin, 'but it tuckers me out.

The next few days were terrible for Billy. The weather was bad, the road were lousy, and Billy's knees were swelling up more and more. The left one popped and began oozing yellow pus. Billy didn't let Lear—or anybody else—see it. He wrapped it up tightly at night. On the road, Billy started singing and humming songs, trying to keep his mind off the pain, songs like *Swing Low, Sweet Chariot, Comin' for to carry me Home*—Sometimes he was doing more screaming than singing.

"I'm very worried about you, Billy," Lear said, "You're looking weaker and more tired all the time."

"I'm doin,' all right, Mr. Lear. Be there soon."

"There's some yellow stuff oozing out of your pants leg," Lear said.

Lear reined in near a tavern along the road, dismounted, made Billy pull up his pant leg, took one look and said, "No wonder you're moaning; I would, too."

He found a serving girl from the tavern and had her clean up Billy's leg—both legs. The girl didn't look too happy doing it, and Billy figured maybe his legs smelled a bit. She tried to smile but couldn't make it work.

Lear said, "Billy, it's no disgrace to be in so much pain. Mr. Washington said that if it gets too difficult he hoped you would stop and rest for a while, maybe in Philadelphia, even in a hospital, if necessary."

Billy sighed heavily and said, "I know damn well I cain't go on this way, Mr. Lear. I got a fren' in Philly, name a' Jeremy Ennis. Served at Valley Forge. I know he'll take me in—y ou jes get me to the edge a' town, an' Pll go the rest a' the way mesself."

"I should go with you, Billy."

"Ain't necessary," Billy said. "Jes help me sling up my banjo an' my blanket roll. You best be helpin' the General. I know he needs you."

They argued up an' back a bit, but Lear finally shook Billy's hand and rode off.

As I'm grindin'my way into Philly I oney think a second on Margaret. Even if she's there I ain't gonna let her see me like I am. I fine Ennis 'place pretty easy. Got a nice little brick house wi' a little white fence. I tie Sarge to the fence an' walk very slow to the door.

Ennis came running out. "Billy!" he said, put his arm under Billy's and half carried him into the house.

"Please," Billy said, "take the saddle offen' my horse an' feed him."

And then he passed out. When he woke up, he was lying on a bed in Ennis's house, and his wife, Mary Rose, and their children were staring at him.

Embarrassed, Billy asked, "Where's Jeremy?"

"He went to Mr. Biddle's house to tell him you's here."

Mr. Biddle was a very important man—the one the General wrote to in Philly when Billy asked him to track down Margaret. "I don' wan' Mr. Biddle to bother wi'me."

"Jeremy be back here soon. You talk to him," Mary Rose said.

Pretty soon Jeremy came home, smiling and happy to see Billy awake.

"It's nice a' you to speak to Mr. Biddle," Billy said, "but I don' think the General—the president—got time to bother wi' a broken down ole black slave."

Jeremy laughed. "You bettuh sleep some more, you broken-down slave, an' mebbe we'll be able to put you togethuh again."

After they left, Billy tried to stand up and couldn't do it.

I'm in the wors 'pain a' my life. I also has to pee like crazy. I'm startin' to roll off en the bed as a way a' standin' up to go to the outhouse when I see a bedpan lyin' there. Thank the Lord.

Second day, a doctor name a' Smith come to see me. Says he's sent by Mr. Biddle. He don'smile at all. Works real slow, tryin'not to hurt me. Shakes his head when he unwraps my knees. Cleans 'em an'rewraps 'em hisself. Then he's outta there real quick.

The next day, Mr. Biddle came by. Billy tried to get up, but couldn't make it.

Biddle said, "Doctor Smith is very worried about you. He wants another doctor to look at your knees—name's Hutchinson."

A couple of days passed and Doctor Hutchinson arrived. He was very young and full of smiles.

"Pleasure to meet you Mr. Lee," he said. "Some very important folks think very highly of you."

"Thankee," Billy said, "please call me 'Billy.' Don' know how anybody can think high on a feller who's feelin' so low."

Hutchinson chuckled, opened his doctor's bag, and began listening to Billy's chest. He lifted and turned Billy's legs, while Billy bit his tongue so he wouldn't scream. Hutchinson took a good long time, then frowned.

"You're in terrible shape, Mr. Lee," he said with a very serious look. "I think we best chop off both your legs above the knees."

Billy screamed and tried to stand up, but the doctor pushed him back down with one hand.

"Hold on, Billy. I'm just teasing—I'm not really going to do surgery on you, although I admit I never saw a better case for choppin' off legs and starting over, maybe with wood."

"I'm useless, Doctor, jes a useless ole man."

"You're not old, Billy," Doctor Hutchinson said. "You're not even forty years old. Your heart is strong and so are your lungs. You've got terrible knees, but the rest of you is fine." He shook his head and said, "You don't really want to go to New York, do you?"

Oh, I do. In my deepes' heart I surely do."

"Then I'll do my best to help you."

For the next week Hutchinson and Smith came almost every day. They used a salve that really burned, trying to clear try to clear up Billy's infections, but it didn't seem to make much difference.

Figure 28 Washington's inauguration on April 30, 1789

Days go by. Finally it's April 30. Inauguration day an' I ain't there.

Doctuh Hutchinson says he 's gonna have a metal brace made for my left knee—the wors 'one, an' then maybe I kin walk wi'lesspain. Biddle okays it, an' nex' thing you know I got this beautiful metal brace. Hutchinson straps it on, test my leg as bes' he kin an' then asts me to stan' up.

Billy stood up very slowly, pressing on the right leg first, so it would carry most of the weight.

"Very good," the doctor said. "Now, try walking, Billy." Biddle was there, Doctor Smith, Ennis and his family—all watching.

Billy took a step, which hurt a lot. Then he took another, which still hurt, but not as much as before. He gave everybody his very best smile. "I kin do it," Billy said. "I'm ready to go to New York!"

Everybody clapped their hands. Billy was smiling his hardest, believing he had everybody fooled.

"I have good news for you," Mr. Biddle said. "The president sent a carriage and it's waiting at my house. Tomorrow, I'll bring it here and you'll be in New York very soon."

Billy almost kissed Mr. Biddle, and sure enough, he was crying.

CHAPTER 25

Let Down

The ride to New York in a two-horse carriage ain't as bad as I 'spected. They was plenny a' cushions inside, an' the carriage has these big springs that takes some a' the bumps outta the road. They's windows, but I keep 'em shut tryin' to stay clean, but dust an' dirt gets in anyhow, so by the time I reach New York I'm pretty filthy. I figured on that so I don' wear my good shirt or jacket on the road, but keep 'em wrapped in a big sheet I borrows from Ennis.

When the coachman first saw whom he was driving, he dropped his jaw, but recovered quickly. Billy doubted he had ever driven a black man before. The coach traveled more slowly than Billy had expected—making no more than five or six miles every hour. Of course, a lot had to do with the poor road–mostly just dirt—and heavy traffic. Billy wanted the driver to get there fast, and he was certain the driver wanted to get rid of him as quickly as possible. But the full distance was nearly a hundred miles, and it took the better part of two days.

They didn't travel after dark, and Billy slept overnight in the carriage—figuring it was cleaner than the filthy inns where the driver stayed; anyway, he didn't want to argue with the innkeepers about putting up a black man.

***

The Washingtons greeted Billy very warmly. The President shook his hand vigorously. He smiled and said, "William, I knew you'd get here somehow, even if you ended up crawling the last few steps."

Billy couldn't even laugh—he was trying so hard to walk without limping. He put on his finest important white man's voice and said,

190

"Thank you, Mr. President, for the carriage ride. I'm very proud to be here."

Christopher was standing right there and he was smiling, too.

Washington said, "Christopher, please take Will to his room."

Billy was thrilled to hear he was going to have his own room—not sharing one with Christopher, and the best part of it was that the room was on the ground floor—no stairs. The next question was, what would he do to earn his keep in New York? He was prepared to work in the kitchen, where limping wouldn't matter as much. It would be a comedown, but he was prepared to do anything to remain in New York with the president.

Then Christopher told him the news. The General was putting together all his personal papers from after the war, and Billy was assigned to working with Tobias Lear, the General's secretary, cataloging the documents.

I'm gonna write down stuff that Mr. Lear tells me. My han 's already pretty good -an' I know it's gonna git bettuh. Fact is, I knows a lot 'bout the General's papers, since I had care a' 'em durin' the war an' for years at home at Mount Vernon. The ones from durin' the war had all been filed an' boxed by the General's secretaries, but the ones from aftuh still need work I din't know Mr. Lear had brung so many documents to New York—they was so many carts followin' the Washingtons I din't realize some's full a 'papuhs.

Other good news is I'm workin 'wi 'Mr. Lear on the groun 'floor a' the house. They's stacks an' stacks a' cartons piled up nice an' neat, but all that's marked on 'em is April, 1784, May, 1784, an On an' on. We got to go through all this stuff an' organize it, make little written notes, attach some to a pile here an' a pile there.

Billy found the work pleasant for about two weeks, but after that he could hardly keep his eyes open. He soldiered on, happy to be in New York and doing something useful. Still, it wasn't much fun. Mr. Lear began to see that Billy was almost dozing off. He said, "Will, would you like a little time off from this boring work?"

"Oh no, sir. Din't sleep too well las' night, but I'm happy to do this importan' work. Thankee for askin'."

The nex 'couple months woulda been pretty bad, 'cept for my meetin' a nice lady from the kitchen. This lady an'me, Isabel's her name, we become fas 'frens, an' my havin 'my own room don 'hurt at all.

But finally Billy said to Lear, "I don' think I'm doin' my best at this papuh work. I 'pologize, but mebbe somebody else could help you better'n me. Gonna tell the president I don't mind workin' in the stable. I'm good wi' horses."

At first the General said, "Billy, I'm worried about you having to muck around in the stables. You're built for finer work." But Billy convinced him that it was really all right with him, and the rest of the time in New York, he worked in the stables—not too hard, but just enough. Every once in a while, the General gave him some easy inside work, as, for example, when he had visitors, and Billy dressed in fine clothes and stood around smiling, which beat cleaning up horseshit any time.

The General, who was inventing the American presidency as he went along, decided to hold an open house at the presidential mansion every week, called a levee. It was partly a formal occasion and partly a republican occasion for the president to interact with the public. The bows and curtsies were a bit formal, but the discussions were not. Mostly, Billy thought (and the president agreed) it was just boring.

At one of these events, Billy spotted a stunningly familiar face. "Margaret!" he called out, and hurried to her side, his face creased in a vast and benign smile. But Margaret did not smile back, and in a moment, Caty Greene was by her side, clearly protective. Billy ignored her.

"Margaret, honey," Billy said. "Been tryin' to track you down forevuh."

"I'm not your honey, Mr. Lee."

"But you's my wife."

This little contretemps was attracting the attention of everyone nearby, and Caty deftly drew Margaret, Billy, and a tall, distinguished looking black man aside.

Caty said, "You were never married to Margaret."

"You was right there when it happens," Billy protested.

"That was an amusement," Caty said, "an entertainment. Margaret has been truly and legally married to my manager, here,

Jonathan Stafford, for over a year." It was obvious that Stafford was totally under the control of Caty Greene; he merely nodded his head and smiled faintly.

Billy was furious, and he was about to say so, when Caty broke in. "Are you a free man, Mr. Lee? Has the General freed you?"

That left Billy speechless.

They all turned their backs on Billy, who would have liked to melt into the floor if it had been possible. He stiffened his back, utterly crushed, but unwilling to lower his head and show his despair.

***

In 1790, the government moved to Philadelphia. After a while the General asked Billy if he wanted to take a short trip back to Mount Vernon. There was a law in Philly, different than New York, which provided that if a slave stayed in the city for six months, he became a free man. Washington didn't want to lose Hercules, who was Martha's favorite cook, Paris who also worked for her, or Billy and a couple of others. They planned a turnaround trip so they could start another six months.

Soun's pretty smart to me, but ol 'Here, he's really mad. Ast Washingtons why they don' trust him—goin' on an' on . Finally it's all worked out somehow—although the idea a'goin' to Mount Vernon don 'seem bad to me at all.

On the other hand, now that Billy's dreams about re-uniting with Margaret in Philly—or anywhere else—had been crushed, there seemed to be little point in being there. He didn't deal well with that disappointment, and one night he got really drunk, falling down drunk.

He was fortunate that Isabel, who had moved with the Washingtons from New York to Philadelphia, found him near the stable and she tried to help him stumble inside, but he was very heavy. At that moment, Tobias Lear, who had been out for the evening, came along. Except for a flickering lantern, it was very dark in the stable, but not so dark that Lear couldn't see what shape Billy was in. It was obvious that Isabel was having a difficult time dragging him along. Lear didn't hesitate.

"I see you're not feeling, well, Billy," Lear said. "Let me help you to your room. Goodnight, Isabel."

193

Lear, who was very strong, more or less carried Billy to his room, and laid him across the bed. Billy wanted to thank Lear, but he couldn't even speak.

Lear said, "Get a good night's rest," and left.

Lear never told Washington about Billy being drunk, but Billy decided that he didn't want to be in Philly any longer—no matter where Margaret was. He told the General he thought he'd be more useful at Mount Vernon as a cobbler. Washington agreed.

CHAPTER 26

Capital Decisions

Before Billy returned to Mount Vernon, the General occasionally had Billy act as his aide—in effect his witness—at important meetings with members of his government, both friends and (suspected) enemies. After such meetings, Billy would write notes of the discussions to give to Washington; his memory was excellent and his notes proved consistently reliable. One of the most important negotiations involved the location of the national capital. Everyone understood that the location would have an important impact on the power arrangements of the new country. All of the key people were accustomed to the presence of Billy based on their experiences with Washington during the war. It was not clear whether they trusted him, or in fact ignored him.

On one steaming, hot spring day, while Jefferson, Madison and Hamilton waited for Washington in an anteroom of his residence, Jefferson made solicitous inquiries about the president.

"I'm concerned about Mr. Washington," Jefferson said. "He doesn't seem to be himself. He was under such tremendous pressure during the war and was often in heavy combat—anyone would suffer under such circumstances."

Billy frowned at Jefferson, then smiled. "Don' you worry, Mr. Jefferson. The General is as fit an' wise as evuh."

Jefferson said, "I'm certainly happy to hear that. He's been heavily criticized in many newspapers—not that I give credence to any of these scurrilous attacks."

Hamilton and Madison stared at Jefferson, but Billy smiled. "As a mattuh a' fact," Billy said, "the General's been very concerned for you, Mr. Jefferson. People keep claimin' you's sayin' the nastiest things 'bout him, but the General refuse to believe that his dear friend, Jefferson, could be such a mean-spirited wretch." Billy paused for a second. "Yes, that's zackly what the president said." He nodded sagely

Hamilton and Madison seemed to enjoy this exchange; Jefferson did not. He lapsed into silence.

By the time, Billy finally ushered the others into Washington's office, it was so hot that the General immediately suggested the men remove their jackets, which they were relieved to do. Washington did not remove his jacket, but that didn't surprise anybody. Billy quietly served wine and passed out cigars.

After the requisite pleasantries, Hamilton said, getting right to the point, "We should keep the new capital city in Philadelphia or New York. Why create a whole new city in the middle of nowhere?"

Washington was surprised; he had expected Hamilton to support a location in Virginia, which he knew the General preferred.

Madison says, "We're a new country, we ought to have a new capital."

"Yes," Jefferson said, "in Virginia."

Hamilton said, "You southerners have too much power as it is."

Jefferson said, "And you want to take it from us farmers and give it to your merchants and bond-sellers."

Madison added, "Not to the real people."

Hamilton slammed his fist on the table. "If the new government assumes all the federal and state debt, you can put the capital any place you damn please!" Another surprise—they had not been discussing the debt before, but it was now clear where Hamilton's priorities lay.

Jefferson quickly said, "Richmond."

"Well, maybe not Richmond," Hamilton responded, "a new city, close to Mt. Vernon" (he glanced at Washington), "so the president doesn't have to ride too far."

Washington smiled, but didn't immediately speak. They all waited for him to say something. Finally, he said, "What about Hamilton's National Bank?"

Jefferson exclaimed, "A bank, too?"

Madison laughed. "Then you Virginia planters can borrow from your friends here instead of the British. I doubt it's possible under our constitution."

Hamilton asked, "What do you say, Mr. President? Madison tells me there's a place on the Potomac that's exactly half-way between the North and South limits of the thirteen states—and that place is Mount Vernon. A capital on the Potomac would be only a few miles away."

Washington would not be rushed. He asked, "You're certain the central government will assume all of Virginia's debts?"

Hamilton said, "That's a promise. We'll settle the bank question later, for now we'll trade assumption for a capital in Virginia."

They all looked at Washington, who smiled, nodded his head, and stood up. They all stood up, shook hands and left. It seemed obvious from the bewildered looks on several faces, that no one had expected such a quick resolution.

Washington asked Billy, "How does all this sound to you?"

Billy shrugged. "At leas' from Mt. Vernon, we'll be able to keep an eye on those fellers. Hamilton's too smart for his own good, Jefferson says one thing an' does 'nothuh. Madison—I don' know whose side he's on."

Washington agreed. "Precisely my sentiments." Then Washington said something Billy had never heard him say before: "Now pour us a couple of glasses of Claret, Billy, and we'll forget about these gentlemen for a little while."

Billy poured two glasses, while Washington removed his jacket

"To the United States of America," Washington said.

"To freedom," Billy said.

CHAPTER 27

Home Again

The years the General 's away bein' president ain't the bes' for me. Back at Mount Vernon I gits my old room back, an' I do shoe-makin 'for evabody there—who's got shoes. When black folks have meetin's or dances, I go to 'em, an' sometimes I plays my banjo. But I got constant pain an 'I ain't very happy. To tell the truth I get drunk pretty off en. Still there was one thing that was needlin 'my mind, an' I got Preacher in a quiet place an 'talked to him 'bout it.

"Preacher, you tole me you got a key to that safe unduh the house."

"I din't say that. I said there might be 'nothuh key."

"That ain't zackly what you said either, but no fancy words, Preacher, do you know where to get 'nothuh key?"

Preacher sighed. "They's one hidden right near the safe. The ironmonger put it there an' tole me not to say nothin' to nobody. I think he figured some time he'd come back and see if they was any money stashed there. I was gonna tell Mr. Washington, but I heard the ironmonger got kilt in the collapse a' some mine, so I jes forgot about it."

Billy smiled. "We both know there ain't no money in there, but I got the deepes' curiosity 'bout them letters. I'm goin' to go look at 'em. You gonna help me?"

Preacher frowned. "I don' like this, Billy."

"Ain't gonna steal nothin'." Jes gonna read some letters." They argued back and forth, but Billy eventually persuaded Preacher to help him. What he didn't tell him was that he hoped to find something that would help his bid for freedom.

One night, after the lights were out in the Mansion, and they were fairly certain they would not be disturbed, the two men approached the entrance to the storage area under the piazza. They quickly pushed aside the brush which had previously obscured the opening, but was now merely piled over it. Preacher lighted a candle and they slowly made their way through guardian bats and rats. When they reached the safe, Preacher dug in the earth behind the framework, smiled, and brought out a key.

"I knew it was here," he whispered.

Billy took the key from Preacher, scraped some rust from it with his pocket knife and plunged it into the slot. It turned much more easily than the last time. They struggled with the heavy door, but Preacher had brought some wax, which he applied to the hinges, and it finally moved. The noise was considerable, and they hoped the heavy construction of the piazza over their heads would muffle the sound. They waited a minute, but heard no response from above.

Billy hesitated for a moment, then decided to ignore the deeds and charts on the upper shelves because he realized that the information they contained would be of no use to him. In fact, he wondered if anything but insatiable curiosity had led him to perform this possibly criminal act. It certainly wouldn't help his campaign for his freedom if he were found out.

Billy went directly to the bottom shelf where the letters were neatly stacked in separate piles. The candle was guttering, but Preacher lit another one from it. "I kin go now," he said. "You don' need me."

"Stay here," Billy said, a bit harshly. He wanted Preacher to witness whatever he was doing, although he wasn't certain exactly why. Preacher sighed and lowered himself to his haunches.

The correspondence went back to the 1740's and included letters to and from Lawrence and other Washingtons. There was also a copy of Augustine's will, the one where Vitruvius and Leander and eight other slaves had been given to young George.

There was correspondence with the Fairfaxes, young and old— nothing explicit from Sally, except a note that seemed quite flirtatious to Billy.

But the real surprises lay in the correspondence with Martha Dandridge Custis. Billy was well aware that he shouldn't be reading this material, but he couldn't help himself. He had a sense that what he read might change his life.

Washington had actually proposed marriage in writing. Perhaps he had previously asked the widow for her hand personally, but he had followed up with a written proposal. Billy smiled—this seemed stilted and old-fashioned to him, but he understood that Washington was a very formal person at the core; maybe that's what these white folks expected. It didn't seem very romantic to him, but then, what did he know?—he was a slave.

Martha had responded in writing. He quickly scanned her letter, written in a surprisingly irregular hand: "Dear Colonel Washington: I am honored, flattered and greatly pleased by your proposal. There are certain matters that I believe you should be aware of and that may very well have an impact on your offer of marriage."

The letter went on to describe her property, the number and description of her slaves, and a clear statement that these were "dower slaves," and that they would always belong to her family and could not be owned by her husband—even if she married Washington.

Then came what was for Billy, the most interesting part of the letter. "I feel compelled to inform you, sir, that as the result of surgery following my fourth pregnancy, I am unable to conceive another child. If we are married, I will not be able to bear you children. If this should result in the withdrawal of your proposal, I will understand, but I did not think I could respond to your proposal without making this situation very clear to you. Again, I am honored by your proposal, and if you decide to affirm it, I will be profoundly happy to accept it."

Billy was stunned. He understood for the first time that the General had married Martha—the richest widow in Virginia—knowing full well that the line would end with him. Billy would think about that for a long time, and rethink it many times, as he struggled to fiilly understand the man who owned him. It did occur to Billy that whatever the reasons the General married Martha, it was very clear that he loved her very much.

At that moment he recalled Martha's desk, the locked drawers and the papers that were stored there. He wondered if she were retaining copies of the same letters and documents that the General had stored in this safe, and whether they both were aware of what the other was keeping under lock and key. Billy smiled to himself; the duplicate sets—if there were duplicate sets—were being maintained on separate levels of the very same building, the Mount Vernon Mansion. If the British Captain had burned the building, Martha's set of papers would have gone up in flames. Would the safe have protected the General's set? Perhaps.

Billy quickly examined the other letters. As far as he could tell, there was nothing that would affect his status as a slave. He wondered if the knowledge he now had about the Washington marriage would be valuable to him, but his racing mind gave him no useful answers to that question. Perhaps this had been a misguided adventure, and he suddenly wanted to be out of there as quickly as possible.

"Le's go, Preacher," Billy said. "Le's close this thing up an' git out a' here."

Preacher looked at Billy questioningly, but there was nothing Billy wanted to tell him. They closed the safe, exited the storage area and covered it again with shrubbery. Apparently they not been observed.

***

They went back to the Family House, where Billy offered Preacher a drink of the wine he had stashed in his cublicle. Preacher refused and left. Billy finished the bottle himself. He was thoroughly drunk and, although he fell asleep quickly, he woke up with a terrible hangover and was more or less useless for that day. He found himself falling into the same pattern of heavy drinking much too often. He told himself it was because of the pain in his knees, and that was partly true, but it did not explain everything.

Several years later, when the General returned to Mount Vernon, Billy remained a troubled man. The general built a distillery in '97, and the slaves working there let Billy have all the whiskey he wanted. Usually, he was a quiet drunk, but not always.

Overseers complained to the General. Mr. Anderson, who managed the farms including the distillery, also complained. The General called Billy in and said, "I guess your knees are hurting you pretty bad."

"Yessir,"

"Is that why you've been drinking so much whiskey?"

"Yessir, that's it."

He gave Billy a small smile. "I understand, but I believe you're overdoing it. What do you think?"

Billy looked down and then up. "I guess I am, General. I'm sorry."

"You've been a great help all the time you've been with me, William, and I don't like to have folks looking down at you or making fun of you. You're too good a man for that."

"I 'preciate that, General. You won' hear no more 'bout me 'an whiskey from this day on."

"Good," Washington said.

I wish I kep' my word all the time. I did mos' the time, an' for the rest, people tries to protect me from mesself Anyway, as I'm gettin' olduh, the knees gettin 'worse an' worse. I don 'know no way to help the pain 'cept whiskey. I try to drink quiet in my room, an'not wander out when I'm feelin' cantankerous. Once in a while, I jes fail. I don 'think that helps my case for bein 'set free.

CHAPTER 28

Temptation of Hercules

Ain't been back at Mount Vernon very long, when Hercules, who'd been sent to Mount Vernon for a while, comes to me by night. I has my own little room in an outbuildin', not part a' the big buildin' where mos' a' the slaves sleeps. Sometimes Missy visits me here, but not this night. Hercules wakes me an' puts a hand ovuh my mouth.

"Hush up," he whispers.

It's a pretty dark night, but the walls are whitewashed and a slip of moonlight comes in through the window—enough for Billy to see that Here has on black clothes that are darker than he is, a bandanna over his head. He looks so fat Billy figures he has more than one set of clothes covering his body. It's very hot, and he's sweating heavily.

"We's goin'" he whispers.

Billy knows what he means. Here and Daniel and others had talked about running away and going north for a long, long time. Billy always thought it was just big talk, but here he was, looking mighty ready. He apparently believed it would be easier to escape from Mount Vernon than Philly, where the whole government was.

"Get some stuff," Here whispers. "Come wi' us."

"You's gonna get yourself hurt, brothuh," Billy whispers.

Hercules pats his chest. "They's gonna have to kill me."

He looks fierce, eyes big and blazing. Billy knows he means he has a gun under his clothes. That was no big surprise. Some trusted negroes at Mount Vernon had guns, mostly rifles, for hunting. Mrs. Washington thought the General was crazy for allowing that, but the General told her some of the slaves were as good as family and wouldn't hurt anybody.

Billy was confused. He didn't particularly like Hercules, but it seemed to him that it wasn't likely that the General was going to set him free any time soon. He began to feel pretty excited thinking about running away. He would surprise all these white folks and prove he had real courage.

Billy rolled out of bed and pulled a heavy wool shirt over the cotton shirt and pants he was wearing. He shoved his hunting knife in his belt, and reached under the bed for the musket the General had given him

"Good!" Hercules says—speaking a little too loudly.

Billy finds musket balls and powder bags and begins shoving them into his pockets.

"Le's go, Le's go!" Here says in a harsh whisper.

Billy grabs his banjo and begins to sling it over his shoulder.

'You cain't take that!" Hercules says, grabbing at the strap.

Billy backs away from him. "Why not?" he asks.

"This ain't no party, no dance. You leave that shit behine an' take more clothes!"

"I'm takin' my banjo!" Billy says.

"Forget it!" Hercules says, and Billy see's that he's getting very angry. He's had these kinds of arguments with him before. Here wants to be boss, wants to run everything.

Suddenly I has a pitture a 'mesself runnin' low an' jumpin 'creeks, wi' white men behine me, yellin an' yellin an' shootin.' "Nothuh pitture crowds that out: me an' the General ridin' hard after a fox, the hounds bayin', a soft rain fallin,' an' the General an' me laughin.' Laughin.'

Hercules steps toward Billy and puts his face in Billy's. "You do what I say, nigguh, I'm runnin' this show."

Billy thinks Here is going to grab him. He slowly takes the banjo up over his head and props it against the wall.

"Tha's bettuh!" Here says.

But then Billy surprises him. He sits down on his bed and slowly pulls his wool shirt up over his head. He shoves the musket under the bed.

"You crazy?" Here asks.

"Ain't goin,' Here. Better get outta here. Oney a few hours to daylight."

Here reaches out, slaps Billy's face, spins on his heel and runs out.

I lie down on my bed. My heart's slowin' down but my head's still spinnin'. Did I do right? I thought 'bout cryin ', but I din't cry. I jes lay there till near dawn an' then slowly peels the rest a' my clothin' off an' digs the shot out a' my pockets. I nevuh do fall asleep.

***

Hercules an' Daniel gits a little past Alexandria afore they's caught by some white men an' brung back to Mount Vernon. Would they 've escaped iffen I was wi' 'em? I doubts it. Good news is, Miz Washington don' want 'em whipped. Here is her favorite, an' she has him brung up to Philly. He never talks to me agin, but thass fine wi[9] me, an' latuh, on the President 's birthday, he takes off an' disappears for good. Shows y a, that even for Here, fine clothes an' special treatment don 'compare wi 'freedom.

CHAPTER 29

Portraits of Power

Figure 29 Edward Savage portrait of Washington's family with Billy Lee behind Martha.

Don' matter whether we's at Mount Vernon or someplace else, somebody's alius makin 'pittures a 'the General. Some he orders his-self, but othuhs is for the fam'ly, the Congress, "the country," an' "generations aftuh him." He ain 't crazy 'boutposin 'for them things, but he tries to be calm an' good-natured. You gotta 'membuh, this is one busy man. Gets upa' 5 in the mornin ', keeps goin 'till he goes to sleep 'round 9 at night or latuh. He's runnin' a farm, runnin 'a war, runnin 'a country, mebbe all three. Like I says afore, jes writin 'them thousan 's a letters he done in his life woulda filled up ev'ry minute for an ord'nary man. But the General ain't no ord'nary man, thass for sure.

Some of the pictures looked like Washington and some didn't. There was a famous portrait painted at Mount Vernon by a man named Charles Willson Peale in '72, a few years after the General bought Billy. In this painting the General was portrayed with a pot belly. Billy could attest that Washington never had a pot belly— hardly had any belly at all—and he was standing right there when the General was posing for it.

Billy didn't say anything at the time, but he spoke to Peale years later, after the General was long gone, when Peale came to Mount Vernon to pay his respects at the General's tomb. Billy and Peale had a long talk—Peale had been a soldier in the war and Billy remembered him from that time.

Peale told Billy, "I wasn't trying to make fun of Washington. That nice full body is supposed to show that Washington's very prosperous. If I had painted him thin, folks might have thought he was poor." They both laughed heartily.

"At least you liked the General," Billy said. "That man Stuart hated him for some reason."

Peale said, "Dolley Madison, the president's wife, saved that huge painting Stuart had painted in '96, when the British burned down the White House."

Billy shook his head. "In that pitture, the General's almos' full size. Looks like him some, but Stuart's got him standin' stiff, wi' his left hand holdin' the hilt a' his sword, an' his right han' held almos' straight out, palm up. Don' know what he's sposed to be reachin' for, but I nevuh seen him standin' like that. Mebbe he's collectin' money for the parish church over in Truro."

Peale didn't feel comfortable criticizing Stuart. "Some folks seem to like that painting," he said, "but I'm not partial to it."

"Me neither," Billy said. "Not that the General was much of a smiler—them bad teeth you know, but don' they ever paint these importan' folks with a fren'ly look on their faces?"

"I guess that may be illegal in the painting fraternity," Peale said.

Billy said, "My favorite paintin' is the one by Mr. Savage. You know why? 'Cause I'm in it. Me an' the General, an' Miz Washington, an' 'her gran'chillun, Nellie an' the boy named for the General, George Washington Parke Custis. What a name to live up to! Miz Washington's chillun, Patsy an' Jacky, ain't in the pitture, 'cause by the time Mr. Savage works on it, they's both long gone. Patsy dies from the fallin' down disease in '73, an' Jacky, who was in uniform at Yorktown as an aide to the General, gets some kinda infection, dies a few days aftuh the Brits surrender. No way the General can enjoy that victory when his stepson is dyin.' The folks who think Washington's made a' marble, shoulda seen him when he hears Jacky's gone."

"There was a lot more sadness in the General's life than people know," Peale said.

Billy nodded. "Mr. Edward Savage works on this paintin' for a very long time. Starts in '89 while the General's president in New York. Works agin in '90 an' '91, finally finishes in '96 in Philly. Savage don' have us all togethuh any one time. He don' fill me in till '96. He knows I cain't move 'round a lot aftuh my injuries, so he makes it easy on me. Paints me standin' up, but has me pose sittin' sideways on a chair, 'cause he's paintin' me in profile, like they say. I think I look pretty fine. Standin' straight an' tall—which I truly couldn' do no more. My chin's strong an' my hair's tight 'round my head. I'm wearin' nice livery. I'm off to one side an' the paint's a bit dark ovuh there, but still I'm in the pitture 'cause the General insist on me bein' in it."

"I've seen other paintings of Washington with a black man. Are they all you?"

Billy laughed. "In some a' them pittures, the slave'll be standin' 'round or ridin' a horse, wi' a real dumb look on his face an' a huge white turban wrapped 'round his head. These painters got lots a 'magination, but no information. Or maybe they thinks they's bein' funny—I sure do."

"Were you around when that French sculptor made the bust of Washington?"

"Sure was. Stranges' thing I ever seen. In '85, this Frenchman name a' Jean-Antoine Houdon—they pronounce it "Oodawn" -comes to Mount Vernon wi' a couple assistants. It ain't the president's idea, it's Mr. Franklin's an' Mr. Jefferson's. I never did find out who's payin' for this work, but Oodawn an' his men is livin' in fine rooms at Mount Vernon, eatin' wi' the General an' his family at special nice meals, drinkin' some a' the General's bes' wine. Oodawn follers the General 'round tryin' to get the expression on his face that he wants—strong an' stern, but still kinda' human.

"One day the General has some dealin's wi' a horsetraduh, who's trying to cheat him, an' the General gits mad an' throws that feller offen the propity.

"'That's it!' Oodawn says, an' he tries to get the look on his work that the General showed when he was gettin' rid a' that horsetraduh.

"Oodawn says he ain't gonna make the whole statue at Mount Vernon. He's gonna make a bust a' the General—I finds out what a bust is, an' it ain't what I 'spect. Oodawn'll carve the rest a' the statue when he's back home in Paris. Actually, he's plannin' to use the same head with lots a' differen' bodies. Pretty tricky, I think.

"When he tells Washington how he's gonna make a plaster mask right on his face, I near falls over. Wouldn' let nobody cover my face wi' no plastuh mask no matter what they pays me.

"Now pitture this. We're settin' up in the second dinin' room. The General is lyin' on his back on a table. Got a sheet ovuh him from his toes to his throat. Oodawn is layin' thin strips a' cloth with plastuh on 'em ovuh his face from his throat to the top a' his head. General's got his eyes closed so the plastuh don' get in there. He cain't move at all or he'll crack the plastuh. Got two quills—one in each a' his nostrils—stickin' through the plastuh so's he can breathe. But he cain't move a muscle, cain't even take a deep breath or the whole thing gets loused up, an' they'll have to start ovuh.

"The General is fine, lyin' there like a mummy—not movin.' Strip aftuh strip aftuh strip. Oodawn is talkin' low to the General, tryin' to keep him calm, but he forgits sometimes an' speaks in French, which the General don' know a single word. An' even in English his accent's so strong, I cain't follow him half the time—an' I ain't got no plastuh mask scarin' me to death.

"Oodawn's men don't say nothin.' He holds out his hand an' they gives him a strip. He sets it in place. Evabody's covered with plastuh dust an' looks like ghosts. Nelly, the General's step-granddaughter wanders inta the room. One a' the Frenchies tries to shoo her off. She slips 'round him. Now she's standin' right in fron a' this weird creature. She recognizes it's her granpaw. He's lyin' there still an' covered in a white sheet an' a plastuh mask.

"Poor Nelly figures Granpaw's daid. She lets out a piercin' scream an' tries to climb on the table with Granpaw—yellin' an' cryin' an' tryin' to tear that thing offen his face.

"Oodawn gets a hold on her an' I comes over, callin,' 'It's okay, Nelly—Granpaw is okay—jes makin' a mask a' his head."

"But she ain't listenin,' she's twistin' 'round, arms reachin' out to Granpaw, pleadin' with him, 'Get up Granpaw. Don't lie there dyin'—I love you Grandpaw, sit up, please sit up!'"

"Oodawn yells at the General, 'Don't move *M'sieu le General*—you'll destroy the mask!'

"General ain't movin,' but Nelly's still screamin.'

"M'sieu" I calls out, "let the little girl touch her Granpaw's finguhs. He can move his finguhs 'thout hurtin' the mask an' she'll know he's alive."

"Oodawn nods at one a' his people, an' this man slowly lifts the sheet ovuh the General's hand. Oodawn brings Nelly ovuh.

"Go ahead, Nelly," I says. "Touch his han'." Then I says to Washington, "General, when she touches your han,' curl your finguhs."

"An' that's how it goes. Nelly touches the General's han'—he squeezes her finguhs a bit an' she starts smilin' an' cryin' at the same time.

"Now, please, *M'sieu William,* take this young lady to her mother."

"Come on, Nelly," I says. "Let's go see your mothuh."

"Nelly looks up sharply—tears gone. She folds her little arms an' **Stan**'s there, defiant as all get out. 'I wanna see what it looks like when they're finished!'"

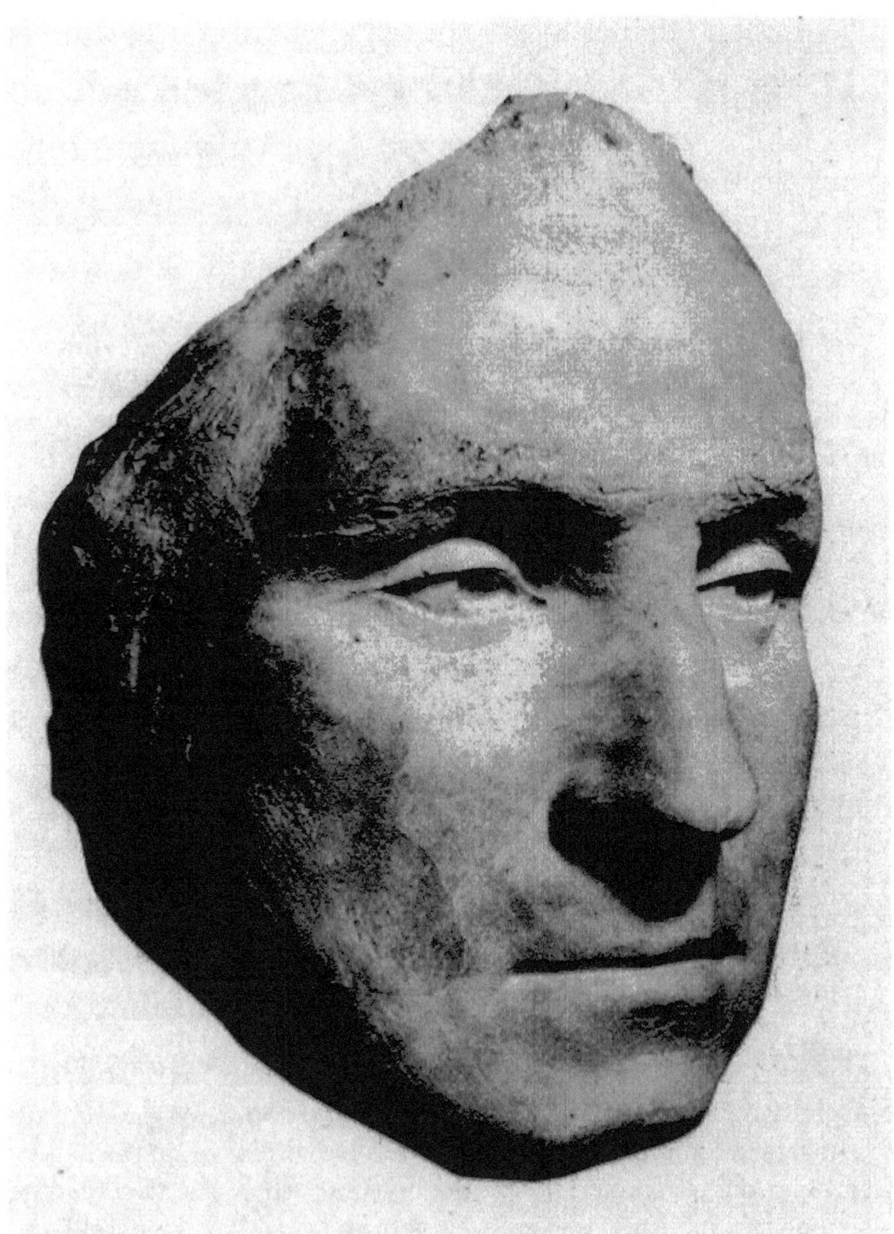

Figure 30 Jean-Antoine Houdon's "life mask" of George Washington.

CHAPTER 30

The Last Ride

I thought that aftuh all those years I 'dfinally got used to not ridin' the five farms wi' the General, but truth is I missed it a lot. I knew I couldn' ride so good no more, but when I seen him ride out that mornin' wi' Christopher 'stead a me, I felt kinda strange. All of a sudden I missed ridin' wi' the General real bad. In fact, I had a bad feelin' all 'round.

Billy was in the open arcade between the mansion house and the cobbler shop, limping along as always, almost thankful for the cold because it made him think of something else besides his knees. Washington saw Billy and tipped the edge of his hat, something he had never done before. The sight of the once powerful Billy Lee, stiff-legged, slow and almost stumbling as he walked, had touched him. Billy noticed the gesture and called out, "Bad day, General!" but if Washington heard him, he didn't acknowledge it.

Washington rode at a steady lope, pacing himself for the five hour ride to check out his farms. It was a ride he took often when he was in residence at Mount Vernon, regardless of the weather. He could have given his horse—a descendant of the half-breed Arabian known as Ranger—free rein and the stallion would most likely have completed the circuit without any direction from Washington. But this was an especially mean December day. A heavy storm had unleashed torrents of snow, sleet and ice that somehow reminded him of another bitter December day at Trenton, twenty-odd years earlier. The wind carried a sound—it might have been Billy yelling, "Bad day, General!" but Washington didn't turn or wave, although he wondered if the reference to a "bad day" had a touch of prophecy to it. He shrugged that off as he and Christopher cantered away.

I seen him come back, too, more 'n' five hours latuh, when I'm walkin' to the Mansion, carryin' some shoes I made for Miz Washington. General'd soon be headin' for a mid-day meal wi' the guests in the Big House. General once said he ain't had a meal alone wi' Martha in twenny years.

The wind was still blowin,' snow 's still drivin.' Christopher 's hunched inta his coat, hat pulled down ovuh his eyes, lookin' like he 'd shrunk a bit. The General 's ridin' tall—like always. Trouble is, his coat's darker than dark—soaked through. An' his face under the tricorn s white as snow. Iffen I was wi' him, I'd a' talked him inta greetin' his guests, for gettin' about dinner, excusin' hisself an' goin' upstairs to rest. I'd a helped him strip off his clothes an' get into some dry ones an' down a few cups a' hot tea. But I ain 't in that job no more.

Washington swung off his horse and landed clean, hitting the ground with his knees slightly bent, and turned the reins over to Christopher who would lead their horses to the stable. Washington felt a sudden chill. *Damn old coat,* he thought, *frayed thin, rain goes right through it. 1 'II buy a new one from a tailor in Alexandria—we don 't do any shopping with England these days. If Billy were still riding, I could send him into town with my order. Too bad.*

Usually, Washington would go upstairs, wash up, and change clothes so that he'd look his best for his guests, but he was late and he didn't want his guests to have to wait any longer. He tossed the heavy, water-soaked coat and his equally soaked tricorn onto a rack, splashed water on his hands and face from a bowl in the anteroom, straightened up and strode into the dining room.

The table was set for a party of eight, who were not yet seated, milling about and chatting, while they sipped glasses of dry sack, a gift from Hamilton. The dishes on the table were English earthern-ware, sedate in blue and white, chosen by Martha, who was moved to purchase the pattern in 1766 because the company that made the dishes, Wedgwood, was founded in 1759, the year of her marriage to George. Of course, that was long before the war.

Washington didn't recognize the guests, but that was no surprise. Many Americans, as well as foreigners, clearly believed that Mount Vernon was the national public hospitality center, and that George Washington should be available for visits at any hour of every day.

Washington had never been able to turn visitors away, despite the loss of privacy and the substantial costs, and Martha had never been able to persuade him that entertaining the universe was not his permanent obligation.

As introductions were shared—two elderly couples from Massachusetts, a man who identified himself as the mayor of a small town in Fredericks County in the northwestern corner of Virginia (from which county, oddly, Washington had once been elected to the Virginia Burgesses), and another man who claimed to be an author seeking permission to do a biography of the great man, one of dozens who periodically arrived at Mount Vernon with the same mission. Washington was usually cordial, but not necessarily cooperative.

When Washington opened his mouth to greet his guests, he was surprised how hoarse he sounded, for which he apologized, but the gravelly tone immediately caught Martha's attention.

"In weather like this, George, you might consider taking some time off from inspecting our farms. I believe they will still be there a few days later."

"Even without my scrupulous attention? My dear, you make me feel ancient and irrelevant."

"Never that, George. You've hardly aged at all since the day I married you."

Washington began to laugh, but his laugh was interrupted by a jarring cough. The others were startled, but Washington quickly recovered, raised his glass and said, "A toast to that ageless marvel, yours truly, and to his ever young and beautiful bride, the magnificent Martha."

"Hear, hear," the would-be author cried, and Washington smiled, imagining him making mental notes of how he would write up this moment.

But Martha was not persuaded by Washington's words or his smile. She ushered the guests to their seats and sped up the serving of the meal as much as good manners and protocol permitted.

After the guests had departed, Washington began to go to his office for his customary review of newspapers and recent correspondence, but Martha caught his hand and turned him toward her. "Not today, my love. You're going up to our bedroom. I can't guarantee romance, but I can promise you a good nap."

Washington bowed his head in assent. He was feeling strangely weak and tired and his throat seemed tight. "You have convinced me, my dear," he said, but it was in fact the unaccustomed weakness and shortness of breath that persuaded him.

***

The next morning, Billy decided to wait in the main entrance hall, to find out how the General was doing. Christopher appeared and told him that Mrs. Washington had talked the General out of riding the farms that day. Billy should have been pleased to hear that, but in fact it worried him even more. He decided to stay around the Mansion until he found out what was really going on. A couple of hours later, he was surprised to see the General come downstairs fully dressed and put on a different overcoat. Billy was afraid he had changed his mind and decided to ride the farms.

"Mis'able day, General. I hope you ain't thinkin' a' ridin'?"

Washington started to answer, but at first no sound came out; then he forced out a couple of words: "Not today, Billy. I'm planning to mark a few trees to be cut down."

"Cain't it wait 'til spring?"

Washington didn't answer, just went outside (with Billy limping along), where he met a pair of men waiting for him by the green-house, hunched in their coats against the driving sleet. The General started to tell them his plans, but his voice was thin and strained. He apologized, said he had a cold, and repeated what he had been saying a little more clearly, but there was no doubt he was ill. The landscape men keeps nodding, and after a while the General shook hands with them and headed back inside. His stride was pretty slow—for him.

"I know you're worrying about me, Billy," Washington said— between coughs—but it won't help me if you get yourself a fine cold like mine."

"Never had no cold, General," Billy said. "My lungs is tough as nails."

Washington didn't respond—his voice wouldn't take it. He entered the house, Billy hustling alongside, and helping him take off his coat.

"This one's a little thin, but bettuh'n that othuh one," Billy said. "That ole thing don' stop water no bettuh than a fishin' net."

Washington nodded, and Billy was pleased to see that he immediately started up the stairs, instead of going towards his office. A few minutes later, Martha came out of the kitchen.

"Have you seen the General, Billy?"

"Yes, Ma'am. He jes went upstairs to your bedroom."

"I think that's good news, but I'm not sure."

"He's gonna need some nursin,' Ma'am. Gotta cough so bad it shakes him somethin' fierce. Generals kin use a lotta tea an' honey an' lovin' care."

"I can supply all of those, Billy. Please find Christopher and send him upstairs."

Washington undressed slowly, and Martha hurried to help him. "I'm getting older, not younger, Martha. You don't have to undress me.

"You would deny me that pleasure?" Martha said, forcing a smile despite her concerns. She began helping him to lift his shirt over his head as she had done many times before prior to love-making, but this time George looked wan, his skin pale, his eyes red and the heat that radiated from him seemed to measure a fever that was far from sexual.

Washington had successfully battled many forms of illness in his life, including cancerous tumors, smallpox and a fierce case of influenza, but he was older now, had fought a long war and suffered the abuse of enemies—and even former friends. George Washington's life, despite his many triumphs had been a life of never-ending stress. He was a very wealthy man, but his wealth was in land, and his cash finances had always been precarious, and the condition of his country equally so. Therefore, his sudden illness in December, 1799, struck a still apparently strong, but in fact, subtly and also not so subtly, weakened man. He had been dodging this realization for several years. It was connected to his earlier conviction that no British bullet could ever strike him, that he was invulnerable. But no longer. Fever was familiar to him, but the tightness in his chest, the steadily increasing constriction of his throat, subjected him to labored breathing comparable to the influenza that had nearly killed him in 1790.

"I'm going to rest for a while, Martha—take a little nap."

As he lay down she kissed him on the forehead, astonished again by the heat of his body. In fact, he did not sleep. Each time he drifted off, he would be racked by coughing. Christopher had brought up some honey-laced tea, and although Washington welcomed the warmth, it was not easy to swallow.

Billy stayed in the Big House instead of the little white-washed house Washington had given him. He wanted to be as close as possible—to help if he could. Even sitting in the hall downstairs, Billy could hear Washington's coughing now and again. Martha bustled out and came back with some hot compresses. Christopher brought more tea, honey and hot lemon-water, but later, before he went back upstairs, he told Billy the General was having a helluva time swallowing.

When Christopher come down in the mornin, 'he tole me the General has a real bad night an' was too weak to get outta bed. He tole Christopher to get Tobias Lear, the General's aide an' secretary. Lear's only in there a few minutes; when he comes out he sends for Mr.Rawlins, the estate overseer. I don' know what's goin' on, but I ain 'tgoin 'to the cobbler shop to fix 'shoes while the General's feelin' so bad, so I hang 'round, watchin 'an 'listenin. 'Achin 'to go upstairs to see for mesself, but don 'wanna bother him. Mr. Rawlins comes in an'almos'runs up the steps.

Rawlins prepared a mixture of molasses, vinegar and butter, but when Washington tried to swallow it he began to choke. As soon as he recovered a bit, he ordered Rawlins to perform a venesection, and to let half a pint of blood. Martha protested and Rawlins was reluctant, but Washington insisted.

Rawlins was very cautious, but Washington said. "Don't be afraid...take more...more..."

After Rawlins finished, Martha, faint, but determined, wrapped flannel dipped in salve around his neck while a slave bathed his feet in warm water.

"I'm getting Dr. Craik," Lear said and hurried out without waiting for approval.

Later in the morning, Lear returned with Doctor Craik, the General's friend and personal physician for forty years. That worried Billy greatly. Even worse, a few minutes later, Craik came down and seeing Billy said, "Billy, you must bring in these two doctors."

He scribbled names and addresses on pieces of paper: Dr. Gustavus Brown, Port Tobacco, Maryland, and Dr. Elisha Dick, Alexandria.

Craik apparently didn't realize that Billy was no longer able to undertake such a mission personally, but he was anxious to help.

"Yessir!" Billy said

Craik said, "You must hurry. He's very, very ill."

Billy hurried (wincing as he moved), to bring the notes to James Anderson, Washington's farm manager, who immediately told his son, John, to take some trusted workers and bring the doctors to Mount Vernon immediately.

The hours went by, and periodically Christopher reported to Billy that the General was doing even more poorly. Eventually— it seemed to Billy that it took forever—John Anderson and the doctors reached Mount Vernon and hurried upstairs. Billy started praying, which was unusual for him, but he was beginning to feel desperate. After a while, he couldn't take just sitting around and he decided to go upstairs. Billy kept his head down and took the steps one at a time.

Martha sat on a chair at the top of the stairs, head held high, expression fixed, eyes staring and almost unreadable. Almost. The tension in her shoulders had raised them to an unnatural level. She went into and out of their bedroom—leaving when they were purging George with powerful laxatives. Billy reached the second floor and nodded towards Martha, but she didn't really see him. He could sense her pain—it was similar to his.

Billy edged over to the door of the bedroom. Then, discreetly as possible, he moved inside.

Washington, stripped virtually naked, lay on the blood-soaked bed. He had requested that the doctors continue to bleed him. When he had first been bled by Rawlins, he had felt a brief moment of relief, but it ended almost immediately, and the constriction in his throat actually tightened. Now he was being bled by Dr. Craik with the assistance of Dr. Brown.

Billy was stunned by the sight of this big, strong man being bled dry, struggling to keep from yelling out, twisting in agony and barely able to speak. As he watched, they continued bleeding him, blistering his neck and forcing laxatives down his throat. Liquids were pouring out of him, top and bottom. It seemed to Billy that this great big man had shrunk before his very eyes. He could not believe they were treating Washington this way. He thought this was worse than war—the General had never been hit by a bullet and now they were hitting him with everything.

Billy leaned close and whispered, "Hold on, General."

Washington nodded and said something Billy couldn't hear.

Craik turned and repeated what Washington had said, "You shouldn't be climbing stairs."

Martha came back in, but Billy didn't know what to say to her. He went over to Lear and said, "These doctors ain't savin' him, they's killin' him."

Craik gave Billy a glare and mouthed the words, "Get the hell outta here."

Lear guided Billy away from the bed. Martha was holding herself in, but her chest was heaving and her shoulders were shaking.

Billy whispered to Lear, "She's gotta git 'em to stop."

Lear lowered his head. "She tried. The president wouldn't listen, and now he's too weak to do anything."

Elisha Dick, the youngest of the doctors, said "We should put a hole in his neck—open his trachea, bypass that blockage and maybe he'll be able to breathe."

Brown and Craik shared a look, and then both said firmly, "No."

"That would be much too dangerous," Brown said. Craik nodded in agreement. They outvoted the younger man.

Billy thought that Dr. Dick was making good sense, but he knew no one was going to listen to him. Billy couldn't help thinking that the others didn't want to go down in history as the ones who had slit George Washington's throat. He was barely able to control his anger as he slowly edged his way out of the room.

Washington felt what was left of his strength ebbing away—relentlessly. He realized that there was no hope. He called Lear to him and, gasping, gave some instructions about his will and testament. Then he told Craik, "I die hard, but I am ready to go." He told the doctors, "I thank you for your attentions, but no more."

Just outside the doorway, Billy was leaning on his cane so heavily that it almost bent beneath his weight. When Washington said, "No more," Billy sighed so loudly that he feared he might be heard.

Washington then gave Lear his final instructions. "I want a decent burial, but no elaborate funeral, and do not let me be put in the vault until at least three days after I die. Do you understand me?" Lear said that he did. He knew that Washington believed that others, including Jesus, had been buried while still alive and he did not want that to happen to him.

As Washington's breathing slowed, Martha sank down on the bed and took his hand. "Tis well," he said, and then exhaled one last time.

"Is he gone?" Martha asked.

Craik nodded.

"Tis well," she said, repeating her husband's words. "I shall soon follow him. I have no more trials to pass through."

Billy just cried.

Figure 31 George Washington on hi s deathbed.

CHAPTER 31

Free at Last

They buries the General four days latuh in the ole family vault on a hillside overlookin 'the Potomac. They was a lot a sincere mournin' 'roundMount Vernon an' lots a 'ceremony—drums, 'guns firin ',folks makin 'speeches. Miz Washington dint attend the funeral, but I was pretty sure I saw her lookin 'out a' window from the Mansion.

Miz Washington has tole me it's okay if us black folks plays some music, too. Banjo, flute, fiddle an' such ain't usual funeral music, but we also got a drum. We plays slow an'deep.

There were many frightened black people at Mount Vernon—some frightened white people, too. Everyone was wondering whether Mrs. Washington was going to close down the plantation and move into town. Would she perhaps keep the Mansion and sell off the slaves? Billy, for one, was aware that Washington had considered these and other ideas like them for years. The General had often said there was no way that Mount Vernon could earn enough to support all the indentured servants and more than three hundred slaves. During his lifetime he had not solved the problems, partly because he didn't want to break up families. He had promised Billy he wouldn't do that more than twenty-five years earlier at Williamsburg. But now he was gone.

Some slaves didn't wait to see what would happen, and they slipped away as quickly and quietly as they could. The manager and Mr. Lear decided not to track them down, and Mrs. Washington agreed. Billy didn't even think about running away—with his bad legs there was nowhere for him to go.

Preacher told Billy that Mrs. Washington had him burn some papers—secretly. She didn't want him to tell anybody. He said some came from her sewing room and looked like letters, but they were so bundled up he couldn't be sure, and she stood over him while he burned them in a fireplace, so he didn't have time to check them over. Preacher didn't know whether Mrs. Washington had a key to the safe under the portico, but it hardly mattered because the General could have emptied the safe out any time after he returned home from the war.

A few days passed and Mr. Lear gathered everyone together inside the big room in the Mansion. Some slaves had never been in the Big House before, and they were staring around, looking here, there and everywhere. Mrs. Washington was there, Anderson the manager and all the overseers. They were sitting down and the slaves were standing up.

"Oh, oh," Billy was thinking, "here comes the bad news." He figured they couldn't get much for him unless somebody needed a shoemaker somewhere; he was feeling pretty sad when Mr. Lear stood up and began to speak.

Lear said, "General Washington loved Mount Vernon and he appreciated deeply the work that all of you folks did for him. Some, like Billy Lee, have worked for the family for over thirty years. I'm going to read to you from his will:

'Upon the decease of my wife it is my Will and desire that all the slaves which I own in my *own* right shall receive their freedom..."

There was a funny sighing sound from the slaves. Mr. Lear hurried on:

"I...forbid the sale, transportation out of Virginia of any slave I may die possessed of *under any pretence whatsoever...! do...* solemnly enjoin my executors...to see that this clause respecting Slaves...be religiously fulfilled...without evasion, neglect or delay.'

Mr. Lear looked up from the will and said, "I want you to understand that General Washington didn't own all the slaves himself. Some belong to Madam Washington, and she can't free them because her family has rights, too. But Mrs. Washington wants you to know that she intends to fulfill every word of her husband's will."

Mrs. Washington was listening with her head down, but now she turned in her chair, looked at us and nodded firmly.

Mr. Lear went on: "General Washington wants all of you to be taken care of, free or not. He said that all old and sick slaves shall be 'comfortably cloathed and fed by my heirs while they live.'"

Billy thought that sounded pretty good—pretty good but not special good.

Mr. Lear then read: "The younger, healthy slaves are to be supported until they are twenty-five years old, and taught to read and trained in a useful occupation."

There were more low sounds from the slaves. Billy realized some didn't quite understand what Lear was saying.

Billy thought that was the end of it, but Mr. Lear looked straight at him and said, "William Lee, General Washington made special provision for you. He wrote that you should be set free immediately when he died–you are free as I read this, Billy. And he said even more. You are to receive free room and board for the rest of your life and an annual payment of thirty pounds a year to do with as you like. You may live here at Mount Vernon or wherever you choose, and you will still receive all your necessities and the payments. The General wrote that he did this 'as a testament to my sense of his attachment to me, and for his faithful services during the Revolutionary War.'"

I chokes up pretty good. I cain't hardly b'lieve I'm free—free at that very moment—free aftuh near fifty years as nothin'but a slave. Then I thought 'bout the way the General was providin'for me. Thirty pounds is a lotta money. I ain't nevuh gonna have to worry 'bout money again—long as I lives.

I feel humble that the General says what he says—right in his will—'bout my attachment to him an my loyal service. It's true: I been deeply attached to the General, more 'n to any man in the world, and to any woman, too. I'm extremely proud that I'm the only slave— formuh slave—mentioned by name in the General's will, the oney one wi' a reg'lar payment for life.

All the slaves were smiling and talking as they walked out of the room. Mr. Lear came over and shook Billy's hand. Mr. Bushrod Washington, too, the General's nephew, son of his late brother, Jack. Bushrod was one of the executors of the General's will.

Mrs.Washington said, "Bless you, Billy. Bless you for all you've done for us."

Aftuh that I done a lotta thinkin.' I got the money. But Margaret still don 'want me; she got somebody else. I got some lady friends at Mount Vernon an' they don' seem to mind my troubles—prob 'ly like me even bettuh wi 'my new money

I try to think a'what I kin do off the plantation, an 'I cain't figure it out— not so's it work for me. !fin 'ly decides to stay. My brother Frank stays, too, workin 'as the butler. His wife, Lucy, stays in the kitchen. Chillun called me 'Uncle William. 'Feels good.

Cain't help thinkin' a' Mama. Woulda liked to tell her iffen she was still alive that I was free—jes like in that song she liked to sing:

Free at last, free at last,
I thank God I'm free at last.
Free at last, free at last,
I thank God I'm free at last.
On my knees when the light pass 'd by,
I thank God I'm free at last.
Tho't my soul would rise and fly,
I thank God I'm free at last.
Some of these mornings, bright and clear,
Goin'to meet King Jesus in the air,
I thank God I'm free at last.

EPILOGUE

To: Editor, *The National Intelligencer*
From: Marcus Ames, Reporter
Date: September 1, 1825

I appreciate the generous coverage you have granted my reporting about the life of Billy Lee, a former slave, and the late American president, George Washington. My manuscript ended with Washington's death in December, 1799, Lee's freedom soon thereafter, and his emotional recital of the slave's song, *Free at Last*. You inquired about Lee's life after his emancipation, and as you surmised, he lived a radically different but nevertheless fascinating existence.

I confess that I anticipated your possible interest and I continued to interview Billy (We're now on a first name basis). I made copious notes and concluded that it would be best to present his story in as close an approximation of his own words as I can manage. You may judge how well I have done in the document that follows. I have divided these autobiographical materials into "chapters" where I considered appropriate and provided captions for each section, but otherwise have left these materials in the form I jotted them down as Billy, never shy, spoke to me.

A few days ago, I had the unexpected privilege of meeting the Marquis de Lafayette who was visiting Mount Vernon, and if I ever had any doubts about the importance of Billy Lee in American history, they were finally and completely disposed of by my personally witnessing the profound affection and shared reminiscences of these two stalwarts, Lafayette and Lee.

MARTHA'S SADNESS

Figure 32 Martha Washington.

I thought that'd be it. Livin' at Mount Vernon an' slowly gettin' older—not walkin' any better, but not feelin' so bad either. Frank an' Christopher keep tellin' me I shouldn' drink so much, but they don' have the pains like I do. Hercules never tole me nothin'—he run away for the las' an' final time 'bout when the Washingtons leave Philly. Ain't nobody seen him since.

I'm really thinkin' I'm gonna live peaceful for the rest a' my days, an' I ain't 'spectin' a lotta years, but thass all right. What I'm forge-tin' is what's gonna happen wi' all the other slaves—the ones whose lives depends on how long Miz Washington lives an' what happens aftuh that. Fact is, aftuh she dies all the slaves the General owned when he died is gonna be free—right then, wi' no more legal mumbo jumbo

Soon aftuh they buries the General an' things settles down jes a bit, Miz Washington calls me in to talk to her.

"Billy, even though you're free, you're staying on at Mount Vernon and doing your regular work, which I appreciate. Not all the folks who are still slaves are still working. I'm sure you know that."

I nods my head.

"You know the folks here better than anyone. I'm beginning to feel very uncomfortable, like some of the slaves are looking at me and wishing me dead, so they'll be free. I'm even afraid some of them may do something to hurry the day."

I know she's right—even 'bout wishin' her dead. Couple a' 'em has mumbled stuff like that to me, but I don' know if they's jes makin' noises or really means it. I sure ain't gonna tell Miz Washington what I been hearin.' Won' do nobody no good.

"Miz Washington," I says, "you've alius been kind to the black folks here, nevuh havin' none beat, givin' 'em special treats at Chrissmas—lots a' nice things. They cain't help worryin' that kine as you are, one day you'll be gone, an' they'll have to shift for they-selves. Jes natural to think like that, but none a' 'em I knows would evuh harm you. They ain't that kine a' people."

She don' say nothin' so I know she ain't convinced.

"I knows evabody here an' they knows me. I'll keep my ears an' eyes wide open, an' if they's the slightes' chance anybody's got any bad ideas, I'll git the good people here to stop 'em. I'll surely let you know any thin' at all that might be a danger for you."

I can see she's relaxin' a bit. "Thankee, Billy, I know I can trust you."

"Yes, Ma'am," I says.

I'm thinkin' real hard. Folks is getting' restless, specially 'round the Mansion House. Somethin' might spill over an' turn mean. Once people's stirred up, you nevuh know how it's gonna end. Now my life's pretty good. I'm free—cain't move 'round all that much—but I got plenny a' money an' plenny a free time. Don' want nobody lousin' that up. They's othuh places in Virginny an' elsewhere that slaves has started rebellín.' Nevuh, evuh turns out good, an' the black folks alius ends up worse off, maybe even dead. If somebody starts somethin' here, all a' Martha's family gonna come down on 'em. An' that ain't the half of it. Othuh slave owners, militia, prob'ly regular soljers gonna be here right soon. Among the folks that's gonna git kilt could be me. I ain't got no sign on me that says, "Don' mess with this nigguh—he's free."

I know who's been sayin' what 'round Mount Vernon. I figure the feller who tried to cut me an' I beat up on—Caesar—he's the wors. Been talkin' mean stuff, 'specially when he gits a little rum in him. I been tryin' to stay away from Caesar, but now I know I gotta face him.

I waits till the right time. I puts my iron brace on my knee—gives me some movement—an' I use the cane I carved outta hickory. It's a real hot day. Caesar an' some othuhs, men an' women, is comin' in from hayin.' Theys sweatin' good, an' breathin' pretty hard. That's how I wants 'em.

I takes up a position near the greenhouse—nex' to the housin' the General built for the workers aftuh he took down the Family House. I'm standin' in the shade—feelin' what little breeze they is. Com-pared to them workers I'm very cool. They comes in, some nods to me, some says a few words. Caesar, he don' say nothin'. As he's goin' by, I slides my cane ovuh jes a bit an' trips him. He stagguhs an' falls face down. Starts to turn ovuh an' git up, madder'n' hell.

"What you—"

"—Hold on," I yells, pokin' him in the chest wi' my cane. "I'm tryin' to save you from gittin' kilt!"

Stops him for a second. "You been talkin' big 'bout what you gonna do to git youseP free. Word's got all over—evabody knows what you been sayin.'"

Other folks is gatherin' 'round.' Ain't easy for Caesar to stand up wi' my cane in his chest, an' all these folks pushin'nex' to him, an' him still tired an' drippin' wet from the fields.

"Word's got to the guvament in the Federal City. Got to Judge Bushrod Washington. Know him? That's the General's nephew. Gonna inherit Mount Vernon one day. Meantime he's a judge on the U. S. Supreme Court. Anythin' goes wrong at Mount Vernon, you gonna have the Judge, the President an' the whole darn army all ovuh you."

Folks is "oohin'" and "aahin.'"

Caesar's tryin' to sit up now, but he ain't lookin' real hostile. Eyes flickerin' 'round in circles. I knows Caesar ain't the oney one, but the othuhs is happy to have him be the one's takin' the punishment for 'em.

Nothuh slave, Eustis, says, "You wanna git us all beat to death, Caesar?"

He don' ansuh.

I says, "You think Miz Washington is hard on you?" I'm talkin' to the whole bunch a' 'em.

"No, No," they's sayin.'

Rosabelle, Caesar's lates' girlfrien' says, "She's very nice to me. Give me a fine dress las' Easter an' some pretty shoes to go wi' it."

Caesar can see it ain't goin' good for him.

"I was jes talkin,'" he says. "Don't mean no harm."

"Thass bettuh," Eustis says.

Others nod an' agrees.

I takes my cane offen his chest.

"Help this man up," I says.

Eustis puts out his hand.

Caesar ignore it, pushes himself upright, but not straight-backed, kinda hunched ovuh. I ain't sure what he's gonna do.

"I'm hungry," he says. "Rosabelle, you git me somethin' to eat."

That's the end a' it. At least for then.

I tell Miz Washington what happen, but I kin see she ain't convinced she's safe. I try to keep the slaves from doin' anythin' they's gonna regret, but you cain't stop the whisperin.'

In Decembuh, 'bout a year aftuh the General dies, Miz Washington calls me in again, shows me this letter. I looks at it, an' I kin see for sure it's the General's handwritin'—know it anywhere.

"Please read this, Billy. Read it aloud. You can go past the first paragraph, which is very personal."

"Yes, Ma'am," I says, an' begins to read: A' course I ain't got that lettuh in fron' a me now, but from readin' it aloud an' knowin' how 'portant it was, I kin tell you mos'ly what it says.

General starts wi' tellin' Miz Washington she kin free his slaves any time she pleases. Figures almos' all a' 'em will leave Mount Vernon, which'U be that many less mouths to feed.

He says he thinks Billy'11 stay at Mount Vernon an he kin help Martha a lot.

Goes on to say that Miz Washington's slaves, the dower slaves, is more'n enough to take care a' Mount Vernon, but if she don' wanna be responsible for 'em, she can release 'em to her family. General says he's talked to her fam'ly an don' believe they'll free they slaves—either to be rid a' 'em or wi' the intention a' rehirin' 'em as free workers.

General says both he an' Martha regret the fam'ly feels this way, but cain't change it—the fam'ly ain't givin' up they property 'thout bein' paid.

Then the lettuh says somethin' I nevuh even thought of—that if the General's been able to sell some a' his farms they coulda bought them dower slaves an' freed 'em theyselves. He hopes thinkin' 'bout that don' upset her too much.

Also says if he'd been able to persuade othuh planters that the Virginny legislature should authorize abolition—slow but sure— would a'been real good, but he was scared that iffen he pressured the othuh plantuhs too much, they might a' killed off the whole United States a' America experiment. If they'd done that evabody, includin' the slaves woulda been worse off. He believes in time the abolition thing sure to happen.

Lemme see now. Resta the lettuh's about Miz Washington maybe givin' the dower slaves to the fam'ly, sellin the western lands in Ohio an' such, an' havin' enuf to purchase a town house in Alexandria an' live a comfortable, peaceful life. He hopes he'll have a chance to do that afore he dies, but she can do it herself if he's gone.

General says Bushrod'll take over Mount Vernon when she's gone. Since he don' fancy farmin', he'll mebbe sell the property. At least the new owners'll have it free a' slaves, an' that won't be so bad for the General's an' Martha's reputation—name a' Mount Vernon won't be forevuh saddled wi' slavery.

He says he don' know what Bushrod'll do if an' when he comes into MountVernon aftuh they's both gone, but hope he'll sell his own estate, free his slaves an' rehire 'em at Mount Vernon. It may even be possible to run Mount Vernon that way an' make some money.

General writes he's tried to let Bushrod know his feelin's, but Bushrod ain't promised nothin'. He b'lieves there'll be plenty a' pressure on him on account a' the General an' Martha havin' freed they slaves. Says Bushrod's a fine judge an' very honorable but don' know if that'll get him to do right by his slaves.

Thass mos'ly it. I asts Miz Washington why the General writes her this lettuh, 'stead ajes tellin' her.

She says, "The General would have put these thoughts into his will, but didn't want to give others the means to force my hand, and he didn't want me to feel any sense of obligation to do anything other than what I choose."

She hesitates for a second. "The General said he had complete trust and faith in Billy's judgment, but can't say as much for the others. He wanted me to have his thoughts in writing if I should need them."

I hands the lettuh back to Miz Washington.

"What are your thoughts, Billy as you read this?"

"Like the General says, it's up to you."

"What would you do—if it was up to *you?*"

"First, let me say, that the General's right 'bout me. I'll stay at Mount Vernon as long as you want me. For the rest, I think the General's also right—you'd be bettuh off lettin' the rest a' his slaves go. They ain't likely to try an' kill you, but they's always rumblin's. An' they don' do as much work as they should—but don' tell 'em I said so."

"You've confirmed my feelings, Billy. I'll have Bushrod draw up a certificate freeing General Washington's slaves. Please don't say anything to anyone until this is done."

Miz Washington does what she says, writin' up this papuh that sets all a' them slaves free on January 1st of '01—'bout a hundert twenny a' 'em, since a few has died or run off. She has to go to the Fairfax County Courthouse to file the papahs settin' them slaves free. Mos' of the freed formuh slaves leaves Mount Vernon fast as they kin. Don' know where they's goin' Din't ask. Othuh ones wi' nowhere to go stays on the plantation.

Turns out they wasn' much reason for any a' those folks to think on hurtin' Miz Washington. She wasn' a well lady—sick many times—an' in May a' '02, she gets real sick an up an' dies. Big shock

for evabody who's still there. A few more slaves slips away, but mos'
is jes waitin' to see what's gonna happen. I thought it might be a good
time to read the General's letter to Miz Washington again— mebbe
even read it to some a' the Mount Vernon people. Gonna stir up some
folks, but it might help some othuhs.

Don' matter, we hear Miz Washington has burned mos'ly all the
lettuhs she evuh receive from the General—the slave lettuh among
'em. I kin tell folks anythin' I wants to, but 'thout the lettuh it don'
mean nothin.'

Folks begin to realize what I already knows, that the othuh
slaves—the dower ones that b'longs to Miz Washington while she's
livin'—now b'longs to Miz Washington's family. Those folks don' ask
no questions. They takes all the slaves they owns to they own homes
an' plantations. Most evabody I know since I was a young man is
leavin.' Men, women, chillun—some as whole families, some broken
up, say, with a wife goin' here an' a husban' there, chillun someplace
else. They separate brothuhs an' sistuhs, ole folks from young folks.
It's terr'ble. Lots a wailin' an' cryin, but ain't no one listenin.'

Hits right at home for me. My brothuh Frank is a free man now,
but his wife Lucy is a dower slave an' so is' his chillun. They takes
Lucy an' the chillun away—chillun has to be pried loose from they
Daddy. Lucy's tryin' to quiet 'em, but she's cryin,' too. Frank's gittin'
desperate.

"I cain't go back inta bein' a slave," he says, "but I cain't afford
to buy my family outta slavery. What'm' I to do, Billy?"

"I ain't got no answer," I says. "I'm plenny sorry."

Folks that own Lucy won't lissen to nobody. If Frank ain't careful,
he's gonna end up even worse off. They's nobody lef here to protect
the freedmen—no General, or Martha—nobody. I'd been thinkin' my
life was gonna be pretty good—havin' my freedom an' a few dollahs
a month, my own little house an some chillun to call me "uncle." It's
ovuh. 'nothuh dream squashed by selfish white folks.

They divvies them people up an takes 'em away like they was
furniture or silvaware. An' then they takes that stuff, too—carts an'
wagons piled high with evathin' the General an' his wife evuh owned.

I says a thousan' goodbyes, turnin' this way an' that, happenin' so
fas,' my head is spinnin.' Sometimes don' even know some old frens is

gone till latuh. Ain't time to cry or I'd drown in my own tears.

By the time they's finished, Mount Vernon is empty—I mean empty. All they leave behind is a key to some prison in Paris that Lafayette gave to Washington and a heavy white marble mantel from a fireplace—'cause they cain't move it. It's scary to walk through them empty rooms, 'memberin' all the folks thass been there, white an' black, slave an' free—thinkin' on all the meals that was et there, parties held, weddin's an more. Empty a' people as well as things. Oney us scared old folks roamin' 'round, lookin' lost.

Some a' 'em asts me, "What now, Will? Whass gonna happen now?"

I try to git them to be calm, but it ain't easy. I tell 'em to do they reg'lar work—whatevuh that may be—an' feed theyselves with whatevuh's lef in storerooms an' barns. Tell 'em to go fishin' in the Potomac, or huntin' in the woods—still some a' 'em got muskets. When I figured out what was goin' on, I hid a bunch a guns in the cellar undah the Mansion House. Preacher an' me had covuhed the entrance wi' bushes an' such, so if you don' know it's there you might not notice. Some food's in there, too. Not much for all them years a' struggle.

BUSHROD AND BILLY

Figure 33 Bushrod Washington.

I knows somethin' mos' a' the othuh folks don', 'cause I heard the General an' Miz Washington talk about it wi' Bushrod. He's the zecutor a' General's an' Miz Washington's wills, but more'n' that, the simple truth is the Mansion House an' four thousan'acres 'round it now b'longs to Judge Bushrod.

He's the opposite a' the General—a squirrely little guy wi' scrawny shoulders and a skinny body, a face that looks like marble, wi' oney one eye workin.' Very polite, but don' smile much, suppose to be very smart, a good lawyer, an'jes before the General dies, John Adams, who's president, puts him on the Supreme Court.

Eustis, one a' the free slaves that's left ovuh from Washington's time, comes to me an' says, "You was right to tell evabody to be patient. Now Judge Bushrod's bringin' his own slaves to Mount Vernon, an' he's gonna set 'em all free, jes like his uncle done."

"I nevuh tole you that," I says. "I got no idea what Bushrod's gonna do. But I knows you better be careful 'round him, he's got the whole guvament behind him."

Bushrod's slaves—'bout forty a' 'em—comes to live at Mount Vernon. They takes ovuh the place, 'long wi' his manager. Folks like us, who's left ovuh from the General's time, is pushed aside. They don' stop me from fixin' shoes, but they don' pay me eithuh. None a' these folks knows me from when the General owned the place, an' they got no respec' for me, or Eustis, or anybody else from before.

One thing we learn is Bushrod's real religious. Has services mornin' an' night—'cludin' evabody, slave an' free. His own people's used to this, but us folks from Mount Vernon nevuh seen such goin's on. Lotta folks don' work on Sunday, prays some, an' some even goes to services in Alexandria, but not ev'ry day. Don' pay to argue 'bout it, we all prays wi' Bushrod. Prob'ly it's good for our souls—jes don't like to be forced inta it.

When Bushrod don' free his slaves right away, folks starts grumblin.' Some a' the folks who was the General's slaves tells Bushrod's slaves that they's free men—the General set 'em all free, an' they's proud of it.

As the months an' years go by, the judge don' do nothin' to free his slaves. He ain't there all the time, workin' on the Supreme Court an' ridin' the circuit, an' the place begins to look run down. Slaves ain't free, but they ain't workin' very hard, eithuh.

Sometimes Judge Bushrod brings folks to Mount Vernon to entertain 'em, like his fellow judges from the Supreme Court. When that happens, the manager an' overseer gets evabody workin' to clean up the house an' prune the trees, so at least the Mansion House looks decent. If anybody takes a good look, they'd see Mount Vernon ain't spit an' polish clean like when the General an' Miz Washington owns it. But mos'ly, folks don' care. The Judge talks to 'em 'bout his uncle, an' the guests is pleased to be where the General lived an' worked. They don' say nuthin' 'bout slavery, an' Bushrod sure don' bring it up.

They's othuh folks comin' to Mount Vernon all the time. Visituhs from all ovuh America, all ovuh the world. The judge don't stop 'em—for a while—but he don' encourage 'em eithuh. I talks to some a' 'em—sometimes it's a general or othuh officer I served wi,' sometimes jes a' ordinary soljer. In fact, many officuhs an' soljers asts for me. Like in the days when the General an' me use to set on the big piazza facin' the Potomac, talkin' 'bout folks we knew, battles we was in. These folks'll ask me the same things. I'm happy to tell 'em—sometimes they's carryin' a little liquor an' I gits a nip—altho I ain't sure Bushrod likes me showin' 'em 'round an' chattin' em' up. Fact is I know lots more 'bout his uncle than he does, an' I thinks maybe he's a little jealous. Or he's afraid it makes him look bad. Don' stop me, whatevuh he thinks.

Some a' Bushrod's slaves is more favored than othuhs. They's Oliver Smith who's been wi' Bushrod a real long time. Oliver an' his wife Doll is treated bes' of all by Bushrod an' his wife. Funny thing is when I goes 'round Mount Vernon wi' visitors, tellin' about the General, the war, an' evathin' else, Oliver likes to foller me. When we's alone he'll question me 'bout the General. One a' the things he's curious 'bout is what it was like when the General dies.

"I was oney in the bedroom part a' the time, but my brothuh Frank an' my nephew Christopher was there lots, an' they tole me all 'bout it. I seen when they was bleedin' him an' othuh painful an' disgustin'stuff. He was very brave, but it was terr'ble to see."

Oliver question me more an' more, an' I tell him 'bout my life wi' the General from when I first come to Mount Vernon. I'm kinda flattered by his interés,' but aftuh a while it become tiresome.

Then one day, I see Oliver go up to a group a' visitors an' start talkin' wi' 'em. I trails behine, listenin' as bes' I can. I'm flabbergast. Oliver's tellin' these folks 'bout the General as if he was at Mount Vernon all his life. Acts like he was sittin' wi' him when he dies. Ain't a thing he's sayin' he din't learn from me. I don' know whet-huh to laugh or be mad. This feller din't show up at Mount Vernon till three years aftuh the General was dead an' buried.

Fin'ly I says to myself,' let him do it. I cain't talk to all the visitors, specially since I cain't walk 'round too much. Mebbe it's bettuh that *somebody* tell's folks 'bout Washington if I ain't there to do the job.

I says to Oliver, "I'm on to you, Mr. Smith. You're talkin' to visitors like you was here an' friendly wi' the General. He nevuh heard a' you."

Oliver gets flustered, red in the face, an' starts sayin' he don' mean no harm.

I says, "I don' care, long as you gets the story straight. You can put y ousel' in the story, long as you don' take me outta it."

He's real grateful. "That's very nice a' you, Billy. I 'predates it. Fact is, I loves to talk to these folks, an' I got real respec' for the General.—an' you, too. I'll try to clean up my tellin' so it don' bothuh you."

Sometimes it happens that I talks to folks before or aftuh Oliver does. I alius wonders if they hears the same story from both a' us, an' if they don,' who do they b'lieve is lyin?'

That gets me to thinkin.' General's gone, Miz Washington's gone. So is Patsy an' Jacky. Rest a' family 'ceptin' Bushrod has moved away—slaves is mos'ly all gone, 'cept for me an' a few othuh old folks. I coulda been kilt in the war, but I wasn.' Coulda got some terr'ble diseases, but I din't. Lost Philomena an' the baby when I was young, don' know where Margaret's gone. I mighta had cancer like the General, but I din't.

Why am I still here? I ain't as religious as some folks, but I'm a good bit more as I gits olduh, I knows the Good Lord could take me away any time he wants.

I think I'm beginnin' to figure it out. I'm here to keep tellin' the story a' George Washington an' the war an' Mount Vernon, 'specially 'bout slaves an' freedom. Ain't nobody left here to tell it. So I tells it to visitors an' I also tells it to Oliver Smith so's he kin do the same—an' git it right! He's 'bout ten years younguh than me— might las' longuh than me.

But they's also a younguh generation. They's a real smart, young feller name a' West Ford. He's near thirty years younguh than me. I know he likes to show visitors 'round Mount Vernon, tellin 'em what he knows, not makin' up stuff like Oliver done, or copyin' me. I decides I has to tell him even more. We got to keep it goin.' Seems to me it's importan' an' I'm mighty proud to be a part of it.

Thass why I'm doin' more than tellin' the story an' teachin' othuh people to tell it, too. I'm also tellin' it to folks who's writin' it down, so maybe it'll las' longuh than jes folks talkin' to othuh folks. Sorry I din't keep no diary like the General done, but I din't seem to have the time. Cain't 'membuh evathin', but do 'membuh lots. Handlin' the General's papers was a help to me, an' I commit a good deal a' what's in 'em to mem'ry. Things gettin' more distan' an' fuzzy as time pass, but I'm doin' my bes'. Still 'membuh that Declaration of Independence 'almos' word for word. Turned out to be true, sorta, an' thass good enuf for me.

Figure 34 West Ford.

REBELLION IN THE AIR

Some a' the visitors is surprised to learn they's still slaves at Mount Vernon. They thinks they was all set free long ago by the General. I'm listenin' when a visituh asts one ole man iffen Washington set him free.

Ole feller laughs an' says, "If Washington had set me free, I wouldn't be here talkin' to you."

Visitor says, "You mean you were a slave of President Washington's an' he din't free you."

"No sir, that ain't it. I wasn't even here in those days. Judge Bushrod brung me here from his place."

Some othuh slaves is gatherin' 'round, an' a few visitors that was nearby. Makes a li'l circle wi' the ole feller in the middle. He seems to like the attention.

Anothuh visitor says, "I didn't know the judge had slaves."

Ole feller laughs. "Got more than forty. Brung mos' a' 'em from his own plantation."

One of the visitors is a tall man wi' a broad-rimmed hat, flat on top, black jacket an' pantaloons, black long stockin's, buckles on his shoes. Got a white, starched lookin' shirt on his chest. I know from bein' in Philly, this man's a Quaker. They's hunderts, maybe thousand in Philly. Hardly evuh seen one at Mount Vernon afore.

Quaker speaks kinda sof, but also kinda sharp—if that makes sense.

"I told the president many times, all the slaves in America should be set free. He didn't argue with me, but he didn't do anything about it while he was alive. I thought all that ended with his death. I'm very surprised to see slaves on his ancestral estate."

I figures it out. This man is givin' a sermon. He's speakin' a bit quiet so people has to lean in' to hear him. As people gather 'round, othuh slaves an' visitors sees the group an' they comes ovuh, too. Mr. Quaker got hisself a nice I'll congregation.

Sudden-like the preacher turns to me. "You're William Lee. I remember you from the Constitutional Convention when you were at Washington's side the entire time."

I don' recall this preacher, but they was plenny a' Quakers in Philly, an' he might a seen me almos' any day, so I nods my head. Ain't real anxious to get in this man's audience, but don' see no way out.

"I heard you were set free. How come you're still at Mount Vernon?"

"It's my home," I says. "Been here a long time an' ain't plannin' to go nowhere else."

"How can you tolerate these poor souls being in slavery right before your very eyes?" His voice's gettin' a bit louduh now that he's got a good crowd.

"They's many thousan's a slaves in Virginny. Ain't got the tears to cry for 'em all."

Some folks laughs—white folks. I wasn' makin' no joke, but I don' feel this whole slavery thing is up to me.

The preacher is shakin' his head. "Those of you who are slaves of Judge Bushrod should complain to him. Tell him to follow the example of his uncle. The whole world is watching him. I intend to speak to him myself." He pauses for a second, then says, "This is an evil deed and a price must be paid, both on earth and in heaven."

I think he's waitin' for folks to applaud, 'specially the slaves. They's too smart to do that. Cain't tell who's listenin.'

Quaker takes one last look around at all the black people, shakes his head an' strides away. I'm thinkin' this feller wants to start 'nothuh revolution. Maybe he's right, but it's easy enuf to make a big speech an' then walk off an' leave the problem behine. Soon as he starts off, the othuh visituhs leaves real quick. They don't want no part a' this, eithuh.

Alexander, one a'Bushrod's slaves who was listenin' to the Quaker, says to me, "General din't set you free when he was alive. You only got you freedom when his wife dies."

"Not true," I tell him. "I was set free the moment the General dies. Miz Washington set the othuh black folks free soon aftuh that— afore she dies. Ain't really a long time, but she din't know she was gonna die so soon when she set 'em free, so it's almos' the same thing."

Alexander says, "Mebbe the judge plans to set us free in his will, like the General done in his will."

My ol' friend Eustis says, "That satisfy you—waitin' for Bushrod to die so's you can be free? He ain't that old."

"Maybe we won't have to wait so long," Alexander says, smilin'a bit.

"You plannin' to speed things up?" I ask.

Alexander look 'round real quick.

"Don' mean nothin," he says. "Jes thinkin' out loud."

Some a' Bushrod's slaves laughs. I don'laugh an' neithuh does Eustis. We think this is dangerous talk—bound to come to no good.

Alexander likes the laughter he hears. Stands straightuh an' says, "I figure one way or 'nothuh, we's gonna be free. Maybe he'll do like his uncle, an' if not, when he dies, he's sure to set us free in his will."

Folks is noddin' all 'round.

"You bettuh hope the judge don' hear you," Eustis says. Now the othuhs is lookin' scared, wonderin' if somebody's gonna tell the judge what they's been talkin' 'bout.

"You gonna tell him?" Alexander asks me.

"Don' have to," I says. "Word gets 'round fas' in these parts."

Little meetin' breaks up 'thout 'nothuh word. Folks is whisperin' to each othuh, but I cain't hear what they's sayin.'

Eustis tells me, "I think you scared 'em, good an' proper."

"Hope so," I says. "I'd love to see 'em all free, but I don' know if this is the right way to go about it."

Nex' day one a' the Mansion House slaves comes to the cobbler shop an' tells me the judge want to speak to me. Don' like that at all, but I puts aside my tools an' heads for the Mansion House.

Judge is waitin' for me in the room that use' to be the General's library. Whole house now got Bushrod's furniture in it. Ain't as much an' not as nice as the General's, but it's neat an' fair made.

Judge looks up from his desk, an says, "I understand there's talk around Mount Vernon about the slaves being unhappy."

He don' ask me to sit down, or nothin.'

"Don' know what you mean, Judge. A'course, mos' slaves ain't happy bein' slaves as you well know."

"That isn't what I mean, Billy. Lots of rumors are flying around, and none of them are flattering to me. Some people who have no business here have taken it upon themselves to stir up my property— my slaves."

I waits. Don' know where this is goin.'

"I believe you know what I mean, Billy. My uncle thought very highly of you and I'm certain you wouldn't do anything that he would have considered unworthy."

"Your uncle was alius good an' fair wi' me."

"I'd like you to be the same with me."

"I gotta tell you, I hear the General talk to you about slaves, an' he said they should all be freed."

Bushrod sits silent for a minute, eyes down.

"My uncle was talking about his wife's dower slaves, not the ones I own."

"That ain't how I heard it," I says, a little scairt, but not goin' to back down.

"You heard wrong, Billy. It wasn't like that at all."

He's starin' at me with that one eye a' his, an' believe me, even wi' oney one eye a feller kin look pretty mean.

"I think you bettuh talk to your people, Judge. Make sure they know what you plans for 'em. Right now they's plenty worried."

He smiles for the first time. At least I think it was a smile. What with his funny features an' his one eye, I couldn' be sure. I nod and start to walk outta the room.

"Please call the slaves together for me tomorrow," he says. "I will speak to them."

"I think it would be bettuh if you had your own manager call 'em togethuh, Judge." I continues walkin' outta the room. I wasn' gonna carry no water on my shoulduhs for that man, even if he was the General's nephew. I din't see nothin' a' the General in him—not a thing. I sure wouldn' want to be his enemy—but I knew I wasn' goin' to be his fren, eithuh.

Sure enuf, he has his manager call the slaves togethuh. He brings 'em to the piazza overlookin' the rivuh, an' climbs on a little box to talk. Oney makes him look more like a shrimp than he already does.

Judge don' say nothin' fren'ly, jes starts right in:

"I hear some of you believe I am obligated to set you free because my uncle set his slaves free, and others believe I'll set you free in my will. Well, you're wrong. I have no intention of freeing a single slave during my life or when I die, so get that idea out of your minds. And don't fall for the speeches of people who come to Mount Vernon to stir you up. It's none of their business and you'd be foolish to listen to them. They have no right to tell me what to do with my own property— and you all are my property. I will treat you as fairly as I can, but I will never, ever, set you free!"

He Stan's there starin' wi' his one eye, as if he's waitin' for some-body to disagree wi' him. Ain't nobody sayin' a word. They ain't talkin' an they ain't movin.'

Fin'ly, the judge's face turns a bit red, an he says, "Now all of you, get back to work." He steps down offen the box, turns an' stomps into the house, slammin' the door behine him. We hear that slam echo a couple times 'tween the house an' the river.

Then the folks slowly walk away. I'm watchin' real careful, an' I can see some a' 'em is plenny mad. Feels like they been cheated, an' then insulted in the bargain. Judge ain't got many frens left at Mount Vernon—iffen he had any in the first place.

Couple days latuh, four slaves disappears in the night. They ain't waitin' for Bushrod to change his mind or die. Bushrod's plenny angry—sends out the usual word 'bout runaway slaves. He gits two a' 'em back, but he has to pay the 'bounty hunters two hundert an' fifty dollahs. That makes him pretty mad, but he's smart enuf not to beat the slaves he gits back. Woulda made things worse, I b'lieve.

Still, slaves is now a surly lot. If they wasn' too happy 'afore he made his big speech, they's a lot less happy now. If they wasn' workin' all out 'afore, now they's hardly workin' at all. Manager an' overseers complain a lot, but they's come to the place they's gettin' scairt a' these slaves. Word's comin' to us a' slaves revoltin' here an' there in Virginny an' South Carolina. The ownuhs is beginnin' to worry that maybe they's's gonna be a major rebellion. They's also a lot a' abolition talk—some from Quakers, but some from othuh folks, an' that's stirrin' up slaves even more.

In the year 1800, 'bout two years afore Miz Washington dies, we hears 'bout some slave name a' Gabriel down by Richmond, who's planned a slave rebellion. He was suppose to a' been a bright feller who kin read an' write an' works as a blacksmith. They say he was a big strong man—mos' blacksmiths is. Somebody spills the beans an' the guv'nor an' the state militia stops Gabriel afore he gets started. Gabriel an' twenny-six othuh slaves was hanged, but that ain't enuf for the white folks . The numbuh a' slaves is gittin' bigguh all the time, an' the numbuh a' black freedmen is growin' too. White folks is scared all the slaves in the state is gonna rise up at the same time an' start killin' people. White folks starts passin' laws agin black folks gittin' educated or hired out to white folks on some othuh plantation. Some years latuh, they's sayin' any freed black people gotta leave the state or get enslaved all ovuh again. I don' know iffen that includes me, but I ain't goin down to the guv'nor an' ask him. I'm stayin' where I is.

Even earliuh, we has heard 'bout Saint-Domingue down in the Caribbean. They's a genuwine revolution there, an' the black folks lick the white folks good. They throws out the Brits an' the French, an' they starts the second republic in the whole world—the first bein' the U.S. The battles goes on for a long time an thousan's a' people is killed—black an' white—but slave ownuhs in Virginny is gettin' even more scairt. Gettin' strictuh all the time, an' that don' help keep black people calm. They's thinkin' on how to get free all the time. Some day the whole thing's gonna blow up. Don' know as I wants to be 'round when it happens.

Bushrod don' really know what to do. Even if the slaves was workin' hard, Mount Vernon wouldna' been producin' enuf to support itself—ownuhs an' slaves. Bushrod tells me private-like he's losin' five hundert to a thousan' dollahs ev'ry year. I guess I'm s'pose to feel sorry for him, but I don'.

THE BRITISH ARE COMING—AGAIN

Then comes some new troubles.

The General tried to avoid 'nothuh war wi' the 'Brits long as he was president. Aftuh the French has they revolution, they gets into war wi' the British, an' lots a' folks think we should be on the side a' the French 'cause they helped us so much in our revolution. But the General says we ain't ready—won' be for 'bout twenny years, an' he was right a' course. In 1812, long aftuh the General's gone, we gets into war wi' the Brits. Ain't the smartes' thing we evuh done, but there you are.

When the new war starts, slaves at Mount Vernon says, maybe Brits'll capture this place an' set us free. I think they's crazy, but I don' argue wi' 'em. For a while it don' look like the war will get anywhere near Mount Vernon.

But the 'mericans lose a lotta battles an' we hears rumors the Brits is gonna come up Chesapeake Bay an' attack the Federal City— Washington. It's the capital now, an' President Madison's livin' in the White House. The General nevuh did get to see the White House— wasn' bilt till aftuh he was gone. He got to set the corner-stone for the Capitol where the congress sits, but never seen that bilt up eithuh. He le's me ride wi'him to the ceremony in his carriage. I'm dressed real fine in my uniform, but the General's wearin' an apron like a workman—a mason. He's got this big square a' limestone settin' there, some mortar an' a trowel. Don' say no prayers or nothin' but it's still kinda like a religious thing. Evabody is real quiet while he sets the stone, and then they applauds. He smiles, takes off his apron, shakes a few hands an' we heads back home. Looked silly to me, but the General was mighty serious 'bout it.

Like I say, we begins to hear the British fleet is comin.' Judge Bushrod comes home,'an starts to cart away stuff that's valuable— mos'ly b'longs to him an' his wife. The judge is also rightly worried that some a' his slaves is gonna run off to the Brits. Aftuh the battle a' Yorktown back in '81, near six hundrert slaves that was freed by the Brits an' was workin' for 'em in the army, tries to run off, stead a' bein' surrendered to the General. He don' like that at all. Sends out word, captures mos' a' them poor folks an' turns 'em back to they owners.

Still, they was four or five Mount Vernon slaves who sailed off wi'the Brits when the army goes home in '83.

Judge is right to fear folks'll run off, an' I cain't tell 'em not to do it. I ain't goin' nowhere mesself. In a few days, we gets word the Brits is sailing up the bay for sure. A couple a' slaves runs off, figurín' to hook up wi' the Brits when they comes up the Potomac. Don' know if they made it or not—we nevuh seen 'em no more.

Bushrod's still pilin' stuff on wagons, when I says to him, "Judge, you ain't nevuh gonna git all that stuff outa here afore the British come. They's a big cellar under the house. You kin put lots a' stuff down there an' covuh the entrance wi' some more plantin.'"

He looks at me with that one eye a' his an' says, "That's a fine idea, Will. I'm going to put you in charge of that."

Me an' my chatterin' mouth. All I gits from helpin' him is more work. I cain't do any heavy work myseP cause a' my bad knees, but I kin shuffle 'round an' tell the workers how to get the job done. Freedmen don' mind, but slaves is kinda mad at me. Climbin down unduh the house wi' a load on you back is heavy goin, an' they don' like it. But firs' me an' Preacher takes a coupla' rifles what's unduh the piazza an' stashes 'em in my little house.

Bushrod nevuh been down unduh the piazza an' he is surprise by what he sees—specially the big black safe, which is standin' open, empty.

"What's in that safe?" he asks.

"You kin see for you'self, ain't nothin' in there."

"What was in there?"

"Oney the General an' Miz Washington knows. They don' tell me." I ain't zackly tellin' the truth, but close enuf an' no use stirrin' ole stuff up.

"Where's the key?"

I has to keep from laughin.' Maybe Bushrod's one eye ain't workin.' "You can see it's in the lock."

Even in the dark I kin see Bushrod turn red.

I think I bettuh talk 'bout somethin' else. I ast Bushrod, "You plannin' to fight for this place?"

They's lots a' guns at Mount Vernon. Even some a' the slaves has 'em to hunt with, though the judge took some away aftuh he told 'em he ain't evuh gonna set 'em free. My sel,' I'm pretty slick wi' a carbine since the war—not that I evuh shot nobody in battle—but I do know how to fire the darn thing. I still got my carbine an' I also got the guns I took from unduh the piazza, iffen I needs 'em.

The judge shakes his head. "If they send troops here, we'll only get ourselves killed. No, let's leave all the guns hidden in this cellar. Besides, there's Fort Washington just up the river from here— you can see it from the landing—with two thousand soldiers who'll make it hot for the British. Let's just stay calm."

Well, ain't too many folks who's calm at Mount Vernon. Some don' want to be saved by the Brits, but's afraid they'll be grabbed anyway, an' they drifts off inta the woods or finds an excuse to go to 'nothuh farm. I'm pretty nervous mysel,' an' I'm pitched to disappear if I needs to.

Durin' the Revolutionary War, a British ship come up the Potomac whilst me an' the General was out fightin.' British officer takes some slaves, but agrees not to destroy Mount Vernon, an' Mr. Lund, the General's manager, gives the Brits some supplies. When the General hears, he's very angry, an' he tells Mr. Lund, he wishes the place had been burned down rather than collaborate wi' the enemy. I think thass pretty hard on Mr. Lund, an' in my heart I know the General has to be glad they din't destroy his property.

This time we figure it'd be a bad blow to the country to hear the Brits had captured Mount Vernon—includin' a judge from the Supreme Court. Bushrod decides he's gonna stay an' do his best to keep the Brits from destroy in' the place, 'thout shootin' at 'em. Don' seem very likely to me. I know where my guns be, an' at the firs' sign a' Brits landin' at Mount Vernon, I'm gonna get 'em. I'll figure out what to do latuh.

Eustis an' a couple othuhs figure the same as me. We don't know wethuh we's gonna fight or hide, but eithuh way we's gonna have guns. I don' tell this to the judge, a' course.

Pretty soon the Brits shows up, sailin' smoothly up the Potomac. It's a bright, shiny day, an' we kin see all them great big cannon stickin' out the sides a' the boats. Lots a cannon. Well, ain't no 'merican ships there to stop 'em. Washington an' Adams built up a navy, but Jefferson got rid a'almos' all a' it. I guess he nevuh figure anybody's gonna come across the sea an' attack us—or come up from the Indies. Don' really know what that man was thinkin.'

I'm standin' on the big porch aside the judge, watchin.' Seven warships unduh full sail, wi'some troopships behine' an' I do admit it's a pretty sight. But then, they's a flash a' guns an' the roar soon aftuh. I jump a bit an' try to think on where I kin hide. The judge don' move at all—surprises me.

I'm jes holdin' my breath, waitin' for them cannon balls to blast in an' tear up the place. But none comes. Guns flash agin an' agin, smoke flares up, but no cannonballs.

The judge says, "I'll be damned. They're firing a salute to Mount Vernon—to my uncle." Never saw Bushrod tear up afore or since, but that day he sure did.

Seein' as they ain't tryin' to kill us, Bushrod starts down towards the landing, me follerin' as fast as I can—still ain't sure they ain't gonna turn 'round an' start shootin' at us. When I reach the landin,' I see them ships is past us, firin' on Fort Washington, up the river. But the fort don' fire back. I know they got cannon. I seen 'em mesself. But they ain't shootin.' Matter a' fact they strikes they colors, an' puts up a white flag.

They's surrenderin' 'thout firin' a shot. Good thing the General ain't there to see such cowardice. I seen anothuh Fort Washington surrender near New York in '76, but at least those boys put up a fight—not a great one, but they wasn' no cowards.

The judge is standin' there, shocked as I am. "My uncle would have skinned those soldiers alive."

I nods my head.

The Brits send a landing party to Fort Washington, but mos' of the ships keep sailing. After a while, we hear guns—distant like—but no way to mistake the sound. I heard cannons many a time in my service.

Judge said, "They must be firing on Alexandria."

Turns out the folks in Alexandria welcomes the Brits so warm the Brits don' burn the town. They goes on to the Fed'ral City.

At night the sky's lighted up towards the city a' Washington. We din't know it right away, but they has blasted the capítol buildin' an' burned the White House. Nothin' lef but a shell. 'Course Congress has run off long afore, an' President Madison don' stick around to get captured.

His wife, Dolley, was a real hero. She saves mos' a' the furniture, linens, silver, ev'rythin' not nailed down. An' she carries off that great big paintin' a' the General. Get's it outta the White House jes afore the Brits shows up.

Meanwhile, the 'mericans burns down the navy yard. Don' want the Brits to get them docks an' piers an' ships that's partly built.

While smoke's driftin' down the rivuh, all of a sudden there's a terr'ble storm—high winds an' pourin' rain. One a' the wors' I evuh seen. Rain puts out the fires in Washington, or damage'd be much worse. Hand a' God? Cain't truly say.

Some days goes by—mighty quiet days—an' the British fleet comes back down the Potomac. This time they gits a fight. 'Mericans set up some cannon on a hilltop jes west a' Mount Vernon an' starts firin' on the Brits. They fires back an' they got bigger cannon wi' bigger balls. Lots a men an' guns on shore is blasted.

But at least they fights, an' they wasn' no stray shots that hits Mount Vernon. We 'scapes clean, but feelin' a little dirty.

***

Slaves an' 'dentured servants, white workers an' all, start comin' back to Mount Vernon. Lots a whisperin,' but no cheerin' or noise-makin.' When Mr. Bushrod checks things out he finds a few slaves has slipped away. He don' try to get 'em back. We hears latuh that thousans' a slaves in Virginny an' othuh places goes ovuh to the British. They keeps they word an' makes them free. Some goes back to Englan' wi' the troops. Othuhs goes up north to a place call Nova Scotia. Blacks by the thousan' make a home there. Good for 'em.

"The best workers are still here," the judge tells me.

Mebbe. An' mebbe not.

ANOTHER PARTING

As years go by, the slaves gits more an' more restless. The judge ain't the bigges,' healthies' lookin' feller, but he ain't sick much, an' it looks like he's gonna live a long time. Despite what he tole 'em—which was plain enuf—many slaves is still thinkin' when he dies either he'll set 'em free or his heirs will. He ain't got no chillun a' his own an' his wife is a sickly creature. Some thinks her mind is far gone. I don't spend no time wi' her so I cain't say. But I seen her in a wheelchair mos' a' the time, hardly movin,' sayin' less.

We olduh, leftovuh freedmen an'slaves, guess Bushrod'll give his property to some nieces an' nephews. When they learns that Mount Vernon don' earn no money, they ain't gonna wanna keep it. Some figures that then his fam'ly'll set they slaves free. At leas' that's what the slaves is tellin' each othuh. But I ain't buyin' that at all.

Meantime, Bushrod ain't particular good to his own slaves, an' they's workin' less an' less for this man they don' care for.. Part a' they thinkin' is maybe if they ain't earnin' no money for him, he'll set 'em free 'afore he dies. At leas' thass what they's pray in' on. But Bushrod gittin' more an' more unhappy. He talks to me—tells me these folks don' know what they's up against. He ain't givin' in to no slaves. I sighs a bit, an' repeats what his uncle says, if you treat slaves bettuh, you'll get more work outta 'em.

That jes makes Bushrod mad. "I'm supporting them," he says. "They don't earn their keep. I've had to sell property just to feed them and they don't appreciate it."

I tell him some a' these folks been workin' for him for a long time, an' they thinks he owes 'em they keep—even owes 'em they freedom in return for what they's done for him across many, many years.

The judge cain't see it that way. "I'm regarded by friends and enemies alike as a man of great integrity. Other judges say I'm one of the fairest men on the bench. Why don't these people understand that?"

I shakes my head. Iffen he thinks the slaves care what some othuh white folks thinks a' him, he ain't very smart. But I kin see I ain't gonna convince him. I jes smiles an' repeats wha' I said about tryin' to get more work outta folks by treatin' 'em bettuh.

The judge don' listen to me. The slaves an' Bushrod's gettin' furthuh an' fiirthuh apart. Some slaves won't even obey a straight out order. Some'd rathuh get whipped than do what Bushrod says. Nevuh seen nothin' like that afore.

Gettin' to be rumors agin—like 'bout Miz Washington. Casesar's long gone, but othuh slaves is mumblin' about doin' the judge in. I talks to 'em hard, but they jes laughs at me.

"You jes a drunken ole man," they says. "You don' know nothin.'"

Makes me feel real bad. What they's sayin' got some truth in it. I been havin' trouble wi' drinkin' since I broke my knees, more'n' twenty years ago. When Frank an' Christopher was 'round, they helps keep me in line. But they's gone, too. Frank dies in '21, an' Christopher left 'afore that. Even Eustis dies a couple years ago. My old frens is mos'ly gone. I drinks for the pain, an' I drinks for the company it gives me. Sometimes my han's shakes a little. But I kin still cobble shoes real fine—mos'ly. An' I know what's goin' on at Mount Vernon good as anybody—mebbe bettuh 'cause by now I knows the history of ev'ry thing. When folks comes to visit Mount Vernon an' asts to speak to me, I handle mysel' all right. I 'members some a' 'em on sight an' I knows the stories a' all the battles an' conventions. I kin quote the General from mem'ry, an' ain't too many folks kin do that.

Anyway, it's the young black folks what makes fun a' me, not the olduh ones. An' even some a' the young ones will hush up their frens when they says somethin' mean. Whatever anyone thinks, I'm a free man, an' I was freed by the greates' man in all America— greates' man whoevuh lived—an' I'm proud of it.

I don' tell the judge what these young people sayin.' Treat it like they's jes talkin' big an' don' really mean it. Cain't bring mysel' to be the one who gets these young'uns in trouble, mebbe whipped real bad. Or shipped to Barbados.

But, no mattuh what I think or anybody else says, things is gettin' worse at Mount Vernon. Bushrod's gettin' madder an' madder— slaves gettin' madder an' madder. Cain't come to no good end.

Back in 18 an' 16, the judge an' some othuh white folks form somethin' they calls the American Colonization Society. Actually, the name's longuh, but that's the gist of it. Purpose a' this society is to take free people a' color an' move 'em back to Africa. They was a black man, Paul Cuffe—he's both African an' Indian— who starts a colony in West Africa they calls Liberia, but he dies afore he can get many folks there, an' the Colonization society takes ovuh. Lotta big people is part a this thing—Henry Clay, Daniel Webster, James Madison, James Monroe, many othuhs—an' Bushrod's named the first president.

We ain't sure what they's up to. Some think they's well-meanin' people who's tryin' to avoid a war 'tween blacks an' whites, maybe find some clean, beautiful place for 'em to live. Othuhs don' believe it. They thinks these people hates black folks—or at leas' wants to git rid a' 'em. Some thinks it's 'cause they's scairt of an uprisin,' some othuhs 'cause they thinks free black folks is gonna take jobs from white folks. One thing for sure—William Lee may be free, but he ain't thinkin' a movin' to Africa. Ain't gonna take the chance. When I was young I sometimes wonduhed what it would be like to go back to Africa—was it paradise like some folks say or Hell? But mos' of all I fears that if I was evuh free an' went back to Africa, somebody'd capture me an' turn me right back intuh a slave. No thankee.

Well, Judge Bushrod may mean well by this Colonization Society thing, but his slaves feel difieren' 'bout it. They think that if he wants to free people, he kin start wi' his own slaves—an' he kin save the expense a' sendin' them to Africa. Bushrod don' unnerstan' this right away, but in time he begins to learn what his slaves is really thinkin.' This drives him 'bout crazy. He likes to believe he is one fine man wi' very noble ideas, includin' helpin' black folks that's free—but not *his* slaves. They's his property an' they's worth lotta money. No way he's gonna give 'em away.

By the spring a' 1821, things is comin' to a head. Slaves is madder an' madder -Bushrod's madder an' madder. One day, a couple a white men appears at Mount Vernon—I latuh learns their names is Horatio Sprigg an' Archibald Williams. They talks to Bushrod a long time, but that don' tell us anythin's wrong. Lotta white folks comes to Mount Vernon for one reason or 'nothuh. Then Bushrod takes 'em 'round the propity, has slaves come out an' face these men. I'm follerin' 'em as bes' I can, limpin' on my bad knees, wigglin' on my cane. I don' wan' 'em to notice me, but I gets a sharp look from one a' the white fellers now an' then. Bushrod's got some paper an' a pencil an' so's these white men. They's countin' the slaves an' lookin' 'em ovuh.

A deep pang a' fear goes through my heart.

Sudden-like I know zackly wha's happenin'—the judge is plannin' to sell his slaves. Oh Lordy, no.

The white men kinda wave Bushrod away—I guess they wanna talk private. Bushrod don' look 'happy, but he walks off a ways, sits on a stump, head down, not movin.'

I gits to him fas' as I kin. He hears me comin' an' looks up. He ain't fren'ly at all.

"I'm very busy, Will. Don't bother me."

For sure that ain't gonna stop me. "Mr. Justice Bushrod (firs' time I evuh call him by his formal name—he sits up at that), I know you's plannin' to sell slaves—not jes a few, but a large numbuh. Thass gonna be the end a' Mount Vernon as a workin' plantation, an' a very sad time for the slaves you's sellin.'"

The judge don' say nothin,' but I b'lieve he's lookin' at me wi' some respect.

"I am askin' you sir, to please reconsiduh. Save these people's lives an' fam'lies."

"I can't afford to—they're throwing me into bankruptcy, and they're defiant and lazy in the bargain. I've given them every chance."

"Please sir, let me talk to 'em. I know I kin convince 'em to work harduh an' make sure you don' lose so much money. They'll listen to me, sir, I promise you."

"It's too late, Will. It's gone beyond my ability endure any longer. I wish I'd never seen Mount Vernon. My uncle didn't give me a prize, he gave me an anchor that's twisted around my neck. I can't bear the weight of it any longer."

"The General nevuh thought you'd bring your slaves to Mount Vernon."

"I never promised my uncle anything about Mount Vernon or my slaves."

His tone's so bittuh, I cain't speak for a secon,' but I realize I gotta keep tryin.' "When you sell the slaves, you ain't gonna have no one to work the place. You'll be worse off."

"I'm not selling everybody. I'll have enough to keep going."

"How many you sellin?"

"Not really your business, Billy."

"Sir, I've lived on this plantation since 17 an' 68. Thass ovuh fifty yeahs. Coulda lef here when your uncle set me free, but I love Mount Vernon—in my own way."

He looks at me strange for a bit, then shakes his head. "You can stay here if you like. I'm not planning to drive you away."

"You ain't said how many you's sellin."

He sighs an' says, "I think they'll take about fifty."

They's less than ninety slaves on Mount Vernon—he's gonna sell more'n'half a' 'em. I shake my head tryin' to clear it.

"Wi' respect, judge. Let's try some more—maybe 'nothuh year. I'll git them folks workin' hard, I promise you."

This time, he laughs. "Look at you Billy, you can hardly work yourself."

That smarts, but I ain't givin' up. "Tell you what, I don' need much money while I'm livin' here. 'Stead a payin' me the pension the General set up, you keep it an' use it to help support the othuhs."

He starts to laugh, then I see he thinks bettuh of it. He jes shakes his head.

I don' know what to do. "You gonna break up fam'lies?" I ask.

He nods. "I've tried my best to avoid it, but some families will be separated. That's how it is."

"You's the smartes' man 'round here, Judge, you kin do bettuh."

His face get's real red, his eyes bulge. "I'm getting paid ten thousand dollars. They would pay me another two thousand five hundred dollars, except that I'm keeping as many families together as I can!"

Them numbuhs sounds big to me, but don' really mean nothin.' All I can think on is people—real live people, mothuhs, fathuhs, husban's, wives, chillun. Oh Lordy.

"Where these men takin' my people?"

He sighs again. "Loosiana," he says.

Now's my turn to get red in the face. "Thass a terr'ble place—mos' as bad as the Indies!"

"They've promised me to treat these slaves with decency and care."

I cain't help laughin.' "An' you b'lieve that?"

Bushrod's redder'n ever. "That's enough!" he says, gits up an' walks away.

I dunno what to do. I gotta be careful—cain't get caught tellin' folks to run away. They'll put me in jail. Now I ain't young no more—ovuh seventy years old, an' the way I feels I ain't gonna last a long time more. What have I got to lose? Cain't figure out where my loyalties belong. Bushrod's oney the General's nephew, but he ain't been treatin' me bad. Coulda made my life a lot worse, iffen he wanted to. 'Specially since I got this problem wi' the liquor—nevuh so bad as now.

WEST AND ME

They's this younguh feller I tole you 'bout afore, name a West Ford. He's born in 1784 or '85 at Bushfield, the plantation belongin' to Bushrod's mothuh an' fathuh, Hannah an' Jack. I know his mother was name Venus an' she's a young house slave at Bushfield. Ain't clear who the father is, but almos' certain it's somebody name a'Washington. Which one? Mighta been Jack Washington or one a' his sons, Corbin or William. Might even a' been Bushrod.

Some slaves thinks it's the General, but that don' seem likely. He wasn' 'round Bushfield much, an' Venus was nevuh at Mount Vernon. One time I ast West what he thought. Shakes his head an' smiles. Mothuh nevuh told him, an' neither did anyone else. He doubts it was the General, but cain't be sure.

West is a smart, strong feller, learns to be a carpenter an' does fir' class work. Hannah has taught him to read an' write, an' sometimes when Bushrod ain't 'round, West keeps bus'ness books for him. Also, like Oliver Smith, shows folks 'round Mount Vernon—when I ain't up to it. Somewhere, sometime, Hannah has set him free, but he don' leave Mount Vernon.

West become a good friend a' mine. Loves to lissen to my stories a' the General an' the war. Din't know nothin' bout it hisself 'cause he's born too late. He thinks it's fine that the General set me an' the othuh slaves he owns free. Thinks Bushrod is wrong not to foller his uncle's example, but don' say nothin' to him 'bout it. He figures the judge'll oney get mad an' treat evabody even worse.

Sometimes, West is a big help to me. When I gets the shakes an' the shivers, oney thing that seems to help is if someone bleeds me. Now I know that the doctuhs prob'ly helped the General die soonuh rathuh than latuh by bleedin' him, but they carries it too far, they nearly drains the life outta him, an' fin'ly he makes 'em stop. Dies hard anyway.

One time, they's a doctuh visitin' Mount Vernon, who served in the Revolutionary army when we was near White Plains, New York. He asts for me an' I shows him 'round the place. The doctuh asts if I was there when the General died—an' I tells him how it was— even how they bleeds the General till he's near dead. Doctuh says sometimes that works. Says he notices my han's shakes now an' then. I's surprised he notices, but I tells him the truth. He says with this thing I got—he calls it a long name that starts with a "D" an' ends wi' something that soun's like "Treemens"—He shortens it to "DT's"—kin be helped wi' bleedin.' He offiihs to do it for me, an' I'm scairt, but I lets him try it, an' it seems to help. 'Course, the doctuh goes away aftuh his visit, but the DT's don'. I'm thinkin' who could I trust, an' it comes to me— West Ford, an' not jes 'cause he's a carpenter. When I firs' tells him, he laughs. But then, one day when it's real bad, he bleeds me. Does it pretty good, an' I feels some bettuh aftuh. From then on, West bleeds me now an' agin. A crazy thing to do, but I needs the help. Ev'ry time I tries to quit drinkin' I gets them DT's.

I tells West what Bushrod tells me, 'bout sellin' dozens a' slaves. He's shocked as I am, but he don' know what to do, eithuh. Says he'll talk to Bushrod, but I says, ain't gonna help unless you got the money to buy the slaves. West shakes his head.

We thinks on it some more. We figures that Bushrod ain't gonna be able to sell old slaves or sickly ones—the ones that cain't work much or at all. That knocks off at least twenny slaves, but they's still nigh unto seventy lef.' Then they's chillun too young, mebbe ten a' em. We also think if Bushrod ain't sellin' Mount Vernon—an' don' look like he is—he's gonna need some workuhs jes to keep the place from fallin' down, an' some to feed the ones thass too young an' too old. Bushrod, when all's said an' done, gonna only have 'bout fifty slaves to sell, an we pretty much know who they'll be.

We feel we's pretty smart, but then we asts ourselves—so what? If we gets the whole place to rebel, they's gonna be a slaughtuh. If we tries to get half a' 'em to run away, thass gonna alert the whole state a Virginny, an' end up real bad.

West says to me, "We cain't save too many, but if we pick some real strong ones who could run away an' be tuff enuf to 'scape through the swamps an' woods, we'll be doin' some good."

I thinks on that, an' fin'ly says. "Better some then none."

We comes up wi' three couples—young couples who ain't got no chillum yet. Marilu an' Thomas, Alice an' Aurelius, Lorelie an' Phillip. We talks to 'em alone an' in couples, then all six togethuh. We tells 'em they gotta make up they minds real quick. Marilu an' Thomas, Alice an' Aurelius says yes. Lorelei too scared, but Phillip says he'll try 'thout her. Lorelei promise she won' tell, an' we all b'Heves her.

Then I gets anothuh idear. That preacher—the Quaker feller—preaches at this meetin' house in Alexandria. Maybe we can use him to help wi' our plan. I'd like to speak to him, but I cain't get all the way to Alexandria on my legs, so West says he'll go. The idear is that he'll tell the Quaker what's happenin' an the Quaker'll write a lettuh to the local papers tellin' 'em that the Supreme Court justice—the nephew of George Washington—is sellin' his slaves down the river to Loosiana. Maybe they'll be enuf noise to shame him intuh changin' his mind.

It ain't but nine mile to Alexandria, but West cain't find the Quaker right off, an' he cain't put an article in the paper hisself—he's black an' nobody'd print it, so he's stumped. But on his way back to Mount Vernon, West is real lucky—bumps inta this Quaker an' tells him the story. Quaker says he'll do all he can to get the story out fas' as possible.

But Bushrod beats us to it. Same day West talks to the Quaker, them two slave-buyers shows up at Mount Vernon wi' half a' dozen riflemen. Bushrod has an overseer call out the slaves he's got on a list. I hear names bein' called, an' I comes out a' my cobbler shop. Evabody else startin' to come to the oval in front a' the Mansion House where the overseer's standin, yellin' names. They's fifty-four *names—fifty four!* Ain't no old ones or sick ones or chillun, jes' mos' a the healthies,' stronges' slaves on the plantation, 'cept Oliver Smith an' his fam'ly. The rest a' us—a mos'ly sad lot, old an' tired an' small—standin' wi' our arms folded, listenin,'wi' pain in our hearts.

Evabody on that list shows up—'cept five—the five that me an' West picked to run away. They lef the night before, an' nobody knows it till Bushsrod orduhs that roll-call.

I'm standin' there, somebody touches my arm. I turn—it's West. Whispers what he done. Hopes it ain't too late.

Bushrod's gunmen herd them slaves inta they cabins an' rooms, watches ovuh 'em while they rolls up they propity. None a' 'em got much, but whatevuh they got's precious to 'em. One man objects to bein' rushed. A gunmen hits him 'cross his head wi' the butt a' his rifle. Black man's gonna get up an' fight.

I screams, "Don' do it! They'll kill you!"

Slave backs off. Gunman smiles at me, "Thankee, my fren." Iffen I was a bit younguh I'd a knocked him down an' taken away his rifle.

West is there, pullin' on my arm agin—he senses what I'm thinkin.' I back outta there.

When all the folks is gathered wi' they things, the judge comes out an' makes a speech. "I hope you understand that I do this with a heavy heart. It was not my desire to sell you, but I had no other choice. I couldn't pay your costs and keep up Mount Vernon, including the expenses of the folks who aren't going with you."

Woman yells out, "At least, send my husban' an' chile wi' me."

It's a woman name a'Shirley, good workuh, husband's Jonathan, a carpenter, works wi' West.

"I'm sorry," the judge says. "I need Jonathan here."

Echoes in my head. Years ago, I ast Washington to let a feller name Junius fight in his army. Genral says the same thing—cain't do it, needs him at Mount Vernon. Somehow these white folks seems to think what black folks need don' really mattuh. At least, the General fin'ly frees his slaves. Bushrod ain't nevuh gonna do it.

When he can oney turn up forty-nine slaves, traders say they wants five more. They argues a bit, but don' come up wi' any more slaves. Me an' West breathes bettuh aftuh that.

We ain't got no way a knowin' if the newspapuhs gonna report on Bushrod's sellin' his slaves. We watch these poor folks finish they packin' an' start the long walk to Loosiana, jes like twenny yeahs earlier when Miz Washington dies an' all the slaves is eithuh freed or goes off to othuh plantations. I felt terr'ble when the General dies, but I had Frank an Lucy an the chillun to bear me up. Then Miz Washington dies an' Lucy an' the chillun is torn away. I still got Frank. But the same year Bushrod sells off his slaves, Frank dies. He was younguh than me an' I thought he was stronguh. But he up an' dies.

With mos' a the frens I made in Bushrod's time bein' sold down the rivuh, I feels truly alone. Oh, I got West an' a couple othuh frens left, but ain't the same. Most is as old or olduh than me, an' they got more aches an' pains than I do. They's a few younguh people that Bushrod keeps to take care of the place, but not many. I sees oney the past. Don' see no future.

Them slaves is gone a couple days, an' we don' hear nothin' 'bout nobody complainin,' nobody tryin' to save 'em. Then we gets word from the Quaker. He tole West he was gonna alert othuh Quakers to follow the path a' these slaves, an' see what newspapuhs might be saying.

First newpapuh to tell the story is from the town a' Leesburg in Virginny. We git a copy that says:

A drove of negroes, consisting of about 100 men women and children passed through this town for a southern destination. Fifty-four of the unhappy wretches were sold by Judge Washington of Mount Vernon, president of the Colonization Society(Quaker don' know we saved five).

Then, from Baltimore, a writuh say he visited Mount Vernon, "... where the slaves were very sad, saying fifty of their people were sold the week before. They said husbands were torn from wives and children, and many relatives were left behind" . The writer says," George Washington set all his slaves free at death and Judge Washington is his nephew."

Heaviest fire comes from a paper in the Federal City a' Washington. Says while the judge got the right to sell his slaves, it's "revolting ...that the herd of them should be driven from Mount Vernon, sold by the heir and nephew of George Washington. Sold like they were hogs or horned cattle." Goes on attackin' Bushrod an' says he "...hopes Bushrod knows that what he did was a mistake."

Bushrod is furious. He publishes a letter sayin' nobody but him got the right legal or moral to dispose of his property. Says he got no choice—blames folks who come to Mount Vernon an' stirs up his slaves. Goes on an' on, but don' convince nobody—might a' been bettuh off jes shuttin' up.

Fin'ly the editor of that Washington papuh says, "Bushrod may be a judge, but he has not rendered justice." Says it proves even a Supreme Court Justice may commit errors.

Oney good news is that in all the excitement, the five slaves West an' me sent runnin' away ain't caught—at leas' we nevuh hear they was caught. An' the judge is so upset wi' what's happenin' to his reputation, he don' plant no adds in the papuhs offerin' rewards for gittin' 'em back. Wasn't much, but we's happy we done some good.

ME AND THE MARQUIS

The first time I seen the Marquis de Lafayette was in '77 at Valley Forge. He wasn' twenny years ole then, but you could tell right away that he was somebody. Goodhearted, smart an' brave— though we din't learn that till Monmouth a while latuh. General takes to him almos' right away. At firs', he's afraid Lafayette is jes 'nuthuh a' them fiirriners the Congress makes intuh major generals, an' won' even be worth his rations. But Lafayette 's a dififren' kine a' feller—humble, straight up an' plenny tough. He made a big diffrens in the war—gits the French in on our side, which changes evathing.

He goes home in '81, but come back in '84 and '85. Travels the whole country, makin' frens wherevuh he goes. Alius stops at Mount Vernon an' gets hugged pretty good by the General, who don' hug lotta folks. Me an' Lafayette gets along jes fine. He tries to push the General into settin' me free. General puts up wi' it, but don' go along. Lafayette tells me he's sorry.

Latuh, in '89 an' aftuh, Lafayette's in his own country, gets a big job in the army, tries to stop all the murderin,' tries to stop Napoleon, cuz he thinks he's a bad man, fulla hisself an' gonna lead the country to Hell. Lafayette gits arrested, goes to jail, near gets kilt, but 'scapes somehow. Afore he dies, the General struggles to keep 'merica outta that war. Makes lotta folks mad, 'specially Jefferson, who thinks we owes it to the French to take sides. But General's wiser. Knows we ain't in no shape to fight the Brits again jes yet.

Lafayette's back to 'merica in '24 an' '25. In August a' '25 he visits Mount Vernon, an' I'm tellin' my story to this reportuh feller, Marcus Ames. Marcus is nearly knocked ovuh to actually meet Lafayette. Stumbles all ovuh hisself tellin' the Frenchman how honored he is an' such. Lafayette jes smiles an' says, "I'm very happy someone is planning to write the story of William Lee, one of the finest gentlemen I know, and a great hero of the great revolution."

Figure 35 Marquis de Lafayette in later years.

Marcus near chokes up, an' nods his head. He ain't got no words, which makes me laugh 'cause Marcus kin be a great talkuh mos' a' the time. But then Lafayette an' me hugs for a good bit, an' we kinda forgits the reportuh. I cain't help noticin' that while he's follerin' us 'round an' listenin' close, he ain't makin' notes like he usually does.

Lafayette, who was then 67 or 8—I was goin' on 75—strolls wi' me on the piazza of Mount Vernon, facin' the Potomac. Tells me he's been travelin' the whole country agin, visitin' with all the heroes from the war that's still alive.

I says, "You looks pretty good for a man who's traveled so much, fought so many battles, been in jail, called a hero an' a traitor."

"You've had your own ups and downs, Billy," Lafayette responds. "I see you're getting around with a cane. Are your knees any better?"

I cain't help laughin.' "I'm so used to the pain, I hardly notice it— and when I do, a couple a' glasses a' wine helps a lot. Sometimes, when it's real bad, an' the wine gits to me, I starts a' shakin,' an' I got a young friend here, name a West Ford, an' he bleeds me to settle me down."

Lafayette frowned. "Does that work?"

I nods. "Sometimes."

"I came to visit the General's tomb, maybe for the last time," Lafayette says, eager to change the subject. "Can you walk over there with me?"

"A pleasure—sort of."

We walks towards the tomb, Marcus a few steps behine. I'm strugglin' wi' my cane, trying not to let Lafayette see my pain. But I ain't foolin' him, an' he slips his arm 'round me to help me walk.

"I can't say the place looks as good as it did when the General was alive," Lafayette says. His face tells me that he hates to say anythin.'

"No," I say. "His nephew, Bushrod, don' love this place like the General did."

"Not many people working here."

"After Miz Washington dies, the General's slaves mos'ly leaves. Martha's slaves git parceled out to her fam'ly's heirs an' they leaves. Even my brothuh, Frank, dies, an' his chillun, my nieces an' nephews is gone. Most evabody I growed up wi' from the age a' eighteen has jes disappear.' Bushrod brung in some a' his own slaves—but some years ago he sold 'em, 'cept a few, down south to plantations where they'll work 'em to death. Lotta people 'round 'merica complains, but Bushrod ain't really listenin.'"

"I read about that in the French newspapers. Caused quite a stir over there."

'You wanna talk to Bushrod today?"

Lafayette shrugs. "I'll probably have to stop by before I leave, but it isn't easy for me. He doesn't look like the General, doesn't act like him."

"You got that right. Nowadays wi' 'most evabody gone, I feel like my Mama used to read in her bible—I'm a stranger in a strange land."

We reach the tomb, a big stone buildin' cut straight inta the hillside.

I felt like prayin,' which I usually do out here. Ain't sure if I should, but then I see Lafayette press his han's togethuh an' close his eyes. Him an' me pray silently.

Aftuh a couple quiet minutes, Lafayette opens his eyes an' smiles.

"Do you spend lots of time out here?" he asks me.

I reach into a little chamber nex' to the tomb and pull out my old spyglass, still bent from when I hit the Hessian soldier wi' it at Trenton. I polish it wi' my sleeve.

"'Most ev'ry day, I sit here, lookin' out at the river, an' chat wi' my old friend, the General. Sometimes I aim my spyglass towards the Potomac, an' iffen I see a tall man ridin' a horse real good down by the rivuh, I think it's him an' I scrunch up my eyes an' I figure, iffen I kin get up on a horse, I kin ride with him agin, jes like we done for all them years."

I hand the spyglass to Lafayette, who puts it to his eye.

"My sight isn't what it used to be, Billy, but with this magic glass of yours, I believe I can see him, too."

Figure 36 Mount Vernon.

NOTE FROM RON CHERNOW

After viewing the stage version of *The Ballad of Billy Lee,* author Len Lamensdorf's one-man play from which this novel is derived, Ron Chernow, historian and Pulitzer-Prize Winning author of *George Washington, A life,* wrote the following email:

Dear Len Lamensdorf:

Thank you so much for sending me a DVD of "The Ballad of Billy Lee." As I was writing my biography of George Washington, I developed a soft spot for Billy Lee, who was always standing in the shadow of history, just out of camera range, You have done a beautiful job of coaxing him out into the sunlight and giving him the attention that he most assuredly deserves. My sincere congratulations.

From this distance, and with the sparse evidence at our disposal, we can only guess at Lee's voice and personality, but I always imagined him much as you presented him: garrulous and funny, warm and achingly human, as well as very perceptive about the momentous events he observed from Washington's side. I especially liked the way that you concentrated on his craving for freedom, the secret grief that he must have felt beneath his evident pride at participating in historic moments. We don't know whether he and Washington ever discussed slavery so frankly, but, if they did, your dialogue is always plausible and true to what we know of the two men. I also liked the way that you expanded on the few clues that we have about Lee's relationship with Margaret Thomas and turned it into a tender, if ultimately very sad, love story. And you have conveyed the painful story of Lee's broken knees and subsequent alcohol problems with great tenderness.

I must say that you are very lucky to have secured the services of Henry Brown. He is so convincing in the role, and creates such a love for the character, that we quickly forget that the actor is reading from a loose-leaf notebook and become engrossed in his narrative. He has so many fine moments—I especially liked the story of jumping the broom, his agonizing over his flight from Mount Vernon with the redoubtable Hercules, and the magnificent moment when he receives his freedom. Could you please convey to him my admiration of his wonderful performance, which is so full of dignity and tender feeling.

I can see that you tried as much as possible to remain faithful to the historic facts. Every now and then, I detected small errors in those parts of the story that weren't invented. Washington's mother never lived at Mount Vernon and the blue-and-buff uniform that he wore to the First Continental Congress came from the Fairfax militia. But these are trivial points and you will forgive me for even raising them. Far more important is your scrupulous fidelity to the historical record. Of course, I fully understand the need for poetic license to round out the portrait of Billy Lee and this you have done with consistent sensitivity and understanding of the period.

If it ever proves helpful in the future, please feel free to quote my comments in this email. I share your strongly held view that it would be wonderful if more Americans were acquainted with the remarkable Billy Lee.

Wishing you the best, Ron Chernow

AUTHOR'S NOTE

William (Billy) Lee was the most fascinating African-American of the late 18th and early 19th centuries. His personal story is intensely compelling, but his impact on George Washington—the most dominant figure in the creation of the United States—was even more important.. As Professor Joseph J. Ellis, Pulitzer Prize and National Book Award winning historian has noted, Billy's unique story has been in danger of being lost in the swirling mists of founding times—especially because he was a black man and a slave. After I was first introduced to Billy in Joe Ellis's *His Excellency: George Washington,* and David McCullough's *1776*, I was so intrigued that I researched him in books and articles, online and off, and with Mary V. Thompson, historian and research specialist at Mount Vernon. It was soon evident to me that Billy's story must be told, and my conclusion was further confirmed by the multiple references to Billy in Ron Chernow's 2011 Pulitzer Prize winning history, *George Washington, A Life.*

The major issue for me has been how best to tell this story. The record will not support a strictly non-fiction version of Billy Lee's life, and yet, in my opinion, there is enough information to construct a compelling and plausible account. As Professor Ellis has said elsewhere, a historian is not required to surrender the use of his imagination. In the case of Billy Lee, the confirmable information available about him personally, as well as of the people he served and the milieu in which he lived, has permitted me to create a tale that is, for want of a better phrase, historical fiction; but the ultimate goal is to enhance the search for the truth. This, I humbly believe, I have accomplished.

By referring to the Historical Timeline, *infra,* the reader can confirm most of the important actual events that occurred during the life of Billy Lee, a great many of which he personally witnessed and others that he was informed about by Washington and other historical figures of his era. There are many, usually cryptic, references to Billy in Washington's diary, including notes about purchasing clothing for Billy, sending him to a doctor for medical attention, etc. Not the least of these is the remarkable provision Washington made for Billy in his will, quotations from which are included in the text of the novel.

There are comments about Billy's remarkable horsemanship in a number of sources, including the following by the Marquis de

Chastellux, in his book, *Travels in North America (1-111),* referring to both Washington and Billy:

"The General himself...breaks in all his own horses, and because he is a very excellent and bold horseman, leaping the highest fences, and going extremely quick, without standing upon his stirrups, bearing on the bridle, or letting his horse run wild." De Chastellux also wrote about Washington's huntsman, "... sturdy, and of great bone and muscle. Will...mounted on Chinkling, a French horn at his back, throwing himself almost at length on the animal...this fearless horseman would rush, at full speed, through brake or tangled wood, in a style at which a modern huntsman would stand aghast."

One of the most interesting documents was written by Washington's step grandson, George Washington Parke Custis: *Recollections and Private Memoirs of Washington* (see Selected Bibliography) which also provides an extraordinary account of Billy's remarkable horsemanship. Thomas Jefferson said that Washington was the greatest horseman of his era and it must be noted that Billy rode beside him for decades. When Washington's horse died under him from the extreme heat at the battle of Monmouth, Billy promptly brought him another mount—in the thick of battle.

The following is a quotation from Chastellux, page 306

"George Washington Parke Custis, grandson of Martha Washington, lived at Mount Vernon from infancy until George Washington and Martha died. In 1826 he began to compose "Recollections and Private Memoirs of Washington," which is the only firsthand account that describes in any detail Billy's active years as Washington's huntsman and body-servant as well as offering glimpses of Billy during the Revolution."

Custis also revisited (Page 224) the tale of Billy at Monmouth, escaping a cannonball fired at him and other valets as they watched the battle from a small hilltop.

One of the most interesting commentaries by Custis involved a later trip to Mount Vernon (Page 450):

"Among many interesting relics of the past to be found....at Mount Vernon, was old Billy. The famed body-servant of the Commander-in-Chief....Of a stout athletic form, he had from an accident become a cripple....when [a visitor was announced] with a military title, the old body-servant would send his compliments... requesting an interview at his quarters. This was never denied, and Billy after receiving a firm clasp of the hands, would say, "Ah Colonel, glad to see you...." These interviews were frequent, as many veteran officers called to pay their respects to the retired chief, and all of them bestowed a token of remembrance upon the old body-servant of the Revolution."

***

I wrote the story of Philomena, Billy's wife, based on a discussion with Mary Thompson the research historian at Mount Vernon. In many of the most highly regarded histories of the era, including those referred to above by Joseph J. Ellis and Ron Chernow, you will find entries thanking Ms. Thompson for her assistance in researching and developing their books.

Mary Thompson told me there was some information in the historical record indicating that Billy had been married while he was at Mount Vernon, preceding his relationship with Margaret Thomas. The development of this story is my own responsibility.

***

Billy probably first saw Margaret Thomas in Cambridge, and then again in New York because she was working for headquarters during those times, and their romance may have begun earlier than in the novel.

***

My book also refers to a safe under the Piazza (the columned portico) at Mount Vernon that faces the Potomac. The substantial space under the piazza still exists, and during Washington's time it was used for storage of various items. It has a dirt floor, not a very high ceiling, has no provision for lighting, and entry remains difficult today.

It is considered to be historical fact that Washington instructed his wife to burn their correspondence after his death, and there is little doubt that she did so. It is also true that Lund Washington, the General's estate manager, met with a British ship captain, gave him provisions, and was unable to persuade him to return the slaves the British had taken aboard their ship. Washington claimed to be outraged by Lund's conduct, equating it with collaboration with the enemy.

It is also factual that as the American army approached Yorktown, Washington and Billy rode full out to Mount Vernon, and then almost immediately returned to the army. Washington worried about his estate virtually incessantly and Mount Vernon was the subject of a great deal of correspondence between him and Lund. No doubt he was anxious to visit his family and his property at the first opportunity, although it is somewhat curious that he left the army, if only briefly, at such a critical time. Although he had been away from Mount Vernon for several years, Martha traveled to his winter encampments on several occasions and had remained with him during the annual suspensions of hostilities including the horrible winters at Morristown and Valley Forge.

There has long been speculation about the fact that the Washingtons had no children, although Martha had borne two children with her deceased husband. George became guardian of the children and treated them with great fondness. Washington was rumored to have claimed he was not infertile, but there is no solid evidence about either Martha or George in this regard. Whether they had no off-spring by choice or necessity is impossible to ascertain.

I have put my own imagination to work on this situation and I hope the reader will find my reconstruction plausible and compelling.

***

Caty Greene was indeed known as the Cleopatra of the Revolution. When she first appeared at the army's encampment in Cambridge, she was pregnant, and in February she gave birth to a boy whom she named George Washington Greene. There is little doubt that during the entire war period she flirted—perhaps outrageously—with Washington. Ron Chernow said of her :"A woman of stunning good looks [she] was coy and high-spirited....Even as local gossips whispered about her flirting with the Commander-in-Chief, he seemed enchanted by her company. .." Chernow further stated, "Inasmuch as Martha was fond of the younger woman, Caty could hardly have enjoyed an illicit romance with the general." Chernow, *George Washington: A Life,* page 219 (See bibliography). Yet, I can't help wondering. In 1779, Washington specifically asked that Caty come to the army's winter camp, and she did, bringing her son with her, and Nat Greene reported that, "His Excellency and [Caty] danced upwards of three hours without once sitting down." That seems not to have disturbed "Brother Nat." or Martha for that matter. What is even more remarkable about Caty is that from her marriage to Nathanael in 1774 (Caty was 19 years old),until his sudden death in 1786, she bore him five healthy children. Now there's a woman. And by the way, in 1779, Washington was 47.

***

The parallel to the "battle on the bridge" is an actual historical event in which Washington and Billy in headquarters at Cambridge heard loud yelling from somewhere in the encampment. They mounted their horses and raced towards the uproar. Billy dismounted to remove the top rail of a fence rail confronting them, but Washington didn't stop, jumping his horse over the rail. Billy hurried after him. They found over a thousand soldiers engaged in a riot—city boys against farmers. Washington jumped off his horse, waded into the middle of the mob, grabbed one big soldier by the throat with his left hand and another man with his right. Holding them at arms length, he lifted both men off their feet, yelled at them to stop fighting and cracked their heads together, then dropped them. They scrambled to their feet and ran away—and so did the rest of the soldiers who immediately stopped fighting and scattered. The riot was over. Washington and Billy returned to headquarters. See illustration Figure 9, supra. Although I feel passionately about Billy Lee and his impact on the world in which he lived, I have tried not to allow my own feelings distort the tale. I am humbled and honored to have the reader share my own interest and enthusiasm for this truly remarkable human being and his impact on the greatest American of all time.

NOTES FROM THE SUMMIT

The Comments of Mary Thompson Research Historian at Mount Vernon

I have had the great good fortune of having this manuscript reviewed by Mary Thompson, the Research Historian at Mount Vernon Estate and Gardens. This has enabled me to correct several errors and to expand my commentary in these notes to explain certain significant matters. Please understand that these comments and corrections are solely my personal responsibility, and Mary

Thompson bears no responsibility for my words and views.

I am pleased that Mary commented generally, as follows:

"...I really enjoyed reading the manuscript and hope that others will as well.

You are very good at helping people understand the feelings and personalities of the characters involved."

I was pleased to receive this overall evaluation of my work, but Ms. Thompson also commented on a number of specific matters which do not significantly affect this book and which are covered on my website: www.lenlamensdorf.com.

I am very grateful that Mary Thompson has provided me with the information set forth above. My work can only be improved by utilizing her meticulous research and other illuminating suggestions. All I can do, in all humility, is to express my profound and abiding appreciation.

HISTORICAL TIMELINE

Actual historical events that relate to GEORGE WASHINGTON and BILLY LEE

1732	February 22	George Washington's birth.
1750	April 12	Death of George Washington's father Augustine. George inherits 11 slaves.
1750	Unknown	William (Billy Lee) born on plantation of Colonel John and Mary Lee, Westmoreland, Virginia.
1751	September – December	George and brother Lawrence in Barbados for Lawrence's consumption. George contacts Smallpox, but survives.
1752	July 26	Lawrence dies.
1754	May 28	Lieutenant Colonel Washington of Virginia Regiment defeats French at Jumonville's Glen. Rumors of massacre; beginning of French-Indian War.
1755	July 9	Braddock's defeat and death on Monongahela; Washington cited for bravery.
1759	January 6	Washington marries Martha Custis, richest widow in Virginia. She brings 100 dower slaves.
1759	February	Washington seated in Virginia House of Burgesses; speaks privately against British control of Colonies.
1768	April 3	Washington buys Billy and Frank from Widow Lee. Billy becomes Washington's huntsman.
1769	Unknown	Billy marries pregnant "Philomena," who dies in childbirth.
1774	September 10	Washington, delegate to 1st Continental Congress accompanied by Billy.
1775	April 19	Battles of Lexington and Concord.

1775	June 15	Second Continental Congress, Washington named Commander-in-Chief.
1775	July 2	Washington and Billy arrive at Cambridge. General takes command of the Continental Army. Washington breaks up riot of 1000 soldiers with his bare hands.
1776	January 10	Publication of Thomas Paine's "Common Sense."
1776	March 4-5	General Knox and 57 cannon arrive. Americans occupy Dorchester Heights threatening Boston and entire British fleet.
1776	March 17	British evacuate Boston. Americans occupy city.
1776	April 13	Washington arrives in New York.
1776	July 2	Largest fleet ever assembled arrives at New York and British troops occupy Staten Island.
1776	July 4	Declaration of Independence.
1776	August 17	Disastrous battle of Long Island. Joseph Reed and Billy barely able to drag Washington back from front.
1776	August 29	Defeats at Manhattan, Kips's Bay, Harlem Heights.
1776	November 16	Fort Washington falls. Americans abused by Hessians.
1776	November – December	Washington's decimated army retreats across Delaware into Pennsylvania.
1776	December 26	Battle of Trenton, New Jersey.
1777	January 3	Battle of Princeton, New Jersey.
1777	September 11	Battle of Brandy wine, Pennsylvania, Lafayette wounded.
1777	September 16	British occupy Philadelphia.
1777	October 4	Battle of Germantown, Pennsylvania.

1777	October 17	British (Burgoyne) surrender 8000 troops after defeat at Saratoga, New York.
1777	December 19	American army establishes winter quarters at Valley Forge remaining until June 18, 1778.
1777	December 23	Thomas Paine publishes "The Crisis" ("These are the times that try men's souls … ")
1778	January – June	Lafayette becomes "surrogate" son to Washington.
		Nathaniel Green appointed quartermaster; his wife Caty vamps Washington.
		Martha Washington arrives bringing provisions; winters with General.
		"Baron" von Steuben, an unannounced volunteer persuades Washington to let him train troops; by May 18 he is named Inspector General.
		Billy Lee begins romance with Margaret Thomas, a young black free woman working for housekeeper Mrs. Thompson on headquarters staff. Billy and Margaret marry in civil ceremony unsanctioned by Washington.
		Washington refuses to permit Margaret to accompany Billy as they break camp.
1778	June 18	British evacuate Philadelphia. Washington's army follows them.
1778	June 28	Battle of Monmouth Courthouse. General Charles Lee retreats. Washington turns defeat into victory. In intense heat, Washington's horse dies under him. Billy brings fresh replacement in thick of battle.
1778	December	British capture Savannah, Georgia.

1779	June – December	Sullivan's campaigns against hostile Iroquois.
1779	December 1	Army winters at Morristown, New Jersey. Conditions worse than Valley Forge.
1780	May 12	British capture Charleston, South Carolina.
1780	May 25	American troops mutiny at Morristown ruthlessly put down by Washington.
1780	July 10	French fleet under Rochambeau arrives at Newport, Rhode Island.
1780	August	Battle of Camden, South Carolina.
1780	September	Benedict Arnold's treason at West Point.
1780	October 7	Battle of Kings Mountain, South Carolina.
1781	January 1	Pennsylvanian's mutiny is crushed.
1781	January 5 – March 15	Battles of Richmond, Cowpens (Virginia), Guilford Courthouse (North Carolina).
1781	May 20	Cornwallis arrives at Petersburg, Virginia.
1781	July 20	American and French armies link up at White Plains, New York.
1781	July – August	Cornwallis moves army to Yorktown, Virginia. No one has ever figured out why he did it.
1781	September 14	Washington arrives at Williamsburg. Washington and Billy make hurried trip to Mount Vernon and return.
1781	September 28	Siege of Yorktown begins.
1781	October 14-15	Attack on redoubts 9 and 10.
1781	October 19	British army capitulates; Cornwallis evades surrender ceremony. Brigadier attempts surrender to French who refuse his sword as does Washington, sending him to lower rank officer.

1781	October 20	Washington holds reconciliation dinner. British consort with French and ignore Americans.
1783	March 1015	Continental Army almost mutinies at Newburgh, New York. Washington's moving speech quells rebellion.
1783	September 3	Treaty of Paris ends Revolutionary War.
1783	November 3	Washington's farewell orders to army.
1783	November 15	British evacuate New York.
1783	December 4	Washington's farewell to officers at Fraunces Tavern.
1783	December 23	Washington submits resignation to Congress at Annapolis, Maryland. Gala dinner and dance. Washington and Billy ride off to cheers.
1783	December 24	Washington and Billy arrive home to Mount Vernon.
1784	July	To accommodate Billy, Washington tries unsuccessfully to have Clement Biddle locate Margaret and arrange travel for her to Mount Vernon.
1785	April	Billy breaks kneepan while surveying with Washington. Despite misery Billy continues to serve.
1787	May 25	Constitutional Convention in Philadelphia. Washington elected president of convention. Billy, away from dais, keeps notes and papers for Washington.
1787	May – September	Constitution drafted and debated. Washington, silent in public, lobbies behind scenes. Many compromises, including representation: 3/5 of "other persons" included (i.e., slaves and Indians) in population count.

1787	September 17	Constitution adopted by members of convention. Sent to states for ratification.
1788	Summer	Constitution ratified. (Federalist papers)
	March	Billy breaks second knee; can no longer ride full out on horseback. Brother Frank and his nephew Christopher Sheels share his duties.
1789	January	Electors unanimously choose Washington to be First President.
1789	April	Billy tries to ride to New York for inauguration with Tobias Lear. Pain forces him out on Philadelphia.
1789	April 30	Washington inaugurated in New York.
1789	June 22	Fitted with a knee brace and riding in a carriage Billy finally reaches New York. He will act as a more or less immobile butler at levees.
1790		Government moves to Philadelphia.
1790	June – July	Deal made (Jefferson, Hamilton, Madison) for Federal government to assume state debts and Capital to eventually move to Potomac location.
1790	Fall	Billy returns to Mount Vernon to work as cobbler.
1793	March 4	Washington inaugurated for second term.
1794	August 20	Anthony Wayne's victory over Indians at Fallen Timbers.
1794	August – September	Washington suppresses Whiskey Rebellion in western Pennsylvania.
1796		Bushrod Washington, George Washington's nephew appointed to United States Supreme Court.
1796	Fall	Ona Judge and Hercules (chef) favorite slaves run away, never to return.

1797	March 4	Washington retires from presidency and he hopes from public life.
		George Washington builds distillery at Mount Vernon. Workers sneak liquor to Billy.
1798	Spring	Washington tries unsuccessfully to recapture Hercules.
1798	July 13	Washington accepts commission as Commander-in-Chief of United States Army during quasi-war with France.
1799	December 14	Washington dies at Mount Vernon setting Billy free and awarding him lifelong pension and all expenses. Billy elects to stay at Mount Vernon at little house Washington has set aside for him.
1801	January 1	Martha emancipates the rest of George Washington's 123 slaves. Most leave including Billy's brother Frank.
1802	May 22	Martha dies. Subsequently her heirs acquire her dower slaves (approx. 200). Only a few dozen of Washington's former slaves remain.
1802		Bushrod takes possession of Mount Vernon bringing his crippled wife and 40 of his own slaves.
1823		Bushrod sells 54 slaves to be transported to Louisiana. Many groups and periodicals protest but Bushrod is adamant.
1824 – 1825		Lafayette makes final trips to Mount Vernon visiting Billy.
1828		Billy dies alone.

SELECTED BIBLIOGRAPHY

BOOKS

Brookhiser, Richard. *Founding Father: Rediscovering George Washington.* New York: Free Press, 1996.

Bryan, Helen. *Martha Washington: First Lady of Liberty.* New York: John Wiley & Sons, 2002.

Casper, Scott E. *Sara Johnson's Mount Vernon: The Forgotten History of an American Shrine.* New York: Hill & Wang, 2008.

Chernow, Ron. *George Washington: A Life.* New York: The Penguin Press, 2010

__________. *Alexander Hamilton.* New York: The Penguin Press, 2004.

Custis, George Washington Parke. *Recollections and Private Memoirs of Washington.* New York: Derby & Jackson, 1860.

Dalzell, Robert F., Jr. and Lee Baldwin Dalzell. *George Washington 's Mount Vernon: At Home in Revolutionary America.* New York: Oxford University, 1998.

Ellis, Joseph J. *His Excellency: George Washington.* New York: Alfred A. Knopf, 2004

__________. *American Creation: Triumphs & Tragedies at the Founding of the Republic.* New York: Alfred A. Knopf, 2007.

__________. *American Sphinx: The Character of Thomas Jefferson.* New York: Alfred A. Knopf, 1997.

__________. *Founding Brothers: The Revolutionary Generation.* New York: Alfred A. Knopf, 2000.

Flexner, James Thomas. *George Washington.* 4 vols. Boston: Little, Brown, 1965-72

Hirschfeld, Fritz. *George Washington and Slavery: A Documentary Portrayal.* Columbia London: University of Missouri Press, 1997.

Hochschild, Adam. *Bury the Chains: Prophets and Rebels in the Fight to Free an Empire's Slaves.* Boston: Houghton Mifflin, 2004.

Lengel, Edward G. *General George Washington: A Military Life.* New York: Random House, 2005.

Lefkowitz, *George Washington's Indispensable Men: The 32 Aides-de-Camp Who Helped Win American Independence.* Mechanicsburg, PA.: Stackpole Books, 2003

McCullough, David. *John Adams.* New York: Simon & Schuster, 2001.

__________. *1776.* New York: Simon & Schuster, 2005.

Marshall, John. *The Life of George Washington.* Reprint: Indianapolis: Liberty Fund, 2000.

Martin, Joseph Plumb. *Private Yankee Doodle: Being a Narrative of some of the Adventures and Sufferings of a Revolutionary Soldier.* Edited by George E. Scheer. Reprint, N.p.: Eastern National, 2006.

Paine, Thomas. *The Complete Writings of Thomas Paine.* Vol. 2, Edited by Philip S. Foner. New York: Citadel Press, 1945.

Rees, James C. with Stephen Spignesi. *George Washington's Leadership Lessons: What the Father of our Country can teach us About Effective Leadership and Character.* John Wiley & Sons, 2007.

Schwarz, Philip J., ed. *Slavery at the Home of George Washington.* Mount Vernon, Va.: Mount Vernon Ladies Association, 2002

Thompson, Mary V. *In the hands of a Good Providence: Religion in the Life of George Washington.* Charlottesville: University of Virginia Press, 2008.

Thompson, Mary V, ed. *Memorandum for the Martha Washington Anniversary Committee* Compiled for Mount Vernon Ladies Association between 7/31/2001 and 4/7/2008. Typescript in Mount Vernon Library.

__________. ed. *Statements Regarding the Physical Appearance, Traits and Personal Characteristics of George Washington (1732-1799).* Compiled for Mount Vernon Ladies Association between 1/31/2005 and 2/5/2008. Typescript at Mt. Vernon Library.

Washington, George. *George Washington, Writings.* Edited by John Rhodehamel. New York: Library of America, 1997.

__________. *George Washington's Diaries: An Abridgement.* Edited by Dorothy Twohig. Charlottesville: University of Virginia Press, 1999.

Wood, Gordon S. *Revolutionary Characters: What Made the Founders Different.* New York: Penguin Press, 2006

Wood, Gordon S. *Empire of Liberty: A History of the Early Republic, 1789-1815* New York: Oxford University Press 2009.

ARTICLES

Thompson, Mary V. "'They Appear to Live Comfortable Together': Private Life of the Mount Vernon Slaves." Presentation to the symposium: "Slavery in the Age of Washington," Mount Vernon, November 3, 1994. Mount Vernon website.

__________. "'The Only Unavoidable Subject of Regret': George Washington and Slavery." Presentation to symposium 'George Washington and Alexandria, Virginia: Ties That Bind." Alexandria, February 20, 1999. Mount Vernon Website.

__________. "The Lives of Enslaved Workers on George Washington's Outlying Farms." Presentation to the Neighborhood Friends of Mount Vernon, June 16, 1999.

__________. "Houdon's bust of George Washington." *Mount Vernon Annual Report, 2000.*

VIDEO AND OTHER MEDIA

Joseph Ellis: The Founding Fathers
http://www.youfebexom/watch?v=mZFp9MZHa0w

Q&A: Ron Chernow (Part 1)
http://www.youtube.com/watch?v=_y4PpfeVbqk

Q&A: Ron Chernow (Part 2)
http://www.youtube.com/watch?v=8KLybZDahzQ&feature=results_
video&playnext=l&list=PL99CAD37336FAEA8F

Washington, Ron Chernow–9781594202667
http://www.youtube.com/watch?v=UKAnW62X8vU

George Washington Insights by Historian David McCullough
http://www.youtube.com/watch?v=cCWifqclJYw

George Washington, Oath of Office
http://www.youtube.com/watch?NR=1&feature=endscreen&v=JgC-
QDZdlMdc

George Washington (Part 1)
http://www.bing.com/videos/search?q=george+washington&view=-
detail&mid=764E8445D84E0372721E764E8445D84E0372721E&-
first=0&FORM=LKVRl4

George Washington (Part 2)
http://www.bing.com/videos/search?q=george+washington&view=-
detail&mid=764E8445D84E0372721E764E8445D84E0372721E&-
first=0&FORM=LKVRl4

The History of Slavery in America (Part 1)
http://www.youtube.com/watch?v=JclRbUxQv4E

The History of Slavery in America (Part 2)
http://www.youtube.com/watch?v=YPXHrMDvBmO

The History of Slavery in America (Part 3)
http://www.youtube.com/watch?v=MZkpU_ioRKw

IMAGE ATTRIBUTION

AUTHOR BIO

 Len Lamensdorf is an award-winning author of nine novels, three full-length plays, and one motion picture. A three-time Silberman Memorial Scholar and an honors graduate of the University of Chicago, Len studied play-writing at UCLA with Theatre Arts Department Chairman Kenneth Macgowan, founder of the world-famous Provincetown Players and the original producer of the plays of Eugene O'Neill. Lamensdorf also received his J.D. degree from the University of Chicago Law School, where he was Associate Editor/Managing Editor of the University of Chicago Law Review, and completed his post-graduate work at Harvard Law School. Len's career in law and business spanned more than thirty years and he draws on his extensive travel experiences on five continents to create realistic settings for his work. Len's first novel, *Kane's World,* was published in hardcover by Simon & Schuster, in paperback by Dell, and translated into several languages. Delacorte published his next novel, *In the Blood.* His prize-winning Juvenile/ Young Adult *Will to Conquer* trilogy won the 2000 Gold Benjamin Franklin Award for Best Juvenile/Young Adult Fiction, an "Ippy," the Independent Publisher's Award as Best Juvenile/Young Adult Novel and named finalist for the *Fore-Word Magazine's* Book-of-the-Year Award. *The Raging Dragon* was named a "Children's Choice 2003," a program sponsored by the prestigious Children's Book Council and the International Reading Association.

Booklist called Len's adult novel, *Gino, the Countess & Chagall,* "...a glowing tribute to the world of art through the life of a talented and charming painter who personifies a zest for life." *Gino* won a Silver Benjamin Franklin Award, an Ippy, and *ForeWord* magazine's Book-of-the-Year award.

Len is married, the father of two children, grandfather of six and lives in Westlake Village, California.

www.ingramcontent.com/pod-product-compliance
Lightning Source LLC
Chambersburg PA
CBHW020320180726
47991CB00018B/124